CODE 936

Bill Kimbrell, Jr.

AuthorHouse™
1663 Liberty Drive
Bloomington, IN 47403
www.authorhouse.com
Phone: 1-800-839-8640

First published by AuthorHouse 8/24/2009

ISBN: 978-1-4389-7482-8 (e)
ISBN: 978-1-4389-7480-4 (sc)
ISBN: 978-1-4389-7481-1 (hc)

Printed in the United States of America
Bloomington, Indiana

This book is printed on acid-free paper.

In loving memory of my parents, Billy and Dorothy Kimbrell,
English major and English teacher

ACKNOWLEDGMENTS

Writing your first novel is not a singular effort. I have many, many people to thank:

Thanks to my good friend and colleague, Dr. Joe Halcomb, who was the source of the title, *CODE 936*, and who played the villain in the novel, Brice Billups, so well in our skit at our Distributor Meeting in St. Augustine. And thanks for your friendship

Thanks to renowned author, Sue Grafton, who kindly read my first chapters and actually called me with advice

To Beth Dickey, publicist at Doubleday, daughter of my previous associate, Carey Dickey, who really said, "Send me your manuscript..."

To Jason Kaufmann, head of Doubleday, who actually read my complete manuscript and took his valuable time to write me a critique helping my then primitive dialogue

To my dear friend, Dr. Virginia Smith Carter, with sharp #2 pencil, thanks so much for your support, encouragement, and sage counsel

To my late friend and mentor, Dr. Thomas D. Clark, author of thirty plus books, Historian Laureate for Kentucky, and his wonderful wife, Loretta... I miss you badly

To Angelique Cain, then Editor at University Press, who edited, reedited, and helped immensely early on

To Dr. Richard Taylor, author, English professor, ex-Poet Laureate of Kentucky, who read my first chapters and said, "*CODE 936* is another *Erin Brockovich*."

To well-known author, Ed McClanahan, who read and critiqued my first chapters

To Lynn Pruett, author, editor, and teacher, who read, reread, and advised me professionally

Thanks to Jan Isenhour, head of The Carnigie Literacy Center, and all the Seniors Writing Group

To Jenny and the Barnes & Noble Writing Group back then, you helped

To the Writers' League of Texas--what a terrific Workshop in Austin! Y'all have really got it all together...I wish that I lived closer

To the late Steve McCallum, author, to Ed Marheine, and all at the Writers' Group that used to meet at Southern Hills United Methodist Church, thanks!

To Sena Jeter Nasland, famous author and professor, for all your encouragement

To David Dick, who coined the phrase, "One-Book Bill," and his lovely wife, Lalie

To Dr. Jim Klotter, mega-author and professor, who said, "Get away from passive voice..."

To Dr. Jim Gifford, Jesse Stuart Foundation, for your encouragement

To Carol Voss, superb AP English teacher, who helped early on

To literary agents, Annelise Robey, Mary Evans, and Demaris Roland who read my entire manuscript.

To *Writers Digest*, thanks for all your "how to" books...I practically read them all.

To Ken Atchity, AEI, Beverly Hills, agent and movie/TV producer, who read my complete manuscript and said, "Yes, *CODE 936*, will make a great movie, but you need to get the novel published first..."

To Lindsey W. Ingram, Jr., my trusted attorney and friend—thanks so much, man, for everything; and to Sharon Lykins, his wonderful administrative assistant

To the late Dr. Don Herren, my previous minister, dynamic preacher, prolific reader, who read my entire manuscript, and wanted and loved the adjective "innocuous"—it's done, Don!

To Dr. Bill Moore, my current Senior Minister, the greatest storyteller I've ever known, and his associates, Rev. Dennis Burrows, Rev. Clyde David Burberry, and Rev, John Hatton, thanks for your prayers

To Dr. Len Sweet, author of 30 books, Dean of Drew Seminary, dynamic speaker, respected theologian, thanks for your inspiration

To Dr. David B. Stevens, my long-term friend and benefactor, who supported me early in my career and afterwards, as well; thanks so much, DBS

To Dr. Roy "Sonny" Waller, who read my entire manuscript and "did not want it to end..."

To all the dedicated, honest surgeons, nurses, hospital administrators, purchasing and Central Supply personnel who made my career such a joy, you know who you are, thank you...you honored my life

To friend, Elwood Scott, and his wife, Jean, who both read my manuscript simultaneously, thanks for your support

Thanks to my good friend Reed Polk, gifted speaker and reader, who read, commented, critiqued, and helped

To Nell Main, prolific reader and English teacher, a great combination which provided great help; thanks "flower of Allen County" for your early enthusiasm

To all my dear fellow Rotarians of the fabulous Lexington Rotary Club, who counseled, comforted, and encouraged me during the long, arduous, sometimes painful writing process

To Kelli Lane, who read my manuscript, helped, and laughed, when I needed it, and to Julie, Angie, Karen, Tonya, Heather, Chuck, Sabrina, Jennie, Yvonne, David, and all my friends at the excellent Lexington Public Library, thanks for all your help

To Dr. Joe Bark who reached out to me, read my manuscript, and actually referred me to his literary agent, Rosalie Heacock, who really helped. Thanks, friend!

To Coach D, "my brown-eyed brother," and his beautiful bride, Tammy, for friendship, inspiration, and prayers; and more of the same to my comrade Eddie Hammond, and his wife, Roxanne, The "Tres Amigos Brothers" will ride again!

To Mike Cooper and Mike Thompson, Cooper Management, who saw me through some valleys.

To my old running buddy in high school and college, Myles L. (Mike) Williams, who inspired many stories, most of which we dare not tell.

To all my super dedicated, strict, inspiring teachers at Greenville High School, you contributed more to this than you'll ever know.

To those demanding, dedicated professors I had at Millsaps College and Southern Methodist University, thanks for making a difference in my life.

To my daughter, LeVan and son-in-law, Pete's good friend Bill Stearns, writer, English professor, missionary, who helped with my first chapters

To friend Bill Thurman, who introduced me to author and gentleman, Eric Fruge, who introduced me to AuthorHouse

To Rory Beall, my Publishing Consultant at AuthorHouse, Megan Leary, and everyone at AuthorHouse for all your help

To Teri Watkins, AuthorHouse, thanks so much for your support and expertise! And, in addition, Jamie Schnieders and Team Gambia, Tim Reeves, and others at AuthorHouse... thank all of you for such a super quality product with *CODE 936*

To Gary Cremeans, manager of Joseph Beth Booksellers, the total source of knowledge and inspiration, to Brooke Raby, marketing manager, and to Neil Um, its superb owner and founder

To my buddy, the late Bob Abercrombie, who lit up the room playing a great Lenny Shortt in our *CODE 936* skit; I really miss you, man

To my friend, the late Harley Baxter, who read the complete manuscript and his lovely wife, Betty, who won the Academy Award playing Trish, the heroine of *CODE 936* in our skit; you are missed, Harley

To good friend, Bob Wesson, who read the manuscript and brought down the house playing George Driskell in our *CODE 936* skit

To my dear friends, the late Earle Blakely and Orlie Shaffner, I miss you both

To all my fellow Distributors and past business colleagues—Fred Thomson, thanks for your leadership, Keith and Gordie Bartow, Alan Larsen, Pete Lieffring, Tony Pasion, Gary Cook, Fred Rowland, Chet Bartol, Jack Docherty, Jim Docherty, Jim Colbourne, Ward White, Ed Carrigan, David Cox, Paul Daniel, Carey Dickey, Bill Schilling, Dan Fletcher, Norm Hatfield, Neal Smoyer, Jesse Jackson, Mike Burton, Mark Randall, Larry Braillier, Dick Kramer, Mike McKernan, John Powell, Steve Maxon, Jake Wright, Bud Newell, Wade Frey, Mike Baker, Danny Ray, Eric Christopher, Larry Davis, Pete Pietrykowski,

Bill Morris, Tim Walker, Jim Jones, Mike Johns, Syd Pond, Steve Otell, Daryl Westphalen, Al Lucas, Roy Richarson...what a ride we had!

To Good friends Charlie "Boss" Deeds, Terry Egan, Larry Harvey, George Kempsell, Mark Hoffman, J. Alan Morgan, Tom Hughes, Ron Davis, Ed Graham, Dick Bauer, Ed "Fast Eddie" Haushalter and many, many more

To Ken Fallon, whom I ran into in Puerto Rico while I was researching *CODE 936*

To my dedicated team through the years: Donna Watts, great office manager, Pete McLain, Duane Beasey, Simone Nalli, Rick, Kevin, Kathleen, Cindy, Linda, April, Jan, and many more; thanks for all your hard work and loyalty

To family friend, Diann Roundtree, who read my manuscript and prayed, and her husband, Gerald

To my cousins, Dr. Walter Harrison, Rev. T. O. Harrison, and the late Rev. Ray Harrison, thank you for your inspiration and all your prayers

To my little sister, Ragan, dame of New Orleans, always a marvelous inspiration and dear Charleen; thanks for taking up for me for many years

To my favorite Uncle Earl, banker extraordinaire, Southern gentleman, and the shrewdest businessman I ever known, thanks, Uncle, you taught me so, so much, and thanks, too, to his beautiful wife, my dear Aunt Lura

To my cousin, Bill Henry, close friend of John Grisham, who read my entire manuscript, and his wife, Maureen; thanks Cuz for all your encouragement

To Becky, my sister-in-law, thanks for reading my manuscript early on and being there

To my three wonderful daughters, LeVan, Trish, and Kristin, two wonderful sons-in-law, Pete and Todd, and eight fabulous, brilliant grandchildren, Lauren, Ashley, Ali, Grace, Isabel, William, Amani, and Habtamu; I love y'all more than you'll ever know

And, last but certainly not least, copious thanks to my dear first (and only) wife, Pat, for all of your deep abiding love, tolerance, and patience.

Vengeance is Mine, I will repay, saith the Lord. Do not be overcome by evil, but overcome evil with good.

Romans 12:19, 21 (KJV)

PROLOGUE

James looked down at the bloody mass in his hand. Squinting, he tried again to read its lot numbers. He could not make them out. And it was not because of the blood or poor lighting.

"Damn."

Only the monitor beeps and the methodical drone of the patient breathing, in and out, slowly in and out, punctuated the mortal silence.

Frowning, he rotated the implant, tilting it towards the bright operating room lights. Something was definitely wrong here.

The numbers were smeared. He still could hardly make them out. The size, too. Altered? Could the blurred "14mm" have been altered? Could this be the cause of the problem? This component was not right. Is it why the femur split?

James shut his eyes, lowered his head, his chin almost touching his chest. Sweat stained his green scrubs— his surgical gown was now a morbid, green shroud.

No. This can't be. Stale, rancid breath behind his surgical mask parched his mouth.

A defective Total Hip component? From his company? The leader in the industry? *No way.* It would be a medico/legal catastrophe. Worse, with over 600,000 Total Hip replacements done each year, it could be an ongoing surgical disaster. An atrocity. *Damn.*

"This can't be happening," he muttered. He bit his lip. His stomach wrenched at the donut he wished he had not eaten earlier.

How did these numbers get smudged? Was it on purpose? This implant caused the femur to split...without a doubt. *Aw shit.*

"Sponge."

"Wire passer."

Immersed in shock and denial, James heard the familiar sounds of an operating room, but they seemed distant, unreal.

"Lap. Clamp..."

The high pitched alarm on the cardiac monitor shattered the silence.

"CODE! CODE!" the anesthesiologist shouted.

The shrill tone got louder as the straight line went off the screen.

"CODE 500!"

"Damn...."

PART I

Unrequited Betrayal

Thou preparest a table before me in the Presence of mine enemies...

Psalm 23:5 (KJV)

CHAPTER 1

It's all in the day's work.

Anonymous

The afternoon sun baked the asphalt on the Mountain Parkway. Multicolored heat waves shimmered from the black surface. The freshly unfurled leaves of spring painted contrasting hues of green, sprinkled with the white of dogwood blooms and the cream from the bark of the stately sycamores. *Majestic,* he thought. But, traffic was heavier than usual for mid-afternoon.

Suddenly, James slammed on his brakes and swerved, barely missing the coal truck. *Damn it!* All of the surgical instrument sets stacked on the back seat crashed into the back of the front seats, jolting him. The sounds of metal against metal, surgical instruments smashing against each other, into the sterilizing cases, was deafening, drowning out his screeching tires.

He grasped the steering wheel furiously, his knuckles blanched white, his forearms trembling. Another damn coal truck barreling down mountain roads, ignoring yellow no-pass stripes, oblivious to the poor mortals driving cars. Of all the ways to die, getting hit by a coal truck was not James' favorite way to go. Another close call. Too close. He looked at the recent crack in his windshield caused by a chunk of coal thrown from a speeding rig, just one more battle scar from the coal-truck mafia.

As he pulled off on the shoulder of the parkway to straighten out the mess in his car, his hands were still shaking. He got out of the car, still cursing the truck and praying that his expensive instruments weren't damaged. Thankfully, all of the sterile implants were stored in large plastic containers in the trunk. They should be okay. The fresh smell of diesel exhaust from the truck hung in the torrid air. Sweat dripped from his forehead.

Rattled and ragged, James headed toward Lexington. It had been a long day. He had left home at 4:00 A.M. this morning, driving the three hours on dark mountain roads to arrive at the hospital for surgery before 7:00 A.M. He had to cover the surgery for one of his salesmen who was on vacation. He had not only supplied the instruments and implants for a total knee replacement, but had also assisted during the operation, providing technical support for both the surgeon and the operating room personnel. "Stood in" on the surgery was the jargon of the trade; "stood in," such a simplistic idiom for such a complex, labor-intensive, occasionally life-and-death job.

He needed gas, so he pulled off the parkway at the Campton exit. He usually stopped at Jock's Shell Station whether he needed gas or not. He had hired Jock's step-daughter as an intern several years ago while she was attending the University of Kentucky.

"How you doing today? It's a hot 'un, ain't it?" Jock asked in his pronounced Eastern Kentucky accent. Always friendly, he was hosing down a grease stain on the pavement.

"Not too good at the moment, Jock. Another coal truck, just about got me this time. It was this damn close!" James held his hands apart.

"Hell, they're mean . . .'n gettin meaner," he replied, shaking his head. "Where you been? In the operating room, again? I don't see how you do it."

As Jock opened the hood to check his oil, James started the pump, opened the rear door, and got out two of the sterilizing cases to straighten the instruments.

"Lordie, I just don't see how you keep up with them things. Look at that. 'N you show them doctors when to use 'em," Jock said. "I mean, I gotta a buncha tools, but nothing like you here. I just don't see how you can. . . how *do* you do it?"

"Well, Jock, it's my job. I have to study to keep up, but's it's just my job. Like yours and engines. I'd be lost under that hood. You know 'em inside out. How's Cindy doing?"

"Aw, she's got a good job up in Cincinnati (he pronounced it Sin-za-natta). She shore is thankful to you. Still says ya taught her a lot."

"She's a smart girl. A good worker, like her ol' man. Please tell her hello for me."

James bought a Diet Coke even though he had his two-liter jug in the car, paid, and drove back to the parkway.

He reflected back to Jock's comments on his job. Uniquely different from others in medical sales, his business was rewarding but demanding. James *had* to be there in surgery with this orthopaedic surgeon, who was new to his territory. Otherwise, one of his competitors would have moved in to steal hard-earned business away from Cantrill & Associates, Inc. The orthopaedic/surgical business that James had now been in for over thirty years had become very competitive— a dog-eat-dog, really cutthroat business. The total knee surgery, normally a two-hour procedure, had taken this surgeon a little longer, but it had gone well. James was good at what he did, but the business was getting tougher every day. The pressures of managed healthcare had impacted not only the hospitals, physicians, and patients, but also the medical device business, as well. James' role as CEO, President, Sales manager, and Administrator of his own business, James Cantrill & Associates, Inc., had changed radically, too. Market share and profitability were under constant attack. Survival was the order of the day. Hence, James still had to "stand in" on surgeries, sometimes assume the duties of, as well as manage his sales associates, check on the daily surgery calendar, often make emergency deliveries, generally just fill in the cracks, in addition to running the daily business. An awesome task, but he lived and breathed it.

But now, driving home, he was worn out. And frazzled, just narrowly escaping that damn coal truck. He always looked forward to this geographic transition from eastern to central Kentucky— from the stately mountains into the pristine rolling hills of the Bluegrass, a seamless, miraculous piece of creation. Not today. He was so tired he was impervious to the beauty surrounding him— the white fences and the horse farms. Before turning toward his neighborhood, he attempted to focus on the majestic thoroughbreds to get the surgery, the coal truck, and the day's grind off his mind. But he could not. It only served to remind him of that surgery here in Lexington two weeks ago, the one he desperately wanted to forget, the one that still kept him awake nights.

Pulling into the garage, he wondered if he had the energy to climb out of his car. Checking his suit pocket to make sure he had his "brain"

— his little brown pocket calendar with his company's name imprinted on it— he left his briefcase and paperwork sitting on the passenger seat, intending to work on it later if he could keep his eyes open. Entering the kitchen door, he found Trish, his wife and right arm, working on the books and quarterly taxes at the kitchen table. She had on jeans and a sweat shirt with her silver-streaked auburn hair pulled back in a hair-clip.

"Welcome home, hon. How'd the surgery go?" she asked.

"Fine," he answered. "This new surgeon's pretty good. Thank God he doesn't scream and throw instruments like his predecessor. I liked him; the OR staff likes him, too— a refreshing change." He did not tell her about the coal truck. She worried about his driving, especially on the mountain roads.

"Another long day, 'hon?" she said. Trish was his partner in business and life. She did the payroll, taxes, paid the bills, worked on the books, and worked closely with John, their CPA. Even though James had grown the business into a multimillion-dollar operation, she still provided the back-up when they were stretched to the limits— making emergency deliveries and answering phones when the office staff called in sick. More important, Trish was the ever-attentive spouse, his best listener, his port in all storms. She had spent the past three days in Louisville, helping set up the office and logistics center for the newly expanded distributorship he'd been given only a few months before. Her face was drawn, but her deep hazel eyes twinkled with excitement.

She hugged him. "You look exhausted," she said. "Why don't I fix you a cup of coffee while you change?"

He didn't need to answer, just nodded wearily and went upstairs, his feet as heavy as concrete blocks.

Trish was bustling around the kitchen with nervous energy, emptying the dishwasher, a chore she always disliked. When he came into the kitchen, she patted his arm.

"How'd it go in Louisville?" he asked, helping set the table.

She sighed, running her hands through her hair. "I had to buy a new fax machine and copier. Hell, the ones we inherited over there were pieces of crap from the dark ages, and I do mean crap; that's in addition to the computers we'd already bought."

Her mascara was smeared, and she had eaten her lipstick off long ago. But she thrived on challenge. She stood by him through all the tough times. And she didn't just stand there either— she was a worker, working almost as hard as he did. Her criticism of her husband, her major concern, was more than his being a workaholic. It was the fact that he was totally consumed by his business. Though active in their church and Rotary, he was driven by James Cantrill & Associates, Inc. She worried about him, worried a lot, because he was at the vulnerable age for a coronary. She could not forget that James' father, who had run his own office equipment business for many years, had a heart attack when he was exactly the same age as James. She did not want to lose her husband.

"But it's all done now." She gave James that soft, tired smile he loved. "We're having pizza...from Pizza Hut," she said, trying to blot out thoughts of cholesterol— she'd get back to her diet next week.

"Oh, well..." he said, "in that case, I'll stay for dinner." Though it would not be as good as her cooking.

They both laughed at the long-standing joke, though their mirth was a little subdued. James would rather eat Vienna sausages at home with his wife than go out to the ritziest place Lexington had to offer.

She brought the pizza box to the other end of the kitchen table. When she sat down, she reached across and touched his hand briefly.

They said grace holding hands, then, as usual, James fell into describing his day, which had begun long before daylight. He left out the three-hour drive on Appalachian mountain roads in darkness, the coal truck, and cut to the scene in the operating room where he had "stood in" on that total knee replacement, as he had done hundreds of times, making sure the surgeon had the implants and instruments he needed.

"This new surgeon's a nice guy..."

"Honey, quit it! You're talking with your mouth full again," she interrupted.

"Sorry."

"I don't know when you started doing this. It's terrible. You've got better manners than that. So, Dr. Bar-what's-his-name, the screamer is gone?" she asked.

"Yeah. And they don't miss him. All the OR staff is relieved; and really happy with the new surgeon." He rubbed his stomach, trying to decide whether to have another slice of pizza.

"I *know* the nurses are glad that abusive doctor's gone. I remember," she moved the pizza crusts to one side, "that expensive instrument of yours he threw against the wall. Splattering blood everywhere. You and the hospital had to eat the cost. I don't understand it. Why do the nurses put up with someone like that?"

He hesitated after looking outside and noticing pine needles in the gutters. He made a mental note that he had to clean them out this weekend.

"I don't know. Probably because they have to. With managed care, everybody's hurting. Hospitals, doctors, *and* the patients. Good surgeons are hard to find. I just feel sorry for all the scrub nurses— what they have to go through, almost every single day. And speaking of kissing butt, look at the things I have to go through now. It's *not* like it used to be. *Nothing* like it used to be. Just look at the things... all the things we do, all of us, just to make *quota* every month! Quota is going to be the death of me, yet..."

"Where have I heard *that* before?" She was being facetious, but knew that her husband was not— she still worried about him He was so obsessed with making quota.

"I just get this feeling that the business is going to hell. Is the business getting tougher, or am I getting older?"

"Both," she answered.

They laughed, but James also knew how true her statement was. He knew it, felt it in his tired bones every day. He knew way down deep in his gut how much tougher the business had gotten. But, he still loved it.

James went upstairs early. As he sat on the side of the bed making a few notes on his to-do list and checking his appointments for the next day, Trish called up the stairs.

"Jim? There was a message on the machine from George Driskell. He says it's urgent. Said to call him at home."

Even though he did not feel like it, James made the call. Soon he was listening to George's voice demand his presence at corporate headquarters.

"Does it have to be tomorrow?" he asked George. He was way behind in the office and badly needed a full day to catch up; was actually looking forward to it. Plus, he had promised his granddaughters a picnic at Jacobson's Park the following evening, trying to comply with Trish's pleas to spend more time with the grandchildren.

"I need your ass in my office as soon as you can fly up here," George replied.

James was half dead, but he got on the phone, called Delta, and made reservations to fly to Ft. Wayne the next day. *Why did George speak to me that way? Use that tone of voice? He's never talked to me like that. And I even made quota last month.* He had a baleful feeling it was not going to be good.

And he was tired. Not just physically; that was nothing new. He was damned tired of Werner corporate— tired of all their crap, their self-serving agendas, constantly changing the rules, their bureaucratic red-tape, the unethical things going on, the run-around he kept getting about that tragic surgery two weeks ago.

Shit! What are they thinking? With declining sales? Morale that sucks? The possibility of defective products? What have they got up their ass this time? And, now this crap with George?

As he wrote the flight times down, he looked at his to-do list and his pocket calendar. He always slept with them by his bedside, accompanied by a penlight to make notes during the nighttime darkness. He realized for the first time in his life that he was their slave. These two self-made schedules governed his entire life. As their hostage, prisoner, and slave, he was held in human bondage by his own handwriting— all for the purpose of quota. Werner's sales figure he *had* to make every month. Every year. Quota, that infernal word. Quota reverberated around in his head. No wonder Trish worried and complained.

As he said his prayers this night, he made a solemn vow— when he got back from this trip, he was going to take time off, spend time with his family, quality time with his wife, children and grandchildren. Yes, he promised himself for the first time ever, he was going to get a life.

CHAPTER 2

Verily I say unto you,
that one of you shall betray me.
Matthew 26:21 (KJV)

As James sat in the plush, executive meeting room at Werner headquarters waiting on George Driskell, Sr. Vice-President, and Lenny Shortt, Vice-President of Sales, he reflected on how he got here. He, James T. Cantrill, Jr., had achieved the zenith in his long career in medical sales — that of being an independent distributor for Werner, Inc., the leader in the orthopaedic industry. James Cantrill & Associates, Inc. was his own business, his life, his baby. He had hired talented, dedicated people to work for him. Begun with a handshake of implied trust from Werner rather than a written contract, his distributorship resembled a franchise and had become an extremely successful enterprise. It was a unique business, very demanding but very gratifying. He had always enjoyed a good relationship with Werner, and usually had exceeded quota and performance goals. When Werner had recently undertaken a restructuring which terminated over forty of his fellow distributors, James had survived and was offered a larger territory as his new distributorship. This left him with a great deal of ambivalence because many of those involuntarily retired were his close friends. He felt badly for them and their families.

He looked down at the huge, cherry conference table and felt the rich Persian carpet under his feet. As he thought back over the years— all the great times, the conventions, meetings, the wonderful customers who were more friends than customers, the awards he'd won; but he could not put that surgery two weeks ago out of his mind. He had done everything he was supposed to, sent in all the surgical incident reports to Werner, only to get the run-around. The Food and Drug Administration was rigorous in their regulation of medical devices, explicit about Medical Device Reports, about compliance following *any* incident during surgery. And here he was being stonewalled by Werner, his follow-up phone calls unanswered — what in the *hell* were they doing? Something was *not* right. You don't *screw* around with the FDA.

"Hello James. Thanks for coming up," George said, shaking his hand and sitting at the head of the table, right below a Monet painting.

Lenny reached across the table, not smiling, and shook James hand. James' old friend of twenty-nine years seemed unfriendly, strange, aloof.

Something was not right here also, James thought. *Thanks for coming up? Like I had a choice.*

"Have a seat there, James. Would you like some coffee?" George asked.

"No, thank you."

A period of strained silence ensued. Lenny avoided eye contact altogether.

George shifted the stack of papers in front of him.

"We're rescinding the offer to be Distributor in the new territory," George said in his deep, unexpressive voice.

"*What?*" James shouted, feeling as though George had just sucker punched him in the stomach. He sat there in total shock.

I'll stay calm, he told himself. *I must not be hearing what George is saying.*

He felt his face drop, his mouth open, dry. He looked directly across the table at his friend, Lenny Shortt, who again avoided eye contact. Directly behind him a Cezanne adorned the walnut paneling.

James had heard about the double-dealing, back-stabbing tricks George had pulled on other distributors, even on his own best friend, whom he had shafted for a new distributorship. But he could not digest the fact that George was doing it to him. And Lenny just sat there, like a total stranger, refusing to look at James.

James looked past George to the picture windows on the far wall. It was a crisp spring day in the Midwest. The sun framed the fringe of the large Persian rug. What a wonderful day to get sacked. James had been in this very room many times, and he had always been cheered as a major contributor to the growth of the Werner empire. There had always been easy laughter with constructive criticism, optimistic jokes, glad-handing. *Now George is firing me?*

He reached into his left pants pocket, got out his Aloe Chapstik, and rubbed it on his lips. He had to think.

"James?" George said. "James?"

"Are you telling me that I'm *fired?*"

"We are simply having to rescind the offer for the expanded distributorship." George spoke in a monotone as if he had been asked to give name, rank, and serial number.

"I don't believe it," James said. "I've busted my ass these last three months. I have completely set up this huge operation, five offices across five states. I have hired new people, people who have already resigned from their old jobs and are moving their families— people who believed in me— and you're telling me that I am fired?"

"We're sorry, James."

"What in the hell is going on here?" James asked. "Are you going to give me an explanation?"

"We've talked to some of your new sales associates. They don't see you as their leader. They view you as an old granddad. They don't think your old values are what's needed in the new managed-care marketplace." George crunched a couple of Tums and glanced down at the pile of papers in front of him. "It's like baseball, James— we can change managers, but we can't afford to lose one key shortstop."

Talkative and outgoing, James was a popular guy. Though savvy and experienced, he was often misjudged by people because he laughed a lot and spoke with a Southern drawl— though he talked slow, he did not think slow— and sometimes he had a tendency to preach. And here he was, struck dumb. *I can't believe what I am hearing. I can't get my mind around what George is saying.*

"I don't *bee-lieve it.* You're going back on your word. I just do not *damn* believe it. After twenty-nine years, after twenty-nine years of damned hard work, good work, where I have outstripped the company's growth.

Hell, I know I'm not perfect. I've made mistakes, just like other managers. But I've admitted mine. And learned from 'em. And, overall, over twenty-nine damn years, I've grown the business...won awards. George, what in the hell are you talking about?"

"Well, to be honest..." George said.

"*Honest,*" James interrupted. "You've just gone back on your word, here. *Honest?* What does that word mean to you? My word means something— it is *my* bond. My customers *know* that my word is my *bond.* I gave you my word that I would do my best, that I'd set up the new territory, and I did it with zeal, with energy— working nearly twenty-four hours a day, because I dreamed about my new distributorship when I finally slept. You gave me the company's word. I took it in good faith. I've hired new people, new people who *believed* in me, who had *faith* in me...in this company, that this was a long-range plan, a win/win lifetime proposition. Now, you take the word of a few associates who've gone behind my back, stabbed me *in* the back! New guys who don't even know me. And after twenty-nine years, I'm gone."

"As I said," George continued in his monotone, "we will reimburse all out-of-pocket expenses."

Good Lord, James thought, *I've sunk over $100,000 of my own money in this venture.*

"And, of course, you'll be entitled to your buy-out package, as stated in the revised policy manual— a fair, equitable figure, around 150,000, I think."

"*Wait* a *minute,*" James said. He was good with figures, and he was quite aware of Werner's tendency to manipulate them to their advantage. "I have invested over $250,000 for instruments, alone."

"Well, that amount may be negotiable."

"Good will, alone, should be worth..."

"We are not discussing good will," George said.

"Then, what *do* you call it, George? *My* customers don't even relate to Werner," James said. "They only relate to...know James Cantrill & Associates. That's who they call...that's who they buy from. That's *all* they have ever known! For *twenty-nine damn* years! They do business with *me. My* office. *My* people."

George's hand moved towards the Tums bottle, then stopped. "Our offer is more than fair," he said.

"I am *not* finished," James said. "There *is* the half a million dollars I paid, that 5 percent over-ride I paid to Bartle, the ex-Distributor, the *ex*-President of Werner. For over seventeen years, I paid him, as a condition of my employment— franchise fees they're called according to Kentucky law. Over $500,000 worth! That's half a million dollars! Five percent of gross sales. Five percent of everything sold every single day before I even opened my eyes."

George grabbed the Tums bottle and twisted off the cap. He shook out two tablets. Lenny looked away, cleared his throat, and shifted sideways in his chair.

"That is not up for discussion," George snapped. James could hear the Tums crunching when he spoke. "It is not on the table and will not be on the table. The subject of over-rides will not be discussed here."

Beep-beep, beep-beep. At first James thought the shrill tones were in his head, then looked down at his pager. As he shut it off, he checked the digital message. It was his office.

"Do you need to answer that?" George asked.

James shook his head.

"As I was saying," George continued, "we'll offer you a more than equitable package, quite a good one for you... really, and you could continue as a sales consultant at a salary with benefits."

What an insult. Fired as distributor, demoted to sales consultant. James didn't hear another word. He took a deep breath and stood up. He took another deep breath. His brain was on fire.

"Okay, *brace* yourselves," he shouted, slamming his fist on the table. "Y'all are getting ready to see one of the biggest backlashes this company has ever *witnessed.*" His drawl seemed to echo each word off the wall twice.

"There is going to be a complete revolt like you have never seen," James shouted, raising his arms. With his booming southern accent, he seemed like a preacher winding up for the climax of his sermon. "The good people in Kentucky don't like people who go back on their *word,*" he proclaimed, "much less betray one who's true to them."

Finally, Lenny spoke, but it was not as James' good friend, advocate, and benefactor. "Uh, Kentucky is your old territory, Jim," he said, painfully clearing his throat. Twice "It's just a small fraction of the newly aligned one." He did not look at James; he only looked at George. James could see a mental high-five pass between them. Only the expansive width of the conference table prevented James from lunging for Lenny's jugular.

"And how short, how damn *short* your memories are," James said. Saliva had begun to dab the corners of his lips. He saw on George's face immediate recognition— recognition of facts, the events last year when George had called him from a hostile meeting in Dallas where the strong support of his Kentucky surgeons had been voiced. George had called long distance to thank him. Werner had just lost a huge, national HealthCareUSA contract, except in Texas and Kentucky, where James' surgeons had supported him with their loyalty and business.

Finally, George said, "James, there is no doubt about the good job you've done—very fine work— I just wish you'd listened to the consultants we hired... they said all the associates wanted to be employees with benefits and... I even asked you if we were on the same page."

"What! What the hell are you talking about, George?"

"Tell you what we're going to do," George interrupted, "I think we can sweeten the pot." He turned to Lenny. "Lenny, you have another appointment, right? Do you have anything to add?"

Lenny cleared his throat again loudly, looked at George, then at the Monet. "Only, uh, I think James was being a little too conservative with the new territory...like he had been in the past," Lenny said. He stood up, but stayed behind his chair as if he were waiting to be dismissed. Tall, skinny, gawky, he was a vision of Ichabod Crane, which he was sometimes called behind his back.

"Because I— *by damn*— had to be," James said. "Just to stay alive, just to survive with a small, one-lung Distributorship, which included Appalachia, the most impoverished part of America. We had to drive thrift, cost consciousness, and accountability right along with sales. What in the hell do you expect? Oh, for crying out loud, Lenny. We've discussed it a *hundred* times."

Lenny stared down at the table.

"Well... Lenny, I know you have to leave," George said.

And Lenny, now excused, turned and left the room without looking back. No gentleman's handshake, no good-bye, no farewell, no go-to-hell, no it's-been-nice-knowing-you-for-the-last- twenty-nine-years. No I'm sorry. No acknowledgment of the devastation of one human life, the life of a friend. Nothing.

George turned to James. "Now, I'll see if I can get them to sweeten the pot. Let me go down the hall to Legal. Lord knows how long that's going to take," he forced a chuckle in a vain attempt to inject levity. "We've got to bring this to a conclusion before you leave here, James, so... What time's your flight back?

"3:35," he answered.

"You're not going to be able to make that. My secretary will get you on a later flight." Without waiting for a reply, George left the room.

It reminded James of a car salesman leaving the room to check with his sales manager. But, George was lower than any car salesman...

He poked his head back in. "Come with me, James," he said. "We'll get you set up in an office where you can use the phone. You know where the coffee is. How about a couple of sandwiches?"

James shook his head, his stomach curled in a knot. His business had been his life.

"I'll be back from Legal as soon as I can," George smiled— a disarming smile, on the face of the man who had just called a guy up to corporate headquarters, cut off his balls, then tried to feed them back to him, and said, "Let me see if I can sweeten the pot."

CHAPTER 3

per~fi~dy *(pur' fi-de) n.* Deliberate breach of faith; treachery.
The American Heritage Dictionary

James sat in the vacant office, his elbows on the desk, his head held in his cold, damp hands. The loss of his job, his business, his life-force was like the loss of a loved one. Death, divorce, downsizing, destitution— he felt like they had all hit him at once. He picked up the receiver, then put it down. He desperately wanted to call Trish because he knew there lay his comfort— his best friend, his true love, his partner in business as well as his partner in life.

Despite the comfort that sharing his distress might bring him, he knew that he would be delivering a message that would cause her severe pain. It would shatter her world. He dreaded it, especially after she'd spent the last three days moving into, supervising and setting up the new office in Louisville. The freshly laid carpet in that brand new office had just been yanked right out from under the two of them.

James just sat there, staring at the phone. Finally, he punched 9, got an outside line, and dialed home.

He wanted to break the news gently, but found himself blurting out the whole ugly story without even stopping for breath. He finished with "I'm fired— we're done, finished...I just can't believe it. They promote you, give you three months to do the impossible, then take it back three days after you have done it? It doesn't make sense."

"Why? You're over quota...and way over company growth. Why?"

"They said it was because of the salesmen... those two hot-shots... with the 'old grandad' thing...said I was too old-fashioned...."

"*Salesmen.* The ones you inherited? They don't even *know* you." Anger overcame her concern. Her voice raised. "And he believed *them?* Over *you?* After all your...this is *crazy.*"

"Hell yes, it's *crazy.* George said the company could afford to change managers, but they couldn't afford to lose one key shortstop. He said it was like baseball."

"Baseball? What does that mean? Did you tell George that the ball he's batting around is *your life?*"

James thought a moment. *At least she was not giving up yet.*

"Trish, Lenny was there, too, and he didn't say a word to back me up. Nothing. Not a damn word."

"Lenny? Lenny's your *friend.*"

"Was," James said. "He *is* the snake everybody has said he was. Why didn't I see it before?"

"He betrayed us?"

"Absolutely! But I'm afraid it's worse— it was a done deal before I even got there. He *is* the perfidious bastard we'd been hearing about. When the chips are down, and your neck's on the block, he screws ya."

Perfidy had always been one of James' father's favorite words. He never thought it would smack him right between the eyes as it had today, literally turning his world upside down.

"Then, they offered me a sales consultant's spot."

"That's ridiculous."

A pause followed, that seemed much longer than it actually was. James thought about how ridiculous it all was.

"What do we do now?"

"I've already started to fight back," James said. "I protested the package George offered, around $150,000."

"That's a *slap* in the face. A *joke.* Did you tell them how much of our own money we have sunk into this? Setting up the new offices?"

"You *bet* I did. Plus Bartle's 5 *percent.* That $500,000 plus I've *paid.* I told them they'd better get ready for the biggest backlash in the history of Werner. And *Lenny?* That *sonofabitch.* Not only did he just sit there like a knot on a log, but when I warned them that my customers— Kentuckians— don't like people who go back on their word, you know what he said? 'Kentucky is just a small fraction of the newly restructured territory.' Like it was just a *drop* in the bucket."

Another pause ensued. James could hear Trish's breathing, more rapid. And short.

"Oh, James, what are we going to do? I'm scared. The girls...oh, my *God*. Our girls...our little girls?" she repeated almost in a whisper, beginning to cry.

"Honey...Honey?"

A long silence followed. A profound silence, symbolic of destitute emotion.

"Trish," he said, "I'm not taking their deal. They're wrong. Dead wrong..."

"What happened? What have *we* done wrong?"

"Nothing. Absolutely nothing! Honey, don't think like that. Something's wrong here— damned wrong— but we didn't do it. *They* are wrong. I promise you that."

"Just promise me that you won't do anything without calling Lynnwood."

"I'm calling him as soon as I hang up."

"Oh, James, what are we going to do?" she sobbed.

"Trish, I don't know. But, we'll make it. We always have...and I'm not done fighting here, yet."

"I know. I love you." He knew she was trying to be brave.

"I love you, too, Honey."

When he hung up the phone, he felt helpless. His love and his promise came out empty, a vacuous proxy for a lifetime of devotion.

After James hung up the phone, he sat there for a moment, staring at the walls in the empty office, wishing he were dead. *This all has GOT to be a bad dream,* he thought.

He looked up from the desk at one of those inspirational graphics in an elaborate frame titled, FOCUS ON THE TOP LINE. What a bunch of *bull shit.* George had been spouting that line for months— "focus on the top line. You've got to focus on the top line." James had been in business for over thirty years; he knew that he had to watch the bottom line or he was out of business. If he ran his business daily, worked hard, watched the bottom line, allocated resources wisely, and invested for future growth, the top line would take care of itself. Top line meant sales and revenues. But, without a profit, the bottom line, a business would eventually go under. And the crucial thing to focus on was the customer, the key constituent that had been lost sight of in this ivory tower. Focus on the customer, go the extra mile for customer service, build good will, reinvest for growth, and watch the bottom line. That is how you grow, increase sales, and build a business.

James looked around at all the equipment just sitting idle, untouched in this vacant office. The *waste*? And this was not the only completely furnished vacant office. He had passed at least four others between here and the elevator. And that is just on this floor, too. Wonder how many there are on the other five floors? And how many over at the huge manufacturing plant across town? What are they thinking? They are going to need people like me just to keep this ivory tower open. He remembered what his good buddy, Fitch, who had been the distributor in New England for over thirty-nine years, used to say: "They spend money like a drunken sailor in San Diego." It was no wonder that Werner, Inc., was rumored to be up for sale. James wondered what Fitch would say now if he were to see this new corporate headquarters— a gargantuan, marble edifice, cold, gray, and impersonal, with brass elevators, French impressionist paintings, poorly framed, rare imported oriental carpets, all the extravagant appointments and trappings that money could buy— all of which did absolutely nothing for the customer. Nothing for *sales*. All this plastic ornateness only served to create a culture of emptiness. This marble mausoleum looked like it belonged in Warsaw, Indiana, like James belonged in the cockpit of a F-119 Stealth Bomber over the Persian Gulf.

Their priorities were all screwed up. They had moved manufacturing of the vital products out of the country. The quality of those products, absolutely critical to the welfare of patients, had gone right along with it. If the founder, Judson Werner, were alive, he would have a heart attack. And now they were getting rid of the last of their old field generals. *I'm glad, oh thank God,* James thought, *that I saved all those records, those documents, and especially the tapes. I will not suffer this gladly. One way or another, they are going to pay.*

James picked up the phone and dialed his attorney's direct line. Next he needed to call Uncle Earl; then John, his CPA. He heard a strange clicking on the line as he waited to hear the ring on the other end. All this fancy shit and the phone doesn't even work right. Lynnwood picked up on the second ring.

Lynnwood W. Ingle, Jr., was the epitome of professionalism, a reserved, self-assured, urbane, perfect gentleman who never lost his cool. He was truly the antithesis of the popular opinion of lawyers, his legal brilliance surpassed only by his extremely high ethical standards. James knew he was lucky to have him as an attorney and as a friend.

James filled Lynnwood in on what had transpired since he had walked into the Werner building that morning. He finished by saying, "And so, they've rescinded the offer."

"*No. How could* they! They did *not* even have the courtesy to answer the letter I wrote them after you refused to sign that ridiculous contract."

"Well, they dared. And they did," James said.

"What reason did they give you?" Lynnwood asked after a brief silence.

"Nothing that makes any sense. I think you and I both know the *real* reason. But, they said it was a couple of key sales associates seeing me as an 'old grandad.'"

"He used those exact words, 'old grandad?'" Lynnwood interrupted.

"Yes. 'Old grandad.' They offered me $150,000, maybe more if I sign a general release."

"That is *all* they offered?" Lynnwood asked, "Where are you?"

"Sitting in an empty office adjacent to George's, waiting for him to come back," James answered.

"James, trust me. Say very little right now. Call me later from a pay phone," Lynnwood cautioned.

"Got you. I understand."

"Okay, James, continue being the southern gentleman that you are. Work into the conversation that you really felt you were at the pinnacle of your career, ready to make the greatest contribution ever. The key words are pinnacle and contribution. Do you understand?" Lynnwood spoke in his characteristically calm style.

He's so damn cool, James thought to himself. *I'm damned lucky to have him.* "Yes, I understand. Pinnacle and contribution."

"And...sign nothing— is that clear?"

"Absolutely," James said.

George came back in as soon as James hung up. Maybe Lynnwood was right. Or was this precise timing just a coincidence? *Damn*, James thought, *bugged phones? At this point I would not doubt anything from them. They ARE ruthless.*

"Come on in, James. We're ready."

There's that <u>we</u> again, James noticed. He followed George back to the executive suite, where he learned who the <u>we</u> was— Brice Billups, the little dip-shit shyster, himself. *Aw, shit, this has taken a serious turn.* James could feel the adrenalin pumping in his veins.

"You remember Brice from our legal department, don't you, James?" George asked.

"Yes," James replied. No handshake. He kept his voice cool.

"Have a seat," George gestured as he took the chair at the head of the table. James purposefully sat closer to the position of power, one chair up from the position he had occupied earlier. The Monet pond painting seemed larger.

"We have an attractive package to offer you," George began. "We will assume your leases, the building, the automobile for two years. Of course, as I said before, we will reimburse all expenses incurred in setting up the new territory. We want to tether any loose ends. We have cut you a check that you can take with you this afternoon, right now, for $195,000." He placed the check on the table, not quite within James' reach, but positioned so James could read the amount. "All you have to do is sign the standard non-compete/release agreement that Brice has drawn up, and it's yours."

Brice had been sitting there smug all the while. His beady, fish-like eyes looked downward as he reached into his Louis Vuitton portfolio, pulled out some fresh white documents, and placed them right in front of James. *He looked like one of those frogs that wears clothes in one of James' granddaughters' storybooks.*

James smiled inwardly at this vision, but outwardly he showed no reaction. He did not budge. He froze his face and did not even let himself think about the check, only the amount— *$195,000. Sounds like a boat-load of money, but it is not even half what I paid in franchise fees. Doesn't even touch instruments, offices, good will. No. Put it out of your mind. Be cool, stay cool, remain cool, he told himself. Say nothing, do nothing, do not react, don't move, don't even gesture towards those damn documents they are itching for* *you to sign— much less that check. That BRIBE, for crying out loud.* James' mind was raging. He hoped that his face had not turned red because his brain was sizzling. *Be cool, be a gentleman,* he told himself.

Thirty seconds went by— a minute— two minutes. The quiet was broken by the siren from an emergency vehicle passing outside. Brice shifted in his chair across the table. George emptied another Tums from the jar and ate it, crunching it between his back molars. The shrill tone of a fax sounded somewhere down the hall.

James gazed out the window at the expanse of cerulean sky brushed lightly by cirrus clouds. *Say nothing. Do nothing. I'm just a cloud drifting by in a peaceful sky.*

"As soon as you sign off on the agreement," George said, "we have an additional option to enhance your package— another consulting opportunity with our Training Department for a couple of years. We don't have all the particulars worked out, but it could make some nice little pocket change." George cleared his throat and poured out a pile of Tums. Brice looked at him with disgust.

Why, oh God, are both these guys so innocuous? Pocket change! I've built a multi-million dollar business. Invested my entire LIFE... and they offer me peanuts and pocket change.

Brice was getting antsy, opening his Louis Vuitton again, making unnecessary use of his maroon Mont Blanc pen. He had a modified fu manchu moustache which he constantly stroked with his index finger and thumb. *He really is one little pretentious piece of shit,* James noted.

George's breathing was audible, the rasping congestion of excessive smoking rattling like a chain. James strained for restraint, his heart racing and his blood rushing. The thud of silence continued.

Finally, George spoke. "You've probably had the opportunity to call and talk with Trish. I know she's probably upset, but..."

"You have the audacity to bring up my *wife* and her feelings?' he slammed both fists on the table. "Do *not* even mention my *wife*." He then slowly leaned forward, pulling his glasses off with his left hand, tilting them on the stack of contracts, rubbing his eyes with his right hand, his head now just above the level of the table. He exhaled deeply, audibly.

"I only meant that the package would mitigate some of the unpleasantness..."

"Is that what you call this?" James shouted, raising his head, his arms outstretched. "Unpleasantness?"

The silence settled. Seconds stretched into eternity, causing harsh uneasiness for the two corporate potentates. James' body had not budged an inch. His head was still clasped in his hands at the level of the table. The sounds of traffic were more noticeable outside the large picture window. Brice shifted his Louis Vuitton once more. Breathing was labored and frequent.

Beep-beep, beep-beep, beep-beep. James' pager went off.

George and Brice almost cheered out loud, their relief evident.

"Do you need to answer that?" George asked.

James shook his head no.

"Would you care for a cup of coffee, James?" George said.

"No thanks."

Brice moved his portfolio again, carefully placing it by his copies of the oppressive release agreement. All the appurtenant papers had also been precisely repositioned in a tactical arrangement for the attack. The stack of documents begging for James' signature had been straightened and placed squarely in front of his chair. The bait, bribe, or check, as they preferred to call it, had been moved conspicuously closer, now one inch above and parallel to the agreement, which was one inch from and parallel to the edge of the table. Precision, sometimes remiss now in manufacturing, was in force at this setting.

It also appeared that it was to be Brice's turn at bat.

"James," he began in his high-pitched, impish voice, "this $195,000 check represents an increase over your buy-out figure as stated in the January letter. It exceeds the formula laid out in the revised Distributor Policy Manual. It, also, is much more generous than the buy-out other distributors received, distributors, I might add, with larger territories than yours. We feel that it is more than a fair equity, a fair offer for you under the circumstances," Brice said.

"This amount, James, equitable though it is, is further enhanced by George's special arrangement, once you sign off— that is, the consulting opportunities with training. Of course, those opportunities are contingent upon your signing the standard exit agreement." Brice tapped the stack of documents with his middle finger twice, then once more loudly.

Brice reached towards the green check and gingerly slid it three inches closer to James, on top of his "standard exit agreement."

"This is a sizable check, James. Wouldn't it make you feel better to walk out of here with *this* in your pocket?"

James said nothing, trying to ignore the rage welling up in every corpuscle of his being.

George sat there, confused, his eyebrows furled, while Brice's spurious indignation welled up. It was quite obvious that George had been sent to the dugout by Legal. The damn lawyers *were* running the company.

"Your thoughts, James?" Brice impatiently asked.

James still said nothing.

Time went by, slowly.

James slammed his chair back from the table, stood erect, and glared straight across at Brice, whose face quickly turned ashen. James gritted his teeth, breathing so heavily that he was almost snorting.

At six foot two and one half inches tall, strong, in good shape for his years, James was intimidating. He looked as though he were about to pounce upon the more diminutive, now squeamish Brice Billups. At five foot six and small boned, Brice was no match for James. But, at this very moment, neither was a giant.

Then, suddenly James turned his back to the table, inhaled, took two deep breaths, and walked slowly over to the picture window. He looked outside and watched the traffic going by on Highway 37. He heard shuffling and murmuring behind him. Finally, he turned and walked deliberately back to the table.

He picked up the green check and announced, "This check is inadequate. It is over $300,000 short, and you both *know* it . George and Brice looked puzzled, feigning confusion.

"You both *know* that I paid *$569 thousand, 8 hundred 85* dollars and 92 *cents* in franchise fees, that five- percent over-ride on gross sales. That amount is construed by Kentucky state law to be a *franchise fee* and I expect full reimbursement of that amount, which I was required to pay. I have a documented ledger as proof of..."

"*That* is not up for discussion, " Brice said. "This matter was not discussed with any other Distributors. They were not allowed to bring up the subject of over-rides in exit settlements, and it will not be discussed here."

James had heard about Brice's brutal negotiation skills, that he was a genuine barracuda, sometimes intimidating in the courtroom. He put the check back down on the table. "The choice is yours then, counselor. You may either discuss it here with me like a gentleman or in a courtroom in the Commonwealth of Kentucky. It *shall be* discussed. It happened and the debits constitute a fiscal reality. We are talking *real* money here in the amount of over *half a million dollars.*"

Brice leaned back, stared up at the ceiling, and stroked his moustache. George shifted in his seat.

James again walked over to the large window. The sun gleamed through brightly on this spring afternoon. He stood tall there juxtaposed, allowing him to address them while having a view of the street outside.

"Down Highway 37 there you can see the Golden Arches, McDonalds, which is one of the most successful franchises the world has ever known. When the owner started out, he paid the McDonalds Corporation for that franchise. He then proceeded to build his business locally and regionally, incorporating repeat customers, continued patronage, and good will. He increased the revenues of the franchisor by increasing the revenues of his own franchise. He grew their overall corporate business by growing his own individual business. It has been and continues to be a win/win, mutually profitable, fiduciary relationship. Now, if for one reason or the other, he wanted to sell his business, his franchise, how much do you think he would get? What could he sell his franchise for? Less than the amount that he paid for it? *Hell, no. That's insane.*

"My question to you is this: what *is the* difference? Economically speaking, he bought a franchise. I bought a franchise. He has a bottom line. I have a bottom line. He must abide by corporate guidelines. I have *always* abided by corporate guidelines. Other than different product lines, why in *the hell* is there such a difference in his business and *my* business?" James asked.

"A Werner distributorship is not a franchise," Brice said.

"It *is* according to the laws in the state of Kentucky. It is *also,* with legal precedent established, in the state of Missouri, and other states, as well. Why, then, tell me why *you,*" James stared squarely at Brice, "*you* and your Con*fed*erates in Legal have made this subject *taboo?* Just *why* is this germane subject of distributors being required to pay percentage over-rides on their gross sales, *de facto* franchise fees, so damn *taboo?*"

Brice did not answer. George seemed embarrassed, his face flushed.

James was still standing, having walked back from the window to the other end of the long table. During another awkward period of quiet, James gazed down upon these two quasi icons of the corporate hierarchy. "It's *no* damn wonder this company is in trouble, in bad trouble, with ethical issues, *product* liability, that *PDL Hip*, no telling what *else*. And the rumors of impending doom, the company being *up* for sale, are probably true," James concluded.

Brice once again reached over and picked up the green corporate check. He then reached into his Louis Vuitton and pulled out another check.

"Sign the release and this second check, a restricted retainer, in the amount of $350,000, that is an additional three-hundred fifty thousand dollars, will be yours also," Brice added with a smirk.

Un huh. The truth about that cover-up is finally rearing its ugly head, James thought.

"These two generous checks are our final offer to you, Jimmy. Take it or leave it," he said.

James almost exploded. Jimmy! He fought back anger, then picked up his briefcase and stood facing them at the opposite end of the table.

"I walked in here this morning, a successful man, at the pinnacle, the *very pinnacle* of my career, confident of making my greatest contribution *ever* to the company I love. This morning I was a proud man, proud of the business that I have built, proud of what I have stood for all these years. What I have sweated, struggled, and fought to build over the last 30 years, you have, in less than 12 hours, completely destroyed." James' voice quivered.

"You have not only attempted to defile my career, but you have also fought an unethical duel with me, attempting to dishonor the Ethics chairman of the Distributor Network," he added, raising the tone of his whisper. "*But,* I will not allow what I have *stood for* all these years— to be destroyed." He turned and headed toward the door.

Stay calm. Do not tip your hand.

But he could not resist. He owed it to himself.

As he grasped the door knob, James turned around and said, "Oh, and one last thing. I think it is time the *truth* were known, the *truth* about the death of that total hip patient, with that questionable PDL Hip at the Healthcare/USA hospital in Kentucky."

KaBoom!

"In the first place, I diligently exercised full compliance after that tragic incident, sending the Medical Device Reports and Surgical Incident Reports into Werner Regulatory. My office and I went above the letter of compliance. I followed up with repeated phone calls, as did my office manager, only to get the run-around and be stonewalled. Regulatory said to call Legal, and at Legal... guess whose name came up, Brice? On two different occasions I called you leaving a message on your phone mail, as well as a message with your secretary to call me back. Never heard anything. *Twice, Brice.* Both Legal and Regulatory thereafter feigned ignorance. It leads me to believe that this was *not* an isolated incident. How many of these defective Total Hips do we have walking around in patients? *Damn...*" James exhaled, then took a deep breath.

" I have documented the entire account A to Z and tah—" he suddenly stopped himself. *Don't tip your hand.* "Tah...tragic...just tragic. This whole, tragic affair, start to finish, still weighs on my conscience. I've lost a helluva lotta sleep over this. It's just torn me up, night and day...I can't get it off my mind. And I'm not alone. The whole damn thing flies in the face of what I stand for... again, what I've stood for, and I think it's high *time* the *truth* were known."

With his right fist clenched, raised to shoulder level, he concluded, "No, *damn it!* I unequivocally reject your offer."

He opened the door and left the office.

He'd have a lot of time later to think about the threat he had just made.

The way George had gasped and turned ashen.

The way Brice choked, clapped his hand to his throat, the blood draining from his pallid little shit face. The sudden twitching and opaqueness of his fishy eyes.

James walked down the hallway, Monet after Monet, and entered the shiny brass elevator. As the doors closed, the Muzak was playing what seemed like a tune with no melody.

The elevators were opening. James prayed that no one was there. He did not really want to see anyone, especially not now.

Oh, thank goodness, no one here in the hall. Now, got to turn in my security badge to the receptionist in the lobby. Oh, thankfully again she's on the phone, just put the badge on the counter, and, turn and you're almost safely out the door.

James made it through the door and was headed down the sidewalk. It is only a short distance to the parking lot, the rental car, and then you are home free, outta here.

He hurried to the parking lot got into the Avis rental.

As he drove out on the street, he looked in the rear-view mirror and saw his old friend walking out of the building— Henry Terrell, whom he had fondly called S. L., for situational leader. Whenever there was a major problem with a customer, he knew that he could go to Henry, who was *the* leader for distributor-friendly customer advocacy.

James was always referred to as "Blue Sky" by Henry, because he said James was the most optimistic guy he knew, "the genuine eternal optimist."

James was disheartened by the memory. What had his "eternal optimism" gotten him on this day— truly the worst day of his entire life?

CHAPTER 4

The telephone rang with a muffled, low-pitched sound.

"Yeah," the gravelly voice answered.

"Line clean?" the calling party asked.

"Affirmative," was the answer.

"We've had a breach. A Code V at Plant 3," the concerned voice stated. "Repeat. Code V, Plant 3."

"Copy that."

"Neutralize. Code 936," the raspy, concerned voice said. "Repeat. Neutralize. Code 936."

"When?"

"Immediately," was the answer.

"Subject?" came the question.

"Six two, slash half. Two zero zero. Dark brown, slash grey. Glasses. Suit, grey plaid. Tie, red stripe. Black briefcase. Photo, PVT Fax."

"Location?" the voice became deeper.

"Greater Cincinnati. Delta Concourse. ETA 17:15, Comair 3031. ETD 18:55, DL1067," the voice became higher-pitched. "Copy?"

"Copy that. Check. MO?"

"Code 936. Code 936, tonight. Repeat. Procure and Code 936, tonight. Preserve. Repeat. Preserve at all costs. DT interrogate. Locate damage. Capiche?" the voice stated firmly.

"Affirmative. Procurement profile?"

"Low. Para, dot. Or mercenary," came the answer.

"Code 936 legit?" the gravelly voice asked.

"Code 936 legit. Falcon. Ditto?" the raspy voice replied.

"Ditto." Click.

Click.

CHAPTER 5

The death of hope and despair,
This is the death of air.
T. S. Eliot, 1942

Brice rushed back to his office, his mouth dry and eyes twitching like butterfly wings. He picked up the phone and punched the auto-dial button for their manufacturing plant in Caguas, Puerto Rico. He asked for Ruiz Castillo, the Plant manager.

"Ruiz, Brice here. Delay that PDL Hip shipment."

"But Tom's screaming for..."

"*Fuck,* Tom. I'll take care of him. Delay that shipment until you hear back from me."

"But, the 14mm's are already on backorder. We worked all night to... they're..."

"I *said, Ruiz,* delay the goddamn shipment," Brice commanded, smoothing his receding hair back.

"But...why?" Ruiz asked.

"We've got to deviate the specs again. This product would never pass QC."

"... I don't understand. First, I get this memo from Tom telling me to expedite this production run. Then, quit. Shut it down. Then, restart. Expedite. It's *crazy!* He ordered me to cease manufacturing PDLs completely."

"Just *do* it, *damn it Ruiz!* Delay this shipment. *Comprende?*"

"*Si.* Okay...okay," Ruiz replied, shaking his head.

Brice hung up and released the encrypt button, fingering his moustache.

James drove past both the old Holiday Inn and the Comfort Inn on his way out of Warsaw, Indiana. What times they all had enjoyed there, the marvelous memories through the years. They, the Distributor Network and sales force, had such a great fraternity/sorority, such spontaneous camaraderie— all of their frustrations with corporate, how they used to rail at "the factory," the problems they had, the stories they shared of the wars fought, lost, and won. The fond memories would make even the founder himself, Mr. Judson O. Werner, truly proud. Those were good times.

James turned right on Highway 30 East headed toward Ft. Wayne. He opened his briefcase, took out his cellular phone, and punched in his home number to call Trish. The battery had died. *Damn.*

He was close to Columbia City, home of his pal Burford, Werner's Director of Public Communications, who had helped greatly with his Power Point presentations as the newly appointed Ethics Chairman. *Thanks, Burford. Gotta stop and take a leak, get a Diet Coke. Do I have time?* He looked at his watch. He was trying hard not to think about Brice, his bristling impertinence, the cover-up, his higher second offer, but it kept cropping up. How damned corrupt they had become. And now James had unknowingly, innocently become the victim of their treachery. *Damn.*

As he drove Highway 30 east for he thought to be the last time, James tried to think positive, letting his mind reflect back on those memories—*what times they all had.*

But, again he thought about Werner going back on their word. Today was certainly not the first time. They had a history of doing that. James remembered when he had been called up on the hot-seat after writing a letter criticizing the meetings/bioskills workshop manager who had lied to one of his top teaching surgeons. The manager had promised the surgeon support and resources for an important seminar at the medical center, then reneged on his promise– *rescinded the offer. Yeah, they were really good at going back on their word.* James' letter had exposed this manager's dishonesty and incompetence. But, since their manager was one of their "sacred cows," Werner management had instead castigated James for writing a critical letter.

Hence, in the culture of mismanagement, instead of focusing on the customer and the customer's problem, in this case a prominent surgeon, they at Werner would somehow rationalize, whitewash, and find a scapegoat to chastise or annihilate. The most glaring example had been the ex-president of the Implant Division, who was fired for a major manufacturing problem with total hip instruments that he inherited. It had not even been his fault. The snafu had occurred previous to his responsibility for the Implant Division, but he was suddenly terminated and made the scapegoat.

His daddy's song, *The Living Years* by Mike and the Mechanics, was playing in his head. The first time he ever heard that song was the day after his father's funeral. And it had followed him around ever since, playing unexpectedly at very meaningful times in his life. *Aw, Daddy. Thanks and God bless your ol' Magnolia heart.*

He turned right onto Interstate 69 South. The Ft. Wayne airport was not far.

After dropping the keys and mileage in the Avis box, he stood first in line at the Comair ticket counter, the first good luck today.

Then it hit him like cancer! The finality of it all. His life as he had known it had ended. This had been...was his last day. His life was over. The epiphany became utter desperation.

James felt the roller coaster descending again, his stomach knotted, his throat constricted. He did not want to visit that dreaded valley of despair again. All the anger, denial, and disbelief dissolved into nothingness. He grew weaker by the moment. His head spun. Was he losing blood? He felt the life-sustaining substance flowing slowly out of his body. He had been stabbed in the back, and he was finally bleeding. His life substance was hemorrhaging from the wound.

His mouth dried out like cotton. The water fountain didn't cut it. *Get another Diet Coke.* "Sir, your change. Sir, here's your Diet and your change." James was standing at the concession counter, staring off into space.

He couldn't even taste the coke. The P.A. system was announcing flights, but he could barely hear what they were saying. He must be losing his mind.

As he wobbled down the airport corridor, he almost automatically veered into the gift shop to buy little, silly souvenirs for his grandchildren, as he always did. He mindlessly bought five tiny teddy bears wearing Indiana University T-shirts.

James muddled slowly through the airport, leaving a trail of invisible blood. *How much further? Gotta make that gate, find my special phone, the one I always used on trips up here...*

Beep-beep, beep-beep, beep-beep. His pager went off again. James reached down on his belt, brought the pager up, and looked at it with glazed, unreactive eyes. Before he could assimilate the message, the thought pierced the fog in his brain— that he would not be needing the damn thing anymore. He knew it was a necessity in an emergency business, but, it dawned on him, he no longer had an emergency business— or any business, for that matter.

He observed the black plastic box in his hand, unconsciously placed it in the basket held by the security guard, went through the metal detector alcove, picked up his pager and threw it into the nearest trash receptacle. *The hell with 'em.* He heard it start beeping again...beep-beep, beep-beep, until the echoes were smothered by trash.

Only a few more steps around the corner, then to the right, and finally, at last, he saw the bank of three pay phones. Two were taken, but yes! his favorite one was free.

James set his briefcase down, picked up the receiver, and dialed home. The line was busy. *Damn.* He then dialed his mentor in Memphis. Uncle Earl, a rare Southern gentleman, had been a Godsend to James in so many ways after the death of his father. They just didn't come any wiser, shrewder, or more lovingly supportive than his Uncle Earl.

Uncle Earl had walked hand-in-hand, shoulder-to-shoulder with James throughout this entire, sordid Werner affair. Uncle Earl had privately thought the whole thing was a carefully orchestrated, premeditated plan on Werner's part to get rid of his nephew. Boy, was he ever clairvoyant— dead-on right— that James knew of unethical events, and held too steadfastly to his old-fashioned values, much like his father, grandfather, and uncle. He knew that his nephew always spoke out for the truth and against unethical improprieties, which was why James had been appointed to be national chairman of the Ethics Committee, making Uncle even prouder.

"It didn't go well. Your premonition was correct, Uncle," James gasped. "They *rescinded* their offer."

There was silence— a long silence. James could almost feel his uncle's razor sharp mind calculating. He *had* presaged the whole scenario.

"Well, those revolving *sombitches,*" Uncle Earl stated firmly. This was a first for James. He had never heard his uncle say damn. But, his uncle's expletive had injected another breath of life into his anemic veins.

"Tell me exactly what they said."

James proceeded to describe the day's events, chronologically from start to finish.

"That second check confirms their duplicity." Uncle Earl had retired as Chairman and CEO of one of the fastest growing, most profitable bank holding corporations in the South and still had a mind for figures and business like a steel wolf trap.

"I had Lynnwood's office make copies of both the tapes and the files." James looked over his shoulder, half expecting to see a man in a trench-coat lurking nearby. Instead, he saw an attractive woman talking on the adjacent phone, dressed professionally, her briefcase on the floor by his, just a woman on a business trip. James hunched down a little and spoke softly. "I stopped at Fed Ex before flying up here. That package is en route to you. You should get it tomorrow morning."

"Well done."

Suddenly, James felt himself slipping. He was down to the very last of his adrenalin and energy. He heard his uncle's voice in the phone, but he could not answer. His breath shortened. His legs weakened. *Am I going to buy the farm here in the damn Ft. Wayne airport?*

Uncle Earl's voice on the phone was calling, calling from far away, "Nephew? Are you alright? James... James..."

Lord, please don't let me die here...pahleeese not here. His knees were twitching, shaking; he tried to prevent his legs from buckling. He dropped the receiver. It swung on its cord, knocking against the paneled wall of the half-booth. James began to crumble. He grabbed at the booth, but his hands were like clubs. He felt that if he hit the dirty tile floor in the Ft. Wayne airport he would never get up again.

His body twisted. His right leg flew out, kicking over his briefcase, which knocked over the briefcase belonging to the woman on the adjacent phone.

She reached over to grab James with her left hand while hanging up the receiver with her right. She braced James against the steel shelf of the phone booth, buttressing him there with her hip. She took his left wrist, pressed her fingers to it while she checked her watch. "Pulse strong," she said almost to herself. By then, a kind-hearted man in a business suit had stopped to hold James steady.

"Sir, let me help you. I'm a nurse," the woman said to him. She opened his left eyelid wide with her thumb and index finger.

"Are you having chest pains?"

James could not speak. He shook his head. This nice lady certainly seems to know what she is doing.

"Can you tell me what you think is wrong?"

"Fired...my job...loss... ma bizznuss," James whispered.

"Oh, my..." she said.

Slowly, James was able to stand on his own. Her spontaneous sympathy and tenderness seemed to be bringing him back from the void.

"Do you feel light-headed?"

"There will be a slight delay for Comair Flight number 3031 to Cincinnati," the P.A. system announced. "Since it is only a minor delay, we will begin the boarding process now."

"I'm...better," James managed to mutter.

"Do you feel you can make this flight?" she asked. "Your vitals are okay, but you need to be monitored for a while."

James wanted to get home. All he wanted to do was get home to Trish. *If I have to, I'll crawl there on all fours.* "I wanna get on that plane."

"I'll help you," she offered.

"Thanks..." James said. He was so grateful he felt tears brimming in his eyes again.

"Have you ever had an anxiety attack?" she asked as she helped him to the plane.

The phone was still dangling in the air.

"James...James...Nephew...can anybody hear me? Hello? James? Hello?" Uncle Earl's concerned voice called out.

The black receiver at the end of the silver cord swung slowly like a pendulum out-of-sync, barely rotating, left to right, back and forth, back and forth.

CHAPTER 6

"Rescue my soul from their destructions, my darling from the lions."

Psalm 35:17

The woman from the Ft. Wayne airport and the flight attendant helped James to a seat on the DC-9. After she sat down next to him, she asked the flight attendant to bring him an orange juice.

James was now emaciated, his flowing hair disheveled. He had not combed it since leaving Werner, which seemed like several lifetimes ago.

He sipped the orange juice. The tangy taste began to revive him. He could faintly smell the orange scent. His sense of smell was returning.

The nurse took his pulse again. "Good?" she asked. She lifted her eyes from her watch to his face, and he felt a warmth thawing him.

"Thanks, you...saved...me."

She smiled.

How did she happen to be at this place at this time? Coincidence? Providence?

"James Cantrill," he said, extending his hand.

She gave him a firm but brief handshake and said, "Betty Browning."

Her breath was like something very familiar, a scent from his childhood, some flower. He couldn't make the association, but what a sensation it was, just being able to smell, to think, to talk. All the little things we take for granted.

"That was the worst feeling I've ever had in my life."

"I am not a doctor," Betty said, "but I am a nurse. That looked like an anxiety attack to me; a hypoglycemic, anxiety attack. An anxiety attack, however, does not necessarily imply illness. Nor weakness."

James began to pour out his heart, telling her about his career and its abrupt ending this morning. Betty listened intently, patting his hand periodically.

It was a short flight. When it was almost over, James reached into his inside coat pocket and pulled out his leather calling card holder. As he took out his card, another harsh reality revealed itself. These cards were now obsolete. Worthless. James T. Cantrill, President and CEO— no longer existed. *Shit! President and CEO of what?* He no longer had a business. Cantrill & Associates, Inc. had just been eliminated a few hours ago.

He wrote his home phone number on the back. She reciprocated with her card. *I will have to write her a thank you note, big time,* James thought. Then the thought seemed comical to him. *Dear Betty, You were like an angel from heaven, sent to me in the Ft. Wayne airport yesterday. Thank you for saving my life...*

"Oh, by the way James," his angel said, "in the rush of it all back in Ft. Wayne, we may have left one thing unattended. Were you speaking with someone on the telephone before your attack?"

"Oh, my God, yes, Uncle Earl! I'll have to call him as soon as we land. He is in poor health, has Parkinson's, bless his heart."

"Don't worry," Betty said. "I'm sure everything will be fine."

The DC-9 landed at Greater Cincinnati International Airport with a bounce. As usual, all the passengers crowded into the aisles and stood there impatiently waiting to deplane.

But, James noticed something different. Everyone— man, woman, and even child, seemed to be radiating benevolence his way. They all wore warm, well-wishing, sympathetic smiles, transmitting their own personal best wishes, saying, "Hang in there, Buddy. Life sucks, but you're gonna be all right." *Who said man was not an altruistic animal?*

Those who were closer verbalized their kind miens, "God bless you"... "Take care" ... "Good luck to ya" ... "Hope things are better..." all with accompanying gestures of good will— touches on the arm, pats on the back, on the shoulder. This outreaching kindness overwhelmed James. *Some* people were genuinely nice.

And, there was this wonderful lady named Betty Browning, an angel from above in James' estimation. They caught the tram from the Comair terminal to the main terminal, rode the escalator up together, talking as though they had known each other forever.

James thanked her again and, with a gentle hug, bade her farewell.

She turned back to wave and reminded him, "Don't forget to call your Uncle Earl."

How *do* you thank someone for saving your life?

James got off the escalator in the main terminal of the Greater Cincinnati International Airport and hurried to the first bank of pay phones he saw.

He called Uncle Earl and quickly described his near collapse in Ft. Wayne assuring him that he was okay. He had pretty much accepted Betty's suggestion that he had a hypoglycemic/anxiety attack.

"For heaven's sake," his uncle told him, "get off this line and call Trish. She's worried sick. I'll be here for you whenever you need me, Nephew. Call anytime..." His uncle was truly a gentleman.

James dialed his home number.

"What happened to you, angel?" Trish said. "Did *they* do something else to you?"

"No, I'm okay. I'll explain more when I get home. The question is... how are *you*?" he wanted to know, needed to know.

"Better...I still don't believe all this is *happening*."

"I wish we didn't have Kathleen's birthday party tonight. What an awful birthday present to be bringing home— news that I've been fired. What an awful scene..." His glum tone hung in the phone.

She said something, but James was distracted by a flight announcement coming over the speakers. The main terminal was packed, weary travelers crowding, bumping, hurrying, all rushing to get home for the weekend. Popcorn and sweat tainted the hot air. Five people stood staring at the phones waiting for their turns.

"Honey, I've got to go. I'll be home in just a little while. I love you." James wanted more than anything to be at home with his wife. He hung up the phone and headed toward the gate for his Delta flight.

Two uniformed security officers stopped him

"Mr. Cantrill? James T. Cantrill?" the taller man asked.

"Yes... Why?" asked James, thinking *what is it now?*

"Please come with us. Just for a few minutes. To a private phone..." said the taller one.

"Wait a minute. I can't miss my flight," James protested.

"You will not miss your flight, Mr. Cantrill. We've already talked to Delta. This'll only take a few minutes. Come right this way, just over here." The taller man had an eastern accent, out of New England, with short a's.

"What in the hell is going *on?*" he asked the man. He did not like the looks of the second man. He was shorter, stockier, and had a hunted, beady look. Sometimes, for some obscure reason, James, a real people-person normally, did not like a person the instant he saw him. He thought this guy, with a very noticeable tic in his right eye, to be downright shifty.

They took a left down the corridor back toward the main lobby where all of the ticket counters were. The two men then motioned James to the down escalator toward the baggage claim area.

James was feeling uneasier by the minute.

"Where in the hell are you taking me? This is getting farther away from my gate, " he said.

"It's right down here, Mr. Cantrill. Don't worry. I a'ready tol' ya, Delta will not leave without ya," the tall one stated impatiently. James felt a warning flutter in his belly.

As they were getting off the escalator, James said, "You tell me what this is all about...I'm going back up to catch my plane." He turned doggedly toward the up escalator.

Suddenly, he felt a sharp jab in his back rib cage, sending bolts of pain up his torso.

"Aw, *SHIT!*" he gasped. His briefcase dropped with a thud.

"Shut your *fucking* mouth, or you're dead," said the stocky guy, jabbing the gun further into James' ribs.

The men grabbed him firmly by both arms and marched him toward the automatic doors.

About thirty more feet and they would be outside the airport.

Two business men stood by the bank of phones at the door. They turned to look at James being escorted out like a criminal. Their eyes slid away as if he were a bum or a bomber. Then one of the men glanced back, and James locked eyes with him. James raised his eyebrows as high as they would go, gnashed his teeth openly, and, darted his eyes quickly left and right, trying to signify some alarm.

Then, just as James was about to shout "Help," the stocky one poking the gun noticed and shoved him into the exit.

The automatic doors whisked open, and James found himself on the sidewalk with the two goons. The tall man had James' right arm bent up behind his back so he was forced to walk on his tiptoes to keep his arm from twisting out of the socket.

"What's going on? Where in the hell are you guys taking me?" James grunted through clenched teeth.

"Shut up, *asshole!*" Stocky shouted, jabbing the barrel in James' back and tightening his grip on his other arm. His fingers burrowed into his flesh through his suit.

James saw a uniformed policeman directing backed-up traffic.

"Hey!" he yelled. "Hey! Help!" Stocky hit James in the back of the head.

The roar of the shuttle buses drowned his cries for help. The policeman did not hear or see him.

On the other side of the pillars, a van with black-tinted windows waited. The men pushed James inside. There were two rows of seats in back. Stocky shoved James into the front row. He pushed him toward the dark window on the driver's side, and yelled, "Put your hands behind ya" He grabbed James' hands and handcuffed him. The tall one tapped on the black window behind the driver, signaling him to leave.

James could not see the driver.

The van pulled away from the curb and moved quickly into airport traffic with the shuttle vans, buses, cars, and cabs. They passed the cop who hadn't heard James' call, and he waved them into the flow.

"Just what do you guys want with me?" James asked.

"Shut up!" Stocky quickly answered.

James angled his head to the back, trying to address the taller guy, "Is he the spokesman for your group?"

With that Stocky whacked James' head again saying, "Ya better shut up, *asshole!*"

After a short drive, the van turned under a sign that read, "Aero Aviation-Air Charter." The van stopped behind a chain link fence. The tall man got out first, taking James' briefcase with him. Stocky then pulled James out, throwing a trench coat over his shoulders to hide his handcuffed hands. It was dusk, the daylight of early spring slowly dwindling.

They marched him over the tarmac to a plane, a twin-prop like a Kingair. Lanky climbed the stairs into the plane first. Next James, then Stocky prodded him from behind. The pilots in the cockpit paid no attention to any of them. Lanky pulled the door to the plane shut, wheeled the safety crank to the lock position. He then called to the pilots, "Roger. Ready." The pilots revved the engines, which were already running, and they taxied to the runway.

Stocky slammed James down in the aft seat of the 8-passenger cabin and fastened the seatbelt over him. He and Lanky sat in the two front seats facing each other, saying nothing.

The pilot tested the engines one final time and took off.

James was possessed more with shock and disbelief than fear—disbelief that yet another incredible thing had happened on this day from hell. He had been kidnapped.

As the Kingair leveled at cruising altitude, James looked out the window at the clouds reddened by the setting sun and pondered his fate. *Having spent the worst day of his life in the fiery depths of Hell, where was he headed now?*

PART II

"THE AGONY OF SALVATION"*

*"No free man shall be taken or imprisoned
or dispossessed, or outlawed or exiled, or in any way
destroyed, nor will we go upon him, nor will we send
against him except by the lawful judgement of his
peers or the law of the land."*

The MAGNA CARTA, 1215
Clause 39

***from Pearl Buck**

CHAPTER 7

— the actual enemy is the unknown.
The Magic Mountain, 1924
Thomas Mann

As the twin-prop began to descend, James tried to look at his watch but could not with his hands handcuffed behind his back. Damned uncomfortable it was— the cuffs were really chafing his wrists now. He guessed that they had been airborne for a little over an hour. He would have been home by now, but he could not allow himself to think about that. *Aw, Trish....*

James' shock, consternation, and disbelief regarding his present circumstances all converged together. He had to think, to concentrate, really focus on the present. As he always used to say to his salespeople— focus and stay focused on the *now.* Distinguish between short and long-term goals. Well, he didn't need a seminar in goal-setting, especially on this ominous mission. His goals were simple:

1. STAY ALIVE and #2. ESCAPE!

His two uniformed henchmen still sat up front facing each other. They did not talk to each other, and, as best James could determine, were not reading anything. They simply sat there, with blank stares, real mental heavyweights, these two. They were drinking something but had not offered him anything.

James called to them, "Can I go to the bathroom? I need to go to the bathroom."

Stocky got up and walked back to him, unbuckling his seatbelt.

James stood up slowly, his joints creaking from stiffness. He could not stand completely erect in the cabin, but Stocky could. Even bent over, James towered above him.

"Will you please take off the handcuffs? I might have difficulty relieving myself with them on," he said, flexing his elbows.

Stocky stared at him and hesitated.

"C'mon," James grinned, risking another swat, "where am I going to go, anyway?"

Thinking this to be a rational conclusion, the enlightened escort, through a series of reluctant grunts, unlocked the captive's handcuffs.

His hands free, James immediately began rubbing his aching wrists, which felt so good that he once again appreciated things taken for granted — circulation.

They walked to the rear of the plane. Stocky went in first to check it out, as one would expect of a dutiful valet, probably making sure no one had left a straight razor on the sink. He pushed James in and pulled the door semi-closed, leaving his big boot as the door stop.

James looked all around the interior for something. He didn't know what he was looking for, but anything that he might be able to use later. He took one little mini-bar of soap, slipped it into his coat pocket; several paper towels, folded them over, and put them in his hip pocket. Aha! Carefully placing a paper towel on the counter, he took out his monogrammed Parker ball-point pen that used to be his father's, and wrote:

> "HELP! I NEED HELP! KIDNAPPED! on this KINGAIR from AERO AVIATION, CINCY, OH. Please CALL FBI! Then my WIFE (859) 278-4469. FRI 4/4/97 10:35 PM. Thank you!!
>
> JAMES T. CANTRILL
> PLEASE HELP! HELP

"C'mon. C'mon in dere," Stocky said impatiently.

James had to quit writing quickly.

"Okay. Okay," James called back, running the water in the lavatory and flushing.

He carefully replaced the paper towel in the dispenser, a little over midway down in the stack, hoping that someone might find it on the next charter. Or whenever.

As James walked back to his seat, he waited until he was closer to Lanky to ask, "May I have something to drink? I'm real thirsty."

"Whaddaya want?" Stocky asked after Lanky's nod.

"Orange juice, if it's not too much trouble. Or water," James replied. The orange juice had such a reviving effect after his last episode. He needed to maintain his carbohydrate/blood sugar level as best he could, because, for all he knew, he might be on a starvation diet in a dungeon soon... if he made it to his destination alive.

Stocky brought him a small can of Donald Duck-brand orange juice, then re-handcuffed his hands, in front so he could hold the little can.

"Thank you," James said.

Stocky grunted. He did not want to be accommodating.

James sipped it as slowly as he could, trying to make it last.

The plane continued its descent. Where could they be landing? It had to be around an hour's flight time from Cincinnati. If he had to hazard a guess, it would be roughly 300 to 400 aeronautical miles. That would include a radius circumscribed by Charleston, West Virginia; Canton, Ohio; Clarksville, Tennessee; Danville, Illinois; and...*damn.* It hit him like a thunderbolt! Warsaw, Indiana. *No. Surely not. That can't be. Could those bastards have stooped this low? To brazenly break the law like this?*

The Kingair landed smoothly, turned around, and taxied down what seem to be a long runway. It was pitch-black dark outside.

Stocky came back to fetch him, unlocked the left handcuff, repositioned both hands behind him, and relocked the handcuff. Then he threw a trench coat over James' head.

"Look down, ya hear? Don't try ta look up, or yo ass's dead," Stocky commanded.

James intended to comply.

They walked him down the stairs from the plane. James could only see the concrete of the runway, followed by a much finer paved, cleaner concrete that echoed from their footsteps. They must be in a hangar. Through the strained silence he could feel the presence of others just by motions or gestures. These goons were crafty. Standing there with Stocky gripping his left arm, James could only see scuffed paratrooper boots and the shiny pavement.

Jet engines started, their roar deafening. They walked James back onto the rough concrete and guided him up another set of stairs into the cabin of a corporate-type jet. More plush than the Kingair, it had green leather upholstery, which smelled new like a brand-new car. The cabin was also larger with ten seats, minimum— four big captain's swivel chairs in front and two three-seaters on either side of the aisle aft. The plushness was enhanced by the thick pile of the beige carpet. There was a stylish salon, more than a galley, in front of the cabin, where, once again, the pilot's cockpit was closed. The door to the restroom in the rear was open making visible the black marble lavatory with brass fixtures.

Definitely first class, James was impressed. While he was not a connoisseur of corporate jets, it did not require an economist to realize that this aircraft cost millions, in excess of eight-figures.

Of much greater concern to James at this point was his unanticipated realization— this jet probably had long-range fuel capacity.

Where in the hell are they taking me?

Trish was really getting nervous. James ought to be home by now. The flight from Cincinnati takes less than thirty minutes. Maybe the planes were running late. That happens.

Trish had left a message on their daughter's answering machine telling her that she was ill, that her father was tied up on business and would not make it home in time for her birthday celebration. She hated to lie, but until she knew more about what happened, she did not want to upset anyone else. She was going to plant herself by the phone until James got home and she could put her arms around him. She knew this message would seem odd to the girls since their mother was so seldom sick. And less likely was the chance that she would miss a cozy family gathering at Alfalfa's, where James would laugh while he ate his favorite hoppin' john and she would relax with a glass of wine and Jamaican beans and salsa.

The phone rang. Trish jumped.

Kathleen, their oldest daughter, asked, "Can we pick anything up for you? Advil or anything?"

"No, thank you, Honey, I'll be fine," Trish said. *But I don't feel fine. I am scared, I am angry and I'm bent on revenge. But at least I'm not crying.*

"Thanks for calling. Happy birthday, Darling." She tried not to sniff. Her children were very perceptive. And James would definitely have to tell them tomorrow, but not tonight. Not on his daughter's birthday. *What have those damned asses at Werner done to my husband? They will not get away with it.*

She tried to quit looking at the clock but could not. She got no comfort from seeing how little the hands had moved since the last time she had checked. How slowly time goes when you don't want it to? *Do I want it to go faster or slower? Am I crawling toward the moment when I learn that James is dead— oh God, would he hurt himself— he wouldn't, would he? — no, he would never willingly leave me. I know him. Quit thinking like that!* Perhaps it was only a minor delay. She could call the airport and see if the flight was delayed, but then she'd know the answer, and if the answer was no, she'd have to reevaluate what she was worried about and come up with another scenario. *This is the worst day of my life. I want James here so badly. I need him.*

She considered calling a friend, but she wanted to keep the line free for James. *He's been in some kind of accident. I just know it.*

The phone rang. She lunged at it.

"Mom?" It was their youngest daughter, Christine. "Mom, I'm sorry you're sick. We're going to miss you at Kathleen's birthday dinner. Can I get you anything?" she asked.

"No, thank you, Angel, but thanks for calling."

"Is Dad there? I used his Visa card to get Kathleen a present. I just needed to tell him."

"No, he's not back yet. But, he'd appreciate your letting him know. Just save the charge slip."

"I will, Mom."

"I love you," Trish said.

"Love you, too, Mom. Bye."

Oh my God, what are we going to do about Christine? Her college tuition's due in two weeks. How are we going to come up with that? Now that James is out of a job? What time is it? 7:55.

He should have made it home by now. Maybe the luggage was delayed at baggage claim. But he wouldn't have checked any luggage. All he had was a carry-on and his briefcase. Maybe there weren't any cabs at the airport. Maybe the flights were really running late.

She called Delta. Flight #1067 from Cincinnati to Lexington departed at 6:58 and arrived Lex at 7:39. *He will be hungry, so let me go down to the kitchen and fix him something.*

She heated some of her home-made vegetable soup and prepared a tray.

An hour passed and he was not home yet. *Maybe he missed the flight.*

She called Delta again, asking that they check the passenger list. She stayed on hold forever while the agent checked. Finally he came back on the line and said, "I am sorry, Mrs. Cantrill, but I don't show a James Cantrill on that flight. It was overbooked. Perhaps he took the option for a later flight?"

"He *called* me from the airport in Cincinnati," Trish said. "He was headed to board that plane when he hung up the phone!"

The agent was polite, but there was nothing else he could do. He advised her to call back in the morning. *The morning! How am I going to get through the night?* Trish asked herself.

Her hands were cold, clammy, shaking so badly she could not hold the paper she had in her hand, much less drink her iced tea.

Oh God, dear God. What could have happened to him? Oh, where are you James, my love? Where are you? Come home to me...

She had to do something to occupy her mind before she went crazy. She went down to the kitchen and got out all her church stuff. As President of the United Methodist Women, she was continually busy, as well as challenged— and that's putting it politely. The Board meeting next week was an important one, because they had to finalize funds for all their mission projects. In addition to the matter of tablecloths. Those *damn* tablecloths. They were the bane of her leadership. The wonderful ladies of the UMW were going to drive her absolutely batty over tablecloths. After moving the corporate books over on the kitchen table, then laying out her church paperwork, she discovered that she could not concentrate. Nor could she write with her hands still trembling.

She got up, went over to the kitchen counter, and rearranged James' dinner tray, moving the soup to make room for a small plate of cheese and crackers. She dropped the plate, breaking it into hundreds of pieces. *Damnit. Shit.*

Agitated, she cleaned up the broken plate, and went back to her bedroom. Paralyzed with fear, her body quaking, Trish was coming apart at the seams. She fell to her knees and began to pray.

The Falcon 50 corporate jet had been airborne for about three hours. Each time James dozed off, the handcuffs would wake him up, gouging into his wrists. His two abductors were asleep in the swivel seats up front, both snoring noisily. He had some thinking to do, some very serious thinking. He could sit there, hoping this whole thing was a bad dream or a big mistake that would sort itself out. Or he could formulate a plan.

He took stock of what he really knew about the situation. One, he was being taken somewhere he didn't want to go and he had no idea where that might be. Two, he was being held by two strong but stupid captors who were very obviously not working alone. On their own they'd have absolutely no reason to abduct him. He was determined that he would not die in some secret location leaving his loved ones forever wondering. *Trish would die from that.*

In his heart of hearts, he knew. It depressed him, but he knew that the culprit behind the scenes, the perpetrator of this situation was Werner, Inc. — though he had trouble believing that the company he'd worked for most of his life, that he loved, would stoop this low, to unabashed criminal acts.

And, if indeed it was Werner, he did not think they would kill him, at least, not right away. Because he had something which they badly wanted. *Why did I broadcast those tapes? All that evidence? How could they set this up so fast?* Even if he told them everything they wanted to know, could they afford to let him go? He knew the answer. *I have to escape.*

So, his first tactic would be preparation. He must prepare himself to be mentally sharp, alert, wired at all times, ready to pounce upon any momentary opportunity. Drink as much water as he could, eat snacks, squirrel away snacks when possible, and sound the internal alarm. Forget yesterday. It happened. So what? He was still alive, and that's all that mattered. Focus on the minute and prepare for the moment. Yes, he knew that it would come. That would be his slogan, his motto: *focus on the minute, and prepare for the moment.*

He began to prepare "bread crumbs," like Hansel and Gretel in the forest. James pulled out his father's pen, then with his hands cuffed, wiggled out his wallet and removed a stack of business cards. The captors snored on as he scribbled messages on the backs of the cards. He slid credit cards out of his wallet along with his old frayed fishing license, his Kentucky Colonel card, his Rotary membership card, his well-used Lexington Library card, and an AARP ID card. He stacked all the cards together and put them in the front pocket of his pants.

He leaned his head back and tried to conserve what little strength he had left. He was wired in the survival mode. He repeated his new motto: *focus on the minute and prepare for the moment. And escape*

CHAPTER 8

Something is rotten...

Hamlet, 1601
Shakespeare

The view from the corner executive suite on the forty-sixth floor of the office tower was spectacular, almost breathtaking. Central Park was directly to the right and the Statue of Liberty could be seen in the distance on the left. The sun had dropped behind the twin towers of the World Trade Center. The warm spring weather added an extra kick to the joggers' sprint and a lilt to the crowds on the sidewalks of New York City.

But Rob Hempstead, Group President, Medical Division of Brecken, Mersak-Strauss, Inc., was not having a good day. Two representatives from the Inspector General's office of the FDA had just left after an unannounced, official visit. It was *not* a routine visit by an auditor from FDA, but worse. Much worse. It was the IG's office— *the* Inspector General from the Food and Drug Administration, the most dreaded nightmare for a medical industry executive. They had come to corporate headquarters because of "an uncooperative attitude" with their investigation at Werner, Inc., Brecken's subsidiary in Warsaw, IN — his responsibility. This was undoubtedly the worst day that Rob Hempstead had ever experienced in his professional career.

His promotion six years ago to Group President of the Medical Division of Brecken-Mersack Strauss, the multi-billion-dollar pharmaceutical conglomerate, included responsibility for Werner, Inc., a subsidiary where he was told "there are problems." *Problems? It was a smoldering can of worms.* Werner was saturated with executives, upper managers, and middle managers known for their incompetence— *particularly a Vice-President of Sales who had never been in sales, never sold a damn thing*— known for their self-serving hidden agendas, polemics, covert dishonesty, blame-shifting, and backstabbing. As a result, there had been a decline in sales and market share. He had tried diligently to conduct a long past-due, thorough house-cleaning, purging the unclean and hiring new highly ethical leaders. He had anxiously hoped to reestablish the proud tradition, to reconstruct the positive, reassuring culture begun almost one hundred years ago by Judson Werner. He was now on his third CEO— three in six years! He surely understood that you could not radically change and ameliorate a corporate culture in a short period of time. It took years. Quite obvious in the present circumstances, all the chaff had not been separated. The only reason that Werner still barely held on to their leadership position in the orthopaedic industry was clearly due to the strength, longevity, and franchised good will of the distributors, most of whom were exceptional businessmen and women who deserved their success. Moreover, they deserved to be commended, to be praised for their hard work and success. However, for some inexplicable reason, they, the distributors, had been denigrated by the previous management. And, now for some other incomprehensible reason, this refractory attitude had invaded Werner's historically unimpeachable manufacturing practices.

Rob still had his angered chief Counsel for the Medical Group, Ross Carswell, in his office. He needed him there to hear the long-distance call he was about to make.

He direct dialed the number himself.

"Lenny Shortt," was the answer.

"Lenny, this is Rob Hempstead in New York."

Shock jolted Leonard R. Shortt, the Vice-President of Sales at Werner, like a Taser stun gun. He had only seen Robert Hempstead at meetings, had never had a one-on-one conversation, much less a direct call from the Group President.

"... How are you today?" he said, still trying to recover from the shock.

"NOT well at all. I've just had two people from the Inspector General's office of the FDA here."

"We have a *major* problem. We have had a breach," Hempstead stated.

"...What do you mean?" Lenny questioned, his hands and voice shaking simultaneously.

"You know *exactly* what I'm referring to, Shortt. The death, the quality assurance," Hempstead exclaimed. "We are ALL in deep shit because of this!

"And I understand that you terminated the Distributor in that territory yesterday morning."

"... George... George rescinded the offer. And Brice," Lenny murmured.

There was a brief, awkward period of silence. It made Lenny's left cheek twitch.

"You have a history of backing out of ugly situations, Shortt, of attempting to cover your tracks, just like a damn crawfish. Well, this is *one damn* situation that you are *not* going to *crawfish* out of! Is the Distributor, what's his name, gone?"

"Yes sir. James Cantrill, sir," Lenny replied, the knot in his throat and stomach were growing together. The "crawfish" accusation had socked him right where the truth really hurts, right between the eyes.

"I understand that Cantrill claims to have taped conversations regarding the...incident?"

"That's what I heard. I wasn't in the final meeting with him. That was...George and Brice. George's out of town...in LA, I think. He had Brice come over from Legal."

"Shortt, you go get Brice right now. I don't give a damn what he's doing. Have him call me back immediately! *Both* of you. ...understood? Is *that understood?*"

"Yes... sir," Lenny replied, thinking the knot in his throat was going to choke him to death, while the one in his gut burned its way to his spine.

Robert Hempstead and Ross Carswell, both usually cool and composed during crises, stared at each other in concomitant shock and consternation. Neither could believe what they were hearing—that a Distributor without a written contract had been fired, further complicated by the fact that he had witnessed a litigious intraoperative incident, had documented Werner's lack of response to it, including taped phone conversations— all sensitive information that they badly needed. And needed to contain.

Hempstead glanced down at the device sitting on his desk that he had just used— a hand-held sweeper used to detect bugs. Certainly, Brecken, a prominent international corporation in the competitive global marketplace, was very security-conscious. But these functions were normally handled by Technical Services, the department in charge of and highly experienced in electronic surveillance and all its applications. His office and conference room were routinely "swept" every evening.

The sirens and notorious New York City traffic bustling below on this warm afternoon. somehow seemed an appropriate background to the agonizing fallout in the executive suite. Both Group President and head counsel, unwilling co-conspirators, did not bother to look at each other. Their mutual silence communicated their worst suspicions. They both knew the severity of the situation.

The intercom buzzed, and Hempstead's secretary announced the call they'd been waiting for. He punched the Tape/*Private button on his console.

"Shortt? Brice? Is your speaker secure?"

"Yes sir. Uh, yes sir, it is," they both replied in unison.

"Brice, are you aware of the FDA's visit there yesterday? The Inspector General's office?" the Group President asked.

"Uh, yes sir. I just heard about that. I was in a meeting being debriefed on that when Lenny came in to get me," Brice's high-pitched voice strained, his fish-eyes already beginning to flicker.

"And?" Hempstead questioned.

"... I believe they were on a fishing expedition. They did not even mention any of the QA snafus we had, you remember, when manufacturing moved those hip implants offshore, to Puerto Rico, you know...the 936 initiative."

"And none of that seems to concern *YOU!* These— snafus, as you call them?"

Ross Carswell, red-faced, both hands extended, did everything he could to restrain himself, control his anger at this blase` attitude. He had always thought Brice Billups to be competent but pompous, having reserved his opinion because of his other pressing priorities at Werner. He had never dealt directly with Billups, always having worked with his two superiors in Legal, but knew of the two hallmark suits Brice had won for Werner, saving the company millions. While having heard of his courtroom prowess, he had also heard that Billups' ruthlessness and arrogance were present outside court, evidenced by an inflammatory case of "the little man's syndrome."

"I'm sorry, Mr. Hempstead. I was just placed over Regulatory last year. This is the first QA problem..."

"Oh, I see, Billups, that's not your area of expertise. It is *your* responsibility, *but*! Well, what I've got, here, is another *goddamn CRAWfish!* And, what about the termination yesterday? Of that Distributor? Cantrill?" Hempstead asked.

"Oh, *him!*" Brice perked up, " Well, he had it coming..."

"*Had it* coming! *Had it* coming to him," Hempstead shouted. "After *how many years!* Just tell me, Billups," he said, trying to lower his voice, "how many years had Cantrill been with Werner?"

"Uh...twenty-nine...isn't that right, Lenny?" Brice stroked his moustache continuously.

"*Had* it coming to him after twenty-nine years! I don't *damn believe* this — a wrongful termination and the FDA on the same day! And, you two are cavalier...*cavalier* as *hell* about it!"

Hempstead jumped up. "Don't either one of you move!"

He slammed down the disconnect button and remained standing behind his desk, trying to catch his breath and slow his hammering heart. His disbelief and bewilderment overpowered him.

He feared legal repercussions with the now *ex*-distributor in question, James Cantrill. It was just plain common sense. One simply did not promote a long-term, proven performer during a major restructuring, then, turn around and take it away, "rescind," go back on one's word on the *fourth* day of the new operation. Not without criminal or major cause. He strongly differed with George's opinion, with his baseball metaphor — you could take the raw talent of an inexperienced salesperson and with a proven, ethical leader, mold, nurture, and turn him or her into a productive team player.

Hempstead jabbed out the number to Shortt's office again and hoped to hell that those two crawfish had obeyed him. Billups answered.

"And the *tapes?*" Hempstead asked without preliminaries.

"You don't have to worry, sir. That's been contained," Brice smugly answered. "What do you mean *contained?*" the Group President asked.

"It might not be wise to discuss it here, over the wires, sir...even with our security consoles... with all due respect." Billups' false bravado attempted a comeback. "I think he was bluffing anyway..."

"Bluffing! What do you mean, bluffing!"

"James Cantrill was ...shell-shocked...he had to say something... to..."

"Jee-sus Christ! I don't be-*lieve this!* It's getting worse..." Rob's fists were clenched, his lips parched.

He took a deep breath, lowered his voice to almost a whisper, leaned over the speaker, and said, "We will get back to you." And hung up.

Ross Carswell had bolted from his chair and was pacing back and forth, staring out the window.

Hempstead felt as though he was exploding and evaporating simultaneously. He literally raised his hand to his head to make sure it was still there. He sat, deflated, behind his desk, thankful that Billups was five hundred miles away. Otherwise, he might have strangled the little bastard. *This is a fucking nightmare.*

After the phone call Brice looked over at Lenny, who avoided eye contact. Brice thought he was shook up until he scrutinized Lenny— his bald, fluorescent head, morbid face, ashen jowls, bottom lip almost purple, his hands shaking on top of his desk.

What a pathetic wimp, Brice thought. It helped him try to compose himself; he could still feel his eyes twitching— he hated that. But, compared to Lenny, he was a centurion.

"What are we going to do?" Lenny finally asked.

"Well, I don't know about you, Lenny, but Hempstead's *not* going to talk to me like that...*ever* again. *Fuck 'im!*"

"What... are we going to do?"

"I'll handle it, Lenny," Brice cut him off. "I gotta go think."

As he got up to leave, he looked around Lenny's office— over three times the size of his, two big windows. Brice had none. Even had his own mahogany conference table. *Shit!* Brice had to schedule his meetings in a dingy conference room that he had to share with Engineering and

Regulatory. *Look at all this shit.* And for a VP of Sales who never sold a goddamn thing!

"Just keep your mouth shut, Lenny. I'll get back to ya," Brice said as he left, trying to summon his courtroom bravado.

The idea of Hempstead yelling at me. I'll get his ass for sure. He'll pay for this. This whole company is all fucked up. Lenny, a no-talent nerd, nada sales experience, and promoted to Vice-President! And they ignore ME— all my talents, advanced Doctor of Laws degree. And my office is a little fuckin' broom closet. Then, they stick me with this Regulatory abortion. What fool made the decision to move Hips to Puerto Rico, anyway? A premier, high quality/tight spec product manufactured by a bunch of stupid spics? It's insane. Code 936's ass! Tax savings? Bullshit. Arm slings in Mexico are different than Total Hip Femoral Components. These Werner assholes don't know shit. I'll show them, by God.

Brice continued to mumble madly to himself as he walked down the Impressionist-lined hallway.

CHAPTER 9

The telephone rang with a low-pitched ring.

"Yeah," the gravelly voice answered.

"Line clean?" the calling party asked.

"Affirmative," came the answer.

"Code 936? Status?" the raspy voice asked.

"Code 936 check. Falcon, current, 37-slash, zero, zero, zero."

"Falcon 5-zero?"

"Affirmative. November 391 Alpha Zulu."

"Legit?"

"Affirmative. Plan, flight service, Great Circle, 1856 statute. Legit. Cover— on board, new computer-advised, CAD/MFG specs, print-outs, to deliver."

"Subject?"

"Secure," was the reply.

"Preserve to interrogate. Clear?"

"Ditto."

"ETA?"

"Approx flight time— 4:42. With tail W., 4:17."

"Ditto?" the raspy voice asked.

CHAPTER 10

Vengeance is mine;
I shall repay, saith the Lord.
Romans 12:19 (KJV)

Trish had spent a wretched, sleepless night, crying fitfully. Her TMJ was killing her, the pain splintering from her jaw. Worried out of her mind, she was sitting at the kitchen table in the dark drinking her third cup of coffee, wishing that she had not quit smoking years ago. What she would give for a cigarette. The only light in the room was the red LCD on the coffee-maker. Each time she thought that she had heard something, she ran to the living room and looked out the window. She had called Delta first thing this morning. Getting no satisfaction there, she called the Kentucky State Police and reported her husband missing. She called hospitals, airport hotels, airport security, and car rental desks. Not a trace. Nothing.

She kept picking up the phone, checking the dial tone, hoping that something was wrong with the phone— that would explain why James couldn't reach her.

She thought of their three daughters. *Oh, God, how was she ever going to tell them? What would this do to them?* All three were beautiful in their own way, strong, opinionated, and as distinctly different as snowflakes. Kathleen, their oldest, was brilliant, a Phi Beta Kappa, very religious, a loving mother to their two youngest granddaughters, married to Sam, James'...*dear God, what was this going to do to them?* Ann, their middle daughter, was outgoing, talkative, and smart, too, a paralegal in a large law firm in Austin, Texas. Married to Tom, an architect, she was also a wonderful mother to their three granddaughters. Christine, their youngest daughter, had a great sense of humor and loved to party like a lot of college kids. An exceptional artist, immensely talented in many ways, she was an art major at the University of Kentucky. *Damn. Her tuition? How are we going to pay it, now?* All three daughters had sound values and were optimists, each with their own individual faith. *How on earth was she going to explain to them that the company to which their father had devoted his entire professional life had fired him? Had called him up there and fired him! Had taken away his business, his very lifeblood. How could Werner do this to him? Werner— those asses. Those absolute asses.*

Slowly the same conviction that had dawned on James, halfway around the world, came to Trish. *Werner has something to do with this, with his unexplained absence.*

And just as certainly as she knew that, she knew she wasn't going to let them get away with it.

Damn them. Damn them all to hell!

The corporate jet had begun its descent. To where? They had been airborne for three hours and about forty minutes, which made James think that they were definitely out of the country. Mexico? Canada? Surely not Canada. The Caribbean? Central America? Must be Mexico. He would find out soon enough.

He had listened as his abductors talked. However, he had difficulty understanding their conversation, a vernacular punctuated with grunts remindful of the caveman.

James had asked for and consumed two bottles of Minute Maid orange juice, one Evian water, an apple juice, a pack of Nabs, a Granola Honey & Wheat bar, and a Butterfinger. He had been eating and drinking like a king. Plus, he had been able to squirrel away another granola bar in his pocket, in addition to the four Sweet 'n Lows he had swiped from the coffee shop yesterday. His "win-all-friends-and-influence-people" policy seemed to connect, his armed escorts now loose and much more lenient. Was this the end of the line?

The captain illuminated the "Fasten Seat Belts" sign as the jet prepared to land. James almost hated to leave its plush atmosphere of contained safety. He had been able to temper his state of shock with concentrated strategic thinking in these executive confines. Yet, fear of the unknown hovered over him.

Stocky replaced the handcuffs, more gently this time without yelling or shoving.

The Falcon 50 landed smoothly and taxied up what must have been a long runway, meaning that they were not in some podunk airstrip. Stocky placed the trench coat over James' head again, but without threats this time. They led him off the plane into darkness. The heat and humidity were stifling. The pavement was asphalt, not concrete. There were shrill, high-pitched, tropical sounds filling the night air, like nothing he had ever heard before. The tropics. It had to be Mexico.

They led him into a corrugated aluminum hangar where a gray van with black-tinted windows awaited. Removing the trench coat from his head, they took off his glasses, slipped them into his suit pocket, blindfolded him, then put him in the backseat of the van, pushing his head down as he entered. Whoever was in the van remained silent. The air conditioning felt good.

They drove on smooth roads for, he guessed, about an hour. There was traffic, but not much. He could hear cars and noisier trucks passing in both directions. There was no stopping for traffic lights, so wherever they were, it had to be a suburban or rural highway.

James practiced honing the sharpness of his senses. He listened to all sounds, not just the traffic, but everything else over the drone of the air conditioner. He heard someone shouting as they passed by. While it he could not understand the language, he knew it was not English; probably Spanish, confirming Mexico. He smelled body odor, different from Stocky's and Lanky's. It belonged to someone else in the van; no mistake about the hotter, tropical climate.

The van slowed, turned to the left, then drove slowly for a few minutes. He could hear dogs barking. There was a stop, a turn to the right, then a turn off the road onto a driveway that crunched like gravel.

The sliding door opened and James was led out of the van, stepping down onto gravel, then sparse grass and dirt. The hot air sucked his breath away. The exotic tropical night sounds were intoxicating. He walked up three rickety steps. A squeaky screen door opened. He entered a room that had vinyl or linoleum floors, then walked down a short hall, past two doorways, which he was able to identify by the change in their footsteps, then into a room. He was shoved down on a cot. The room smelled bad— fetid, sweaty, unclean. Scents of fried foods hung in the air. His right wrist was freed, his left arm extended, then the cuff clamped on to something metal. Another cuff was locked on his right wrist and snapped to something on the wall. James was locked down, arms spread, practically immobilized. The footsteps retreated. The creaking door closed.

James needed to take a leak, but decided he would not ask. He was scared, but not scared shitless. Not yet, anyway. He repeated his motto: *focus on the minute, prepare for the moment.*

They had not only changed the ball park, they'd changed the rules of the whole damn ball- game.

Trish had accomplished the most difficult task in her entire life as a mother. How does a mother inform her own children that their father had suddenly been called to company headquarters, dispossessed of his business, fired from his job, and that he was now missing? Missing! There was no etiquette book or published protocol on how a mother should perform that task. But, with all the strength and courage she could summon, she had done it. She had told their daughters the whole, unbelievable story.

Kathleen, concerned for her own family as well as her parents, was angry then fearful. Ann was upset and very sympathetic. Christine was shaken but brave. They all had ideas on how they could help.

Trish resolved to set up a command center right there in her kitchen, where the remains of the soup she'd heated for James last night were still on the stove. She also resolved a more difficult task— to stop crying, pull herself together, and do something.

She called Werner headquarters and asked to speak to George Driskell first. Then Lenny Shortt. George was out of town, and Lenny was "in a meeting." She asked Arleen, their secretary, to take down a message to be delivered verbatim.

"Please tell them," Trish said, "that my husband, who devoted twenty-nine years of his life to this company, has been violated and betrayed by people who pretended to be his friends. Furthermore, James is missing, and I am holding them responsible."

After Trish dictated her statement, Arlene asked, "May I say something before you go? I want you to know that this whole matter with James has made me sick. He is a wonderful man. We all loved him up here. For whatever it's worth, Mrs. Cantrill, I am sorry. Please rest assured, I'll deliver your message just as you've given it to me. And I will be praying..."

Trish was moved by what Arlene had said. She knew James had a lot of friends within the company. Most people really liked him, though a few disliked his Southern accent, especially that damn female, the new Area Vice-President.

However, Trish took nothing for granted when dealing with corporate Werner. This was a conditioned response learned many times through the years. She hung up, called back, and left that very same message on both George Driskell's and Lenny Shortt's phone mail, with special emphasis each time she pronounced the most pertinent word, *betrayed.*

She had called Uncle Earl, too. Just hearing his voice and discussing her shock, disbelief, and anger had been good, as it always was with an older and wiser father-figure. She hoped she was not consoling herself at the expense of his health. Since she and James had lost their parents, Uncle Earl had meant so much to them. He was going to make a few calls on his own to some of his contacts. The good feeling she had down deep inside after her conversation with Uncle Earl defied description. She knew that it was not like everything was going to be all right. It would not. But, a wise uncle who genuinely cared, who loved you and your husband unconditionally, conveyed a sense of support, calm, and comfort.

"Call Lynnwood and tell him to get in touch with the FBI," Uncle Earl told her.

"*Missing?*" Lynnwood, their attorney, asked. "What do you mean?"

Trish gave him the details, some of which he occasionally asked her to repeat. He meant to contact the FBI as soon as Trish hung up.

"One more thing," she told him. "I want you to be careful. You could be in danger."

"You let me worry about that," Lynnwood told her. "Do you want me to come over?"

"I'll be fine...but, thanks."

"I will be available for you twenty-four hours a day. All you have to do is call."

"I know. Thanks, Lynnwood." Trish said.

After Trish hung up, she recalled something Lynnwood had said, "what fine Christians they all were." Trish had a problem with that— a real, burning internal problem. She was not feeling too Christian at the moment. Certainly, she still believed in God, had prayed and prayed for her husband and her family, but there was something else in her heart—another emotion that was large and growing larger, slowly beginning to displace the plethora of anxiety and grief which had been saturating her being for the last two days. This emotion was the desire for revenge—sheer, unadulterated revenge. Those bastards! How dare they do that to her family! And, as if that were not enough, she knew they had something to do with James' whereabouts. He did not just turn up missing on a lark. No, down deep in her heart, she did not feel too genuinely Christian. She knew the verse from the Bible, *"vengeance is mine saith the Lord,"* but she had a great ambivalence with it at the present. She wanted vengeance. She wanted vengeance herself, and she wanted every *bit* of it for herself. That was all there was to it.

Trish had a splitting headache, her TMJ cracking her jaw, but she formulated a plan. She called a family friend, Chuck Thursgoode, a private detective who used to be a policeman. She and James had hired him once to help with a technical business matter.

Over the phone, Chuck asked the right questions, and by the end of the conversation she was actually feeling hopeful. And he had given her something to do: she was to reconstruct what she'd heard in the background of James' calls. The announcement over the PA calling the flight, the conversations of people on adjacent phones, the "clutter," Chuck called it.

"But, Chuck— I have those calls on tape!"

"You what?"

"We— we've just been in the habit of taping things lately."

Chuck sounded enthusiastic. He planned to drive to Cincinnati that afternoon, and he had a contact at the airport there. "I'll get the ball rolling," Chuck told her. Trish was to write down everything she could think of that would help. Chuck would pick up the tapes from her when he returned.

I don't know how I'll ever pay him, she thought as she hung up the phone. She would think of something. But for now her hands had stopped shaking.

Trish got her sweater, hurriedly put on some lipstick, grabbed her purse, and stuck the cassette inside. She went downtown to have the tape copied. She wasn't about to give Chuck the only copy of the last conversations she'd had with her husband.

CHAPTER 11

Who controls the past controls the future:
who controls the present controls the past.
Nineteen Eighty-Four, 1949
George Orwell

James heard sounds outside, children playing in the distance. Speaking Spanish. That's it — Mexico, for sure. Probably Monterey. Must be the outskirts of Monterey. Since the NAFTA Treaty, numerous companies in the United States had relocated their manufacturing plants there because of cheap labor and reduced taxes. He knew that Werner had moved some of its softgoods manufacturing to Mexico— arm slings, swathes, vest restraints, knee immobilizers and others were now made offshore. They would have a legitimate reason for corporate flights to that destination.

James lay there with his arms outspread for hours, just listening. Finally, strong, calloused hands unlocked the cuffs and shoved him down the hall into the bathroom. By tilting his head back, he could see a sliver of light under the blindfold, revealing a filthy commode and lavatory that had definitely never been touched by the wonder of Lysol or Comet.

His escort said nothing. Slightly shorter than James, he had a rancid body odor, inclusive of cigarettes and marijuana, which would explain his cough. James thought one, maybe two others were in the house. But not Stocky or Lanky. He kind of missed them, especially after they had reached a higher level of understanding. His new custodian recuffed him on the cot.

Dogs were barking. He could hear a truck or car with a loud muffler coming. Lots of loud mufflers here. There was the crunch of the gravel in the driveway, then voices coming into the house, but he could not make out what they were saying. Or their language.

James' adrenalin was pumping. Something had changed in the air. He could hear someone rustling something into the adjoining room.

One thing that he felt confident of— they were not going to kill him. At least not right now. They wanted those tapes, his copies of the surgical/medical device reports, his legal pad documenting every little thing, the memos, the files, all the incriminating evidence implicating them in that patient's death— the cause as well as the cover-up. If there were no culpable cause, then why all these extraordinary measures to obliterate everything? To eradicate every single detail remotely associated with that surgery? All the stonewalling? The feigned periods of ignorance? The lapses of memory? The run-around with Corporate? From Regulatory to Legal and back again. James had decided that he was just one piece of a big puzzle that could expose Werner. This whole situation was bigger than he could guess.

Without question, that mis-marked femoral component had caused the patient's femur to fracture, precipitating the tragic circumstances which ultimately resulted in his death. How many more of those defective femoral components have been implanted in patients? How many more were walking around in patients right now waiting for the inevitable to happen? For their femurs to split? Walking accidents waiting to happen? *Damn.* Walking...? *Hell, they were walking time bombs. Walking time bombs! Shit.* The thought of it made James shudder. *Walking time bombs...* Yes, this *was* high risk. High stakes. Playing for keeps.

But, for now— *Focus. Be cool, be friendly. Smile. No matter what, keep smiling.* He would recall the whole tragic scenario of the surgery that had started this whole mess; categorize the culpable circumstances, events, and actions at a later time. Now, best to put that out of his mind, clear his head, and psych himself up for whatever was about to come. *Get into their heads. Play mind games.* He used to be good at that. Real good.

He heard the sounds of shuffling feet on the slick floor. Coming nearer. There were two of them now. They unlocked the handcuffs on his wrists. Took off his suit coat.

James worried more about their finding his "Help!" business cards than his glasses. Should he mention his glasses in the pocket?

They walked him into the adjoining room. It smelled equally squalid. They sat him down in a hardback chair with flat, wooden arms.

There was a third person in the room. This new player was obviously in charge. After James was seated, they removed his blindfold. Even though the window was covered with a worn counterpane, the brightness was blinding. James winced at the burst of light. He squinted, trying to adjust. He couldn't focus on the faces of his captors. Then, suddenly he felt chills starting at the top of his head, rolling down to his feet. Sitting over in the left corner of the room he recognized an electrosurgical cautery machine. *Damn!* Did he ever recognize it — an Aspen MF-360A Electrosurgical Generator. He used to sell them. For crying out loud. In the operating room, where it was commonly called a Bovie machine, it was used to concentrate electrical current into a hand-held Bovie "pencil" or "knife" to make incisions while coagulating the bleeding. It was also used to stop "bleeders" by cauterizing them with the tip, which coagulated and stopped the blood flow. Was it a coincidence? Hardly...

The man standing before him was neither Mexican nor Latino. Pale, gaunt, with sunken jaws, he had a tapered Erroll Flynn-type mustache over angular lips. Tall and thin, he had to be over six feet. His wrinkled white shirt with a stained brown foulard tie made him look more like a tired research scientist than whatever he was— or was about to become. He had blue-green eyes that sprinted through the muffled sunlight, bushy gray eyebrows behind wire-rimmed trifocals, with thinning grey hair combed straight back. His body, like his eyes, moved with a weird series of jerks.

"Mr. Cantrill," he spoke with an accent. "We have several things to discuss. The discussion could be very brief"— his accent made very sound like ferry — "or it could be very prolonged and painful for you. You must decide, Mr. Cantrill," his voice deep, harsh. And with that he directed the other two men to proceed.

They were both Latinos. Both wore jeans, dirty T-shirts, had mustaches and long, tousled dark hair— one's was shoulder-length and the other's in a pony tail. Both had multiple tattoos— a cross in a sunburst on a forearm, a large, coiled snake on the other's bicep. They took off James' tie first, next his white dress shirt, then his V-necked undershirt.

Their eyes darted quickly to the inch-long, lightening bolt tattooed on his right shoulder, a remnant from his hell-raising, college days. James caught their quick glance of secret admiration. Using silver duct tape, they strapped his arms to the flat surfaces on the large armchair. Next, they pulled up his pants legs, then strapped the exposed area to the chair legs.

The alpine man watched intently.

"Now, Mr. Cantrill, let's make this easy and brief, so that you may be on your way. Tell us the location of the tapes," he stated.

James looked straight into his cold, azure eyes, studying him closely, while trying to assess the level of danger. He then replied, "Before we begin our discourse, you have me at a disadvantage. We have not been properly introduced," he said with a smile. "You seem to know who I am, and I have not had the pleasure of making your acquaintance. If we are to share information in an open, cordial forum here, I believe we should at least know each other, don't you?"

"Yes, please forgive me, Mr. Cantrill. My name is Doctor Horst Frommacht and my assistants are Ramon and Alfredo.

"Ah, in that case, '*Wie geht es Ihnen?*' and '*Como esta?*'" James asked, looking to each person as he spoke in their respective languages. James was going back to his college German learned under Herr Professor Guess and his border town Spanish learned on those hell-raising trips to Mexico on college holidays.

"Sehr gut, danke."

"Muy bien," the two replied. They smiled, revealing their gold teeth.

"Wo kommen Sie hier, mein Herr Doktor, aus die Deutchland?" James thought himself clever. His two Latin *amigos* were still smiling, obviously thinking him clever, too.

The doctor's expression changed; he looked him squarely in the eye. "Let's cut the bull-shit, Mr. Cantrill. We do not have time to play games. We mean business here, serious business, as you are certainly about to ascertain. Now, where are the tapes?"

James smiled and said, "I do not have any tapes."

The doctor turned, pulled a surgical glove on his right hand, and backhanded James across the face with a vicious blow. His complete facial expression had altered, a sinister glare in his eyes.

The abrupt force shocked the two Latinos. Their faces had changed, as well. Blood trickled from the right corner of James' mouth.

"Where *are* the tapes?" Dr. Frommacht shouted. The timber of his voice rattled the room.

"Dr. Frommacht!" James retorted with his own strong voice. Again, the Latinos were surprised by the assertiveness of his quick response. "Dr. Frommacht," lowering his voice, "I did not intend to anger you. I answered your question honestly. I do not have any tapes in my possession, here or elsewhere."

The doctor's face reddened with agitation, "Then let us phrase it differently. *WHERE* can we find the tapes, Mr. Cantrill?"

"I honestly do not know. I have not seen them in months," he replied, trying to come up with a sincere smile.

The doctor, now sanguine with rage, began shaking. He pulled the glove over his wrist and struck James again in the same place on his face. The blood now became more than a trickle.

James and his two Mexican *amigos* had just witnessed one of the most dynamic alterations in personality, countenance, and character they had ever seen. It was scary. This Doctor Horst Frommacht, from wherever but hell, was a modern day Dr. Jekyl and Mr. Hyde.

Ramon's and Alfredo's facial expressions changed, indicating that they weren't particularly fond of their current job descriptions and probably were not real sure of their own job security.

"Very well, one last time. Where could we find the tapes?" he asked getting right in James' face.

"It has been weeks since I've seen them, Doctor. They are not in my possession — not at my home, not at my office, not in my warehouse. I don't honestly know their exact location," he answered.

"That does it."

He madly swung his hands, directing Ramon and Alfredo to secure James' back to the chair.

They tied two heavy ropes around him, one under his armpits, the other around his waist. The two moved quickly, anxiously, hoping not to incur the good doctor's wrath, as James had just done.

The doctor pulled two Baxter isopropyl alcohol preps from a dispenser box, opened a peel-packed, sterile Aspen Hand-trol Bovie pencil, plugged it into the Aspen Electrosurgical Generator, set the Cut knob on "3" and the Coag knob on "5," opened a sterile pair of size 8 ½ Perry Surgical gloves. He pushed a stool with casters over closer to the chair, sat down, and used the isopropyl preps to wipe the back of both James' hands and wrists.

Well, it wasn't Betadine, but, at least some aseptic, sterile technique was being employed, James thought, trying to divert his mind. He knew exactly what Bovie machines were used for. He had stood in surgery too many times, smelling the burning flesh, the stench of smoking tissue.

Doctor Frommacht leaned closely over towards his face and said, "Ve vill find those tapes."

Taking the yellow Bovie in his right hand, he adroitly placed the blade on the back of James' left hand, just below the wrist. With his index finger he punched down the cut button.

The electric current sizzled into James' flesh, making an incision about an inch long and a half inch deep. Blood oozed slowly from the wound as the coagulating action of the blade simultaneously cauterized the bleeders, smoldering and blackening the skin, fascia, and dermis.

James gritted his teeth for as long as he could stand it, then let out a blood-curdling scream that had to wake the dead within a five-mile radius.

Ramon and Alfredo winced.

The doctor scooted the stool over, depressed the cut button and began making an incision in James' right hand in roughly the same place.

This time he started screaming at once.

The smell of his own sizzling, smoldering, blackened flesh was sickening, the pain excruciating. The heat was more than a burn. It exceeded burning.

James had burned himself before. He had experienced a severe burn in college. In Organic Chemistry lab an experiment blew up, causing concentrated sulfuric acid to hit him in the chest and face. The blast was so hot that he bolted and ran. His fellow students had to catch him and hold his face under running water before taking him to the hospital. It even burned through his lab apron, shirt, and undershirt. Fortunately, it just missed his left eye, but he still had a scar on his left cheek where it had splashed. James remembered it being hotter than fire. But, that acid burn was mild compared to this.

"Now! Now, Herr Kantrell! Tell me. Where are the tapes?" Dr. Frommacht shouted. His eyes were demonic, flickering from side to side. This man had a razor's edge to his demeanor that intimidated not only the captive, but also the guards.

James' brain ceased to process pain. He experienced an eerie lucidity. He saw the doctor frozen, staring at him— evaluating him. He saw the shocked expressions of his assistants, their attempts to conceal their reactions to the sizzle, smell, and sight of James' burning skin, the sound of his screams. Written on their craggy faces was their dismay at the doctor's vicious methods.

"Doctor," James said quietly, "Doctor, I would tell you this— the honest truth. I do not know where they are."

The doctor's eyes darted like flames. Saliva coated his thin lips, dotted the corners of his mouth. The man is psychotic.

"You *vil* tell, *gotta-damnit!*" he yelled activating the Bovie again on James' right hand. The sparks flew as the sizzle burned its way deeper into his flesh.

Screams— louder than before.

"Once more, where *are* they!" the doctor yelled. James had slumped down in the chair and was struggling to maintain semi-consciousness, now. He shook his head and stared down into his lap. A thin string of drool hung from his lip.

"I...I...don't...know..." he barely murmured. The drool dangled.

The sizzle was immediate, this time cross-ways on the right hand.

James' screams pierced through the walls...before he fell into a merciful blackness.

CHAPTER 12

Perpetual devotion to what a man calls his business, is only to be sustained by perpetual neglect of many other things.

An Apology for Idlers
Robert Louis Stevenson, 1881

As he drove I-75 north toward Cincinnati, Chuck Thursgoode thought back on how his and James' careers had paralleled each other. After working as Detective, Special Investigations, in the Lexington Police Department for ten years, he had been promoted to lieutenant. Likewise, James was promoted to Distributor for Kentucky by Werner, Inc. after having worked ten years as a sales associate, then sales manager. They had both worked hard to earn their promotions, which occurred the same week. From time to time, they had discussed the problems and setbacks with their respective jobs. While their work was entirely different, their work ethic, ambition, and continuous extra-effort were similar, making their concurrent promotions more than coincidental. Another coincidence was the birth of their daughters on the same day at Regional Baptist Hospital. Their friendship became grounded upon honesty, integrity, hard work, and a common value system. Their shared experiences had bonded them together through the years.

Chuck had taken his twenty-five-year retirement option with full pension benefits from the police force and started a second career. Now busier than ever, he had built his private investigations business over the last three years. Hearing the terrible news of his old friend disturbed him. It had really upset him talking to Trish. He had spoken with distraught, tearful wives many times, but none affected him like Trish's desperate cry for help. He was damned determined now to pull out all stops and get to the bottom of this case.

He had called Roger Staub, his previous acquaintance in the CPD, now working for the Pinkerton Agency, which had the security contract for Greater Cincinnati International Airport. No, Roger had not been on duty the night of James Cantrill's disappearance, but a friend of his had been. Yes, they could have coffee together, then arrange for Chuck to meet with that officer.

They met at the Starbucks Shoppe in the center of the C Concourse. Roger now had a big pot belly hanging over his wide gun belt, was almost bald, but his smile was still as spontaneous as ever. Obviously excited to see Chuck, he spoke in rapid spurts.

"So, how's the private dick biz? Must be good, huh? Yeah, the big bucks. Look at ya! Yuh look great, really great, man. Yep, must be agreeing with ya," he rattled on.

Chuck was not feeling very conversational. Distracted, he watched the people scurrying through the airport. James, his friend of many years, had been through here less than seventy-two hours ago, depressed and demoralized, after having his life's work sliced out from under him. Probably felt like part of his body had just been amputated while he watched.

"You were real tight with this guy? Right? What'sis name, Cantrill?" Roger interrupted Chuck's reverie.

Chuck took another sip of his steaming hot, Colombian roasted coffee. "Yeah, Rog, I am."

"What happened to him?"

"He was fired from his job. Outta the blue, he got called to company headquarters and shafted; totally shafted after thirty years! No warning. Nothing. Those assholes..." Chuck quit talking mid-sentence. He stared at someone in the concourse opposite the coffee shop.

"What ya looking at?" Roger asked, turning in his chair to look.

"I thought I'd seen that guy at a gas station back in Lexington," Chuck said, sipping his coffee.

Roger slurped his Hazelnut Supreme coffee.

"I can't believe you're drinking that yuppie Hazelnut *shit*, Rog. You must be getting younger." Chuck explained what he knew about James' trip to Warsaw, his flight back here from Fort Wayne, and his disappearance.

He looked over at his bald friend and saw him, really saw him for the first time in the last hour. He was visibly angered, his eyes squinted, his broad forehead wrinkled.

"It sure does suck, like you said," Roger said. "And I'll tell ya what, ol' buddy, anyway I can help ya on this one, you got it. I'll bend em, go the limits...you damn right I will!"

Roger's sympathy level with James Cantrill, a man whom he had never met, must have been elevated by a personal experience with someone close, like a relative or neighbor. His emotional investment in this situation far exceeded a normal reaction. This was more than simply a reunion of past acquaintances. He was moved by the unorthodox, almost inhuman treatment of an old friend's very close friend. He seemed to genuinely care.

"You think he— you know— did away with himself?"

"No," Chuck said.

He observed the man sitting across from him, now in a much more grave, pensive mood than before. He remembered that Roger Staub drank too much and chain-smoked, but below his casual, happy-go-lucky air, he possessed a strong sense of right and wrong— an unswerving bias for what's fair, especially for the common, everyday citizen, an unspoken commitment to basic justice that transcended contemporary law.

"Okay, Chuck. What have we got to go on?" Roger inquired. His demeanor had completely changed now, seeming ready to get down to serious business.

Chuck summarized the sequence of events: James Cantrill's arrival in the Comair terminal on Comair flight #3031 at 6:45 PM on April 4th, his catching the shuttle to the main Delta terminal, C concourse, going to Gate 32, checking in for Delta flight # 1067 to Lexington, going to the bank of public phones in the gate area, and calling his wife. "He was on the phone with her when the gate agent was making the boarding announcement for the flight. Trish heard that echoing in the background. The last thing he said to her was, 'I've gotta go now. They're boarding the plane. See you in a little bit, honey...' "

Chuck sighed. "After those final words with his wife, he disappeared. As far as we know, no one has seen or heard from him since," he concluded.

"Weird. Damn weird! Any photos of him?" Roger asked.

"Yes, several," Chuck replied, reaching into his pocket, "got 'em from his wife."

He spread them out on the table. There were four different photos—one wallet size, with only James' face; another, standing, smiling, at the Tivoli Fountain in Rome; the third, wearing a suit, speaking at a church function; and, the last one, a family picture, with daughters and sons-in-law, showing him to be taller than average.

"These are great, Chuck. This will give us something concrete to show around. Somebody, for sure, will have seen him, either inside the terminal or outside," Roger said.

Chuck asked for a copy of the manifest, the passenger lists on the incoming Comair flight # 3031 from Ft. Wayne and the outgoing Delta flight # 1067 to Lexington, that he was supposed to be on.

"Somebody on those flights, especially 1067, had to have noticed something." Chuck said.

"No problem. No problem, at all. I can get that while you're talking to the Delta gate agent. What else?"

"After I talk with the gate agent, I'll probably have more. And, of course, I will want to check the airport hotels and motels, the rental car agencies for rentals within two hours of the arrival of the Comair flight, all the private charter flying services here, and maybe later, the commercial international flights that left that night. I can track most of those things down on my own. You've already been very helpful, Rog," Chuck commented.

"Hadn't done a thing, yet, 'cept buy you a cup of good coffee. And, there's plenty more where that came from. I'm looking forward to it, I mean, working some with ya again, no matter what it takes. *Capisce*, ol' Buddy?"

"Thanks, Rog. And thanks for the great coffee. I'll buy the next round," he replied.

Chuck wrote down Roger's pager number, the private line into Airport Security, made a few notes, made arrangements to pick up the passenger lists and any other recent information. Roger insisted that he take down his home phone number, too. Chuck thanked his friend, and promised to keep in touch.

Chuck introduced himself to Jim Drew, the agent with Delta. Yes, he quickly recalled flight # 1067 to Lexington two nights ago, because it was overbooked. The flight stopped in Lexington, then continued on to Atlanta. They offered their usual concessions to passengers who would consider taking a later flight, free round trip tickets to anywhere within the USA, but had no takers, which increased the bedlam. All of those irate travelers were anxious to get home on a Friday night. Yet, the plane took off 12 minutes late with one empty seat— seat 23C that belonged to James Cantrill, who had checked in at the gate, approximately 15 minutes before departure. Jim Drew could not forget flight #1067 because he was taken to task, called up by his supervisor to explain that empty seat, as if it were his fault due to negligence. It was like he had caused the airline to miss its passenger-load capacity quota for the month. While he did not remember James Cantrill specifically, his pictures did look familiar, particularly his grey temples and height, since Drew was 6' 2" tall, himself. Whatever happened, he was just as confounded by James Cantrill's sudden disappearance, too.

Frustrated, Chuck felt he was right back where he started. On a routine case, this would be expected. But this time things were different. He wanted to have something to tell Trish when he called tonight. He dreaded calling her because he, too, was beginning to empathize with her utter sense of desperation and knew how anxious and expectant she would be.

CHAPTER 13

The fear... sent packing which
...troubles the life of man from its deepest depths,
suffuses all with the blackness of death, and
leaves no delight clean and pure.

Of the Nature of Things
Lucretius, 60 B. C.

The stinking odor enveloping the room awakened James, accompanied by the stabbing pain. The smell of his own burnt flesh was nauseating. He looked at the open, oozing wounds on his hands framed by the craters of charred skin. They made the raw abrasions the handcuffs had caused on his wrists seem like nothing. The I-shaped wound on his right hand was cavernous— so deep that he could see the bone in his third metacarpal, encased by reddish-brown, bloody tendons and muscles, yellowish-brown adipose tissue, all surrounded by his black, charred, burnt skin. Grotesque. The constant throbbing, stabbing pain radiated all the way up his arms into his shoulders.

James could not believe his eyes— his very own flesh surgically ravaged, so repugnant that it was indescribable. He inadvertently glanced at the red and black Grand Canyon carved into his right hand. He started to retch. Then the picture of his vomiting all over himself flashed in his mind. *Oh God, don't get sick. Not now. You don't need your own vomit complicating an already intolerable situation.*

As quickly as he started gagging, he called up all the control he could summon, diverted his mind, and forced himself to stop. *Don't look at them again. Quit thinking about the wounds. Quit dwelling on them and your misery. Quit the self-pity. Get off the pity pot, James. Get a grip. Get hold of yourself, man!* Just thinking "man" did him good. *Think strategy, think survival. Think escape. Remember again your survival motto, your battle cry: Focus on the minute, and prepare for the moment.*

To even think of escaping, James, you've got to analyze the situation. Recall all your excellent analytical skills, conduct a thorough situational analysis, and build confidence on it. Develop a plan that begins with your adversaries, old boy. First and foremost, the good Dr. Horst Frommacht has a light out in his sign— several lights out. No telling what might set him off. Rule out any sort of humane connection with that monster.

James needed to find a way to appease the doctor, at least enough to avoid any more torture. He knew that the horrendous wounds on his hands doomed his normal return to the everyday world. He didn't know how much more disfigurement he could stand. How could he buy time with his demonic interrogator?

The door squeaked open. James flinched.

Ramon brought in a cup of steaming coffee in a dark green, ceramic mug.

"Buenos dias, Ramon," James said, trying to be cheerful. *"Como esta?"*

Ramon, quite taken with the unexpected greeting, smiled, showing his gold tooth. He replied, *"Bien. Muy bien, senor. Y tu' ?"*

"Bien. Muchas gracias," James said, slowly sipping the strong coffee, holding the mug with both hands. *"Ahh... muchas, muchas gracias, Ramon. Como esta Alfredo?"*

"Bien, tambien," Ramon answered, still smiling, probably at James' brave attempt to be friendly, to converse in his limited Spanish with his Southern accent.

"Um, bien," James said as he took another sip, *"bien. Que rico. Que rico cafe, Ramon. Muchas gracias."*

"De nada," he replied, almost laughing. Ramon seemed to be genuinely receptive to James' spontaneous gratitude.

James decided that very minute to employ the same strategy of affability that he had used effectively with Lanky and Stocky.

He smiled as big as he could, nodding his head up and down, as in yes, and stated, "*Ramon, mi amigo, muy bien; Alfredo, mi amigo, bien.*" Ramon was smiling even wider, trying to passively agree.

Then, James frowned, shook his head back and forth, in a serious no gesture, and said, "*Senor Doctor, no amigo. No amigo, es loco, muy loco, Doctor Loco.*"

Ramon could no longer control himself. He burst out laughing, slapping his left leg with the arm that had the cross tatooed on it. He continued to laugh louder, making a hoarse, coughing sound. He laughed so loudly that Alfredo came running into the room.

Ramon raised his right hand, waving him off, shaking his head from side to side, and continuing to laugh, nodding his head toward James..

Ramon threw his arm around Alfredo's broad shoulders, and they both left the room, with Ramon repeating, "*el loco, el loco, Doctor Loco*" over and over, laughing all the time.

James had connected, scoring an unplanned overture of good will.

The unexpected coffee had stimulated his metabolism and his languid brain. He went back to planning. Even if it were impossible to achieve the goals he settled on, the process served a purpose in stimulating his mental capabilities, giving him a sense of accomplishment.

How could he play a mind game with the deranged doctor?

Dr. Horst Frommacht seemed totally devoid of any compassion or sense of humor, completely focused on getting what he wanted. Was he strictly results-oriented or was there something else driving him? He had a deep sense of frustration. Certainly torturing people was not why he had studied long years through medical school. Otherwise, why would he have bothered to put the anti-bacterial Neosporin on James' gaping wounds? Why would he care? The answer is he did not care. The bactericidal ointment was the result of his medical training. The doctor had failed at whatever had been his original career choice, whether it was medical practice or some kind of research. Research, that's it. It had to be research because he did not possess the people skills or bedside manner to be a practicing physician. That sense of failure contributed to his frustration, impatience, and volatile temper. He must have been employed by a medical company with a manufacturing plant here in Mexico.

If that scenario was even close to being true, James at least had a psychological profile as a backdrop. He had to buy himself some time, because he now felt that it might be possible to win Ramon and Alfredo over to his side.

At that moment, Ramon reentered the room and asked, "*bano?*"

"*Si. Gracias,*" James politely replied.

Ramon unlocked the one handcuff from the cot and, almost apologetically, motioned for James' other wrist. As he locked it, placing both hands in front, he said, "*el Doctor Loco,*" and laughed.

Since his last trip to the bathroom, the Mini Maids had not found the place. The white porcelain commode and lavatory were both a dark rust brown from neglect. The toilet stank. James' acute sense of smell was getting a real work-out in several different arenas.

After Ramon had recuffed James to the cot, he asked, "*Mas cafe?*"

"*Oh, si...si. Gracias, Ramon,*" James answered.

The pain was now shooting up both of his arms, into his shoulders, causing his shoulder blades to throb. He diverted his mind once again by strategizing.

The second mug of coffee was even hotter than the first, bringing tears to his eyes. He sipped it gingerly. What a refreshing sensory response—definitely a contrast to all the others that had racked his nervous system. In the last two and a half days, James had endured more variations of mental and physical pain than he had experienced in his total life.

There was no easy way, probably no way, to humor Dr. Frommacht. James heard gravel crunch in the driveway outside. *Oh, no, not yet— just give me a little more time to think.*

The footsteps entered the hall and moved to the next room. Ramon and Alfredo came to get him. *Damn.* They were no longer smiling. They consciously avoided eye contact with him, as well as each other. Whatever the new agenda, it had totally altered the loose decorum in the shanty safe house.

They led James back into the next bedroom, now the torture chamber. They sat him back down in the stiff, wooden chair. Without a moment's hesitation, they proceeded to strap his arms and legs down with the silver duct tape.

The doctor said nothing. Busy preparing all of his instruments of torture with sure, studied dexterity, he did not look up. If this silent exercise was meant to enhance James' anticipation of further mutilation, it was working.

James watched the doctor's hands moving rapidly, laying out the isopropyl preps, the sterile gloves, the yellow plastic Bovie pen, a sterile back-up blade, an abrasive pad, and Neosporin ointment. His hands did not waste a stroke. The doctor was as good at setting up the operating room as any circulating nurse/scrub technician James had ever seen.

James could not see Ramon and Alfredo. They were both standing behind the chair, probably on purpose. It was apparent that they were not enjoying their participation.

"*Guten morgen, Herr Artz Frommacht. Wie geht es Ihnen?*" James inquired.

No reply. Dr. Horst Frommacht did not move, much less acknowledge James' friendly overture in his best college German.

The ignored question bothered Ramon and Alfredo as well. James could sense their discomfort directly behind him. He could hear their feet shifting and practically feel their eyes glancing back and forth at each other, avoiding *el Loco*.

The doctor plugged the Bovie machine into the loose wall outlet, dropped off the Bovie cord from the sterile pack, then plugged it into the machine. He reset the CUT button on 6 and left the COAG setting on 5. What did that say to James? What did turning up the surgical cutting mode of the Aspen Electrosurgical generator indicate? That the doctor was dead serious? He was dead set on making more incisions in James' already mutilated body.

The next few minutes passed in ominous silence. He could detect changes in each individual's breathing patterns, the doctor's growing longer and deeper, while Ramon's, Alfredo's, and James' grew shorter and shallower.

After Dr. Frommacht pulled on the sterile gloves, he sat down on the rolling stool just like a self-respecting hand surgeon. He picked up the Bovie pen in his left hand and a sterile isopropyl prep in his right. He turned to face James.

"Okay, Mr. Cantrill. You have exhausted my patience. I expect the correct answer immediately. Where are the tapes?"

James drew up as much courage as he could, raised his voice, and stated authoritatively, *"Achtung! Herr Doctor Frommacht! Ich habe nicht tapetes. Ich habe nicht!"*

The doctor looked shocked by the loud vehemence of James' reply. It took a minute for him to recover.

But, whatever James had hoped to accomplish with this novel approach was futile, except for the short-lived, suppressed snickers of Ramon and Alfredo.

Without hesitation, Dr. Horst Frommacht zapped the Bovie blade against James' left hand, making a deep incision one inch long in line with his little finger. The sizzle, the smell of his burnt flesh, the blood, the black, charred tissue all presented a cornucopia of excruciating terror.

James' screams were far louder than those of yesterday. The sounds of his screams began lower, in the bass register, almost a verbratto— emanating from his abdomen, progressively raising to a higher pitch with time— the longer the time the higher the pitch. Until it pierced through the cinder block walls, and the ceiling of the little house simultaneously. Each phase in scream pitch was more prolonged, lasting for what seemed like hours. James had always possessed a resonant voice, an ability to project his speech, accustomed to using his voice to command attention. These capacities were even more expansive in the screams.

The refractory period for recovery was also more prolonged— for the tortured, the torturer, and especially the two attendants. The shambles of a shack they all occupied also required its time to settle. The force of the decibels generated by the tortured screams reverberated its walls, making them vibrate so that the cracked mortar and cracked plaster cracked more, while its infirm foundation rattled. The loose concrete blocks and timbers in its shoddy construction literally shook from their joists.

James sat limp in the chair, his head drooped, his chin against his chest.

"How much more do you want, Herr Cantrill?" the doctor asked. He rolled his stool to the other side of the chair. He forgot that James right hand had much larger wounds, therefore less surface area to gouge. He rolled back to the center.

"Look at me, *HERR CANTRILL!*" the doctor shouted, sitting practically in his lap. He slapped James' forehead with the back of his right hand. James' head jerked upward.

"Tell me now. Vere are ze tapes?" The doctor's accent always returned when he raised his voice in anger.

It took James a minute to find his voice. When he finally did, it was hoarse from abuse.

"Herr Doctor...*bitte*. Please...allow me to explain," he muttered. James swallowed, and struggled to express himself.

"As I tried to tell you, they are not in my... possession...uh...that is... they are not anywhere on any of my...uh...premises...my home, my office... uh...my warehouse...uh, not my bank, or safety deposit box, nor any..."

"*Um Gottes willen,*" Frommacht yelled, interrupting. " *Gotta-damnit! CANTRELLL!* I told you... you...*YOU!...*"

And with that, Dr. Horst Frommacht jutted the Bovie blade behind the base of James' left thumb, almost parallel to his left wrist, pressed down on the cut button activating the heat. The current burned through his flesh, sizzling the skin black, the red blood oozing slowly out, turning brown as it was coagulated. The blade worked its way deeper. And then it hit! Lightning bolts of razor sharp pain bolted up James' forearm. Through the elbow. Up the humerus. Into his left shoulder. Up his neck, causing his face to burn, his left cheek on fire. Up his temple, left ear. Into his brain, making it explode. Rolling fireballs and lightning rods of blazing hot, excruciating pain. Pain— unbearable, indescribable, unspeakable pain. Rifling faster than the speed of light. Radiating throughout his complete left quadrant. Terminating in his brain. And... and then— ricocheting back downward.

His screams far surpassed the ones just previous, eclipsing the crumbling concrete block structure, piercing the walls, the roof, the hot, humid air, the atmosphere, the skies, the clouds, the stratosphere, into heaven.

The mad doctor had purposefully, flawlessly zapped James' radial nerve.

Ramon and Alfredo were both physically shaking. They unconsciously clasped their hands over their ears, trying desperately to shut out the heart-shattering, blood curdling screams— the likes of which they had never heard before— like no animal within a five-mile radius had ever heard before.

CHAPTER 14

Important principles may and must be inflexible.
Last public address, April, 1865
Abraham Lincoln

It would be the only pleasant thought that he would have all day.

Rob Hempstead loved his new corporate jet. His new Falcon 50EX Wide Body was similar in some ways to his previous Falcon 50, but improved in many others— the larger capacity, 10-seater versus 8-seater; head and leg room, he could stand erect with his 5' 10 ½" muscular frame in the cabin now; the appointments, wow, the appointments, the imported Afghan calf, black leather seats, the 18-carat, Italian Gold embossed fixtures in both the cabin and head; the power and speed, 550 + mph or .84 Mach at 43,000 feet; the fuel capacity and range, enabling him to fly non-stop with his staff to their offices in Brussels, Belgium, as well as Osaka, Japan; the flexibility; the reduced landing requirements, allowing it to land at smaller airports, particularly the one this very morning. He was on a vital, duty-laden trip to Warsaw, Indiana. And he dreaded it.

This was the regularly scheduled quarterly review at Werner, Inc., Brecken, Mersack-Strauss' orthopaedic manufacturing subsidiary. Rob, as Group president of Brecken's Medical Division, did not attend each quarterly review, but his Executive Vice-President, David Zuckerman, and Chief Financial Officer, Terry Meissner, always did. He needed to go along today. Rather, he *had* to go today due to the disastrous circumstances just reported to him. First, the sudden, premature termination of a long-term Werner distributor named James Cantrill, an unethical, litigious event itself; however, the questionable circumstances before and after Cantrill's dismissal gravely compounded the matter. Second, an official visit from the Inspector General's office of the FDA! An unannounced visit, *at* corporate headquarters, calling on *him* due to "the blase' attitude about compliance issues" received with their inquiry at the Werner plant two days before. *Inexcusable.* It represented an overt violation of company policy *and* Federal Regulatory guidelines. What he, the Group President, faced today was a legal quagmire of multiple dimensions— a grave situation which could easily present a serious threat to the combined future of both companies.

In addition, performance results had been and continued to be horrendous.

Rob thought this time he had recruited and hired the right man for president of Werner. He was certainly better than the two predecessors, both of whom he had to terminate.

All the feedback and reports on the new president, Ronald Salter, during his first year had been mostly positive. Salter had a track record showing a market-driven, customer-oriented, hands-on leader. But, the last nine months did not reflect any of these attributes. On the contrary, he had apparently been just the opposite. Both distributors and senior management complained that he had become distant, ambiguous, disingenuous, sometimes arrogant. And Werner's disappointing, unacceptable performance — the negative growth, the declining market share, and the declining profit margins— strongly supported the latter. There was definitely something wrong within Werner, for years their corporate darling, their champion subsidiary with stellar revenue and earnings growth.

Hempstead used to look forward to his trips to Werner and Warsaw. This small, mid-western town with its historic pride and rigid work ethic, its deep sense of community, warmed the hearts of most business visitors. He tilted his head back against the rich, black leather seat and began to reflect, to recall the rich history of the company.

A history lesson, a story of the American Dream it was. Werner's founder, Judson O. Werner, a local farm boy, was a visionary whose rise to success represented the epitome of the American Dream. Uneducated but fiercely ambitious, he had first proved himself as an exceptional salesman with a local splint company named DuLuth. Back during the Depression, he traveled the country on the railroads, calling on doctors and selling the splint kits, an assortment of wooden splints, which addressed the most common fractures. Price for the complete kit? $25.00. The best mode of travel back then was by train, and he was usually on the road for three months at a time. His original territory—everything east of the Mississippi River. The first salesman he hired was known as "The City Boy." Alvin Harkness, destined to become one of Werner's pioneer Distributors, had as his primary territory, Boston, New York, Philadelphia, Baltimore, and Washington, D.C., hence his sobriquet. Judson Werner was critically objective even during his humble beginning, admitting that he was a less effective salesman in the larger cities. Early on in his career, young Werner became a legend around the country with many doctors who came to depend upon him as their fracture specialist.

Mr. Werner eventually had a falling out with old man DuLuth, primarily over a difference of opinion in the future direction of the business and reinvestment for growth. After Mrs. DuLuth angrily told young Werner one day that he would never amount to anything, he promptly left the DuLuth Splint Company. With the financial backing of three prominent lumbermen in Warsaw, a very determined Judson Werner started his own company, which, beyond even his wildest dreams, was to become the linchpin, the springboard, and eventually the leader in the new orthopaedic industry. He quickly became a shrewd, entrepreneurial businessman, an artful manager, and a dynamic leader.

To promote and sell the company's products, he created and designed the independent Distributor Network versus the usual salaried-employee sales force. He empowered those distributors to become entrepreneurs, too. The distributors, in return, were encouraged to hire independent, commissioned sales people, giving them, also, a sense of ownership of their respective businesses/territories. The corporate structure and Distributor Network which he established produced tremendous growth and success— an ingenious strategy. His core ideology was easily embraced by all his employees, with their enthusiasm becoming contagious within their families as well. The corporate culture, which precluded total honesty and unmitigated loyalty, was founded upon a sense of family, of belonging, of caring, and of commitment to quality and service. Quality and service were not measurements of productivity and performance; they were a creed, a philosophy, which supported Mr. Werner's mission— helping mankind. Employment at Werner was not just a job, it was a way of life. It was the employees' way of life and they loved it. They were dedicated to it, via their customers, doctors and patients, their distributors, and their sales force.

Mr. Werner was, first and foremost, a super salesman, who demanded that all employees support, respect, and pledge themselves to the distributors and their sales associates. He repeatedly stated, "Nothing happens without the sale. No sale, no job." Though he did not intend it as such, that saying became a credo, a motto for the employees. They were even more committed and dedicated to their visionary leader, whom they genuinely loved. Mr. Werner was also adamant about reinvestment for the future, always allocating a certain percentage of the annual budget for Research & Development, though it was not called that back then. He simply called it "New Products." As a result, the customer base expanded steadily— from the rural family doctor's office, to the clinic, to the small hospital, and, finally, larger hospitals and medical centers.

Rob momentarily compared himself, his mission and his job, to that of Mr. Judson O. Werner. Of course, the times and conditions were different then, yet the overall corporate objective remained the same— to ethically grow the business by helping others. One striking difference, however, was the total sense of ownership that Werner had with his own business. Could this have been Judson's purpose? Setting up his sales organization through exclusive independent distributors? That they, the distributors, as entrepreneurs and business owners, would operate with the same love, dedication, commitment and pride as he did? Rob Hempstead was a major stockholder in Brecken-Mersack Strauss, Inc. with some 763,945 shares, he didn't even know exactly how many he owned. But he was eons from having that heartfelt sense of ownership J. O. Werner had. And, through Judson's genius, that every single Werner distributor also had. They treated their distributorships like children— like their very own babies.

Yes, there were definite advantages to being a private corporation versus a public corporation with stockholders. Werner only had to answer to himself— his own conscience, mind, heart, and soul— a metaphysical proxy synonymous with his distributors, employees, and customers. They were one. The man's mind, heart, and soul were incorporated within his universal constituency. Even his financiers, the three lumbermen, his venture capitalists of the time, were on the same wave length.

But Rob had to answer to his boss, who had to answer to his boss, who had to answer to the Board of Directors, who had to answer to the Chairman of the Board of Directors, who had to answer to the stockholders, all of whom only wanted *one thing*— the price of the stock, and its dividend, to go up. Today, an inordinate amount of pressure is put upon corporate executives, having to "answer" in the short-term— with quarterly earning reports. If the quarterly earnings report failed to meet the "analysts' estimates," what "the street expects," it was the kiss of death. Failing to do so, each and every executive, and his/her corporation could realistically expect their stock to "come under pressure," and depreciate in price— or *tank*, in the Wall Street jargon. The aftermath was usually ugly— blood-letting, heads rolling, people fired, all disguised as "corporate restructuring." *Damn*. Rob did not want to think about it.

In other words, the constituency to whom Judson Werner had to answer was centered in his heart and soul. There was no confusion whatsoever about Judson Werner's and the Werner Company's constituents, for they were with him night and day. They were a vital part of his life, a vital part of his heart and soul, his life and breath.

All in all, it was a phenomenal success story. A new, innovative business, which fulfilled a living need in the human skeleton, management of fractures and deformities, evolved and grew into one of the leading growth segments in the then fledgling healthcare business.

Thus, an industry was born. Born in a small lumber town in America's mid-west. A local farm boy and his dream gave birth to this wonderful orthopaedic industry. A little lumber town, rich in timber, furnished the raw materials to make splints out of oak to treat broken bones. Mr. Werner's great invention, his innovation, was to manufacture the splints out of aluminum, making them much lighter for the patients and, more importantly, rendering them radiolucent for X-rays. His vision was even more prescient: he foresaw the practice of fracture management moving more to internal fixation of fractures through surgery. This eventually created a specialty in general surgery, the harbinger of what we know today in modern medicine as Orthopaedic Surgery. Many deemed him crazy, maintaining that all implant metals would corrode in the body, saying, "They always have corroded, like in Greece and Europe, and they always will." Mr. Werner had not only been a visionary, but, in this instance, he was clairvoyant, a genuine futurist. Time *has* proved him right, particularly with trauma surgery, and, even more so, with the highly successful total joint replacements begun in Europe in the late 1960s and the United States in the early 1970s. Certainly, history has recorded his genius as one of the progenitors of a vital, exciting industry, firmly documenting his dream as a contribution to mankind's quality of life. What a legacy— and what a thriving, dynamic growth company! Unfortunately, emphasis is applied in the past tense.

Rob Hempstead could not believe that a company so rich in history and tradition, so blessed with culture and success could self-destruct so damn quickly. How could a company that was so good go so bad? What had gone wrong? What had caused the tremendous loss of morale? What ever happened to honesty and hard work? To honor and dedication? To teamwork and loyalty? What had caused the titanic, downward spiral in sales, market share, and profit? Certainly, the rate of change in the entire medical industry had greatly accelerated in the last three years. So what? This has been true in many major industries— steel, automotive, construction. Radical change was the constant in the marketplace. It is the hourly constant today in the technology industry–computers, semiconductors, software, etc. But, with focus, innovation, and dynamic leadership, the best adapted and succeeded. Was that it? Leadership? Dynamic leadership? Or was it due to managed care and the hostile healthcare marketplace? No, it could not be not the latter, or their competitors would also be suffering from the same downtrend. And they were not. Some were actually experiencing double-digit growth, clearly at the expense of Werner's eroding market share. No, the radical change within Werner was metamorphic— in mission, vision, and culture. The current culture was the antithesis of that inspired by Mr. Werner, probably causing him, not to turn over in his grave, but to stand up! His unselfish values had coagulated into self-serving dogmas. Instead of his old mantra, "Nothing happens without the sale. No sale, no job," it was now, "Nothing happens without *me*. *My* job, *my* way."

Hempstead's pilot announced turbulence at 31,000 feet, that he would change altitudes. *Man, I love this my new jet.* He continued his reflections on Werner.

There was a deep-seated resentment internally of both the distributors and sales associates — a feeling that they made too much money. Upper management, accounting and financial especially, thought commissions were only made to be cut, somehow having lost the reality that commissions were only paid after the sale was made, correctly shipped, received, invoiced, and paid by the customer. Hence, the revenue and profit were recorded on the ledger before distributors realized the first cent of commission. Their immediate response to every budget shortfall was to cut the commission rates on sales, further antagonizing and demotivating the people who "made the sale, put the bread on the table, brought home the bacon," as Mr. Werner used to say. Every commission cut, every reduction in the prevailing commission rate, only made the distributors/sales associates that much more angry, dispirited, and distracted. It literally cut into their pocket books, their enterprise, and their corporate hearts, distancing them just that much more from the mutual objectives and further devaluing their long-standing relationship.

As a matter of fact, one of the previous presidents, a myopic financial analyst, a proverbial "bean-counter," attempted to take the sales force direct. He did away with commissioned sales people, converting four of the lagging distributorships to company stores with salaried employees only. That was a major mistake. It destroyed historic incentive. It established a duplicitous relationship among corporate personnel at all levels, pitting the direct, salaried salespeople against all the traditional commissioned distributors and their sales associates. An ever-deepening rift developed between management and the field, creating an expanding dichotomy of purpose. That same president initiated the first layoffs in the history of Werner, causing a debilitating paranoia among all who worked there. Trust throughout the entire organization was disparate, almost non-existent. Self-serving agendas became the daily internal modus operandi. Power plays kindled fires of hostility. Morale suffered, finger-pointing flourished, backorders increased, and sales were tanking.

Something *was* truly rotten at Werner. Werner had developed a malignancy and it was metastasizing rapidly. Hempstead had to make a quick diagnosis and perform an immediate excision, or exorcism, whichever the case might be.

He would start at the top. Several years ago, there was a comical, rustic saying describing one of the Werner problem divisions, which was paradoxically attributed to James Cantrill, the recently terminated distributor: "a fish always stinks from the head down."

Ironically, Hempstead, himself a southerner, liked its crude, rural wisdom. It was very apropos now. Werner, Inc. literally stunk from its head down...way down.

He would start with the head first. Start at the top. Go straight to the president, Ron Salter, and ascertain the level of mismanagement and depth of denial right there. He would determine how entrenched these pernicious problems were at the pinnacle. If he had to question each and every upper level officer in the Werner corporation, he would do it. Into the night, if necessary. He was sorry now that Dr. Jack Howard had been promoted and sent to clean up and turn things around at their power equipment subsidiary on the west coast. Jack was the only member of upper management whom he could trust.

After thoroughly interrogating Salter, Brice Billups, and other high-level officers, then, and only then, could he begin to assess the extent and depth of damage and begin to develop a expeditious plan for correction. Before leaving today, he had arranged for his chief counsel, Ross Carswell, to be on immediate, twenty-four-hour stand-by back at headquarters in New York. Even though Rob had been an attorney, his first surmise of this deplorable situation would invite consultation with his trusted corporate counsel.

Neither Ron Salter, nor any of the senior officers at Werner, nor Brice Billups, nor any of the attorneys in their legal department knew that the Group President was coming today.

Rob Hempstead wanted the element of surprise.

Since his car was in the shop again, Brice had to drive his stepson's piece-of-shit car to meet with Lenny. This damn car was filthy— stunk like marijuana, stale beer, cigarettes, with an occasional whiff of vomit. The muffler was half off, making it roar each time he accelerated. Plus it was burning oil leaving a trail of smoke a block long. There were weird bumper stickers meaning who-knows-what, probably subliminal treason. *Shit, this was embarrassing. Thank God it was getting dark, so no one will see me.* This boy was a major problem, having been arrested multiple times, kicked out of school, God knows what else. *If I had known what I know now, I would have never married the boy's mother, wonder-full Wanda.*

Brice met Wanda when he was working his way through law school at Upstate University in Brooklyn. A secretary in the Registrar's office—*God she was a great lay back then*— she was sympathetic to his repeated rejections from Harvard Law School and was overly supportive of him in his quest to graduate first in his class, another thing he got screwed out of, finishing fourth behind wealthy law students whose families had donated to the university. He kind of felt sorry for her— working so hard as a single parent and being poor like he was. Both blue-collar misfits swimming with sharks in a white-collar sea, their relationship was bonded more in common background and ambition than in love.

It was Brice's third marriage and Wanda's third also. *Three's a charm,* they said. *Bullshit.* Anyway, Wanda had gotten fat, looked like shit, and, other than being such an infrequent, lousy piece-of-ass now, she had become a social-climbing, demanding bitch. *Hell, he'd had to buy her a used Lincoln Towncar so she'd quit her constant bitching, whining, and crying. Shit.* All they ever did was argue— mostly about her worthless, pothead son and her incipient social status.

Brice was headed for this clandestine meeting because Lenny had freaked out, called him in a panic to get together this evening. They were meeting in the parking lot behind K-Mart, so that no one would see them.

Brice pulled up beside Lenny sitting there in his company car, a Buick Park Avenue. *Shit. I don't have a company car, much less a Park Avenue. My six-year-old Honda is in the shop more often than not, but I'm gonna drive it into the ground to make a point— all these worthless VPs and marketing managers get company cars, and here I've saved this company's ass in mega-suits time and again, and what do I get? I'll show 'em, the stinkin' pissants. They'll see.* Brice got out of the rat-trap he was driving and got into Lenny's car.

Even in the waning light, Lenny looked like a hunted man, his face drawn, sallow, his tic, nervously clearing his throat, in full tenor.

He's pathetic, Brice thought.

Lenny blurted out, "What'd ya mean in that phone call with Rob Hempstead when you said 'contained?' You know, referring to James Cantrill?"

"You don't have to worry about him, Lenny."

"*Jee-zus, Brice.* You don't mean 'contained' as in something bad? Illegal? ...do you?"

"Let's just say Cantrill's on an extended vacation, courtesy of Werner."

"*Aw, Jeezus. Holy shit...I don't...* That's a fed...."

"Cool it, Lenny! I've got it handled."

Lenny's tic had progressed into a throaty wheeze. "Oh God...*damn,* I don't believe it. *Jeez,* Brice, how in the hell're you paying for this?"

"Listen closely, Lenny," Brice said, looking around the parking lot. He reached over, turned the key to accessory, and turned on the radio, as if they were under surveillance. "This stays right here in the car. Do you understand? I mean *right here! Capisce?*" Brice squinted and stared straight into Lenny's moribund eyes.

"Okay. Yeah..." Lenny answered.

"I've got a slush fund that nobody knows about. Remember that huge, knee product liability suit in Florida? I settled it for peanuts. Werner and Brecken, always expecting the worse, fearing class action, had set up an escrow account for a helluva lot more. Then they wrote it off. It was an off-budget item accounting-wise, anyway. You know how they screw the numbers over in Finance— what a buncha *fuckin' crooks.* When that asshole, Zielinsky, the CFO, got fired last year, they forgot about it. I got myself appointed trustee, moved it offshore— it's earning interest as we speak...growing very nicely." Brice could feel his chest swelling.

Lenny was dumbfounded.

"We're not playing T-ball here. This's for keeps. You're not dealing with your Mickey-Mouse marketing managers, Lenny boy. All your sweet little inner circle of ass-kissers can't help you out of this one."

"*Jee-zus Kee-reist, Brice!* That's kidnapping! *Goddamnit,* this is... serious. *Jee-zus,* I can't believe what you've gotten me into," Lenny finally spouted out.

"Listen here, Lenny. You got your own pansy ass into this. You could've stopped this thing with Cantrill, headed it off long before he ever got called up to George's office. And you *damn* well know it."

Lenny swallowed hard and forcefully cleared his throat.

"It was common knowledge inside Werner how much that butch bitch, your new Area VP, disliked Cantrill, hated his Southern charm— she was stirring up things against him, doing everything within her power to undermine him, like she was jealous of his accomplishments and popularity, really a buncha cheap-shit shots. She's a back-biting ball-buster, and she's your report." Brice paused to look at his manicured nails.

"While my professional domain is primarily legal and regulatory, Lenny, any fool knows that is *corrupt* management— to have a manager cutting down a proven performer behind his back. And *she's* been on a rampage on your watch. She's *your* responsibility!" Brice stated emphatically.

Lenny looked like he had just been kicked in the nuts.

"Yes sir, your days of slimy weaseling— what did Hempstead call it? Crawfishing? Yeah, crawfishing. Perfect. Yo' crawfishin' days are over, Lenny Boy. And don't you forget *it!*"

Lenny could not speak. Ashen, slack jawed, slumped down in the seat, he stared out the car window.

Brice got out, walked around to the driver's side, leaned his head in, and said, "You just keep your mealy mouth shut for a change, Lenny. I'll be in touch."

The little car roared. The trail of smoke from its exhaust enveloped Lenny Shortt before he could raise his window, exacerbating his tic into a choking cough.

CHAPTER 15

...how much less man, who is vile and corrupt,
who drinks up evil like water.
Job 15:16 (NIV)

Waves of revulsion engulfed James, temporarily countervailing the acute pain from his wounds. What he had suffered and endured in the last four days was so reprehensible that it defied description. How could the company for whom he had labored for so long, the company to whom he had devoted most of his life, the company he had loved, how in the hell could they do this to him? To any human being? He could not bear to look at his hands and arms— the grisly, bloody, charred excavations in his flesh, permanently disfiguring him for life. How could they order something so macabre, so inhuman? It was worse than a terrorist's behavior, because that's expected with terrorism— worse because it was born in a legitimate, presumably respectable corporation. It was conceived, formulated, and ordered out of a fiduciary business environment, composed of working people— executives, managers, employees, distributors, sales professionals, all of whom were supposed to have mutual goals, respect, and trust. If he could only live through this torture, he swore, swore an oath to his dying day, that he would somehow *make the truth known*. The reprobates, the barbarians who were behind this, those lowly bastards deserved exposure, to have the gruesome truth, with bloody pictures of his mutilated body, blatantly confront them before God and their peers.

He would not dwell on that aspect. Justice, judgment, and punishment were far from his domain now. The torture and permanent disfigurement were also academic at this point. What's at stake here is *his life.* He needed to channel his anger, his energy to his own good. He had to focus on survival, living through this, this gory torture and mutilation so that he could serve up and testify to the truth. He owed it to himself, to his family, to his employees, to his team— his *ex*-team, to his fellow Distributors and to all his many friends— to loudly and proudly broadcast *the truth.*

He had slept very little during the night. The heat and stench in this fetid chamber of death sucked the breath right out of his mouth. Each and every time he attempted to breathe deeply through his mouth to assuage the nausea, he would gag. The malodor of his surroundings exacerbated his condition. Pain, nausea, hunger, thirst, extreme fatigue, mental confusion, nervous exhaustion, disorientation, helplessness, all foreboding death. The place smelled like death.

There was absolutely nothing he could do at this moment to change his surroundings. Get a grip. He had to get a grip. Rid himself of the feeling of helplessness, more physical than psychological. Physically, he was a wreck. But, psychologically, he was still unbelievably strong. And spiritually, as well. His abiding faith and hope, though whacked, were still in tact. Keep on holding *on.* His very desperation should impart strength to his resolve and efforts. He should make a determined, a dogged effort, no matter what, to maintain his selfhood, preserve his personal values, endure, and survive, as he had so valiantly done thus far.

He thought he knew the psychodynamics of the techniques being used on him. He had studied them back in college, especially in Physiological Psychology. He knew what they wanted, and why; he knew what they wanted and how. He knew the so-called doctor, his torturer, was a total nutcase. He should compliment him on his using NeoSporin on his wounds. The use of the medication represented the supreme paradox— first this crazed doctor maims James' arms and hands beyond human comprehension with electrosurgical current, then administers to the wounds with antibacterial ointment. But, thank God for that antibacterial ointment, otherwise infection would have already set in. All Frommacht wanted, had been instructed to get, was the location of the tapes. Why was he, James Cantrill, withholding the information so stubbornly? So resolutely? Was it to save his life? Once they found out about the tapes, how much longer would they keep him alive? Until they had gotten the tapes in their hands? A day? Probably two days at most. If he continued to resist, how much longer could he last? How much more of the torture could he withstand?

Just then, Ramon came in bringing him hot coffee in the same chipped mug. He was smiling, a wider smile, exposing his gold tooth. A gleam of diffused sunlight reflected off the gold, sending a bright flash across the room.

"*Como esta, amigo?*" he asked, upbeat.

"*Bien, Ramon,*" James lied, forcing a weak smile back.

James saw a light. The fact that Ramon had spontaneously called him *amigo* had to demonstrate a tacit friendliness. Maybe, just maybe, given the right circumstance and opportunity, Ramon could be an ally.

The first sip of the steaming coffee burned James' lips, mouth, throat, his esophagus, all the way down into his stomach. The trail left a wake of sensational stimuli, beginning with tears in the corners of his eyes— welcome signs, reaffirming his sensory responses and the fact that he was indeed still alive.

"*Ahh, gracias. Muchas gracias, Ramon,*" he said, taking another sip.

"*De nada. De nada,*" he repeated, smiling ear to ear, before turning to leave.

The strong coffee stimulated his brain waves, too. He needed to think— think positively, think creatively. He was not dead, yet.

He recalled from a spy book that he had read that it was usually the third successive day of progressive torture that resulted in conversion of the subject. Whoever conceived this torture was ingenious— the symbolism, using a system that James used to sell, an instrument from his livelihood, one that painted the entire sensory landscape. It was not so much the pain, the sense of touch; not so much the smell, of his own burning flesh; not so much the sight, the bloody, charred caverns of his own skin; not so much the sound, the sizzle as the blade incised his flesh, but it was the abhorrent anticipation, the concurrent fear and full knowledge of what was about to happen. Granted, the extent of mutilation and level of pain inflicted upon him had been increased by the hour each day. That last lightning bolt of current to his radial nerve was the sharpest pain he had ever experienced in his entire life. Had he reached his threshold? His limit? He needed to create some kind of diversion, change the pace, change the sequence, alter the process, anything, so that some glimmer of opportunity might present itself. He hoped that his suspicions about Ramon and Alfredo, especially Ramon, would prove correct. James suspected that, if even the slightest opportunity, Ramon would maybe look the other way. The adrenalin rush, the sudden thrust of optimism felt good and boded well.

He heard the sounds of gravel crunching outside, indicating the arrival of his torturer.

Ramon rushed in through the door, carrying an old, dented coffee pot with steam rising out of the spout. He carefully poured a little warmer into James' mug.

"*Copita?*" he smiled and quickly left.

"*El loco?*" James asked.

"*Si,*" Ramon answered, laughing. "*Doctor mui loco.*"

As James finished his piping-hot, high-test coffee, he heard raised voices echoing through the thin walls of the shoddily constructed house. He recognized Frommacht's voice, already shouting orders to his subordinates. He treated Ramon and Alfredo like low-life dirt. His voice got louder. He was raving mad about something.

Ramon came in to fetch James. The contrast in his countenance was cosmic. Alfredo stood in the doorway extremely glum. The effect of Dr. Frommacht's tirade was noticeable on their faces.

They half forcefully led him back into the adjoining room, the Torture Chamber. Dr. Frommacht was already sitting on his stool, first turning the power switch on, then adjusting the cut/coag knobs on the Aspen Electosurgical generator. Next, painstakingly conducting his preoperative routine, he began laying out the sterile gloves, isopropyl preps, Neosporin, and sterile Bovie pencil with cord on a small, draped table, which acted as the Mayo stand. He did not speak.

They again strapped James to the high-backed, wooden chair with the silver duct tape. Ramon and Alfredo made a studied effort to avoid eye contact with him, as well as with each other. He noticed they both had do-or-die, ominous expressions on their now sullen faces.

James patiently sat there, composing himself, waiting for the mad doctor to turn and face him.

After meticulously opening the sterile Bovie and gloving, Dr. Frommacht turned on the stool to address his subject. He held the Bovie in his right hand, an isopropyl prep in his left.

James immediately spoke with strength and confidence, " Dr. Frommacht, before you begin, allow me to tell you that today, in no uncertain terms, I shall give you the information which you desire."

This unexpected announcement by the victim of his sadistic torture caught the doctor totally off guard. His expression changed. He moved the stool back, seemingly disappointed that he was not going to be able to activate his surgical handpiece. Yet, at the same time, a faint trace of relief penetrated his sinister demeanor.

"First, Dr. Frommacht, allow me to thank you for using Neosporin ointment on my wounds. If you had not done so, infection would have already developed and I would be in a much more severe, more morbid condition than I am," James stated, enunciating his words carefully and succinctly.

The doctor nodded subtly, but did not smile or speak.

"Secondly, I wish to compliment you as a physician and as a surgeon," James continued, pouring it on.

The unsolicited compliment also caught Dr. Frommacht by surprise, almost momentarily softening his heretofore evil appearance.

"I have watched your sterile technique very closely, your dexterity with instruments, particularly the electrosurgical electrode, the Bovie, your methodical, very meticulous attention to proper procedure and protocol, Dr. Frommacht. Your psycho-motor skills are excellent. As you may know, I, myself, have a medical background, went to medical school briefly, not nearly as long as you, however, then did graduate work in physiology. In my professional career over the last 31 years, I was fortunate to have had and built my own orthopaedic/surgical business. During that time, I have worked with many surgeons, stood in with them on hundreds and hundreds of surgeries in the operating room, have helped train and assist surgical and orthopaedic residents from many different nationalities, and have trained all my personnel in proper surgical technique. I have seen and observed professional capabilities at all levels, from incompetent to highly skilled, from very bad to very good. Your skill set, Dr. Frommacht, is, quite simply stated, exceptional and, accordingly, your education and training in Germany had to have been superior, as well."

James could see that his compliments, these qualified assessments of the doctor's professional ability, were being well received, really hitting home. He thought that he was on a roll. Horst Frommacht, *the person,* the repressed Horst Frommacht, still existed and was struggling internally to express genuine gratitude. There was an intermittent, dim glow on his mien of a smiling "thanks." But, at the same time, the schizophrenic twin, the Dr. Jekyll/Dr. Frommacht suppressed any attempt at good behavior via affable self-expression. Rather, the sadistic personality component dominated the bipolar conflict within, as manifested by the textbook, short attention span. In other words, the alter ego, the internal Horst tried to smile, but the dominant ego, the external Dr. Frommacht was becoming impatient and testy.

James perceived it and needed to get on with his dissertation.

"That said, Herr Doktor, there are two critical items which I need to clarify before I divulge the information which you were contracted to obtain." James hit a sensitive area with the latter part of his comment. The doctor frowned, recoiling slightly at the word "contracted."

"I can certainly appreciate the fact that your initial specialty in surgery, medicine, did not involve the practice you have employed here the last two days. Rather, and this is speculation on my part, you were probably hired at a high salary for medical research by one of the large, multinational corporations taking advantage of the NAFTA Treaty here in Mexico." At that, Dr. Frommacht smirked, a gesture which James could not interpret.

"Something untoward occurred, due entirely to no fault of your own, and your career was suddenly compromised. They, these global corporations, deficient in ethics and devoid of loyalty as many of them are, did not appreciate and value the excellent skills which you possess, Dr. Frommacht, and they unjustifiably compromised your exceptional professional career. All of which has reduced you to..."

"Cut the bullshit, Herr Cantrill. Enough! *Und*...and for your information, you are not in Mexico, you fool! You are in Puerto Rico," Dr. Frommacht shouted, growing red-faced.

Damn. Puerto Rico! thought James. *Well, damn. That explains a lot of things— all the pharmaceutical plants located here due to U. S. tax incentives,*

Code 936, I think they call it. Yes. The medical device manufacturers, too. Werner had a plant here. That explains his flight here. Hell, that explains the whole damn, bloody horror show. Light bulbs went off in rapid succession inside James' head. *And the mad doctor, too. He was working for one of the huge pharmaceutical companies and got fired. No wonder. With his sadistic personality disorder — speaking of schizoid, split personality.*

James realized that he was pushing his luck, exhausting the limited patience of his demented torturer, but obviously he had hit a nerve when he said "reduced." The incendiary reaction was evoked right then. James had really been on a roll, taking control of the situation, changing the sequence of the interrogation and torture. How could he recover? How could he regain Frommacht's attention?

"Well, Puerto Rico. Puerto Rico, Herr Doktor, further emphasizes what we were discussing. Over one hundred big pharmaceutical companies are located here. Even more if you count medical manufacturers. Why? Why are so many of them located here in Puerto Rico, Dr. Frommacht?" James had momentarily recovered his impatient attention.

"Why? Why, Herr Doktor? You know," James raised his assertiveness, "you know. You know better than I, Dr. Frommacht. No *taxes!* Not one cent of tax on every product made here. No damn taxes means fatter profits. Fatter profits mean *BIG BUCKS! BIG BUCKS,* Doctor, not to you. Not to me. To their execs, big bonuses, stock options for the insiders, their internal power elite. Do you think they care about you? *Hell no.* They don't give a shit about you. They don't give a shit about me. Just look at what's happened to *me!* Why do you think I'm here in Puerto Rico? On vacation? No way. It's because of them. Look at *me,*" now shouting, using his chin to point to the grotesque wounds on his arms.

Ramon and Alfredo looked aghast, shocked by James' outburst of authority.

"Look at *you!* A superbly trained physician, a highly skilled *surgeon,*" James yelled, maneuvering the only part of his body free to move, his head, for emphasis.

"Just take a good hard look at yourself," suddenly lowering his voice, "look at you. They, the no good, self-serving bastards, have compromised your fine career, your great potential...just like they've done to me," tilting his chin downward again toward his gashes. He thought he might have penetrated Horst Frommacht's psychiatric armor. The doctor still held the Bovie in his right hand, but his stone grey eyes focused on James and what he was saying.

"Look at you," James kept his voice low, intent on continuing to hold forth, "an ingenious researcher and practitioner, a physician, surgeon, and, here you are, in a shit house, a dilapidated shit house, using an obsolete Aspen Electrosurgical generator on a, uh... well...the question is why? *WHY?* Look what they've done to *you!* Why? For what reason? Who did this to you? CellGen? Clark-DuBoise? Brecken-Mersack Strauss? They're the bastards who betrayed me."

The doctor was getting redder, his cold, gray eyes beginning to twitch, his jaws tightening. Could James be getting to him? At last?

"Werner, the sons-of-bitches and their parent company, Brecken-Mersack, betrayed me. Who did you in? Who shafted you? Siebert & Siebert? The Spellmann-Ross Company?"

James was getting bolder and bolder.

"Who brought the ax down on you? Fromm-Rice? Pfaelger? They're all down here. Over a hundred of 'em, all the drug companies. Medical device manufacturers, too. Who was it? Zeitz Medical Products?"

"SCHLIESSEN den MUND! Schliessen den Mund. GENUG! Genug. Gotta-damnit! Cantrellll! Ze tapes! Geben sie mir ze tapes, ze documents!" Horst Frommacht blew, mixing his German and English again.

James did not know what had triggered this, his latest volcanic eruption— a name, a company, THE company, impatience, or sheer psychosis.

"Geben sie mir, Herr Cantrell, ich verlangen, Gotta...Gotta-damnit! Wo ist...where are they? Where are the tapes?" he shouted, moving his stool closer.

Dr. Frommacht had already activated the blade of the Bovie, which was incising, sizzling, charring the skin on the inside of James' left elbow, right next to his funny bone.

"No, Wait! No, not again...pahleese. Noo!" James shouted.

As the smoke and now familiar, repulsive odor of his burning flesh rose in the rancid air, James gritted his teeth fiercely, groaning with a guttural sound, a loud but muted bellow, bravely attempting to hold back.

Then it hit him! The current blasted his ulnar nerve.

James' resounding scream far surpassed those of the previous two days.

It was not just the riveting pain, which shot up through his arm, shoulder, neck, by the left ear, running up his skull, into his brain, where it exploded. But, worse than that razor sharp pain was the motor response, the sudden, severe muscle contractions in his arm and hand— the tetanic contractions, converting his left hand into a giant claw, stretching the silver tape and digging into the arm of the chair. Like the claws of a tiger, his finger nails ground into the flat wood, causing splinters to embed themselves beneath his nails. His left wrist curled as his hand cramped, scratching, clawing aimlessly. The contractions continued for what seemed like hours. His hand, wrist, arm, and shoulder shook violently, with accompanying vibrations throughout his entire body.

There were milder, sympathetic contractions in his right arm, up his right shoulder, causing his lightning bolt tattoo to flutter. The concurrent waves of pain were insufferable.

Ramon and Alfredo shuddered. They pointed at the tattooed skin fluttering, quivering, making the lightning bolt seem real. They whispered to each other about... they knew, *El Diablo.*

James' scream increased by the milli-second to super-human decibel levels. The resultant vibrations were spine tingling, supernatural in their forceful timber, nearly resembling diluted jet propulsion.

Ramon and Alfredo winced miserably, bending at their waists, turning their backs to James, facing the wall, clasping their hands over their ears, trying in vain to shut out his blood-curdling scream.

The layers of peeling pastel paint on the eroding cinder blocks fluttered. The cheap, trashy construction of the house was never more apparent, as it seemed to rise, lift up, creaking into the stratosphere. It shook, seemed to vibrate— foundation, floor, walls, plaster falling from the ceiling, and, either from a wind as well as the reverberating sound waves, the corrugated aluminum roof rattled like a broken cymbal.

His bombastic screams sliced the hot, humid air outside into sections like pizza. If a neighborhood had existed previously here, it had now disappeared. The horrific sounds of torment radiating from the torture house had converted this once peaceful neighborhood into a miniature ghost town.

The laughter of children playing had been rudely displaced by shrieking, wailing screams of horror.

The fall-out from the incomprehensible pain were evident—the torturer wheeling his stool around so as not to countenance his victim; the bystanders striving to distance themselves from the carnage; the very structure of this dump falling apart; the neighborhood vacated in fear; even the hot, humid air outside, the atmosphere somehow altered; and finally, the poor victim, a bloody, charred, limp heap, barely qualifying as a piece of humanity.

The contractions continued in James' left flank, but were slowly beginning to subside. The suffering had not.

James was slumped way down in the chair; the only thing which prevented his falling out was the wrinkled silver duct tape. His head had dropped onto his right shoulder, his chin drooped, mouth slanted open, drooling saliva down his chest.

He let out another howl, almost like a wolf, but more grating. It lingered while more contractions recommenced in his left arm, then receded in involuntary jerks, one after another, each lasting about twenty-five seconds, then finally diminishing.

The final howl persisted, tapering off to spasmodic groans... each time snapping James' chin off his shoulder.

Finally, it stopped.

He crumbled— a crumbled up, maimed, twisted, mutilated mass.

He was struggling to maintain consciousness, drifting in and out, his eyes only slightly open. The barely visible whites of his eyes were now a blood-shot, hideous yellow.

After the last howl, Dr. Horst Frommacht turned on his stool, leaned over closer almost in his victim's face, and asked in a quieter, bass tone, not quite a whisper, "Okay, *Herr* James Cantrill, tell me now, fere are ze tapes?"

James did not reply, having again lost consciousness.

Then, Frommacht grabbed James' chin with his gloved, left hand and slapped his right cheek with his right hand, making a resounding splat.

James yelled, recoiling from the shock.

Ramon lunged forward, as if ready to attack the demoniacal torturer. Alfredo quickly restrained his *compadre*.

"Where are the tapes?" Frommacht shouted, still holding James' jaw with his left hand.

James muttered something, speaking unintelligibly, as much from the forceful hand on his chin as from his groggy state of semi-consciousness.

"Where? Where, Herr Cantrill?" the doctor repeated.

"...at my attorney's..." James mumbled.

" What? Where? Where are they?" Frommacht bludgeoned again.

"At my attorney's office..." he murmured, barely conscious.

" Is that Herr Engle? Herr Lynnwood Engle?"

"...Yeah..." James answered, hardly audible.

" In Herr Lynnwood Engle's office?"

James had lost consciousness, again.

He had also lost his last vestige of resolve, the last shred of strength, the last ounce of resistance, so courageously, so tenaciously, so steadfastly maintained for so long.

James had mentally departed the chamber of torture, not fully knowing what he had just done. He was now drifting deeper and deeper, descending downward into the dungeon of death, his grossly lacerated flesh a macabre beacon to the morbid keepers there, the dark, black abyss he had visited so many times in the last seventy-two hours, but from whence he had valiantly returned to fight again,

and again,

and again.

CHAPTER 16

The telephone rang with a muted, low-pitched ring.

"Yeah," the gravelly voice answered.

"Line clean?" the calling party inquired.

"Affirmative," was the answer.

"Status? Code 936 package?" the raspy voice asked.

Objective accomplished," the voice firmly stated.

"Location?"

"One niner five Main, Suite one two zero zero. Firm, S-t-a-h-l pause K-e-n-d-r-I-c-k pause H-a-r-t . Office, A-t-t-y L dot W dot Ingle, nee L-y-n-n-w-double O-d. Copy?"

"Affirmative. City?"

"Same. L dot E dot X dot."

There was a prolonged silence. Only breathing— deep, weathered breathing could be heard on the phone.

"Subject?"

"Impaired. Markedly impaired," was the answer.

"Eliminate. Repeat. Eliminate. And dispose of. Repeat. Dispose of. No trace. Copy?"

"Affirmative," the gravelly voice replied.

"Confirm," the raspy voice commanded.

"Affirmative."

"Repeat. Confirm objective," even more sternly stated.

"Ditto."
"Ditto?"
"Ditto." Click.
Click.

CHAPTER 17

...expectation whirls me round.
Troilus and Cressida, 1602
Shakespeare

The phone ringing startled Trish. She must have just dozed off, because, again for a second night, she had not slept.

"Hello," she answered expectantly. It was 7:23 A.M.

"I'm sorry I didn't call you last night, but I didn't have enough to report," Chuck Thursgoode apologized.

"I'm so worried," she said.

"Trish, I think you are holding up unbelievably well. As you already know, I can't do anything about James' job or business, or about the damn people at Werner who treated him so abysmally. But, what I'll solemnly promise you is this: I shall go to the ends of the earth to find James, and, in the process, I'll never mislead you... or give you anything to create false hope. I'm not only searching for your husband, I'm also looking for my friend," he swallowed hard, "a special friend whom I hold in high regard, uh, have great respect for... and, I think you know how much I care."

"Yes, I do, Chuck. Thank you," she bit her quivering lip. "What on earth's happened to my husband..." she choked.

Chuck summarized his meeting with his security contact at Cincinnati International — his circulating the pictures of James, helping obtain the commercial flight information, ingoing and outgoing, with passenger manifests, helping with the complete canvass of the airport area auto rental agencies, hotels, motels, private air charters. He continued with his interview of the Delta gate agent who was on duty that night for flight #1067 to Lexington/Atlanta, his recognition of James' photo.

"That positive ID corroborates your last phone call from James, when you heard this gate agent making the boarding announcement for flight #1067. This concretely establishes James' last known whereabouts. It places him right here at Delta gate # 34 in the Greater Cincinnati International Airport on Friday, April 4, 1997 between 6:25 and 7:16, which is the last time James was seen or heard."

Trish sighed a small sound of hope.

"I've discovered a suspicious private charter, a twin-prop, that took off shortly after James arrived. I'm pursuing it further, the flight plan, etc." Chuck talked faster as he enthusiastically related the events.

" Good," she wanted to share his enthusiasm but it was hard for her.

" Now, I need your help. I want you to think back to James' corporate relationships. Who were his enemies, maybe not so much enemy as being anti-James..."

"Nobody, but that damn bitch, the new VP. She's the only one, Trish thought.

"...anyone jealous or envious, opposed to his values, principles, what he stood for, spoke out for, his position as Ethics Chairman. Was Werner doing any unethical things?"

" Oh, my God, *yes!*" Trish vehemently interrupted, "you wouldn't *believe* some of the things."

"Not yet, Trish, don't tell me now. Write down everything; everything, even trivial things. Think back to conversations you had with James, recently, as well as months ago, even years ago, his comments, things that were bothering him, keeping him awake nights, not quota, necessarily," they both chuckled at the same moment.

Just the mention of the word, "quota," brought back memories for both of them, because James was always, monthly, annually, perennially, always struggling, fighting to make quota, a constant preoccupation, an obsession. Of course, quota was secondary to his mission, his vision, his undaunted code of ethics, his love of people and guiding purpose to help them. But, sometimes to hear him talk about it, complain about it, his very employment, his job security depended upon "making quota." It was a do-or-die proposition, a make-quota-or-get-fired kind of mind-set. The pressure, the stress that this abstract, theoretical number placed on so many hard working, committed, commissioned sales people was absolutely appalling.

"Yeah, 'death by quota,' James used to say," Chuck mused. They laughed together.

Trish recalled how James felt— that Werner constantly manipulated the numbers, keeping him and most of his fellow distributors, their sales associates, and their offices unbalanced, unnecessarily stressed-out, and under the gun. The corporate gods issued edicts pertinent to quota attainment, quota achievement, and meeting budget, like popcorn coming out of a popper. And if business was good, putting him over quota, they would camp on growth, sales increase, balanced selling, or one of their other contrived, arbitrary measurements. It was a numbers game in which they made the rules, fudged them, then, changed them. Whenever James or one of the "respected" Distributors presented a documented challenge to their figures, exposing one of their manipulations, such as a conflicting disparity between quota and growth or a disputed addition of percentages, they would not admit making a mistake or apologize, but attempt to gloss it over, just sweep it under the rug. It was comical, yet tragic.

"No, not quota, but any incident, any..."

"Well, Chuck, there *was* a major incident, and I mean *major* last month— a patient died after surgery, almost died in surgery..." and then Trish caught herself.

" *NOT* over the phone!" they both said in unison.

" Right, Trish. When's the FBI coming in and setting up?" Chuck asked.

" They're supposed to be here this morning," Trish replied. "And so is our attorney."

"Well, you understand what I need. Write down anything and everything, and not just corporate matters. Also, surgeons, surgeries, customers, hospitals, managed care things, HMOs, hospital groups. I recall James' apprehension and distrust of that HealthCare USA chain when they started buying up all the little rural hospitals in Kentucky."

" Oh, my, *yes*. They were a real problem for him and all his associates. He did not hold them in high regard, at all," Trish interjected. "As a matter of fact, James felt *terrible* about the whole managed care thing, what it was doing to his surgeons, the hospitals, the nurses, and especially the poor patients," she added.

"Amen to that. It's going to hit us all, going to really hurt all of us. But, back to what I want from you. You are going to become a walking stenographer, making notes on everything that comes to mind. You are going to be amazed at how much you are going to recall. And don't consider anything too trivial. While that gate agent doesn't seem like any big deal right now, it could be later. You're right about phone discussions. The FBI will 'sweep' your house anyway before they bug your phones."

She told Chuck that she wanted to tell their attorney, Lynnwood, about having hired him, but not tell the FBI yet.

Chuck agreed.

Trish was still in her old security flannel nightgown, her hair looking like it had been rubbed between two bricks. But she felt some relief because she was no longer in this alone.

Only 8:45 A.M. the next day, Trish was still in her bedroom. It was late by her standards. The FBI had rung the doorbell at 6:05 A.M. this morning. Thank the Lord that Lynnwood had come over shortly after the FBI. Had he not, Trish was certain she might have lost it. She had not slept in days, had been drinking coffee by the gallon, and was strung out tighter than a snare drum. The third FBI man through the door had been the rub. Without the courtesy of a hello or greeting of any kind, loaded with electronic equipment, he had bumped Trish with it while rudely demanding to be shown where to set everything up. In spite of her distraught state, she had psyched herself up to be hospitable, but the brash techno-agent had really taxed her patience with his offensive behavior. The other agents had been nice and very professional.

She was becoming desperate, crazy with worry over James' whereabouts, his well-being. Where on earth could he be? Was he alive? O, dear God, she simply felt helpless, so helpless— and lonely, terribly, terribly lonely.

Her house now swarmed like a beehive. People were everywhere. The FBI had questioned her in detail about her last phone conversations with James, his business, his employees, his sales associates, any disagreements, recent or past, any disgruntled ex-employees? No, James always was and still is a fair man and a fair boss. What about his career, his relationship with Werner, Inc.? Were there any enemies there? Managers?

"Yes, that *bitch*," Trish caught herself. "Please excuse my language, but there was a new female Area Vice-President who disliked James, didn't like his Souther accent, his... really resented his past achievements, his popularity— everybody at Werner likes my husband, officers. And, I'm sorry, but she was just a bitch, who did everything she could to discredit James. Her name's J. M., J. M. Corzone. No one dares to call her by her real name, Jenny Mae— yes, she's one of those. But, she was the only one at Werner I'm aware of. As I said, my husband was well liked."

The FBI noted that on their pads and continued. Subsidiaries? Any product people? Accounting? How about his peers? Fellow distributors? Any jealousy among them? Their offices? Their salespeople? What about his role as Ethics Chairman? Any resentments because of his duty in that capacity? How about competitors? Would any particular ones especially benefit from his absence? What about clubs, professional organizations, Rotary? Church? Friends? Then, after an apology, they asked if there been any major problems in their marriage? After thirty-five years of a happy marriage, that subject had not even entered her mind.

Then, they questioned Lynnwood as James' attorney and friend. What exactly did James say when he called from corporate headquarters? Even though there had been the adversarial exchange between James and the vice-presidents after they had unexpectedly terminated his distributorship, did there seem to be any fear ruminating in his voice? Think back, try to recall your phone conversation verbatim. Certainly he had to have been destroyed after suddenly losing his job and his business after all those years, but was he afraid? Did James in any way communicate a threat, or fear of any type of a threat to his own personal safety? What about his surgical business? Problems with surgeons? Clinics? Hospitals? Malpractice suits? Had he or his corporation been named in any recently? In the last three years? Last five years?

Lynnwood gave them details about the fateful surgery at the HealthCareUSA Hospital. His purposeful glance at Trish alerted her that his reply was intentional of full cooperation.

Lynnwood related James' genuine, heartfelt concern over the patient's death after the surgery. James had been summoned by the orthopaedic surgeon for both the patient's initial total hip replacement, as well as the second procedure, the most recent revision surgery. In the process,

James had gotten to know and had become fond of the patient, a farmer. Lynnwood described James' job, his focused protocol for surgeries, the meticulous, arduous process of having all the equipment the surgeon needed there for the operation. He also described his conscientiousness, his diligence, his absolute attention to detail, his penchant for intraoperative, contingency planning, always having a fall-back option, a "What if?" All of this did not mean that he or his staff were perfect. Where human beings are involved, mistakes can be made. But, James was overly zealous in trying to prevent mistakes.

He went on to relate James' detailed, religious compliance with the Medical Device Reports, the FDA requirements, implant tracking, lot numbers, permanent patient files. He also alluded to James' chagrin with the cool, detached, matter-of-fact, almost cavalier manner with which the corporate office had handled this tragic incident. James had taken exception to their lack of concern, compassion, and attention, furthering his consternation with Werner's Regulatory and Legal Department and their blase' attitude regarding the entire event. No, there had been no negligence, or errors and omissions on the part of James, his office, or his sales associates. Yes, there had been complications with the surgery, which can happen with any surgery, but, none had been the fault of James or any of his staff. Yes, James had documented the entire surgical procedure from A to Z. And, no, he, Lynnwood, was not aware of any formal medico-legal ramifications at this time. There were, to his knowledge, no legal suits filed, yet, with emphasis on the yet.

The agents continued to probe deeper. Could this be the source of vengeance or foul play?

Yes, while a possibility, Lynnwood thought it not very likely. It would simply be too brazen. Were there any other mitigating circumstances or compromising situations involving James? No. Did he, as James' attorney, know of any enemies that James might have or have had? No, Lynnwood replied, that one would really be hard-pressed to find anyone who genuinely disliked James. He was very friendly to everyone. He grew on people and was an endearing sort of a guy. The two agents gave Lynnwood their cards and asked him to call if he remembered anything, no matter how insignificant it might seem.

The revolting, mind-boggling thing had been the FBI's discovery of "bugs" — bugging devices in her home. The unsettling matter, it seemed, for the FBI was the presence of two different types of eavesdropping devices, each of which had to have been planted by two different sources. This seemed to take the investigation to another level. They said they would reserve comment on the seriousness, the gravity of this discovery, pending further lab analysis of the specific devices themselves.

Trish was equally shocked and angered— the very idea of someone violating the sanctity of her home. How dare they? Just the thought perplexed her even more.

Lynnwood was shocked, as well. He was even more shocked by the extent to which *they*, the unknown *they*, were pursuing the Cantrills. He may have previously underestimated the seriousness of their adversaries.

She was further affirmed by her decision to hire a private investigator, her friend, Chuck Thursgoode. She pulled Lynnwood aside to confidentially tell him that. He seconded her decision without hesitation and added that, in lieu of the FBI's uncovering all the bugs, it was really a good idea for Trish to have hired him. She told Lynnwood about Chuck's telephone call to her last night. While investigating James' bizarre disappearance in the Greater Cincinnati International Airport, he had uncovered an air charter on which the timing might be suspect. A twin-prop, 8-passenger Beech Kingair had been chartered at one of the smaller private charter agencies that night. The flight plan was first filed for a flight to North Carolina, but the plane had actually flown almost two hours to a smaller airport in Indiana. Chuck was driving to that area last night and hoped to report back this evening. Lynnwood asked if he had a beeper and suggested that Trish page him right away. He, Chuck, should be informed about the FBI finding the variety of bugs in her house immediately. She agreed.

As Lynnwood left, he stood in her doorway, told her not to hesitate to call him for anything, that Sheryl would always know where he was, even if he were in court, she could get word to him. He gave Trish a big hug.

As she looked up at him, into his light brown eyes filled with understanding, she began to cry, again.

CHAPTER 18

Freedom stretches only as far as
the limits of our consciousness.
Paracelsus the Physician, 1942
Carl Gustav Jung

When James came to, he was slumped over, his chin on his chest, soaked with his saliva and sweat, his wrists still strapped to the chair with silver duct tape. Opening his eyes was blinding, causing him to blink repeatedly. Still daytime. Slowly, he looked around the room. He was alone. No sign of Alfredo, Ramon, or the mad doctor. He listened intently; heard nothing. Was anyone else in the house? The quiet was only broken by his labored breathing.

His last memory haunted him quickly, its evidence written in agony. He looked down at the enlarged wounds on his arms— grotesque, bloody, black, but glazed with Neosporin ointment. The yellow Bovie, the torture instrument, still lay on the sterile-draped table beside his chair. Was it still connected to the generator? Yes.

He listened again— only the usual sounds outside, dogs barking, birds singing. Nothing inside. Where had they gone?

James tried to move his hands. The pain zapped him. In spite of it, he strained again, wincing as he tried to free up his wrists. The tape barely moved. His strength had been sapped.

The smell of his own burnt flesh hung heavy in the hot, fetid room. Nauseating. He gagged.

Quit it. Think escape. Could this be his opportunity? His elusive moment?

He strained to move his hands again. The pain was overwhelming, but it was something he would have to work through. The tape hardly budged. But, at least it was flexible, unlike the handcuffs.

Was the Aspen generator on? No. Could he reach the toggle switch with his foot? Thankfully, they had not strapped his ankles to the chair legs during the last session. He extended his right leg toward it, but the on/off switch was at the wrong angle.

If he could only get hold of that Bovie, and turn the generator on, he might be able to use it to cut the tape. Was it within reach?

Shifting his hips in the chair, he hooked his right foot under the left front leg of the cart and pulled it towards him. Again pain rifled up through his shoulders and neck. He grimaced and pulled it closer.

Made it! He raised his left foot and flipped the switch to on. The beeps of the microprocessor going through the safety check sounded louder than sirens. *Damn.*

Were anyone in the house, they would surely have heard it.

James sat still, his heart pounding in his ears. A minute went by. Felt like an hour. Nothing.

How could he get that Bovie hand piece on the table? He tried again to move his hands. The tape only rolled back on itself, but held tight. *Damn the pain.* If he tried to maneuver the cord with his feet to pull it towards him, it could become unplugged from the generator. A bad move. He'd never get it plugged back in without his hands.

How far could he move his body in the chair? Shifting his hips had helped in moving the cart.

He had to let the pain subside a minute. It was radiating up to his head causing him to see spots. Don't black out. Not at this point.

James moved his body in the chair to the left, leaned to the right, trying to crane his neck over the table. Close.

The tantalizing thought spread through James' dazed mind.

If he could just get the plastic hand piece in his mouth, he could hold it with his teeth. Would it electrocute him? A possibility. The grounding pad was still stuck to his side. Shock him? Maybe.

Could he use the Bovie to cut the silver duct tape? Would it cut tape? If it would slice through skin and muscle, it ought to. Hell, yes, it was worth a try.

He could feel his adrenalin pumping. This was the first real chance that had come his way.

He leaned again, reaching his neck over the table. He leaned down, opened his mouth wide, and bit down on the Bovie. Dropped it. *Damn.*

James forced himself to muffle his groans. Each and every move, armless or not, generated a different bolt of pain. But, the mere thought of escape fired his determination.

This time he bent over more slowly. He methodically inched his face downward toward the table. He levered himself using his injured right elbow; his ulnar nerve sent out fresh reminders of torment. He hesitated, waiting for the dizziness to abate. He resumed, leaning slowly, ever so slowly.

He braced himself. Further spasms racked his body. *The hell with it.* He tried to ignore the distress, overpower it, will it away.

One more inch. He opened his mouth wide, bit down— got it! He sat back up in the chair, his head giddy from the effort as well as the success. His mouth was dry, his chin still wet from drool.

He took a couple of deep breaths. Keep your jaws tight. Don't let go of the Bovie, his secret weapon of the moment. A couple more deep breaths. Regroup. Easy does it.

James bent slowly toward his right hand. He cocked his head to the left, aiming the blade at the silver tape. How would he activate the cut button? With the corner of his mouth? No. He might drop it. With his tongue? Would it electrocute him? Shock him? Think. The entire Bovie hand piece had to be water-resistant, waterproof, to work in blood and saline. Sure it did. Okay, the tongue.

He leaned down all the way. Another half inch and the blade was against the tape. The strain pain on his neck and side made him tremble. Do not lose it. The button on the right was the cut switch, the left coag. He angled his tongue to the right, found the serrated ridge of the cut button. Now for the moment of truth...

With the tip of the blade touching the silver tape, he pushed with his tongue on the cut button as hard as he could.

The sizzle was immediate. That sound which just hours ago brought horror and torture was now symphonic and symbolic. The yellowish orange sparks of the current cutting the tape were a splendid sight. And the smell was like rubber burning, an improvement over his very own flesh. The blade sliced through the tape like a scalpel through whipped cream. His tongue was tiring. Just a little more to go.

Zip! His right hand was now free. Success. He straightened back in the chair resting his back and tongue.

Very quickly he discovered how much the injuries had compromised his dexterity and the extent of pain which movement exacted. He could not make a fist. But, with his right hand he could hold the Bovie, which he removed from his mouth.

James took no time in using the Bovie to cut the tape on his left wrist. Once done, he noticed that it was more painful to move his left hand and arm than his right. Weird.

He tore the grounding pad from his side, stood up, wobbled from queasiness, then struggled towards the light of the window, covered with a ragged old bedspread. He pushed it aside to find no window casing, just a plastic covering.

He looked out. Saw no one. He pushed out the plastic, straddled the cinder block, rolled out, and hit the ground with a thud. The impact riveted up his spine, out the extremities.

His stomach flipped. In spite of the dizziness, he struggled to his feet, stumbled, then ran. He knew not where. But, staggering, hobbling at first, he ran away. With blurred vision, he attempted to survey his surroundings. Without his glasses he couldn't see shit. Squinting, he was able to make out some of the terrain — down from the house, there was an old dirt road, part gravel, part seashells, winding up a hillside. Just on the other side, he saw what looked like another abandoned shack. Rural, remote, unpopulated, and undeveloped, the rough road lost itself in dense, tropical outgrowth.

He needed to get to the other side of the hill, out of sight from the house. He trotted unevenly, his feet crunching the seashells, panting, stumbling, thrashing through the vines, trying to veer away from the center of the road. Slowly, he made his way to the top of the hill.

Once over it, he took a second to look back. No one was chasing him; only the haunting vision of the decrepit shack, his torture chamber, remained. He squinted again. The view from this side of the hill looked the same— two more run-down shanties up the winding road, a beat-up car, bikes maybe? Some toys in front of the furthest one. And more jungle, a lot more jungle.

It was hot as hell. The sun bore down. He guessed it to be mid-afternoon.

James shifted to the right, to the opposite side of the road from the house that looked occupied. He tried to hide himself in the thicket, get a little further, before he could rest a minute. The underbrush tore at his open wounds. He was wringing wet with sweat, panting, wheezing, aching, his heart bursting in his chest.

He came upon a thick tree trunk, far enough into the undergrowth where he did not think he could be seen. He collapsed against it. Gasping the hot air, he had to rest. He knew that he needed to distance himself further from where he had been, but he was totally exhausted. He could not go another inch. Rays of sunlight pierced through the dark canopy of the jungle, one reflecting off the sheen ointment coating the gaping wound on his right arm.

James did not know where the hell he was. He did not know where the hell he was going. Nor did he know what the hell to do next. But for now, for the moment, he did know that he was free. Free at last. Free from that horror show— that seemed to have been staged like a prolonged lifetime, an unreal, horrendous existence. But, now paramount in that prolonged lifetime was his first real semblance of hope. Hope— its sweet touch brought a faint smile.

He lowered his head, winced, yawned a huge yawn that hurt, shut his eyes, said a quick prayer thanking God for his freedom, and passed out.

CHAPTER 19

Life is but a day;
A fragile dewdrop on its perilous way...
Sleep and Poetry, 1817
John Keats

Sheryl Lukens, Ingle's exceptional legal secretary, looked at her watch as she rode the elevator up to the eleventh floor. It was 4:44 A.M. She did not mind coming in early in the morning; no phones, no conversations, no distractions. Just quiet. She could get so much done. She especially did not mind on this particular Friday morning because she would be leaving on her long-awaited vacation after she completed two lengthy briefs for Mr. Ingle. She had not taken a day off in over two years. Having been with Stahl, Kendrick, and Hart, LLC for over nineteen years, she had accrued a lot of vacation time. Recently widowed by a husband with no life insurance and a trail of bad, gambling debts, with two kids in college, she had to work to just make ends meet— no, simply to survive. She had worked straight through last year's vacations to earn extra to get her car fixed and help her children with their college expenses. She needed this vacation, two glorious weeks on the beach in Panama City. She had spent months, many months anticipating this time off, buying plenty of paperbacks from romance junk to bestsellers, including her favorite, Sue Grafton, from *I* to *P*, sun-tan lotions from SPF 4 to 35, even the ultimate splurge, two new bathing suits she bought on sale. Though she rarely complained, by golly, she was really looking forward to this R & R, and heavens, *did* she ever deserve it.

When the elevator dinged the eleventh floor and the doors opened, she sensed that something was not right; call it a second sense or female intuition. She did not know exactly what it was, but something was different. The aura, that calm that usually engulfed her when she came in early was absent. The invisible shroud of quiet, which always complimented her superb productivity, was tentative this dark morning.

As she flipped on the light switch and walked across the black Irian Jayan marble foyer, she thought she heard something.

None of the ninety-seven attorneys in the firm had come in early today as they often did, or they would have left the entry lights on. No, she was the first one here, the way she liked it.

She looked past the Brazilian walnut paneling in the foyer, down the hall, thought she saw a flicker of light. She walked briskly towards her wing, her heels clicking softly on the marble floor.

She turned left and headed down the long hallway to her office next to Mr. Ingle's corner suite.

And, wham! Like a tornado, it hit her. She could not believe what she was seeing — papers, files, briefs thrown everywhere, drawers from the filing cabinets dumped and cast aside. Desk drawers had been emptied, pencils, paper clips, pens all over, strewn across stacks of papers, folders, then piled back on top of the desks. It *did* look just like a tornado had hit the place. She had never seen anything like it.

Her desk had been destroyed, the picture frames of her children flung aside and broken. Sheryl gasped.

Mr. Ingle's office had been totally ransacked, turned upside-down. It looked worse than the tornado's path.

She entered Mr. Ingle's office, aghast, her mouth frozen open, her hand on her cheek. "What in the world," she exclaimed.

With the light from the hallway, in the semi-darkness, she suddenly saw two shapes with ski masks crouched behind Mr. Ingle's desk.

Each of the intruders fired their guns with silencers almost simultaneously. Thoup! Thoup! The first bullet hit Sheryl in the right shoulder. The second slug impacted her left rib cage, propelling her body back through the doorway into the hall, exiting just below her left scapula. Her blood splattered all over the sandalwood grass-cloth wall coverings.

She screamed as she hit the floor, collapsing on the piles of legal documents.

The blood gushed through her beige, brocade suit, staining it crimson. It rushed downward onto the manila folders, flowing, drawing maps, as it dripped towards the edges.

As the two trespassers ran for the fire exit, they tried to jump over her prostrate body, sprawled out across the debris. The tall one's foot came down on her left wrist, which was extended over her head.

She shrieked. Her high pitch then dissipated into a moan, a long, guttural groan.

The crimson stains circumscribed ever widening arcs on her suit, continuing to spill over on the folders, then pooling on the mauve carpet.

Sheryl Lukens lay there bleeding on the work she had done all her life, her life a paradox. Her veritable life's substance, her blood, was now tarnishing her superb accomplishments, her professional productivity, smearing the end results of her personal pursuit of excellence.

"Why me?" she asked. "All I've ever done is work hard...and try to be a good mother. Why me?"

Her mind filled with lucid memories— scenes from high school, Pulaski County High, standing on the stage after being voted "Girl Most Likely to Succeed," the prom, her new dress, green and yellow, her father said she looked so pretty, the only time he ever told her that. Then hazy vignettes— flying away from her, escaping her weakening grasp. Suddenly, her whole lifetime seemed brief and shallow. Succeed? Success? Her life a success? It all seemed so shallow.

She lost consciousness....

As Lynnwood drove up to his office building downtown, he found pandemonium. He saw three EMS ambulances, two television vans, and four police cars on Main Street at the entrance to his office building. Sirens screamed in the distance. He could not pull into his parking garage because the police had blocked the gate with two cruisers. As he parked on the street, he noticed three more police cars inside the garage.

He attempted to enter his building through the rear door, but he was stopped by two patrolmen who demanded identification. After convincing them he was in the law firm occupying the entire eleventh floor, he was allowed to enter. He was confronted with the same request by the officer at the elevator bay.

As he waited, the adjacent elevator doors opened and four EMS technicians emerged pulling a stretcher.

Lynnwood looked down. The pale woman on the stretcher barely opened her eyes, a blank stare, void of recognition.

"Wait! Wait, that's my secretary. Sheryl! Oh, Sheryl..."

The policemen gently restrained him as he tried to reach out to her when her stretcher rolled past him. The EMS people rushed her out.

"What happened? She's my executive assistant."

"There was a break-in up on the eleventh floor," the officer explained, "we believe she walked in on it, surprised the intruders."

"A break-in? Oh, no... poor Sheryl. I don't believe it." Lynnwood was shaking.

"I'm sorry, sir. It is just a crazy world," the officer said, shaking his head.

Lynnwood made a studied effort to compose himself. He put down his briefcase, straightened his tie, and ran his hand over his hair.

When he stepped off the elevator, he found swarming chaos. Linda, the receptionist, Beth, and Rowena, legal secretaries, were all crying fitfully, embracing each other. Police, both plainclothes and uniformed, were busy marking off the crime scene with yellow tape. Crime scene? This was his reserved, sophisticated legal firm.

"Mr. Engle. There's Mr. Engle," Linda sobbed.

Before she could say more, Lynnwood was approached by a man in a light gray suit with a sullen expression.

"Mr. Engle? I'm Lieutenant Briscoe." The man drew Lynnwood down the hall with a practiced manner. "Would you please follow me?" he said, though they were already moving toward an empty office.

As Lynnwood rounded the corner behind Lt. Briscoe, he was horrified by what he saw—blood splattered all over the walls, the carpet, and furniture, file drawers emptied, desk drawers pulled out and thrown, files, briefs, some stained with blood, scattered and strewn about. A white chalk outline marked the form of a body on the mauve carpet in the hallway. Mounds of dried, brownish-red blood were contained within the chalk outline like cow pies in a pasture. Technicians with surgical gloves were busy dusting for finger-prints, gathering evidence in Ziploc bags. His whole hallway was amuck. Yellow tape prevented his entrance.

Dumbfounded, Lynnwood felt his face douche, his breath sucked right out of his mouth. What he could see of his office looked even worse. It had literally been turned upside down, as if struck twice by a two-way tornado. While he disbelieved his eyes, his stomach churned, confirming what he saw. His usually neat, well organized, sternly structured office patterned after a disciplined, orderly lifestyle had been totally ransacked. It, along with this day, was in shambles.... the most horrible moment of his life.

"I need a moment, Lieutenant. Excuse me," Lynnwood said, stepping into a partner's empty office. He sat behind the desk, took off his glasses, and held his head in his hands. The sequence of disasters overwhelmed him. He said a prayer for Sheryl. Then Trish, then his friend James.

He came out and joined Briscoe in one of the smaller conference rooms. Lynnwood W. Engle Jr., erudite master of any situation, urbane leader, had forgotten about his pressing schedule, the two briefs, the court appearance. Someone besides Sheryl would have to call the judge today.

"Mr. Engle, I know this is disturbing, but I need to ask a few questions. How long has Sheryl Likens worked with you?"

"... seventeen years." He yearned for that number to continue.

The sergeant came in and handed a note to the Lieutenant.

"Mr. Engle, it seems quite obvious that your office was the focal point of the break-in. Any idea what someone would be looking for?"

Lynwood Engle's stared straight into Briscoe's eyes, just as he had done in the courtroom so many times.

"Lieutenant, previous to my arrival here this morning, I had just left the FBI setting up surveillance at a friend's home. Her husband, a dear friend of many years and client, as well, is believed to have been kidnapped. As much as I would like to internally deny it, I now believe that there is a connection. Without a doubt, these horrible events must be related. With all due respect to you, Lt. Briscoe, your authority, and jurisdiction, I think that I must report this to the FBI, because it is relevant and could affect my friend's well-being, as well as his wife's. I realize that some local police forces resent the Feds and resist having to work with them. Considering what is at stake here with my secretary, my good friend and client's welfare, my legal firm, I would ask that we all work together on this."

Lt. Briscoe, with raised eyebrows, nodded his consent.

Then Lynnwood described in chronologic order the circumstances previous to James' disappearance.

"Now, Lieutenant, that is all that I can tell you at this point. Allow me to tell Mrs. Cantrill and the FBI about this first, then I can satisfactorily refer you to her for an interview."

The lieutenant thanked Lynnwood, saying that he understood that it would be difficult to ascertain what was missing from his office. After the chaos settles somewhat, if Lynnwood could determine if James Cantrill's file or any other files had been stolen, please call immediately. He gave Lynnwood his card and agreed for him to contact the FBI first, but please tell them it is urgent. Lt. Briscoe was thorough in his questions and courteous in manner, a burnished professional.

They shook hands and Lynnwood quickly left to find an undisturbed office to use the phone.

CHAPTER 20

We are betrayed by what is false within.
Modern Love, 1862
George Meredith

Rob Hempstead's new Falcon 50EX corporate jet landed at the Warsaw, Indiana, airport. The landing was smoother than ice. It induced his second positive, prideful thought of the day— and his last. He smiled what would be his final smile today.

Unannounced, he entered the conference room at Werner, Inc. Lenny Shortt, the Vice-President of Sales, was standing in front at the projection screen presenting the quarterly sales overview. The meeting was less than twenty-minutes old and the drone of his voice was already putting those in required attendance to sleep.

The chart on the overhead screen clearly depicted Werner's poor performance. It showed that the company had not made quota in the last six quarters, concluding with the miserable 79.3 percent of quota for 1997, with a - 39.6 percent decrease in sales. The results from the previous year were equally unimpressive.

Rob Hempstead was determined to be objective, but his anger rose when Shortt glossed right over the unbelievable amount of the sales shortfall— $14,005,366, over $14 million dollars in lost business.

"The ... reasons for this negative performance ... shortfall, are several," Shortt continued. " The ... 3 Q numbers actually make it look worse *net:net* than it ... actually ... is." Shortt went through a litany of excuses— the delayed release of the new Sphinx Hip system, managed care, Medicare, the DRGs, what he called demographic decline, the economy, and vendors. "... that vendor problem. Right, Tom?" Lenny asked. And Tom Tomjonavich, Director of Manufacturing, jerked awake, nodded and smiled. Lenny tried next to appeal to Nick Knodycki, the V. P. of Marketing and Product Development, who was trying to sleep off his usual hangover. Knodycki mumbled something unintelligible.

Lenny's laser pointer trembled in his hand, and the red dot appeared on Knodycki's forehead like a target.

Leonard Shortt just stood there, mute, awkward, melancholy. His gloomy presentation had converted the large conference room into a dark, foggy remnant from Sleepy Hollow, with Ichabod Crane as presenter.

Lenny finally turned to face the audience and choked when his eyes met Rob Hempstead's. Having just noticed the big boss, he was aghast, ghost-white, an upright cadaver in a corporate mortuary.

Rob placed his black, calf-skin leather Gucci briefcase on his knees, popped the gold-plated latches open, and sifted through the printouts, spreadsheets, and the overheads which he had specially prepared for this meeting.

Whispers and shuffling filled the room. The brave ones dared to turn around in their seats to observe the unexpected presence of the big boss; the others accepted the whispers as fact.

The presenter turned to stone. The only signs that he was yet among the living was the inadvertent red beam sporadically emanating from his laser pointer.

Then, with the desperation of one facing death, he made a futile attempt to recover, trying to repeat the overhead still illuminated on the screen. "... the government ... Medicare, HCFA, the ... FDA, Medicaid, cost... DRGs ... capitation, and, as I said, the vendors ... Healthcare USA..." Rob snorted quietly and let him dig himself deeper into this black hole. "... these groups are demanding huge discounts ... 30 percent ... 35 percent ... on implants— " Lenny preceded every other word with an uh.

Rob Hempstead was getting angrier by the moment.

His two surrogate officers knew it. Both David Zuckerman, Executive VP of the Medical Division and Terry Meissner, CFO, knew Rob extremely well and had the greatest respect for him and what he stood for. He was a pragmatic, fair, but demanding boss, a dynamic leader, and an outspoken advocate of honesty and accountability. He possessed a passion for values, especially ethics and integrity, and a driving desire for value-based growth. If there was one thing that stuck in his craw like a flame, it was dishonesty and evasive behavior— not owning up, shifting the blame, denying responsibility, or shirking accountability in any shape, form, or fashion. Anyone who did not take responsibility for their own decisions or negative results, for not admitting their own mistakes was *the worst* in his eyes. It was not that he had a problem with mistakes. He had made them himself. He was not at all risk averse; he espoused change, encouraging his managers to be very innovative, which he understood sometimes fostered mistakes from which they must learn. While failure was allowed, success was promulgated. The quickest, most sure-fire way to the top of Mr. Hempstead's *shit-list* was to make a mistake, then deny it or try to blame it on someone else— in his words, to "crawfish." And the most renown "crawfish" in the history of the company was up in front of the room, one Leonard R. Shortt, who was highly skilled and adroit at slyly, unobtrusively shifting the blame away from himself— "the problem was with this Area Vice-President, that Regional Manager, one of the Distributors, the product/marketing manager, or the vendor..." — as they had just heard twice from him in the last few minutes. They knew. They themselves had questioned how on earth a person who has never been in the field, never worked as a salesman, never worked as a sales manager, never sold a damn thing in his entire life ever got to be the Vice-President of Sales? Rob had questioned this lack of experience on more than one occasion and been told that Shortt's popularity, ability to mediate disputes, his following by local employees, was so entrenched that he was a natural for the position. No damn wonder the company was in dire straits. They also knew that their Group President was exercising a tremendous amount of restraint and self-control. What they did not know was how much longer his self-restraint would last.

"... 35 percent ... 40 percent..." The beads of sweat on Lenny Shortt's bald pate had congealed into rivulets and rolled down his face by his Elvis sideburns.

Hempstead could stand it no longer. His voice rumbled out from the back of the room. "Are you blaming the customer for our shortfall, Shortt?"

Lenny turned. He shook his head furiously back and forth.

Hempstead shot out of his seat. "I have *never* witnessed such gross rationalization, such *denial* of reality in my life. This damn crawfishing *will stop!* Now!" Everyone in the room shuddered in fear, clinging to their chairs. "You're shifting the blame again, shirking accountability. I will *not stand* for it."

Lenny shivered. Both legs twitched.

"Did you purposefully skip over the $14 million decrease in sales?"

"... no sir," Lenny said.

"'A net:net result looking worse than it actually is' — Isn't that what I heard you say, Shortt?"

"... no ... yes sir, but— "

"How do you explain the fact that our competitors— DuLuth, BioMedica, Ortho, and Jones & Jackson, who work in the same identical marketplace— are all achieving double-digit growth?"

Lenny made a choking sound, but uttered no defense.

"Would you please name one product— one single product— that this company has brought to market on schedule?"

Silence.

"Anybody? Just name one product, one system, in the last five years, ten years, that you have released on schedule?"

No one spoke.

"Knodycki?" Hempstead questioned. Knodycki, the supreme polemicist, the master at disputation, on whose shoulders the responsibility for the repeated delays and late new product releases rested, offered none of his usual argumentative antics designed to mask his own incompetence. All that showed on his bloodless face was guilt.

"Thanks to a couple of distributors in Kentucky and Texas, we're still getting the business at HealthcareUSA hospitals, and I was just informed yesterday that James Cantrill, your distributor for nearly thirty years— one of the only two distributors possessing the market strength and surgeon loyalty to hold on to his business in those HealthcareUSA hospitals— was terminated. Is that how you reward success and franchised goodwill?"

Hempstead strode to the front of the room and took over the projector. Lenny started to slink away, but Hempstead said, "Stay right there, Shortt."

Lenny's right leg had now developed a full tremor.

"George," Hempstead said, drawing out the name. George Driskell flushed and looked at the floor. He had almost become smug in that it was not he doing the quarterly presentation today. After all, the quarterly reviews were his job as head of the U.S. Sales Division, but for some quirky reason he had allowed Lenny to do this one today. He reached into his coat pocket for more Tums.

"I commissioned this market research chart on hip products from two outside firms," Rob said, placing the overhead on the projector. "You'll note that it shows a historical overview of both domestic and foreign sales. I hold these *numbers* to be *true*." The impact of his final word was massive. The bell of truth, quelled for years in the halls of Werner, had finally been rung.

Lenny looked as though he were about to faint. He had not moved from the spot since Hempstead took over, his head hanging like a sick dog.

"Lenny gave you a list of reasons," Hempstead said. "And now I'll give you a list of mine: inflated sales figures; manipulated numbers; contrived, massaged data; fudged budgets; slanted spreadsheets; cooked books; and manufactured results. Sound familiar, George?"

"... no sir," he muttered, over the crunch of two Tums caught up by his rear molars.

"Shortt?"

Lenny could not answer, barely able to shake his head.

"In 1970, when total hip replacements were introduced to the United States, Werner got off to a slow start due to lack of product. But by 1985, greatly due to the strength of our Distributor network, we had a market share of 43.9 percent— an unprecedented, unrivaled position of market dominance. That is the end of the success story. In 1990 Werner's market share had declined to 34.2 percent, a major loss by any elementary calculation. All of you here *should* know the value, the investment strategy, the battle over one full share point of the overall market. Then, in 1995, market share had eroded to 25.6 percent, another significant loss. Now... to the tragic present — mid-year 1997, it is down to a pathetic 17.4 percent. That's a *deplorable loss* of 26.5 *total points* of *market share!*"

Everyone present sucked air, cringed, and attempted to escape within their own fractured minds. The discordant vestiges of honesty and integrity in their corporate hearts had been solidly challenged.

Hempstead detailed the precipitous slide from dominance to dismal failure, citing market shares and losses in dollar figures. His speech was punctuated with loud cracks as he whacked his telescoping pointer against the screen showing the figures. Even Knodycki sat frozen, afraid of further reprisal.

"Your *competitors* have *eaten* your *damn lunch* right *here* in *Flat City,*" Hempstead concluded, with his right fist clenched. He lowered his voice, "But the real tragedy I've witnessed here is not in the numbers, or the deplorable performance they depict. Nor is it in the horrendous trend, this seemingly irreversible downward trend. It is in your rationalization and dishonest reaction to them. No, the real tragedy here lies in betrayal—the betrayal of Werner values, of principle, of each other, of self. The tragic, unrequited betrayal, the betrayal of your fellow colleagues. That *betrayal,* ladies and gentlemen, is the real tragedy here."

Hempstead paused and looked around the room. "Where is your president?" he asked no one in particular. "George? Where is Ron?"

George mumbled, shrugged, and fidgeted.

Hempstead glanced at the chart up on the screen. Its repugnant results further exacerbated his mood, releasing all the enmity pent-up for years. He turned to Lenny, "Shortt? You have seen these deplorable sales numbers. Would you mind telling us," he said in a voice that sounded almost kindly, "exactly how a man who has never sold one damn product in his entire life has managed to become the vice president of sales of a billion-dollar company?"

Lenny's eyes glazed over. A dark spot appeared on the front of his pants and spread down his right leg. Perhaps some in the room might not have noticed his disgrace had he not stooped over and looked down at the evidence. Lenny Shortt had just pissed in his pants.

CHAPTER 21

Every art and every investigation...
seem to aim at some good.
Nichomachean Ethics
Aristotle, 346 B. C.

The phone rang that evening. The FBI had said to allow it to ring at least three times before answering.

Trish could barely restrain herself until the third ring.

"Hello."

"Trish, this is Chuck. I'm calling from the airport in South Bend, Indiana. I believe that I may have traced that chartered flight from Cincinnati to here. The flight controllers recorded a private landing at 22:51 hours, uh, I have to think, it's been a long time since Nam, that's 10:51 P.M., which would have worked out right regarding the estimated flying time. The aircraft was a twin prop, which would be correct for a Beech Kingair, and the call letters were PN348Y. I'm going to call Aero, the charter service in Cincinnati to get the exact call letters on their plane. According to Aero, the plane was originally chartered from Cincinnati to Midway, Chicago. They must have filed an en route change of destination and flown IFR into South Bend, which I'll also confirm when I call. Is the FBI still there?" he asked.

"Yes... I told them about you last night," Trish answered with some hesitation. She wondered to herself why she had hesitated.

"Good. That means they are listening on the line, because I want them to hear this, too. The coincidental thing about it is this: at 23:20

hours, less than 30 minutes after the Kingair landed, a private corporate jet took off. The controllers said that it was very unusual in that most corporate traffic is early morning or mid to late afternoon, correlating with executives' work days. Commercial traffic is around the clock, but private traffic is not. They said it was most unusual to have two private aircraft landing and taking off in close proximity of each other at those late hours. Continuing right along with this," Chuck was obviously excited, "the prop, PN348Y, was at Butler Aviation, the private hangar, for less than an hour. Then it taxis around, and takes off again at 23:40 hours, 20 minutes after the private jet took off. Now, what does that tell you? Huh?" he was talking faster than normal.

"I don't know, Chuck. What?"

"Well, it tells me two things: Number 1. That chartered Kingair didn't fly way the hell up here to South Bend, Indiana, on a lark, just to book night hours. No...it was delivering something. It had to have cargo for delivery to someone. The Butler hangar closes at 22:00, that's 10 o'clock, Trish. All they have there after that is one maintenance man, readying the pre-dawn take-offs. So, the pilot and co-pilot couldn't even go in their lobby to take a break, have a cup of coffee, like they always do. They just turned around, taxied back up the runway, and took off again. Number 2. That corporate jet was obviously waiting on something, or someone, to be brought in by the Kingair charter. Right? Had to be! Like the controllers said, corporate jets don't usually take off until pre-dawn. Also, they thought the corporate jet was a new Falcon, which would have long-range capabilities," Chuck was even breathing faster. "We're 'gonna check that out."

"Way to go, Chuck," Trish replied, her sharp eyebrows raised, excited on hearing the first news of any kind since James' disappearance.

"Hold on, Trish, that's not all. I've got some more for you. Remember Roger, my ex-cop friend, the head of security at Greater Cincinnati?"

"Yes. Yes?" she anxiously answered.

"Well, he called me a few hours ago. Seems that someone saw two uniformed security-types quickly escorting a man in a suit with a briefcase out of the baggage claim area on that same night. Also, they said it looked like the man in the suit was being - quote - "marched," against his will. Rog doesn't have all the details, yet. He hasn't been able to speak to the person or persons who witnessed it in person yet, but he is working on it."

"That had to be James. Yes, it had to be!" Trish threw her right arm in the air, grasping at the first shred of evidence she had heard regarding her husband.

"Wait, Trish. It's only a lead. It's not a positive ID. Rog has to locate the witness, first, and that may take time. But, it's definitely the best we've had to go on, along with these flights here in South Bend. Also, I've got something else. There was a lady on the flight from Ft. Wayne to Cincinnati sitting in the seat next to James. Does the name Elizabeth Browning mean anything to you?" he asked.

"No. Who is she?"

"The person who sat next to James on the plane. How about Beth or Betty Browning with a Dallas address?"

"No. Would she know something?" she asked, wondering about her.

"Well, I'm going to run her down. She was one of the last known people to see him. Might not be anything."

"Thanks, Chuck. Thanks so much," Trish said, suddenly optimistic, but puzzled over this Browning female.

"Now, Trish, I want you to do me a favor," he requested.

"Of course."

"As soon as you hear back from the FBI lab with their analysis of the types of devices they found, see if they will tell you. I want you to write down the exact numbers, models, the manufacturers, the companies, then call me immediately. They may not want to give them to you, since they are officially in charge, and that's fine. I may need to talk to them to give 'em my background, qualifications— a major part of my investigative work involves technology— e-mail fraud, money wire transfers, electronic surveillance, competitive field intelligence. I've had a lot of experience with industrial espionage and corporate counterintelligence. I'm familiar with a lot of the tricks they use. That information will be very useful in determining who we are dealing with, what we're up against. So, call me right away. If you can't reach me on my cellular phone, page me. Okay?"

"Certainly, Chuck, the minute that I hear," Trish replied.

"And, now, I'm going check in to the Days Inn down from the South Bend Airport and get some shut-eye," he said wearily, winding down from his enthusiastic reports given earlier.

As she hung up the phone, she let out a deep sigh. It was as if she had just welcomed a long lost friend back home— encouragement. There was a lingering exhilaration that was revitalizing. For the first time in days, she actually felt alive, like a real human being. The call revitalized her depressed spirit and renewed the hope which she had thought was lost.

Trish was knocked off her passive pity pot by the news of Lynnwood's secretary and office. *Oh, my God. How tragic! Poor Sheryl. I pray that she makes it. And Lynnwood, he did not deserve this...what are we up against?*

She was reinforced by her decision to take a proactive approach. She had Chuck investigating James' disappearance; the FBI was on the case at their home. She would take upon herself to investigate the circumstances, the background leading up to this. Yes, she would conduct her own investigation of the perpetrator— Werner. She knew in her heart of hearts, in her gut that they *had* to be behind this. She knew it.

She left their home and went over to the warehouse, where James had an old fire-proof filing cabinet that his dad had given him.

James kept all of his private documents, files, correspondence, etc. there. He had built a huge file on Werner with relevant information proving that his distributorship was indeed a franchise, with business valuation figures and documentation of the nefarious five-percent payments to Bartle, the "franchise fees," as he and Lynnwood called them. He had tapes of phone conversations that were pertinent to his "buy-out" when he retired, because Werner had a history of shafting their old distributors. He also had mounds and mounds of papers, letters, memos, documents, policies, contracts— a legal paper trail that would stretch the Milky Way.

But, most of all, he had made duplicates of all the documents regarding that surgery at HealthcareUSA where the poor farmer had died— copies at his office, copies for Lynnwood, copies for his "Safe File," as he called it, away from the house and office. The originals were sent to Werner, and she *knew* how they were received, with the stonewalling and cover-up. It had torn James up, had been driving him crazy. She knew he hadn't slept for nights, no matter how tired he was.

And, to think, Trish used to call her husband paranoid. Used to call him a pack-rat, because he saved all that junk. *Oh, dear God, how brilliant he had been. Please, Lord, bring him home to me so I can apologize.*

She had a Bankers Box storage box, that she filled to the top. She would take all of this home, hole up in her bedroom, and go through every single detail, listen to every one of the tapes. This was now evidence. Yes. She knew that those *asses* at Werner were behind this. Some how, some way, and she was going to get to the bottom of this.

CHAPTER 22

Stone walls do not a prison make,
Nor iron bars a cage;
To Althea from Prison, 1649
Richard Lovelace

James was still asleep against the tree when they found him. He was jolted from his state of phlegmatic unconsciousness by the cold shock of a machete blade held by a big, sinister guy with long black hair and a Fu Manchu mustache. Behind him, he saw Ramon standing expressionless with a machete in his left hand.

Blinking in the diffused sunlight, James grappled with the harsh reality of the moment. He was caught. He could not fight back. His freedom, brief, somnolent, but sweet, was over.

He was rousted up from the tree by the big guy, who could have cared less about his mutilated arms. Wringing wet, James was dripping sweat into his wounds making them sting like hell. His throat was so dry it made him cough.

"Vamos! Vamos," the big guy said, pushing James forward. Ramon said nothing.

They used their machetes to clear the thick underbrush. It did not take long to get back to the gravel road. This burgeoning path had been much more fortuitous for James earlier.

An old dented, blue VW van waited on the road. Alfredo sat behind the steering wheel. James looked back in the direction of the torture house. No, he had not come very far.

Shit, he thought. *His great escape did not last long.*

The big guy shoved James into the backseat of the van. *"Cabron!"* he shouted. He cuffed James' left wrist to the door handle. He and Ramon sat in the front seat with Alfredo. He gestured with a snarl for Alfredo to drive, heading in the opposite direction from the house. It was quite obvious that he was in charge.

The van groaned through its gears in that unmistakable VW high pitch, bumping along the unpaved road. It was still afternoon, the sun beaming down on the lush landscape. Tropical birds called from the treetops while a hot, sultry breeze slipped in through the windows.

James could not readily assess his current condition. He was exhausted, but refreshed. It was like he was hanging from a jungle vine, suspended in hot air, but no longer over a swamp of alligators. Somehow, mentally he was different. He no longer felt impotent, like the maimed, passive victim— maimed, yes, but passive, no. He had proved to himself with impunity that he was an active participant in his own survival.

As he dozed off in his dismal state, he smiled— because he just had a passing taste of hope....

James awakened, jarred awake by noise and motion. He was still in the van. He opened his left eye first, then his right. It was dusk, still twilight. He was lying down on the back seat. The upholstery was ragged and torn. It stunk, smelling of body odor and gas fumes.

Did he dare try to sit up to look around?

He was lying on his left side. He moved his torso and a thunderbolt of pain rifled up his left arm. He saw stars, not in the sky, but in his head. It radiated up his neck into his skull, throbbing like a hangover. No, worse than any hangover he'd ever had.

But, *but,* he was still alive! "Thank You, Lord," he quietly acclaimed, giving thanks for this unlikely reality.

He had courted the specter of death countless times in the last few days. The process of moving seemed to somehow suspend that ominous specter, that black cloud over him, and its impending doom, that constant threat foreboding his demise. Disregarding the odors, it was almost refreshing, enervating. The change of pace and scene brought a temporary sense of relief.

The vehicle was steadily groaning in a high pitch, just like the old VW vans left over from the hippie generation.

Hot wind blew in through the windows.

Where are they taking me? he wondered.

At the moment, he did not care where they were taking him . This ride interrupted the menacing despair which had haunted him continually back in the torture shack. Motion in this setting meant change; and change brought hope— hope, a foreign term before his escape. Previously, hope was something that James thought no longer existed for him. Throughout the three sessions of torture at the sadistic hands of the deranged doctor, hope was not even a consideration. His only remote reflex was survival. But, after his brief escape, his taste of that precious commodity, hope, was delicious. And sustaining.

He could hear the guys speaking up front over the whir of the wind. He could not make out what they were saying in Spanish. Alfredo, Ramon, what was the big guy's name?

Dogs were barking, roosters crowing in the distance. There was little or no traffic, few lights, approaching darkness. They were still in a rural area. They had to be taking him way out in the country.

The hills were getting steeper. The curves were challenging the tired horsepower of the old VW. It coughed, sputtered, and groaned as the driver ground the gears and fought to keep it climbing. The roads were getting bumpier and bumpier. There were times when the pavement ended, leaving rocky holes.

The VW was swerving and jolting, causing James' body to roll and shift on the back seat. The bolts of pain increased in intensity. *But, stay quiet. Don't moan, don't cry out. No, contain the pain. Grit the teeth. No matter what, don't let them know you are awake.*

The bucking van catapulted and bumped James' body almost completely off the seat.

"Ahh-eee! Conyo!" came from the front seat.

James could suddenly move his hands freely. The only handcuff locked was on his left wrist. The right cuff was swinging free. It clanged against the seat. He quickly shut his eyes as the person sitting shotgun leaned over to look back.

The right handcuff? Had the door handle broken? Or was it on purpose? Hoping he would make another run for it so they could shoot him?

Whatever the circumstance, it presented James with opportunity, food for thought. He had to think, think seriously.

All of a sudden, an air of positivism, a wave of excitement overcame him. It was having an amazing overall effect on his spirit, mind, and body. He could actually feel himself smiling again. The constant, gnawing, throbbing pain started to abate. He began to discover a new-found energy. It caused him to shiver from head to toe, not from the usual rigors of pain, but from unadulterated exhilaration. What a refreshing change.

What were his possibilities? His first idea was at a stop light. When the van came to a complete stop, he would jump out, run, attempt to escape. A town would provide better cover, more streets, buildings, corners, places to hide. But, there had not been anything resembling a town, city, or village. They were way the hell out in the country, in the hills, wherever that was. He didn't care. Even the jungle again would be an improvement over another torture house. *Anywhere beats that damn place.*

What about his legs? Would he be able to run for it one more time? To make a dash? He knew his legs, his body, for that matter; weren't in great shape. He had tested it once. He just needed more stamina. Forget about his arms, his hands, the horrendous wounds. He wouldn't allow himself to look at them, except to tend to them in whatever limited way he could.

An unforeseen opportunity, another possibility? Hell, forget worrying. Worrying about his legs, his capabilities, worrying about anything. It didn't help. Think possibility. Escape. Freedom. He had done it once. He could do it again. This new surge of energy, of light, of hope was worth everything in the world because, just hours ago, his world was bleak, terribly bleak and dark. Indeed, James' entire world was surely headed towards its end, its bitter, flesh-burned, ashen, bloody end. *Dead city. Death. The End* — for one James T. Cantrill, Jr.

The breath of new life, rebirth, rejuvenation, Renaissance; purge the doubts regarding his capabilities, regarding anything negative. Yes, coming from where he had been...

Screeech! Bam! the driver slammed on the brakes. The van swerved, tires screeched.

James braced himself against the back of the front seat with his free left hand. Pain shot up his arm and down his spine.

"*Conyo, Sheeit!*" the one at shot-gun yelled.

Wham! Clunk! Ka-Wham! The dilapidated van had crashed into something. It lurched up and down, whipped like an old, used see-saw. Metal crunched. A cacophony of sounds shrilled through the open windows—a yelping, then braying, shrill, discordant sound, worse than a shriek.

There was yelling in the front seat. Outside the van, too. Sounds James had never heard.

"*Conyo, Sheeit!*" the driver screamed.

James' body rolled off the seat and hit the floor. The bolts of pain zapped his brain.

"*Urgg...urrgg...*" he moaned, trying to restrain himself.

The van rolled on to its side.

The noises were deafening— human screams, metal crunching, glass shattering, animals bleating, chickens clucking, concomitant sounds of alarm, fear, and destruction.

James was acutely aware of his surroundings and circumstance. If his pain had served any purpose at all, it had helped to unthaw his brain and sharpen his senses.

The van came to a rocking, abrupt stop. Dust, dirt. Feathers were flying. A wheel spinning, metal creaking. James was almost standing upright, his feet on earth, a grassy patch of dirt exposed by the broken window.

The sounds of panic and fright continued for a few seconds— the repeated, varied animal howls drowned out the cries of human anguish. The shouts, moans, and swearing from the front seat had subsided, replaced by a morbid contraction.

James felt that he had some maneuvering room created by the angle, the forward tilt of the front seat caused by the impact. He reached up toward the bar separating the front and rear windows. Pain shot like fire through every part of his body. *To hell with it.*

He grabbed the bar, pulled himself up with all his might, grunting, groaning. The raw pain made sharp slices through his long torso.

His head was clear, now for his upper body. He strained with all his might, both right and left arms throbbing as though knives were jabbing into them, deeper and deeper.

He flexed his knees, trying to raise them up, draw both legs out. Cramps gripped both legs simultaneously. Spasms shook his arms. He struggled to lift himself. With all the strength he could muster, he flung himself out of the smashed vehicle.

His body rolled off the van over onto the ground, and he cried out. Pain mesmerized his entire being, so vast that it was non-specific. He first saw blinding white. Then black— his head swimming from dizziness. Everything suddenly went black.

When he regained consciousness, his eyes were met by the distressed stare of an injured old man lying on his side facing him. Only fifteen feet away, the man, unshaven, dressed in tattered clothes, had blood all over his chest and left hip. His tannish-yellow dog lay closely beside him, yelping from its own injury, the bloody bones protruding from its hind leg.

"Por favor, Senor? Por...favor," the old man pleaded.

A donkey lay on the ground in front of a demolished cart, braying, bleating, gasping for air. Chickens, their feathers flying, were flapping around, clucking fast in staccato.

"Uhgg, por favor? Ayudar...por...fav..." the poor old peasant's despairing plea muffled. His dog had crawled over to her master and was licking his face.

James tried to stand up. He staggered, fell to his left knee, *damn, my leg,* righted himself with his right hand, palm down against the ground. Lightning bolts blitzed up his arm.

He was sobered back into full consciousness by the sight of the old man. He immediately empathized with his desperation, which he only knew so well.

"Ayuda me? Ayuda me, amigo..." the man again begged, using James' word, *amigo.*

James wobbled when he stood up straight. He took three shaky steps.

The old man pitifully reached out to James, his calloused hand trembling.

James paused, leaned over, showing him the gashes on his hands and arms, with the left handcuff swinging from his right wrist. The old man grimaced.

"Lo ciento, lo ciento mucho, amigo," James whispered, gesturing with the handcuffs towards the overturned van.

The old man nodded his head, seeming to understand as he glanced over at the vehicle that had totally destroyed him and the precious possessions of his subsistence.

With that, James turned and tried to run towards the dense forest, limping, his left leg almost buckling under him.

He had only made it several yards, when, all of a sudden, the old man's dog growled, lunged, as if it was going to attack James. Though crippled, its loyalty was devoted to its master.

"Oh, *shit,*" James yelled, falling down, distracted by the ferocity of the growling dog.

"No, Sofia, no!" the old man called to his pet, telling it to stop.

The dog, hearing its master, obeyed.

"Sofia! No!" the man again commanded.

Suddenly, a blood-splattered face emerged from the van.

"Conyo sonnaba-bitch," the person shouted. *"Hey esperar!"* Wait, he shouted at James.

"No. No way!" James quickly blurted back, reacting to the bloody face of a captor.

With that the old man raised up on his elbow, rising to confront the perpetrator of his misery. He screamed commands, *"Sofia. Sofia! Hombre! Cabron!"* calling Sofia, his devoted dog, to attack the *hombre* whom he thought had inflicted their injuries. He was cursing and pointing at the *hombre,* as the one who had caused all this destruction and chaos.

Sofia heeded the anger in the commands from her master.

The dog immediately bolted in a three-legged, blind run towards the blood-drenched form climbing out of the van. It leaped, air-borne, going for the throat of the *hombre.* Growling like a wolf, teeth gnashed, Sophia attacked him with frothing ferocity.

It was the big *hombre* who hardly had a chance. Still reeling from the wreck, he could not steady himself before the cannon-ball of growling fur hit him.

"Ah-eeee! Conyo sheeeit!" he screamed, raising his arms, making a vain attempt to fight off the ferocious attack. Writhing on the ground, he and the dog became a frenzied mass, a fiendish blur of fur, flesh, blood, and mud.

The donkey's bleats had intensified, signaling its last, dying moments.

As James looked back, he surveyed the scene strewn with all sorts of debris— plant and animal, material debris and human debris, flesh and bone scattered across the roadside. The whole landscape was painted with the red and black of death.

"Gracias," he managed to call out to the old man.

As he reached the edge of the tropical forest, he glanced back and waved.

Free! Am I free? he thought to himself, as he ran into the cover of thick vegetation. After seizing this unexpected, gratuitous opportunity to escape, he had hardly begun before he was hit with disbelief.

James did not know where he was. He did not know where he was going. He did not know what he was going to do. But, thank God, he was free. He was alive; and he was free, more so than the last time. Make it count. Make it last. It was good. It felt good. It felt real good.

His feet were sodden with pain. His entire body ached. He stumbled, fell, *damn,* now his damn leg, crawled, got back up, stumbled, gutted it, gritted his teeth and kept limping on...stumbling...falling...crawling... running...further...

And further into the lush, green thickness...of nowhere.

Further into the dark, green thicket...of freedom.

CHAPTER 23

The telephone rang with a muffled, low-pitched ring.

"Yeah," the gravelly voice answered.

"Line clear?" the raspy voice asked.

"Affirmative."

"Status?"

"Subject escaped."

"What!"

"Subject escaped," the gravelly voice repeated.

"How?"

"Uh, there was a wr..."

"Never mind. *Fuck!*" the raspy voice interrupted. "Locate subject. Urgent. Locate and eliminate. Repeat. Locate and eliminate," the angry voice commanded.

"Understood. Search under way," was the response.

"Repeat. Locate and eliminate. Im-*med*-iately. At all costs, neutralize and dispose...or else..."

"Ditto," the gravelly voice responded.

"*Shit!* What a...this is a serious..."

"Understood... Ditto?"

"Ditto." Click.

Click.

PART III

Tropical Sanctuary

And he shall be for a sanctuary; but for a stone of stumbling and for a rock of offence...Sanctify the Lord of hosts himself; and let him be your fear, and let him be your dread.

Isaiah 8:13

CHAPTER 24

I pray the gods some respite from the
weary task of the long year's watch...
Agamemnon, 400 B. C.
Aeschylus

James came to, unsure he was still alive. The pain he felt surpassed the oppressive heat. His last memory was of the accident with the van and cart, the old man, the donkey, and his escape. Where was he now?

It was still dark. He was engulfed by strange sounds, strange high-pitched sounds—*co-kee...co-kee...co-kee,* over and over again, rotating all around in a large circumference, from one point to the next, like they were talking to each other, answering each other. He had never heard anything like it. But, the unfamiliar sounds were accompanied by those all too familiar— the unmistakable hum of mosquitoes.

He looked around. It was just beginning to get light. He was on a cot under a make-shift tent, a camouflage netting suspended from trees somewhere in the wilderness. Over to his right was a woman sleeping in a hammock strung between two trees. She had light brown skin and long black hair which draped out of the hammock. She was sleeping peacefully. Was she the one who had found him? She must be, for some Good Samaritan had administered to his wounds. He had dressings on his hands and arms that had some kind of ointment on them. For that he was thankful. Who was she, this tropical Florence Nightingale?

His primary pain was coming from his left leg and left ankle, which must have been injured in the wreck or its aftermath. A rather crude splint bound with fiber cord was attached to his lower left leg. Yes, he was thankful just to be alive, even more so for being found by someone who would actually care for him.

The *co-kee/co-kee* sounds dissipated as dawn broke. James began to see that he was surrounded by dense foliage, tall trees, thick vines, like a rain forest. Wild bird calls were replacing the *co-kee* chants. The woman was beginning to stir, shifting her small body in the hammock, moaning quietly, looking innocent and almost pretty. She could not have been much over thirty.

Suddenly, there was gunfire— *rat-a-tat! rat-a-tat!* short bursts from automatic rifles. She awakened with a start.

James jumped, groaning at the rush of pain. He could not help thinking, "Aw, hell, here we go again."

The woman jumped out of the hammock and was at his side. She gently put her hand on his shoulder and said, "*pobrecito.*"

James noticed her eyes, big and black, still with sleep in them, but kind and gentle.

The gunfire continued. She patted his shoulder again. For some reason, James was comforted. *Will I ever escape this violence?*

"My name is James," he said.

"James," he repeated pointing to his chest with his bad right hand.

With the dressing on his hand now prominently displayed, he gestured to it. "Thank you. Thank you so much...uh, *gracias. Muchas gracias.*"

She smiled. "*De nada. Margarita...me llamo Margarita. De nada.*"

James felt warmed, almost welcomed.

Rat-a-tat! Rat-a-tat! the gunfire was getting closer.

He cringed. Were they being attacked?

Margarita looked up at his wide-eyed apprehension. She had been checking his dressings. She shook her head, no, and patted his shoulder again.

James would have to take her word for it. What other choice did he have? For a diminutive female alone in the wilderness with an incapacitated, debilitated patient, she was self-assured and confident. She touched his skin, checking his dressings, and he noticed that her hands were rough and calloused, in total contrast to the rest of her skin, which looked so soft. Her complexion was completely unblemished, smooth as virgin coffee ice cream. She adjusted the splint on his left leg, loosening the fiber cords. She certainly seemed to know what she was doing.

James wanted to ask her so many questions. He wished that he knew more than five words in Spanish.

"*Café?*" Margarita asked.

"Oh, yes. Uh, *si...por favor. Gracias.*"

After she left the tent, James heard rustling in the brush. *They are coning to get me?*

His heartbeat quickened. His head thrashed back and forth, responding to the noises, looking for anything, looking for everything, expecting the worse.

Out of nowhere, five Hispanic men dressed to kill, in camouflage fatigues with blackened faces, came into the tent. Each carried an assault rifle. Their entrance into the tent was more casual than attack.

The man with the broadest shoulders approached James.

"*Senor, como esta?*" he asked with a wry grin. He had incising black eyes, and porcelain white teeth framed by a *broad* black moustache.

"Uh...*bien. Gracias.* Uh, *gracias. Muchas gracias,*" James stammered back.

They all smiled, probably laughing at James' attempt at Spanish with a southern accent.

James had the jitters, though. They seemed friendly enough. They were smiling, looking like any one of them was about to crack a joke within the next minute. The soldier who questioned him had an air of authority, and James had no doubt that he was in charge.

"Me *llamo James.* Uh...*gracias. Muchas gracias,*" he said, gesturing to the dressings on his arms and, as best he could, the splint on his leg. And he did his best to produce his "mile smile." He always used to say in his sales meetings, "Whenever in doubt, when hesitant, smile a mile."

The commander smiled back and said, "*Me llamo Moises.*"

At that moment, Margarita came back into the tent and handed James a tin of coffee.

"Oh, *gracias,*" he said, repeating his magic word.

They all began speaking in Spanish, much too fast for him to understand a word. But, as he tried to listen, he realized that Margarita was definitely one of them, whoever they were. And, he did not hear the word, *gringo*, uttered once, and he thought that was a good sign. He also knew that *gringo* was a Mexican term, and he was not in Mexico. He was in Puerto Rico.

As they walked out of the tent, he sipped his coffee, which was so hot and so strong that it brought tears to his eyes. The dented, tin mug was almost too hot to hold. But, it enlivened his mind, and he needed to reorient himself, try to get his bearings.

What did he know about Puerto Rico? Not very much. But, for one thing, he knew that there were tons of pharmaceutical companies and medical manufacturers with plants here due to some kind of tax incentives provided by the Federal Tax Code. He remembered it now because of all of the hoopla internally at Werner a few years ago. It was called Code 936. Werner had a plant located somewhere in Puerto Rico; starts with a C, Caguas. That's it— Caguas, Puerto Rico. James recalled the tremendous controversy it had created back at corporate headquarters in Warsaw, Indiana. Code 936 became a buzzword with upper management— so excited about moving the manufacture of high volume total hip femoral stems offshore. Suddenly, corporate executives caught up in the frenzy of globalization more resembled schoolchildren at recess discovering the opposite sex for the first time. This move was *supposed* to accomplish significant cost reductions and greatly expand profit margins, both badly needed with the deep discounts being demanded by national contracts, i.e. the HealthCareUSA chain. With all of the contractual forces of managed care, national contracts, and Medicare cutbacks, *this* was going to be *the* solution to many fiscal budgetary problems. Then, the proverbial shit hit the fan! Faced with an unskilled workforce, they had to import Puerto Rican workers for training. There were second and third generation family employees working on the shop floor— lathe operators, polishers, investment molders, quality control inspectors, etc. whose fathers and grandfathers, whose mothers and grandmothers, whose aunts and uncles had all worked at Werner. They were a proud people, proud of their heritage, proud of their tradition. They took great pride in their hardy Midwestern work ethic. And, after years of hard work and dedication, they suddenly discovered again that their jobs were in jeopardy. Just two years ago, Werner had announced the first layoffs in its history. That sent shockwaves through the employees, most of whom had devoted their lives to *their* company. Conversely, Werner was an integral part of their lives and sense of community. After all those years of loyalty, of total trust, a sense of family and belonging, their future security was being threatened. They felt betrayed.

There was a huge outcry, a borderline revolt. Werner had prided itself through the years in being non-union. Had they been a union shop, there would have been a strike. Morale deteriorated. Backorders increased. Werner and Brecken-Mersack Strauss had to set up a new plant in Warsaw far removed from the other plants, equip it with all the machines and personnel for training. They had to completely separate this facility from any ongoing operations. Called Plant #9, it was hush-hush in the main manufacturing areas, but remained a known fact. Human Resources had to dedicate a special task force for damage control—to hold employee meetings, attempt to restore their confidence, their job security. But, with a secret plant on the other side of town, full of foreigners trying to learn their precious job skills, literally taking their jobs away from them, this band-aid effort was mission impossible.

A huge, raucous parrot perched on the camouflage netting, its calls answered by another parrot far away. It flew off cawing noisily.

Furthermore, this added insult to injury. Still fresh in their memories, just several years before this fiasco, the employees sorely remembered the closing of the Werner soft goods/traction manufacturing plant in their town. Those operations were moved to Mexico and Central America, to Honduras, where there was much cheaper labor. The NAFTA Treaty was not a popular document there in central Indiana. That permanently sewed the seed of discontent, of job insecurity, of distrust in their minds, hearts, and souls. From that moment on, things were never the same at Werner, Inc. Morale continued to plummet, backorders continued to increase, the Distributors and associates complained even more vociferously, and sales suffered accordingly.

Code 936 heaved salt in an open wound. What had all begun with the less-threatening transfer of the manufacture of soft goods snowballed into core products, which was exacerbated irreversibly by the importation of a workforce of Puerto Ricans. The irony, no the insanity of it all was management's decision to set up the on-sight training in Warsaw, Indiana, the rural birthplace of the orthopaedic industry right in the heartland of Midwestern America. The presence of Hispanic foreigners right there in Warsaw served as a physical threat to their tradition, to the legacy of the family workplace, but, even more so, to their cherished, comfortable way of life. Why wasn't that training conducted at the new plant in Puerto Rico? Or any other facility down there? That would have made sense. But, quite to the contrary, management imports an entire labor force composed of foreigners, who were thrust into a hostile situation with which they had nothing to do. No, it was certainly not the Puerto Ricans' fault. They were good, hard working people just looking for jobs. Mostly, it was yet *one more* poor, ill conceived management decision at Werner, Inc. Quite tragically, these self-defeating, counterproductive strategic decisions within the corporation and the parent company had become so commonplace in the last few years that they were the rule, not the exception.

Rat-a-tat, rat-a-tat! He heard more gunfire in the distance.

James knew this: his presence in Puerto Rico was somehow connected to the manufacturing facilities here. That would have made the long flight of the corporate jet to get him out of the country a legitimate expense. Pharmaceutical/medical research would justify the employment/presence of his torturer, the deranged German doctor. Oh, hell, just the thought of him caused James to shudder. What a degenerate! What kind of demented mind could torture a defenseless, helpless individual? With an electrosurgical cautery machine, for crying out loud, cutting, burning, and mutilating human flesh.

Margarita came back and asked, *"Mas café, Senor James?"*

"Si. Gracias, muchas gracias, Margarita. Bien, mui bien," he said, handing her his cup.

She changed part of the dressing on his bad hand, the right hand and right arm. As she leaned over him to adjust the splint on his leg, her yellow cotton tank top shifted. James could not help noticing that she was not wearing a bra. She had small breasts. James shamed himself for looking. If he was a dirty old man, he was sorry. But this was the first healthy, creative diversion he had enjoyed in days. He chuckled. Trish always wished that she could go braless.

"Mas dolor, Senor?" she asked pointing to his leg and arms.

"... pain? *Dolor?* Pain? *Si.* But, better. Uh, *mui? Gracias,"* he replied. He was unsure of just what he had said.

A white soldier wearing fatigues and a green beret walked in. A gold leaf on his epaulets indicated the rank of Major. He was stocky with large, muscular forearms and had flashing green eyes with a distant twinkle. The beret magnified the green of his eyes.

"*Margarita?* Who is he?"

"*El es*...Major Henry," she replied.

"*Bienvenidos,* James. I am Major Frank Henry. Welcome to the humble home of us *Independitos.* They found you about 15 meters beyond that ridge, lying unconscious, bleeding in the wilderness. They brought you here to our rustic First Aid station in our camp here. Margarita patched you up, as best she could with her home-grown supplies. She is our resident doctor, nurse, and nutritionist. And a mighty good one at that. She has more magic herbs and natural medicines than you can shake a stick at. She's got you fixed up pretty good. You are damn lucky to be alive, *hombre!*" The major spoke with a south Texas accent.

"Yes, and I'm very grateful. *Muchas gracias, Margarita,*" James replied.

"What happened to you, anyway, James? You were in some kind of bad shape," the Major asked.

"I ran into some unfriendlies and lost." James did not want to say too much at this point.

"Hell, I'll say you did!" he retorted.

"Uh, Major Henry, I'm really grateful... don't want to wear out my welcome, but, may I ask, where am I and who are the *Independistos?*" he asked as diplomatically as he could.

"Well, Hoss, since you don't look like the type to rat out your saviors...'n it dudn't look like you're headed to the CIA anytime soon, I'm might jus' tell ya. It's known 'monst the faithful anyways...but our location 'n enlistees are top secret... so, I'll trust ya..."

The major proceeded to explain that the *Independistos* were a rapidly growing band of insurgents who were leading the extremely popular movement in Puerto Rico for independence and autonomy. They wanted total separation from the United States, their very own nascent freedom, and their own form of democratic government. The major, an Army Special Forces veteran, was hired as an instructor and trainer for their troops. Their camp, here, was located deep in the *Corderilla* mountains. The camp was extremely well guarded and any incursion by unknowns was met with force. The only reason that he, James, was alive, allowed to live, was the fact that the huge, gaping wound on his right hand was in the shape of the "I."

"That is the sacred symbol of the *Independistos* and their growing movement," the major continued. "It was also evident that you had been tortured. For whatever the reason, the "I" at least hinted to them that you were sympathetic with their cause. They thought that the "I"-wound was inflicted upon you on purpose, quite visibly so on top of the right hand so that everyone would see it. It was some kinda signal, an omen. The fact that you had survived this torture greatly raised your status with them. I mean, man, you oughta be dead. A dead man way down deep in dead city! *Moises,* the leader, the *el commandante,* feels the same way. They took one look at you, no shirt, your ripped up slacks, blood all over ya, those damn gashes, and said *mui mort*...thought you wuz dead. Then they started calling you *macho Americano con cajones grande—* the brave American with big balls!"

James laughed, trying to restrain himself due to the pain. "I'm not sure I measure up to all that," he said.

"I mean to have survived whatever in the hell it was, you suffered," the Major continued, "the torture, I mean, persecution, musta been awful painful, man. I've been through some tough campaigns, been wounded myself, had my foot almost blown off by a land mine in Nam, caught the "crud" in Desert Storm, still bothers me. Yep, I've seen some really bad shit, but you, Hoss, rank up there. The troops found ya, carried ya in here to bivouac, went and got *Moises,* who called in Margarita, his sister, our resident doctor 'n nurse. So, you're in good hands. I mean, the Lord almost called you home, but you landed on safe. Ya gotcha ass a reprieve."

James questioned the leader's name, *Moises.* "Is that *Moises,* like Moses in the Bible?"

"You betcha. One in the same. He was named after Moses. His parents must have been clairvoyant," the Major explained.

"That *would* seem provident. Moses, *Moises* in this case, is going to lead his people out of bondage, away from the evil Pharaoh *vis a vis* the United States of America, grant them their freedom, and take them to the Promised Land, to their own Promised Land. What a historic coincidence," James proclaimed.

"Well, I'm impressed. I can see, my good man James, that not only were you named after one of the prophets, but you also studied your Sunday school lessons well," Major Henry laughed. He rared back and laughed louder and louder. He had an infectious, deep-throated laugh that echoed into the treetops. James was laughing, too. Laughing to the point that it hurt. It was good to laugh again, in spite of the pain.

Then, the Major leaned over James, lowered his voice, and spoke very seriously, "You were right, James. Historic coincidence. This Puerto Rican named *Moises* is powerful, a 'vi-ery powerful man here, committed to freedom for his people, religious in his beliefs, doctrinal in his mission, and unsurpassed with his following. The people here love him. Believe in him. Would follow him to the end of the earth. He is unbelievably charismatic. I mean, you should hear him give a speech. He *is* articulate. An orator? Dy-no-mite! Castro has tried repeatedly to recruit him to usurp, to revive his cause in Cuba. But, *Moises* has very diplomatically declined, telling Castro that his philosophy is wrong, that socialism is not a viable form of government, much less way of life. He has very politely informed Castro that Communism can't last. *Moises* devoutly believes in capitalism."

A lizard fell off the netting above down on to the Major's beret. He reacted blazingly fast, then casually flipped it off. James was awed by the Major's razor-sharp reflexes.

"...as I was saying, *Moises* is an advocate of capitalism and the free market economy. He's brilliant, well educated, went to The Citadel, then West Point, that's where I first met him, at the Point. Then, he got his MBA from Wharton. He is truly a visionary with a strategic plan. Once he achieves the objective of freedom for his native Puerto Ricans, his vision calls for a strategic alliance of other underdeveloped Caribbean nations, including Cuba, much to Castro's liking. This strategic alliance would serve as the foundation for his free market model, somewhat similar to President Reagan's Caribbean Basin Initiative." The major pulled a bandana from his hip pocket to mop the sweat off his forehead. The heat of the day blanketed them.

"But, his plan's got," he continued, "export/import, free trade zones, major investment incentives, venture capital, a buncha' shit. He's phenomenal. His strategic vision ain't just pie in the sky, my man. It is extremely well researched. He wrote his thesis, did his dissertation at Wharton on it. Two of the big profs there went wild over it, took it with 'em to some big global symposium in Hong Kong. But, his intelligence is not his strong suit. It's his inspiration. He inspires the hell out of people.

And the people believe in him! In turn, he makes the people believe in themselves. He *is* awesome. But, 'lemme tell 'ya, he is much more than just a friend to me. Hell, talk about Moses and historic coincidence. How about divine coincidence? It was my friend, *Moises,* who saved my life in Nam. He *saved* my *life!* Carried me on his back for miles with my foot dangling from my leg, carried me 'til the helicopter evacs came, or I would have bled to death! Thank you, God. And thank God for him! Yes sir, I believe in him. That's why I consented to join him to help train for his cause." Major Frank Henry had just given James a convincing documentary.

"It's ironic you mention coincidence, again, Major," James commented. "My favorite definition of that word:

Coincidence is the Lord's way of remaining anonymous.

"Damn, Hoss! It's no wonder you're still alive. That's beautiful," and he repeated the definition. "I mean, that's downright apostolic. You're something else."

Since the good Major was so candid and forthright, James felt the need to reciprocate as to his state of affairs. He related all the sordid details chronologically. When he finished, he was drained.

"*Jesus,* man, who'd believe it? You are a corporate, cowboy hero! I mean, that's *un-damn, un-damn-believable*! A real live horror show!" Major Henry was daunted with his reaction.

"I'm not a hero," James said. "Not a cowboy. Just a simple man who wants to get back to his family." James felt his eyes closing despite the strange surroundings and the strong coffee.

"And *then,*" he said. "I wanna make the *truth* known, to make sure the *truth* is known."

The major nodded his head.

James, fading fast, again responded that he was not a hero, nor did he aspire to be a hero. He was simply an honest, hardworking businessman who was suddenly, for some unknown reason, dispossessed of his own business, kidnapped, and violently tortured. His driving force, his burning desire now was only to stay alive, to live so that he could return home to his loved ones, to his wife and family. And, then— make the *truth* known.

CHAPTER 25

Globalization can shrink the heart, mind, and soul.
Charles L. Deeds, CEO
Snyder Manufacturing Co.

As Rob Hempstead walked down the Monet-lined hallway at Werner toward the Legal Department, David Zuckerman and Terry Meissner, his Executive VP and his CFO, were walking with him, singing his praises step by step. They were not sucking up to their boss. They could simply not contain their awe and pride over the Group President's recent performance in the Werner quarterly review meeting, which they had just left. Though they had witnessed their bosses' masterful prowess many times, his being the true master of the corporate "Dress-down," this had truly been his finest hour in the "mother of all Dress-downs." And this "Dress-down" had been so badly needed, long overdue at Werner, Inc., which had not met budget or achieved quota for the past six quarters. But that fact paled before the more pernicious problem— their growing dishonesty, the denial, the suspected manipulation of their numbers reflecting false results, and their alleged unethical practices.

Hempstead was looking forward to his impromptu meeting with Brice Billups. He had never liked the little bastard. He was not alone in thinking that Brice had a severe Napoleon complex, which at times had compromised Werner's high professional standards and most recently, their cultural principles and legal ethics. Brice had somehow managed to elevate himself into a position of extreme authority, far exceeding his job description as a corporate counsel, his judicial domain, the confines of the Werner legal department, the boundaries of proper jurisprudence, and, last, but not least, his individual capability. The highly questionable termination of the Distributor of twenty-nine years in Kentucky, James Cantrill, was the most recent case in point— a wrongful termination suit by Cantrill seemed secondary to his role as material witness in a daunting product liability death. Rob's phone conversation with both Brice and Leonard R. Shortt yesterday had left a number of pressing questions unanswered. His Breck-Mersack general counsel, Ross Carswell, agreed and was researching the reason for the impromptu, threatening visit from the Inspector General from the FDA back in New York headquarters. He was also investigating the circumstances regarding the James Cantrill issue and the extent to which Werner was culpable for wrongful termination litigation. Both the counsel and Rob had been dismayed by the lack of contrition on Brice's part after they hung up the phone. What an arrogant little prick! Of course, Lenny Shortt's reaction was to be expected. He was his usual crawfish-self — "who can I blame for this one? Oh, it was George and Brice in that, uh, meeting."

As the three entered through the heavy, burnished walnut door marked "LEGAL" in large embossed gold letters, they were met with the friendliest greeting of the week, which was actually the first gesture of sincerity and honesty they had seen all day.

"Why, Mr. Hempstead, what a pleasant surprise to see you today! And, Mr. Zuckerman and Mr. Meissner, nice to see you, as well. How are you gentlemen doing today?" chirped Ellie, the forever effervescent legal receptionist.

"Hi, Ellie. You are your usual cheerful self," Mr. Hempstead replied

"And to what do we owe this unexpected pleasure? Is Mr. Weist expecting you?"

"No, Ellie, we are here to see Brice Billups, thank you."

"Oh, I'm sorry, he isn't in. He left suddenly, said he had to catch a plane. He said something which I did not understand. He seemed quite nervous. I'm sorry."

"Please tell him that I was, that *we* came to see him, Ellie. Thank you," he said, coolly.

"Shall I have him call you?"

"He will know. Have a nice day, Ellie."

As they proceeded back down the hall, Rob Hempstead was thinking how on earth a lovely person like Ellie could work with such a complete bunch of assholes day in and day out.

Both of his companion officers seem to know exactly what their boss was thinking. They were all thinking the same thing.

They entered the ornate, brass elevator to go up to the President's office. There was total silence on the elevator. Rob Hempstead did not really expect to see Ron Salter today. With the unacceptable quarterly results once again, the growing loss of sales, the continued, calamitous erosion of market share, and the deteriorating morale, the President certainly *should* have been there. The only legitimate excuse for his absence that Rob could think of at the moment was emergency hospitalization. With this example for leadership, it was no wonder that Werner, Inc. was in a precipitous decline, in an economic free fall. Unfortunately, the onus was on him. Yes, without a doubt, the poor performance of this subsidiary was his, the Group President's responsibility. He had attempted to correct this problem in the past by starting at the top, making a change in leadership with the appointment of a new president. Ron Salter had started strong, but had somehow totally lost it, *it* being the mission, focus, direction, and employee respect. Now a grave disappointment, he represented yet another Hempstead mistake. The mendacity, denial, finger-pointing, and dishonesty saturating this place was epidemic and Salter had no vaccine.

Thus, he, the Group President, he, Robert Hempstead, the anointed one most favored to be in line as the next President of Brecken-Mersack Strauss, Inc., was under pressure not only from *the* CEO, but also *the* Board of Directors. This damn Werner disaster had caused the Board to scrutinize and criticize him. Hell, he had to do something dynamic and turn things around quickly, just to save his own neck. Neck, hell! His damn career.

As they entered, Rob and company were again greeted with surprise, courtesy, and sincerity by Linda, the President's executive secretary.

"Oh, Mr. Hempstead, how are you? We weren't expecting you today."

"Yes, that has lamentably been quite obvious. Is Ron in?" He fully expected her to say no. He eagerly awaited the excuse.

"Why, yes. He just got here. I'm afraid you'll have to forgive Mr. Salter this morning. He just had a root canal and still cannot speak too well. Just a moment."

They walked in to find Ron Salter dressed in a gray and red ski sweater holding a Werner Quik-Cold Pack to the right side of his face.

The pain emanating from his root canal was suddenly rendered insignificant by the shock of unexpectedly having the Group President walk into his office. His eyeballs exploded like Roman candles on July the 4th. He shuddered in a state of shock. He groaned loudly. As he jumped up to move from behind his huge desk, he stumbled and dropped the cold pack on his right knee causing him to moan again.

Salter muttered, as if his mouth was full of oatmeal. He extended his chilled right hand to shake hands with his boss and missed his hand. His cold red hand just pumped dead air. His awkwardness heightened. He nodded his head at the Executive V. P. and CFO, clumsily trying to direct them to the couch settee. He stumbled over the Persian rug as he pulled up a chair for himself.

Ron mumbled something to all three, which none of them understood. Then, he pantomimed sipping from a coffee cup on a saucer.

All three of the visiting dignitaries shook their heads at the same time.

Then, Rob Hempstead, the Big Boss, the Group President dropped the bombshell question. "So, Ron, why weren't you at the Quarterly Review meeting this morning?"

Ron Salter choked, his eyes widened and bugged out further. The blood flow through his facial arteries drained. His face looked like concrete.

Instead of answering, he pointed to his right jaw repeatedly, *he thought* very shrewdly.

"Oh, you mean your root canal? Is that it?" Hempstead politely questioned.

Salter grunted, jerking his chin up and down, yes, and attempting to smile through his chapped lips, white-caked with dried saliva.

There was silence.

Rob Hempstead looked down, staring at the scorpion patterns in the Anatolian oriental carpet. Yes, he thought to himself, look at that, an extravagant, $58,000-dollar piece of self-indulgence, purchased by the previous president. This gross expenditure could not be blamed on Ron Salter. No, Salter had bought the antique King Louis the XVIth coffee table on top of the Turkish kilim. It had only cost $79,775; Rob recalled the amount to the dollar. What was the return on capital of these strategic investments? These two collectible gems were contributing a naked zero to the growth of sales, revenues, profit, and market share for this company. And that doesn't even take in to account all of the Monets and Renoirs lining the hallways. Not to be outdone, Ron Salter had also purchased a numbered John Singer Sargent portrait, spotlighted on the far mahogany-paneled wall of the suite. Hempstead could not bear to even look at it. It had cost over $175,000. "But, what a steal!" Ron had bragged. He bought it to celebrate the one decent quarter's result *he* had achieved. Here were over $300,000 dollars invested in three *objets d'art* in the President's office, three exorbitant *things* which were doing absolutely nothing for the growth of the business. And the company did not even have a current catalogue! Had *not had* an up-to-date catalogue in their customers' hands in over nine years. This was insanity — an idiotic allocation of capital.

The silence was brutal. It amplified their inattention, their purposefully avoided eye-contact. Salter was being ignored in his own office. His acute pain was now being surpassed by cold, undiluted fear.

"Ron, I don't mean to be brash, but I thought a root canal was more of a scheduled procedure. Was yours an emergency?" the boss conjectured.

Ron Salter's head was throbbing, his heart pounding out of his chest. He first shook his head no, then caught himself, and tried to nod yes.

He grunted unintelligibly, repeatedly pointing to his jaw again.

Hempstead thought he sounded like Dudley Moore in the movie, *"10,"* but this was tragic not comical.

"I'm not sure what that means, Ron. Given Werner's unacceptable results yet one more consecutive quarter, I believe that it should have behooved you, the President of Werner, Inc., to have attended this meeting, in spite of scheduled dental work. You should have been there no matter what— at least made an appearance. So that there is absolutely no possibility for misunderstanding or rationalization here, I'm going to itemize the major shortfalls to current annual/quarterly plan.

Hempstead proceeded to list them: quarterly quota, annual quota, quarterly and annual growth numbers, market share, budget, margin requirements, profit incentives, cost reduction measures, etc. There nine total. He then reiterated the "*catastrophic* erosion of market share from 43.9 percent in 1990 to 17.4 percent in 1998, a total loss of 26.5 points of share... translating to a volume loss of $937,000,000."

Salter grumbled, touching his jaw.

"That is a loss of business confined to the Hip Product Group, lost business in Hips alone of almost *one billion dollars!*" Hempstead shouted.

"*Glorb. Glorb-zha-shun!*" Salter muttered.

"What? What are you saying, Ron? Globalization?" Hempstead asked.

Salter nodded furiously. "*Glorb-zha-shun!* Uh, *noin,* uh *noin-tree...*" he made a 9, a 3, and a 6, by holding up his fingers. "Por...to *Rico!*"

"936. Code 936? In Puerto Rico? Is that what you're trying to tell us?"

Again, Salter nodded anxiously, attempting to smile, looking like what-a-good-boy-am-I.

"Well, Ron, if globalization and Code 936 are your idea of trimming manufacturing costs, that is one thing. Code 936 saves taxes on profits, yes. *But,* for either of these to be effective, the company must first *make* a profit. Increasing sales and increasing revenues are the *direct* opposite of what you are accomplishing here. In addition, Werner morale is rotten, and globalization can further corrode domestic morale. So, your conjecture about globalization and Code 936 are totally irrelevant."

Salter winced from the pain of harsh reality knifing through his brain.

"Ron, these results are unacceptable. This performance is deplorable. An irreversible trend of consummate, calamitous erosion of share, revenues, and margin now seems to be perpetuating itself. It *must* be stopped. However, the real tragedy we all observed today within that meeting room was the gross rationalization, the abject denial, the air of unaccountability and finger-pointing with a proclivity to shift blame, and *the* blatant dishonesty. The morale was rancid. Concomitant with the absence of ethical direction and leadership was the absence of *the*

President of Werner." The Group President shifted in the Kittinger chair and took a deep breath.

The President of Werner, Inc. sunk deeper into dejection and despondency.

"Furthermore, Ron, had you been present, you would have heard me ask, 'What would our founder say? What would Judson O. Werner say today?' The compendium of people and process, that entire situation we witnessed represent the antithesis of the principles, the ethics, the culture, and the vision created by Mr. Werner. Also, you would have heard me do something I never do in a business meeting: that is quote from the bible. A preacher I am not, but this was both germane and historic. You would have heard me quote Mr. Werner's favorite scripture, Micah, the sixth chapter, the eighth verse:

"He hath showed thee, O man, what is good:
and what doth the Lord require of thee,
but to do justly, and to love mercy,
and to walk humbly with thy God?"

Micah 6:8

"...to do justly...to walk humbly. What *would* Mr. Werner say?" Hempstead's impact was again profound.

Ron Salter felt like Lot's wife, then wished that he *could* turn himself into a pillar of salt.

"Now, as if these facts are not disastrous enough, there are two other very distressing issues: the matter with the Inspector General of the FDA, who made an alarming, unsettling visit to corporate headquarters in New York City yesterday, due to compliance problems at Werner, Inc., *your* responsibility. Secondly, there is the issue of the questionable termination of the Distributor in Kentucky for 29 years, a Mr. James Cantrill. Ross Carswell and I had a phone conversation with Shortt and Brice Billups in Legal, which only served to elevate our severe concerns. We stopped off in Legal to see Billups before coming to your office and were informed that he had left suddenly. Are you on top of these issues, Ron?"

Salter's head was now exploding. He fully expected to see his brains splattered on the ceiling at any second. He could not speak. He wanted to defend himself but could not. All he could do was mumble.

"Ahhrrggg, uhhgg, ahhrrgg," is all that would come out of his parched, cracked lips.

Terry Meissner who was sitting next to Salter flinched visibly due to the gust of his horrendously bad breath.

With that Rob Hempstead nodded at Meissner, who quietly stood and left the office.

"In lieu of this litany of unacceptable results," Hempstead continued, "in lieu of this plague of disastrous circumstances with the FDA and Cantrill's sudden termination, neither of which you are on top of, in lieu of the deteriorating morale and the blatant denial within Werner, Inc., Ron, you are hereby immediately terminated. I regret this, Ron. I had great hopes for you. And you started out in a positive direction. What I can *not* understand, what totally confounds me is your critical detachment. These objectionable conditions have exacerbated almost weekly on your watch."

Terry Meissner reentered with two uniformed security guards.

"Ron, your personal effects will be delivered to you tomorrow by registered courier. Enclosed with them will be the number you are to call to set up your formal exit interview, at a time when you are better able to communicate. At that meeting, the HR officer will give you the details of your severance package and answer any questions which you may have. As I said, Ron, I regret this. Good day."

Hempstead stood and the two security officers escorted Ron Salter, ex-president of Werner, Inc., out of the building.

Ron Salter had never endured such intense pain— both physically and mentally. He had never suffered such excruciating humiliation. He had never, in his entire life, ever felt worse.

As he stood in shock on the sidewalk outside the gray marble edifice, his head throbbing, he swore silently, *How dare these assholes do this to me! I raised this fucking company up out of the ashes. These sons-a-bitches are going to pay for this!*

CHAPTER 26

"§ 936. Puerto Rico and possession tax credit.
(II) All electing corporations ...that produce any products
...may elect...to compute their taxable income from
export sales under a different method..."
UNITED STATES CODE
SUBTITLE A–INCOME TAXES, p. 14

Trish had just accomplished the second hardest thing in her life—she had gone to the office and informed all James' employees and sales associates of his termination by Werner and subsequent disappearance. She thought that her previous experience in telling her daughters would make this easier. It did not. Her own emotional trauma was amplified by their shock, anger, and heartfelt grief. Many tears were shed by all there, except for two absent sales associates who were standing in on surgeries. Trish had held up well until Dana, their office manager, and Alexandra, whom James had hired two years ago as an intern from UK, embraced her for what seemed like forever. That's when she lost it. They all cried together, but afterwards pledged to be strong and continue on as best they could, because that's what James would want them to do.

Trish recalled a verse that James had quoted several times when he became exasperated with Werner. She got out the Bible and read from the 37th Psalm: *...fret not thyself because of him who prospereth in his way, because of the man who bringeth wicked devices to pass. Rest in the Lord...*

And Trish had been so damn noble she could not stand herself. When everyone's anger against Werner riled up, she reminded them of James' mission statement: "*We're in the business of helping people...*" ...when down deep in her heart, she hated Werner for what they had done.

Dana followed Trish out into the parking lot, hugged her again with tears in her eyes, and promised to do anything within her power to help.

While the entire encounter was heartening due to the outpouring of caring, sympathy, and support, it left Trish completely drained— in addition to Lynnwood's secretary weighing on her.

She got back home, fixed herself an iced tea, got pissed due to the mess the FBI guys had left on her kitchen counter, cleaned that up, then paged Chuck.

"Are you still in South Bend, Chuck?" Trish asked. Thank goodness he answered her page so quickly. There was static on the phone line. Was it the FBI's monitoring equipment?

"No, I'm on I-90 to Chicago, rolling through the cornfields and flatlands of Northern Indiana," Chuck Thursgoode replied.

"I was actually hoping you were headed back here, back home. We've had a terrible thing happen," her emotions were surfacing once again.

"What, Trish? What is it?"

"Lynnwood, you remember, our attorney? His secretary...got shot, twice...his office ransacked, torn apart. Sheryl had gone in real early that morning, surprised the intruders, believed to be more than one, ripping Lynnwood's office apart. They were obviously looking for something. Oh, it's awful. She's in ICU at the Med Center...they don't think she'll make it. I have never seen Lynnwood like this. The cops and the FBI think it had something to do with James. Oh, Chuck, I wish you were here. This is serious, really serious?"

"Aw, *Jesus!* Hell *yes,* Trish! It's serious. I'm finding more and more, as we go along, we are dealing with some *very* serious adversaries, some real pros here. Damn! Shot her! I'm sorry I'm not there for you, but I'm on to another lead heading to Chicago. Who was the local detective investigating the shooting at Lynnwood's office? Do you know?"

"No. He may have mentioned his name, but I was so upset. Do you... think this means that James is dead?" she started sobbing again.

"No. No, Trish. Think about it. They are not going to kill him until they get exactly what they want. And the fact that they trashed Lynnwood's office means, well... they probably didn't find whatever they were looking for. Sounds to me like a botched job. Sloppy. If they'd gotten what they wanted , she'd be dead. They left quick, with unfinished business. Understand?"

"Well, if you say so. Yes, I guess that does make sense," Trish answered, trying to calm herself.

"I can call the LPD and find out who was on that case. I hope it was one of my old cronies. I'll let ya know, Trish."

"Well, I got more news for you, Chuck. First, the FBI got the analysis back on those eavesdropping devices. There were two different types of 'bugs,' which the FBI thinks were installed by different 'interests,' as they called them."

"Oh, great, Trish. Wait a sec for me to pull off the highway so that I can write this down...let this semi by...now, okay, I'm ready."

"Well, the first type, the ones found in my kitchen phone, my bedroom, uh, I'm sorry, Chuck, I still can't believe this, I mean coming into my home! The kitchen, bedroom and family room phones were all AGR 238 Crystal Transmitters. FBI said that they were pretty standard, except that each one had...and I'm reading this... a bi-phase, voltage activated booster, supposed to enhance clarity and extend their transmission range for up to a half mile radius. Now, the second type, which they said was very sophisticated— *the* newest, *the* latest technology, genuine 'state-of-the-art,' they said, was made in Taiwan. It was modified and improved over a type they said the CIA and DEA had recently found in Burma, now called Myanmar, used in some narcotics war. They said it was a modified Taiwanese YGRb-3300 advanced Laser Reflectometric Transducer. I wrote this on another page...here! Last month a similar type surfaced at some big international syndicate meeting at the Marina Oriental Hotel in Singapore," she took a sip of iced tea.

"Singapore, Chuck. Even though the attendees supposedly had the meeting room swept and had scramblers there— I'm still reading, Chuck— lasers were used to bounce off the big windows in the hotel from a trawler down in the bay below. They, the eavesdroppers on the ship, were able to pick up everything said in that room. Extremely high tech, the FBI said. Well, this one is a modification of that Taiwanese model. Can you believe it! Does that tell you something?"

"Oh, shit, yeah, 'scuse me, Trish. 'Outta sight! Heavy duty. I subscribe to a journal on TSCM, that is technical surveillance countermeasures, and I've just read something about the new Taiwanese technology. Little did I ever suspect any would ever turn up on one of my cases. Jesus, unbelievable!"

"What does it mean? These 'bugs' were planted by separate 'interests,' as the FBI said?" Trish asked.

"Absolutely. In spades! The second Taiwanese device implies a much more sophisticated, international connection. Now, let me tell you what I've found out, which further substantiates the international aspect. I called AeroTech, you know, where the Kingair was chartered in Cincinnati. It was chartered by a Center Systems Corporation out of Tampa, Florida. They paid cash in large bills. No surprise. But, they had to show proof of major liability insurance coverage, a $5-million dollar minimum umbrella, or put up an additional cash deposit. They gave this LucerneRE Reinsurance AG Corp. as the underwriter of their coverage. I checked that out on the internet. It's a Cayman corporation. Then, called a friend of a friend at a bank in Grand Cayman," he was speaking faster and faster. "It begins to smell a little now— this Center Systems Corp. is a shell corporation, nothing new, I deal with 'em all the time. They are a subsidiary of The Baronne-Fong Group, Ltd., Hong Kong...

"Damn. 'Scuse me, Trish. A car just changed lanes on me," he interjected.

"Okay, Hong Kong. Now, listen to this, Trish, it gets deeper— the Baronne-Fong Group, Ltd. have an office in London, but that's just a front for a larger holding corporation on the Isle of Mann, you know, the international tax haven," he was now speaking excitedly in bursts. "This holding corp. is named Global Distribution Associates, Ltd. Sound interesting? There's more. Turns out this Global Distribution Associates, Ltd. is the tax-free asset holding corp. for a bigger conglomerate in Brussels, Belgium, called International Europa Properties, Ltd. Bingo! Finally made it to the core of the nucleus of this criminal consortium. My banking buddies tell me that there has been a lot of traffic, meaning wires, both money and correspondence, from Brussels to Grand Cayman to guess where?"

"I have no idea, Chuck. You lost me back in Hong Kong. Where?"

"From Brussels. Stop Grand Cayman. Stop to Puerto Rico! ShaZaam! That somehow comes full circle, ya see. Why?" he was talking faster and faster. "Because of all of the pharmaceutical companies and medical device manufacturers with plants in Puerto Rico, due to a special tax code. This IRS tax code is called Code 936. It's a real political 'hot potato' in Congress and the White House. All these giant pharmaceutical companies pay *no* taxes, *no tax* at *all* on *all* profits from products manufactured in Puerto..."

"Rico!" Trish interrupted. "Werner has a new plant down there somewhere. I remember James talking about it. Stirred up alotta' controversy up in Warsaw when they brought all these Puerto Ricans in for training...that after the first ever layoffs. James said it was crazy. Puerto Rico. Oh, my... well, well...boy, have you been busy, Chuck."

"Yea. My laptop's still smoking," he laughed. "That's become my niche, my specialty, Trish, since I went private— industrial espionage and corporate intelligence. The reason I know about Puerto Rico and Tax Code 936 is I have had two contracts, big intelligence jobs, with huge multinational pharmaceutical companies. But, speaking of e-mail and my hot laptop, that's why I'm headed to Chicago. I've got a buddy who works at Butler Aviation at O'Hare. His brother works as a flight controller in the tower at O'Hare and, of course, knows some of the people at FAA. We're going to run down the exact flight plan for that Falcon corporate jet that took off from South Bend. Their original flight plan was for Tampa. But, they made an en route change to Miami. Aha! Closer to Puerto Rico. Right on! When I get with them, we can trace that flight down for damn sure. Then, we'll really have something."

"What does all this mean, Chuck? I'm more scared than ever, with Lynnwood's secretary, poor Sheryl, his office, all this international intrigue...and...and James...oh, James...is..." she choked, "is my husband still alive?" She was starting to break again, in spite of all the positive information.

"Remember what I told you earlier. We are obviously playing with some big boys, big multinationals, some real heavy hitters and that reinforces what I said before. Think about it! They're *not about* to get rid of James until they get what they want and begin to assimilate the resolution to their crisis, whatever that is. That situation in Lynnwood's office surprises me a little. Somebody got sloppy. But, they obviously did *not* find what they were looking for. I'll find out more about that, too. We're *hot* on their trail and getting hotter. Listen, I'm still on the side of the interstate, close to bee-uutiful LaPorte, Indiana. I've gotta head on to Chicago. I'll call you from there, okay?

"Oh, yeah, almost forgot. Remember the woman who sat beside James on the flight from Ft. Wayne to Cincinnati? Elizabeth? She goes by Betty, Betty Browning? Well, I've run her down, am planning to meet her at O'Hare. She'll be flying through Chicago on a business trip. So, I'll call you after I interview her. She was the last person we know of who saw James."

"Wait, one more thing, Chuck. I'm conducting my own little investigation— I'm digging through what James called his 'safe file,' a lotta Werner documents, memos, reports about that surgery, you know? And tapes! You wouldn't believe the tapes, Chuck, James recorded. I mean, major," Trish smiled having used her granddaughters' word. "We gotta talk face-to-face."

"Yeah. I know it. I should be back tomorrow...after Chicago. Meanwhile, page me if anything else comes up. Bye, Trish. Take care and hang in there, ya hear?" He was talking a mile a minute.

After he hung up, Trish noticed that there was still static on the line. She would ask the FBI agent in charge about that.

CHAPTER 27

All tragedies are finished by a death...
Don Juan, 1819
Lord Byron

As James was awakened, he heard the *coquis* chanting their melodic song, *co-kee...co-kee...co-kee*. The throbbing pain in his left leg had subsided a little during the night, allowing him to sleep for a few hours. Margarita had applied another one of her paste poultices made of cayenne, plantain, ginger and goodness knows what else. He could smell the cayenne and ginger. She was an amazing medicine woman, for which he was indeed grateful. There was no activity in the camp yet, which was good. Maybe he could think while his mind was clear, temporarily relieved of three of its constant companions— pain, fever, and rigors.

Could it be that what had gotten him kidnapped and whisked out of the country was his mention of the fatality with that total hip surgery at the HealthCare USA? He recalled Brice's and George's frightful, ashen expressions after he mentioned that. They had almost turned into ghosts when he brought up the records and files, the corporate denial and attempted cover-up, and his incriminating tapes of conversations regarding the tragedy with regulatory and corporate personnel. But, there had to be more to this than he had previously thought, more than just product liability, class action and/or malpractice litigation. Yes, for them to go this far— *damn*, the expense, the contract with the two captors, the planes, the flights, the risk; this was a federal offense, for crying out loud, the FBI, the Feds, all to get him out of the country, to this island, Puerto Rico. It had to be something very serious. Hell, criminal to elicit this much more criminal activity. But, why hadn't they just had him killed? Dumped him? Why not? That would have been a lot easier. It had to be because they wanted something, because they wanted something in the worst way. They wanted those tapes. They had to get those tapes!

He needed to reconstruct the circumstances of that surgery, to recall, as best he could, the entire surgical procedure, start to finish, skin to skin, and post-op, again to see if he was missing anything. He thought, *this might be an exercise in futility, but the more details I recall, the better prepared I will be when the day comes. And, for the first time, I hope and pray the day will come when I return.*

He remembered how Dr. Weller wanted him to stand in on the surgery because of the complications that could easily occur with total hip revisions, which often required having multiple instrument and implant systems available in the operating room, affording the surgeon every option possible. It was a hell of a lot to keep up with— sterile trays and cases of instruments everywhere, making the first and second scrub techs, the circulating RN, as well as the surgeon, more dependent on us, the purveyors, providers, and technicians, all in one. He used special laser pointers to point to the correct instrument or correct position without violating the plane of the sterile field. He helped the circulator select and open the correct double-wrapped-sterile prosthesis to be implanted in the patient. In the ideal case, we served best by anticipating the surgeon's next needed instrument in the procedure so that he could concentrate on his or her technical skills with the patient and not have to be interrupted by looking up on the mayo stand or the back tables. The first scrub always had the next instrument available and things went smoothly. In the worst case scenario, the surgeon lacked confidence, even sometimes competence, and depended too much on the orthopaedic representative— usually blaming others for his own shortcomings. Thankfully, that had not been the situation with this particular patient's surgery, because Dr. Weller was extremely capable. The one thing which James could not do was to come in contact with the patient in any way, since this negated the Errors and Omissions insurance.

The patient, a sixty-three year old male with osteoarthritis, had undergone a total hip replacement six years ago. A very active, non-smoking farmer in stable condition, he needed surgery because he was having increasing thigh pain because of bone wear, called lysis/secondary osteoporosis. The fiber-metal implant had simply worn out the bone due to his ceaseless physical labor as a farmer. The patient had been informed that this was not an unusual complication with a cementless implant, one that the bone grew into, especially with his high activity level. He had been pleased with the result up until about eighteen months ago when the bone loss and resultant pain began. He had postponed the surgery until after harvesting his summer and fall crops. That constant activity explained the rigidity of his bone stock, his strong bones, much stronger than average people his age. Anxious to be done with the surgery, he wanted to get on with his farming and his life. According to Dr. Weller, he had no intention of retiring. Hence, the surgeon wanted several options in implant systems available, both cemented and cementless, so his patient could achieve the optimum long-term result.

James had been called in by Dr. Weller because of his many years experience with difficult revision surgeries, his knowledge of the older implant systems, and his familiarity and friendship with the doctor, who had begun doing total joint surgeries back in the early seventies, when the FDA first approved them in the United States. He recalled looking at the X-rays with Dr. Weller, noting the anterior curve of the femur and his small, tight medullary canal. The scallops of bone loss were more prominent distally, meaning towards the end/tip of the prosthesis. Dr. Weller would make the implant selection intraoperatively, after he had removed the one in there now, cleaned out any wear debris, lavaged the bone and wound, inspected for any trace of the worst enemy, infection, and assessed the condition of his bone. The extent of the damage and the integrity of the bone would be the final determining factors in what he would use. Preoperatively, he was leaning toward implanting a longer-stemmed, porous, cementless prosthesis.

In other words, Dr. Weller would not know exactly what he needed until he was well into the surgery, at which time he needed multiple choices.

It had taken a concerted team effort by James and all the office personnel to order in, unpack, put together, arrange, and assemble all of the instrument sets. There was a total of twenty-three sterilizing cases! All of the implants had to be separated by sets, listed, and their individual lot numbers bar coded correctly on the packing slip, which served as the permanent implant record for their office inventory, their office records, the patient's file, and, most importantly, the lot number tracking by implant required by the Food and Drug Administration. This, along with James' office's Medical Device Report (MDR) file, were federal requirements by law. Orthopaedic Distributors had to keep these two files up to date and ready for field inspection by the FDA at all times. One simply did not want to mess around with the FDA. It took two people, two vehicles, and two trips to deliver all of these sets to the HealthCare USA hospital.

James went to the hospital the afternoon before the morning of the surgery to set up, inservice the operating room personnel, then separate the twenty-three cases into specific sets, and label them for Central Supply to sterilize for the surgery. Keeping all of these segregated by sets/systems, a tremendous task, was critical to the success of the surgery. The ever present frustration factor did not need to be exacerbated by having to look for the correct instrument misplaced in the wrong autoclave case. Also ever present but rarely verbalized was the fear factor— fear that some instrument, some implant might be missing, or in the wrong place. For that very reason, James and all of his excellent staff conducted a routine, safety-check protocol for all surgeries— check, recheck, then recheck by a different person. The sales associates were required to fill out a "Preoperative Work Sheet Form" for the office before any surgery packing slip was generated and the instruments/implants pulled for that particular case. On the more difficult revision surgeries, like this one, they went through a "what if?" drill— what if he needs this, what if that happens, what if this implant gets dropped, what if, what if? They conducted time-consuming but productive contingency planning to avoid a crisis. In spite of all of these thorough measures, there was still room for human error.

One of the unforeseen problems, beyond the control of James Cantrill & Associates, Inc., were the unfortunate casualties of managed care reform. Layoffs and staff cutbacks at all health facilities had increased with reckless abandon, especially so within the HealthCare USA group. A national cost reduction initiative, under the guise of "Quality/Productivity Enhancement," was underway in this chain and the "pink slips" were so prevalent that they almost became wall-coverings. The morale was horrendous and it impacted patient care.

The surgery had been scheduled at 7:30 A.M. that morning, so James had gotten there at 6:30 A.M., with three dozen donuts. It always helped when they brought donuts. They changed into scrubs and went back to recheck the implant carts. It took four surgical carts to hold all the implants. They arranged them by priority leaving the least likely to be used out in the hall directly outside OR #4, the OR suite with laminar flow, which purified the ambient air. There never seemed to be enough space in the OR room for all the equipment, much less all of the sterile implants. James had coordinated their plan over and over again. James would focus on Dr. Weller and the technical part of the surgical procedure itself while Dr. Weller would coordinate the instruments with the second scrub tech, and the implants with the circulating nurse. In other words, James would try to be the scout in the trenches while Dr. Weller would be the artillery officer. If their plan worked like they hoped, they could anticipate Dr. Weller's steps in the procedure and have his next need available, as well as a back-up option. James and Dr. Weller worked beautifully together as a team, with each complimenting the other's strengths while compensating for the other's weaknesses.

The surgery was slightly delayed when the nurse anesthetist could not get the patient intubated. The anesthesiologist had to be called in to assist, so that the operation could proceed.

Dr. Weller made the incision and began the procedure. James and Dr. Weller already had the scrub tech pull the slap/hammer extractor for the removal of the problem femoral prosthesis. It was on the back table ready to be passed to Dr. Weller when he asked for it.

The old prosthesis was removed without too much resistance, even though there was significant bony ingrowth on the anterior/proximal surface. Dr. Weller aspirated the medullary canal with a tapered suction tip and asked for the PulsaVac to lavage the canal, bone, and wound. He had the circulating nurse call X-ray. After cleaning and suctioning the medullary canal out thoroughly, he asked for a 12mm medullary reamer, then the 12mm femoral broach. The size of the porous prosthesis he just took out was a 12mm diameter, 140mm in length. This was commonly referred to as a "12." He reamed with the 12mm reamer, then asked for the 12.5mm reamer. He reamed with the 12.5 and incurred bony resistance distally or deeper into the femur. He then took the 12mm rasp, drove it easily into the femur with a 2 lb. mallet, and asked for an intraoperative A-P X-ray. The X-ray tech slid the cassette under the table, and positioned her C-arm unit over the patient, after Dr. Weller had draped the wound with sterile towels. With the exception of the nurse anesthetist at the head of the table, they all left the OR room and stood in the autoclave press to shield themselves from unnecessary radiation. A few minutes later after the X-ray was taken, they returned and Dr. Weller continued working. After removing the 12mm broach, he asked for the 13mm medullary reamer, reamed, then again with the 13.5mm, which incurred a great deal more resistance, meaning he had run into harder bone distally. Dr. Weller muttered, mostly to himself, "I hope I'm in this good a shape when I'm sixty-three— Ezra Jenkins' bone is like oak and his muscles like rope." He then asked for the 13mm broach and drove it partially in, then out with the 2 lb. mallet, in, then out, in, then out again until he had almost seated the collar on the femur. By then the X-ray tech had brought the X-ray back, put it up on the viewer on the wall. Dr. Weller and James were looking at it when Dr. Weller walked over with his bloody gloves held in the air away from his scrub gown.

Dr. Weller said, "The lysis was not as extensive as I had thought. He's still got a lot of good bone. Notice his medial cortex, even distally. Most of the lysis was lateral. I think I want to press-fit a larger, longer stem, under ream a half millimeter, and lock it distally. Doesn't that PDL, what's it called, James, Positive Distal Lock? Doesn't it have cutting flutes distally?"

"Yes, sir, it does, and you were correct about the name," James replied.

"How long is the 14mm?" he asked, still studying the X-ray.

"It's 190mm long, isn't it, Dr. Weller?" James answered, just confirming it with Dr. Weller.

James went over to the implant cart, checked out the label on the sterile 14mm PDL femoral component, just to make sure, and responded, "Yes, it's 190mm in length."

"I believe part of the problem with his thigh pain was due to the shorter prosthesis, with some toggle effect, see that wear on the lateral cortex? This guy works like a trojan, still loads 100-lb bales of hay, in spite of what I've told him. He's really a worker, he'll probably outlive you and me put together, maybe not Dr. Weller. If I can get a good distal press fit, with some ingrowth proximally, that should last him. Don't you think, James?" Dr. Weller was considering his approach out loud, in addition to counseling with his long term provider and friend.

James immediately placed a 14mm x 190mm template over the X-ray for Dr. Weller to see. "Yes, I think the key is the fixation distally, Dr. Weller, and that template really looks good, don't you think?" he always called surgeons "Dr." in the hospital setting, even though he and Bob Weller had been on a first name basis as friends for years.

"Yep, James, that's what we'll do. Plus, we've always got cement to fall back on, if needed in later years."

Little did either one of them know, that it would be sooner than later.

Dr. Weller went back to the table and asked for the 13.5mm medullary reamer again, after removing the 13mm broach. He reamed again, up and down, in and out, with the 13.5mm reamer carefully hugging the lateral cortex of the femur. It went smoothly. He took the 14mm reamer, measured it against the 14mm broach, and made a shallow ream. He then asked for and got the 14mm broach attached to the handle, which he began to pound with the mallet, in, back out, in, back out, in and out, in and out, being careful not to overstress the bone or split the femur. This farmer's bone was really hard, toughened by years of strenuous labor. After several in/out motions with both hands on the broach handle, Dr. Weller seated the 14mm PDL femoral broach inside the femur and detached the handle. In simpler terms, he used the broach as a trial for the real thing.

"OK, let's get another X-ray," he requested again, closing off the wound with sterile towels.

They all walked out into the autoclave room while the X-ray tech took another X-ray. This was usually the time for the latest 'quickie' jokes, but not today since Dr. Weller was all business.

He went back to the table and reinspected the plastic in the acetabular cup. The socket showed very little wear, unlike the femoral component. Usually, it was just the opposite in a real active patient. He decided not to change the polyethylene liner in the acetabular component.

The X-ray tech returned and put the X-ray of the 14mm rasp up on the viewer. She mentioned that it had a little over-exposure at the top, did the doctor want her to take another one?

"No, I can see what I need to see just fine. Thank you. It looks great. That's what we will use. Go ahead and open the 14mm."Dr. Weller replied kindly. He was, as a rule, considerate of the hospital staff and they enjoyed working with him.

James had already pulled the 14mm PDL Femoral Prosthesis off the cart and given it to the circulating nurse for her to confirm with the surgeon and first scrub. They always made it their policy to take this extra thirty seconds to make sure the wrong implant did not get inadvertently opened. It saved a lot of finger pointing, in addition to unnecessary expense for repackaging and resterilization of opened, unused implants.

"14 PDL, correct?" the first scrub said, looking at the implant box that James was holding.

"14, correct," after Dr. Weller nodded his head as he was pounding back out the 14mm rasp.

James handed the box back to the circulator to open. This was another policy they established to prevent the possibility of their dropping an implant when it was passed off. The exception was in really tight situations where multiple implants were being opened at once, and the bone cement was about to set up. Once bone cement set up, it was like concrete.

The circulator opened the implant, passed it off to the scrub tech, and Dr. Weller and James made sure that the impactor was properly pulled and placed on the mayo stand for the surgeon to use.

Dr. Weller irrigated the wound with the bulb syringe again to make sure of his anatomic landmarks before carefully impacting the new prosthesis.

The scrub passed the prosthesis to the surgeon in a lap sponge for protection.

Dr. Weller took the impactor and began to dive the prosthesis into the patient's femur.

He pounded a few times, waited a second, pounded a few more times, waited a second, pounded as the femoral implant went deeper and deeper into the bone. This was the nouveau accepted technique, particularly in revisions, with the thesis being that the second of not pounding the mallet gave the bone an interval to un-stress itself.

He continued very patiently, more than most, for what seemed like an unusually long time. It was taking a longer time due to the extra-long length of the prosthesis. The femoral component was getting close to "home," with the collar seated on the femur. It only lacked about 3-4 cm... almost there.

A couple of more pounds and...

"Oh, shit! Holy shit!" Dr. Weller shouted. "I don't believe this! Aw, shit!" he yelled again.

James didn't have to ask. He knew.

His and the circulating nurse's eyes met and locked in a fearful, knowing stare, amplified by the narrow gap between their surgical masks and scrub caps and hoods.

Everyone in the OR room froze with eyes widened.

Time stood still.

Dr. Weller rarely, if ever, swore; but, never in the operating room.

James knew that the patient's femur had split.

The stress of the long metal stem being driven down the rigid, tight tunnel of bone had caused the femur to fracture.

Dr. Weller winced, his face contorted, which was visible through his space helmet, tilted his head back, and was staring up at the huge OR light.

The only sounds were the beeps on the anesthetist's monitors.

No one said anything...

It was not quite, but almost one of those unforgettable, unbearable *terminal moments*— when you wished you had chosen a different line of work. When you wished you had been hit by a coal truck that morning. When you wished that you were dead. When you wished that you could just melt and flow through the OR floor.

Finally, after what seemed like a silent eternity, James asked, "How bad is it?"

Dr. Weller groaned and replied, "I'm afraid to look."

He adjusted the light, ran his gloved finger down the bone to feel for the fracture.

"OK. Open up the cerclage wiring set and get me some of those Luque loops with the twister," he said, as he calmed down and went back to work. One of the reasons that people liked to work with Dr. Weller, both in OR and on the wards, was that he was such a no-nonsense, go-to-work type surgeon with superb technical skills. And, he was usually courteous and considerate, now more rare in the managed care environment.

He elongated the incision and exposure distally, so that he could see the femur and where the fracture originated.

"Maybe it's not as bad as I thought, non-displaced, spiral just about 2 to 3 cm distal to the prosthesis," Dr. Weller diagnosed, which was good news, if there could be any, under the circumstances. This brought about a modicum of relief among those present, except for James and Dr. Weller. They were both wondering what system, what total hip prosthesis, Dr. Weller wanted to use now and praying that they had it there in the operating room. For the two of them, these were simply known as *paranoid attacks*— "Oh, damn, did I remember to bring this? What about that? Is that system in there? Where could I get one fast if it isn't?

"Let me have the AO wire passer and twister, then the Luque's," Dr. Weller asked calmly.

After he had cerclaged the femur with three separate wirings, and was now working on the fourth, a Luque loop, he said, "We are going to have to use cement now, James. Do you have a long-stemmed, cemented femoral component?"

"Yes sir, we do," James replied with a great sigh of relief. Dr. Weller was smiling ear-to-ear under his mask. He was *so* relieved.

"How long?" Dr. Weller asked.

"200, 250, and 300mm," James answered without hesitation.

"Perfect," Dr. Weller quickly retorted. "We'll use the 250!"

Hence, it seemed as though what could have been a horrible situation with a detrimental outcome was about to be salvaged.

Only after securely placing a fifth cerclage wire around the femur did Dr. Weller begin to very carefully remove the 14mm PDL femoral prosthesis. Once it had been safely removed it was placed in the saline basin with all of the bloody, previously used instruments. James quietly asked the OR tech if he could retrieve it before it got scratched and pass it off to him, since it would have to be sent into corporate with an incident report. James had put on examination gloves to handle the component.

After the OR tech passed the 14mm femoral to James, he quickly examined it, first looking at the electro-etched numbers. All orthopaedic implants were required by law to have the size and lot number on them. James did not like what he saw. The "4" in the 14mm looked like it had been changed and the lot numbers were smeared, were completely illegible. James placed it in a peel pack to flash sterilize later for decontamination. Something was wrong here...

This did not deter or interrupt the location and coordination of the instrument trays needed for the use of a 250mm cemented long-stem, as Dr. Weller had specified. James had been orchestrating that transition as soon as "number 250" came out of the surgeon's mouth.

"Do you have a 250mm trial, James?" Dr. Weller asked.

"Yes sir, we do, but it does not have a collar like the implant," James replied.

"No problem. That's great. Give me the broach for the stem. I doubt that I have to ream any more than I already have, right James?" he asked.

"You are correct. You had reamed 13.5mm distally, 14mm proximally. The 250 stem has an elliptical diameter of 12mm at the tip, tapered up to 13 at the 125 mid-mark, which leaves you ample room for the cement mantle," James answered. The truth was he and Dr. Weller had busily looked those dimensions up a few minutes ago, he in the product brochure and Dr. Weller in the surgical technique.

"OK, let me have the broach, then the 250 trial and we'll get an X-ray. We need to check whether 250 takes us below the line of the spiral fragment," Dr. Weller was always good at cueing his helpers in on what he wanted to do, a refreshing team approach.

When they were all standing in the autoclave room waiting on the X-ray, it was a little more subdued than before.

"Now let me have the bone plug kit with inserter, then I'll need the PulsaVac, again."

Dr. Weller had inserted the bone plug to dam up the medullary canal for the bone cement and was running a long IM tip with the PulsaVac when the X-ray tech put the two films up on the viewer.

"Dr. Weller, I had to take two X-rays to get the full length of the femur. Is that OK?" she asked almost apologetically. "I'll be glad to take them over, or take more."

"No, thank you. You've done fine. I'll be sure to tell Dr. Roy Wallen what a good job you're doing," Dr. Weller answered reassuringly.

"Oh, thank YOU, Dr. Weller. We never get complimented in surgery, seldom in Radiology anymore, either, with all the stress from the cutbacks. Thank you *so* much," the little X-ray tech said, bubbling over.

Dr. Weller came over to the screen with the X-rays. James stood by his side. It looked unbelievably good to James' experienced eye. You could barely see the spiral fracture. The cerclage wires accomplished their purpose, placed ideally, and the 250mm trial was well below the distal fragment, adding more stability.

"I hate to say it, but, considering, that looks pretty good," Dr. Weller was also more than modest. "Mr. Jenkins isn't going to like it too well, though, because I'm going to have to limit his activity. We'll probably put him in a brace, just to be safe," he said under his breath.

Dr. Weller was too modest. The X-ray was fantastic. The true sign of a great surgeon was they made it look easy, especially in difficult circumstances. And Dr. Weller had demonstrated his superb skill once again.

"OK, open the 250mm femoral and we are going to need at least three packs of large bone cement. And I'll need the extra-long nozzle on the cement gun. You can start mixing the cement," the good doctor could have been a coach.

"Also, I'll probably need two of the tampons to prepare the canal."

"Already got them here for you, Dr. Weller," Jeff, the OR tech said.

"Boy, you're good!" Dr. Weller said, encouraging him, also.

James helped Michele, the circulating nurse, open the sterile packs of bone cement since there were so many things at once, then went to get the 250mm femoral for her to open. Each pack of bone cement contained two separate, sterile pouches— one with the powder, the polymer, and one with the liquid in a carpule, the monomer. These were mixed together in a bowl to make bone cement. James just put the stick-on labels in the pocket of his scrub jacket after passing the others on to the circulator for the patient's chart. He had obtained the label from the 14mm PDL femoral earlier.

Dr. Weller leaned toward Rita, the nurse anesthetist and inquired, "Are we doing all right? You know, we're getting ready to use a triple pack of cement?" he alerted the anesthetist.

"Yes, Dr. Weller. He's had some irregularities, a few PVCs, but should be fine," she replied.

"Where is Dr. Bennettan?" Dr. Weller asked.

"He's off today," she answered.

"You anesthesiologists really have the life," Dr. Weller jokingly commented.

"We wish. How we wish!" the anesthetist quickly replied. "No, it's the cutbacks. Dr. Bennettan wanted to work today, but administration wouldn't let him. All of us in the Anesthesia Department are now limited to three twelve-hour shifts per week, weekdays, thirty-six hours per week, max," Rita angrily protested.

"I'm sorry to hear that. Managed care is now telling *us where* to treat the patient, *how long* the patient can be hospitalized, *what medication* to prescribe, Don't get me started. It *is* a sad, unfortunate situation," Dr. Weller elaborated." How's the cement coming?"

"Almost ready, sir. I'm just getting ready to put it in the gun. It seems to be more 'runny' than usual" Jeff, the tech, answered.

Bone cement, polymethyl methacrylate, when mixed, created a chemical, exothermic reaction which often caused the blood pressure to drop in the patient. This was a well known procedure in orthopaedic surgery, clinically documented for thirty years, and should have been well established, routine protocol with anesthesiologists.

"Is the 250 femoral ready?" Dr. Weller double checked.

"Right here, Doctor. We're ready if you are," Jeff reassured, handing the surgeon the freshly loaded cement gun.

Dr. Weller removed the tampons from the dry bone and began injecting the cement into the medullary canal of the femur in a retrograde fashion.

"Boy, this cement *is* gooey today," Dr. Weller commented, as he continued to squeeze the trigger on the injector.

It was very similar to a caulking gun, with the cement actually being more of a grout compound, though it served to cement the metal to the bone. The one thing you did not want to occur, the very last thing desired during total joint surgery was to have the cement set up before the components were in place. If that horrible event occurred, you had better send word you would be late getting home tonight. Because the surgeon was going to have to start all over again with the surgery, AFTER he had removed all of the bone cement, which was a bear to do. It was like taking up all of the concrete from a sidewalk without a jack-hammer, without destroying the sidewalk. Removing bone cement from bone was an extremely difficult, precarious procedure, one hell of a hard job—because he had to preserve the bone while removing locked-in concrete.

Dr. Weller withdrew the cement nozzle from the top of the femur after injecting it full with cement, introduced the long, 250mm femoral prosthesis, pushed it down the femur partially by hand, then took the impactor and began gently driving it home with the 2-lb.mallet.

"Nine minutes," Jeff called out, letting Dr. Weller know how long it had been since mixing the bone cement. He was kneading a little ball of the cement with his fingers, which served as a kind of field test to let the doctor know when it had set up. It usually took anywhere from twelve to seventeen minutes for it to harden, depending upon the room temperature. The room was a cool 68 degrees, perfect. This might take an another minute or two since it was a large batch.

"This cement ain't as doughy as usual. Ten minutes," Jeff said, watching the second hand on the wall clock.

Dr. Weller seated the collar of the femoral component on the femur, and took the little spatulas that Jeff had handed to him to clean up the globs of extra cement which had oozed out of the femur when the prosthesis was inserted. It was like caulking your bathtub, but the clean-up had to be immediate and very thorough. The cement had run all over the place.

"It sure is gooey, less viscous than normal. Are you sure this isn't that Low Viscosity Cement?" the surgeon questioned.

"Naw, Doc, it's the conventional kind. The regular, right Michele,?" Jeff checked with the circulating nurse to confirm it.

Dr. Weller was just cleaning out the last few pieces, when Jeff announced that it had been seventeen and a half minutes and had not gotten hot yet. The exothermic part, when the cement gets very hot, just precedes setting up, when it hardens.

"Now, if we can have our efficient X-ray tech get us another picture..." Dr. Weller was saying, and the circulator headed to the wall phone to call her.

"How long now, Jeff?"

"Twenty-one minutes and it's just starting to heat up," Jeff replied, shaking his head.

Dr. Weller asked for the standard, 28mm neck trial so that he could do a trial reduction of the hip and check the patient's leg length. He certainly did not want there to be any disparity in this farmer's leg length.

Suddenly, the high-pitched alarm of the monitor sounded. It shook the room like a siren. The nurse anesthetist was pulling out the drawers of her portable drug cart all at once and shooting into the IV line with a large syringe.

She yelled, "CODE! CODE!" She couldn't get the words out of her mouth fast enough.

"CODE! CODE 500!" The patient had gone into cardiac arrest.

The circulating nurse hit the intercom and shouted, "We've got a CODE in Room 4! REPEAT! CODE 500! ROOM 4! GET DR. RASHANI, STAT!"

Michele immediately went to the crash cart to assist the nurse anesthetist, who was ripping drawers out and grabbing for vials as some were hitting the floor and rolling across the room.

James' and Michele's eyes locked in shock again, but this time under an avalanche of fear. How could they help? What could they do? They both bent over simultaneously to retrieve vials as they rolled on the floor.

This was profoundly different than the last frightful synapse in OR #4, for this time...*death hath shown its ugly head.*

A female pushing a crash cart came running in through the main door. Her feet flew out from under her as she fell on the vials rolling on the floor. She screamed, hitting the floor hard, and shoving the cart as she fell. It careened off the wall.

James was on the opposite side of the room separated by the OR table, so he could not help the woman, who was writhing and moaning in pain.

The circulator slammed her fist against the intercom again, yelling, "CODE! CODE! ROOM 4! WHERE IN THE HELL IS DR. RASHANI?!!"

Two more nurses in scrubs came wildly running into the room. One of them went airborne as her feet encountered the little bottles rolling all over the place. She screamed, landing on the woman already on the floor, who let out another loud moan.

Dr. Weller had been packing sterile towels, attempting to close off and protect the wound, his first priority as the surgeon in charge. Regular operating rooms, routine OR protocol had trained all personnel to respond to codes, and normally would have had several anesthesiologists here, in addition to other professionals trained over and over again in emergency response alerts.

The frantic nurse anesthetist had knocked off her scrub bonnet, her surgical mask was down under her chin, she had two needle caps held between her tight lips, her left hand held a vial upside down with a syringe in it while she was injecting the IV line with her right hand. The circulator was aspirating another vial into a syringe, while she hit the intercom button with her left elbow and let fly a blood-curtling scream: **"CODE! CODE DAMNIT! ROOM 4! CAN'T YOU HEAR ME! CODE! WHERE the *SHIT* IS DR. RASHANI?"**

She was as shocked as she was angered by the lack of acknowledgment as with the lack of response.

Dr. Weller had broken scrub, ripping off his gown, yanking the hose out of his space suit, and headed around the foot of the table to assist. The anesthesia machines blocked his shortest route to the head of the table.

Two more bodies had piled into the room, now more aptly described as a pandemonium crypt— the tragic result of layoffs and staff cutbacks glaringly evident.

"I've got a pulse! I'm getting a pulse!" the nurse anesthetist exclaimed, still exasperated, but excited. You could hear the beep, beep, beep starting on the monitor, weak but real. She injected another 20cc of lidocaine with epinephrine. His heartbeat got stronger, a regular rhythm was slowly returning.

Dr. Weller told the circulator to punch the intercom.

"This is Dr. Weller. The patient now has a pulse, but is not yet stable. You get an anesthesiologist to this room STAT. If there is not one in the hospital, get a cardiologist in here, STAT. Is that understood? I had to break scrub and now, I've got to rescrub to finish this case. After this code, I expect a specialist, an MD, in here NOW! And call Administration, tell that CEO, Jervis, to expect me immediately after this surgery. Is that clear?" With that, he walked out of the room to the scrub sink in the hall.

Dr. Weller had confidentially voiced his concern to James about patient care because of all these hospital staff cut-backs. James had known Bob Weller for over twenty-five years and he had never seen him so angry. Regarding this incident, it was more than justified. This was inexcusable. It was a cardinal sin for a major hospital to allow all the operating rooms, the entire surgical theater, to be without an anesthesiologist, to have multiple surgeries going on without a single anesthesiologist in the department. That was an overt invitation for risk in life-threatening situations.

Dr. Weller came back into the room, asked how the patient was doing, nodded to the new arrival with the anesthetist, re-gowned, and proceeded with the final steps of the procedure before closing. A physician, specialty unknown, was currently assisting Rita, the poor nurse anesthetist. It was not Dr. Rashani, the anesthesiologist.

"Okay, first I want the standard neck provisional for the trial reduction, a medium Snyder Hemovac, plenty of antibiotic irrigation, my regular staple and suture, then we will quickly close, and get this nice patient out of here. Michele, would you please call out to the desk and have them send in a PA to help me suture," the angered surgeon said, still extremely professional about the task at hand.

The trial reduction was satisfactory and he asked for the standard neck 28mm to be opened. James dispensed with the careful protocol in opening implants on this one. The 28mm femoral head was impacted on to the cemented prosthesis, the hip reduced into the socket, the Hemovac drains placed in the wound, which was thoroughly irrigated with antibiotic solution, and then closed with 2-0 chromic suture and Ethicon staples.

Dr. Weller, who usually thanked the OR staff for their help at the end of a case, said nothing. He was patently focused on getting his patient out of OR room #4 and to the recovery room— alive. When he tore off his gown and yanked off the space helmet, it became apparent how extremely angry Dr. Robert W. Weller was. His face was red, his eyes blazing, his pupils like pin points, his corneas like fire, in color and emission. Just the slightest glance at him put the literal fear of God in you! James had never seen him this way. Given Dr. Weller's huge stature, it was downright scary. After the patient was transferred to the gurney, and wheeled out of the room, Dr. Weller stopped, leaned over the frazzled nurse anesthetist, and said something to her privately. James wanted to say something, anything to his dear friend of over twenty-five years, but was afraid to do so. James, Dr. Weller and all of the worn-out bodies left standing in OR #4 took refuge in unanimous agreement that they were nowhere close to administration. A bomb was about to be detonated there, and for genuine, justifiable cause. James could not imagine what the good Dr. Weller was going to tell Mr. Jenkins' family.

The patient, one Ezra N. Jenkins, face leathered from the hard work in the sun, had only reluctantly consented to have this surgery. It interrupted his farming and his life. Unknown to him, he had a precariously close call, a brief walk through James' dreaded Chamber of Darkness. Did the fact that Mr. Jenkins has no conscious memory of this nearly fatal event make it any less of a morbid reality? His life was delicately held in the balance by one little, very capable nurse anesthetist, and, thank God, she was able to slightly tilt the scale toward the realm of the living. But, how long had the cardiac arrest lasted? Was there going to be any permanent impairment to his heart? Was he brain damaged?

James said nothing to anyone while changing his clothes in the doctors' lounge. He just wanted to leave. James pulled the stick-on labels out of the pocket. He looked again at the one for the first prosthesis, the one that fractured the femur, shaking his head. It had definitely been tampered with, the "4" altered in the 14mm, as well as the smeared lot number. He looked at the labels for the bone cement.

"Oh, shit! This couldn't be! Aw, shit," he muttered trying to conceal his reaction. He frantically laid all six of the labels on the bench, attempting to match them up. They did *not* match! Damn. He couldn't believe his eyes. There should have been three pairs of matching lot numbers, one lot number for each batch of bone cement— the liquid, the monomer, with a lot number, and the powder, the polymer, with the same, matching lot number. There ought to be a total of three different lot numbers. Instead, James had six different lot numbers! The damn batches of bone cement were screwed up, big time. James shuddered again at yet another revolting discovery. This is something that would go undetected 99 out of 100 times, because when the circulating nurse opens the bone cement to pass it on to the scrub tech to mix, lot numbers are not checked. It is not part of the surgical protocol, which presumes that the product from the manufacturer is entirely efficacious. The complete focus in the operating room is on the process, not the product. Usually when "cement-mixing time" arrives, there is an unspoken physiologic change among the personnel in the operating room. The tension is palpable—the anesthesiologist prepares for the patient's drop in blood pressure when the cement is injected; the surgeon consciously quickens his pace due to the risk of the cement setting up prematurely; the scrub tech mixing the cement reflects intense concentration on the timing — how soon the cement "wets out," next going into the doughy phase, next the injection phase, then the exothermic "hot" phase before it sets up or hardens. Everyone in that room is preoccupied with the progress and texture of the bone cement, except the patient who is asleep.

No wonder this damn cement was so "GOOEY," as Dr. Weller commented; "RUNNY," as Jeff, the tech said. Could this mis-matched, out-of-spec bone cement have caused the patient's heart to stop? A split femur and a cardiac arrest, both from suspicious causes— this *HAD* been a case from hell. Thoughts raced through James' head, all of them bad. He and Dr. Weller did not speak. They avoided looking at each other.

A surgeon in the next row of lockers was telling James a joke. But James did not hear what he was saying. He faked a laugh.

He couldn't wait to get back to his office and call Regulatory Affairs at corporate headquarters. This was going to necessitate two separate MDR reports, Medical Device Regulation incident reports. The one on that PDL Femoral Prosthesis with the altered "14mm" and smeared lot number would have certainly been enough. But, now the addition of another, possibly three more— with one for each batch of bone cement—with a patient, who may have been compromised, is too damn much.

James blasted into his office, laid out all of the questionable imlant labels on his desk, and dialed the corporate office and got Regulatory Affairs. He described the PDL Femoral Prosthesis, its altered "14mm" electro-etch and smeared lot number, the three batches of discreditable bone cement with mismatched lot numbers and packs of monomer and polymer in vivid detail. He then generally described the consequences to the patient, the fractured femur, the uncharacteristic, "gooey" properties of the bone cement, the cardiac arrest upon its injection, all of which inferred "out-of -spec" (out-of-specification) implanted devices with alleged improbity. Afterwards, he was asked if the patient was still alive and put on hold.

After being on hold, he was asked, "Where is the patient now?"

"Recovery, then CCU," he answered, and was placed on hold again.

James felt like he was being given the runaround. After being put on hold several more times, he asked if he should report this to the Legal Department, and was put on hold again.

"No, not necessarily," was the ambiguous answer. He had only dealt with Regulatory a few times in his long career, mainly with product recalls, and thought them rather strange and obtuse. They were essentially detail people who dealt with compliance issues, the government, regulations, packing slips, terminology, etc. They were not, for the most part, "people-people." This conversation was certainly not inspiring James' confidence or alleviating his increasing discomfort, fear, and trepidation. As a matter of fact, red flags, alarms, and sirens were all sounding concomitantly in his brain.

Finally, after being put on hold one last time, he tersely informed them that he would be filling out the required MDR forms and promptly sending them in by FedEx overnight letter.

Thank God he had remembered to record that conversation. He ejected the cassette tape, placed it in its little plastic case, and labeled it precisely. There was imputable evidence of product liability, here, and James was determined to mitigate his and his office staff's culpability by discharging his legal responsibilities and professional ethics with impunity.

James then called his attorney, Lynwood W. Ingle, Jr. at Stahl, Kendrick, & Hart and related the frightening details of the surgery in its entirety, including his disinspiring call to the Regulatory Affairs Department at headquarters. Lynnwood, in his usual polished manner, recommended that James continue with what he was doing, to comply, as always, with all FDA requirements, fill out all the MDR reports in scrupulous detail, make multiple copies, photocopy all of the stick-on implant labels, get a Polaroid of the 14mm prosthesis, send all of them in by Federal Express for certifiable receipt and tracking, with copies to the Legal Department at Werner, Inc. Report it to your Errors & Omissions Insurance carrier, and make sure that he, Lynwood, had copies of everything. And, he did not have to tell James, keep a copy away from the office. In other words, CYA, CYA, CYA all over the place.

James almost hated to tell Dana, his office manager, because she was so caring and conscientious that she would worry, even though she had done everything possible to coordinate all that was needed for this surgery. And, thank goodness, she *was* meticulous.

All of the responsibilities of James Cantrill & Associates were discharged with impeccable attention to every detail.

James' follow-up phone calls to corporate regarding this surgery were met with forgetfulness, which had to be feigned, dispassion, and detachment. He recorded every single phone call and documented the tapes with time of day, date, person, department, and Re: . There were no calls back to their office regarding any of the circumstances with this surgery. It was as if it never happened.

The recovery room nurse inspected the IV's in Mr. Jenkins muscular arms and noticed his tanned, calloused hands, strong hands gifted with hard work. She very carefully separated the leads to the monitors and the IVs from the taut traction cord connecting the pulleys, slings, and weights. Dr. Weller and the orthopaedic tech had placed him in balanced suspension traction to prevent dislocating his hip and protect the fractured femur while allowing him some movement in the bed. He was beginning to regain consciousness. The ECG just taken in recovery showed that he had had an MI, a myocardial infarction. This was relatively good news since it primarily involved the heart muscle, compared to other diagnoses which could have been much more serious. Mr. Jenkins was progressing routinely and would be transferred to CCU, the Coronary Care Unit, in a short while, where he would continue to be monitored closely.

Ezra N. Jenkins was taken to the Coronary Care Unit an hour later. He was told that his family out in the waiting room had been notified that he was awake, okay, and would be allowed to visit him briefly in CCU after a few more tests. Now that he was regaining his good senses, especially his rock-solid common sense, just what in the hell was going on here? What in the hell is CCU? Why was he here? He didn't remember being here the last time. How long was he going to have to stay in this damn hospital? He didn't like hospitals at all. Dr. Weller had told him maybe four to five days. He wanted to get out of here and get back to his farm. He had cattle to feed and alfalfa to bale.

Just before his family was allowed to come in to visit him in CCU, they told him the bad news. He had a heart attack on the operating room table. But, he was doing fine, now, and would be all right. Then, they told him even worse news-- that he was going to have to take it easy for a while. No, not him, not Ezra Jenkins, healthier than a horse, tougher than a corn cob. Plus, he had work to do.

He was still reeling from these developments when Naomi, his wife, their son and two daughters came in. Why all the long faces? His wife and daughters had been crying. Naomi, who was a good woman, a hard worker like he was, still had tears in her blood-shot eyes. His son was an environmental lawyer, but liked helping with the farm on weekends when he could. Both daughters still loved working with their dad and were good farmers themselves. That is the way they had all been reared and they were all very proud of it.

They were standing bedside, touching his long, sinewy arms when they gave him the worst news, yet. In addition to the heart attack, his femur had fractured during the surgery, but, Dr. Weller said that it was going to be all right. He was just going to have to take it easy for a short time. Dr. Weller understands how upset you might be, and for us to tell you that he will talk to you in the morning about it. He said for you not to worry, that you are still going to be able to farm.

And that's when Naomi lost control and started bawling, "Praise the Lord! Ezra... oh, praise the Lord." She was being consoled by her children.

The nurse came up and told them they would have to leave. They all bade him a tearful goodbye and slowly walked out, with his son and both daughters holding their sobbing mother.

His wife was a strong woman. This spontaneous display of emotion was unusual for her. What do they mean, fractured his femur, broken his leg bone? He had good brawny bones. Dr. Weller had told him sometimes these things happen, but not to him. And a heart attack, to boot! Two bad things, terrible things, and he didn't know a thing about either one? There was something going on, here. Something was not right. He, Ezra, could always tell. His horse sense always played true. Whenever he got this squeamish feeling in his gut, like a mule baying, it meant there was something wrong. It never failed him, never. And there was definitely something very wrong here. Look at him, all strung up, tubes coming out of his body everywhere. He was a mess. He didn't do this to himself. Dr. Weller sure as hell didn't do this to him. He was a good man, an honest man just like Ezra, a man of his word, and a damn fine surgeon. What is this? Him take it easy? Hell! No way! This is all a bunch of horse-shit! And he was going to get to the bottom of it, too! Just wait 'til in the morning, he'd talk to Dr. Weller.

The nurse came back, checked some things, and gave him some more shaved ice. She told him that he might be able to have some juice in a little bit, was he comfortable, did all the noises scare him, the sounds, the beeps in CCU could be unsettling to some, told him that he was doing fine, not to get anxious, try to rest, just call her for anything. Her name was Kathy if he had any questions. She was trying to alleviate his anxiety about his condition and the CCU environment. She was nice, she was, and compassionate and all that, but she could save her energy for the real sick people. There were a bunch of 'em in this place. Anyway, he was NOT going to be here that long.

They were short-staffed in the Coronary Care Unit, just like in every other department. There were ten beds in CCU and Mr. Jenkins was the tenth patient, so the unit was full. The recommended patient care protocol in coronary critical care called for a ratio of one registered nurse to every two patients. Currently on this shift, there were only 2 RNs on duty with 1 LPN. They were stretched dangerously thin. And only one of the RNs was a CCRN (Critical Care Registered Nurse) and ACLS (Acute Care Life Support certified), trained to handle any grave, life-threatening emergency that might arise in CCU, or anywhere, for that matter. Of the two remaining, one was a regular staff RN and the other RN was from "pool," with limited experience in cardiac care. The one LPN was a "night house circulating assistant," sent to the floor or department with the greatest staffing need. She unfortunately had no experience with critical care. Therefore, saying they were stretched thin applied only to the nurses comprising the ratio, not the qualifications, experience, or competence of each. The superb training, dedication, and competence of the one CCRN/ACLS nurse, who happened to be the one caring for Mr. Jenkins, did not compensate for the lack of training, experience, and competence of the others working this shift. The stage was unintentionally set for serious, medical risk.

And, it was not going to take long.

Ezra Jenkins, meanwhile, had asked for something to drink. His nurse had brought him some crushed ice with a little water. He was admonished by his nurse to sip it slowly lest he become nauseated.

She checked his cardiac monitor, made a few notations on his chart, said he was doing better, to continue to rest. She would be back to check on him shortly.

The ER had just called with the kind of news that CCU did not want to hear. They had another patient with an MI that they would be sending up after admission, and EMS had alerted the ER that they were en route with a patient who had recurrent, acute angina. The natives were getting more restless and there was no room. That meant two more patients to a CCU that was already maxed out, from 1 RN:3 1/3 patients to 1:4. This was almost a red zone. CCU's overflow was supposed to be channeled into ICU.

And, to make matters even worse, Surgery had also called. They had sent their redo-CABG (called a "cabbage," a coronary artery bypass graft, that had to be revised) to recovery, and she would have to be sent to CCU, because ICU was already over-capacity. That meant thirteen patients, a minimum of seven of whom were seriously ill, extremely high-risk, and they, CCU, only had 3 Rns, only one of whom was unquestionably trained and capable to handle high-risk patients. Something had to give. The night supervisor was going to have to make some tough decisions while distressingly calling for people to come in, reinforcements, any kind of skilled help.

The question was, "Who was working the house? Who was the night supervisor tonight?"

Ezra pushed his call button, and his nurse quickly responded.

"And what can I do for you, Mr. Jenkins?" she asked.

"I hate to bother you, but could I get another drink."

"Why certainly," she answered, in her sweet voice, checking his fluid output, monitor, and vitals in one fell swoop.

She brought it back to him in a jiff and told him again how well he was progressing, but to continue to take it easy, and be sure to only sip the crushed ice.

And then things started getting worse.

The redo-CABG was brought in from recovery, had to be put in the ante-hall instead of a regular cubicle, because the ten were occupied, full. The meticulous, but volatile CT surgeon walked in almost smiling, but that didn't last long. What in the hell do they mean sticking HIS patient out here?

"What in the hell kind of care is that?" Dr. Singh yelled in his East Indian accent.

They tried to explain that it was due to circumstances beyond their control. They were under-staffed and over-capacity. They needed more help, desperately. Even though Kathy, the CCRN, had a reassuring manner, it was inadequate for the irate surgeon. He informed them that he had been up all night the night before and he'd "be damned if he was going to stay up all night again just to make sure that HIS patients got the care they needed! He had three patients already in ICU, and this situation in CCU was intolerable! Call the night supervisor STAT!"

Oh, no. It was Mrs. Roth working house tonight. Of all people, not Roth. She was obtrusive, offensive, antagonistic to employees, incompetent, and afraid of high-strung surgeons. What a synergistic combination of core competencies for problem solving in life-threatening situations!

Yes, the stage was set this night in CCU in this HealthCareUSA hospital for disaster.

Mrs. Roth came in, in her usual kick-ass, take-names, ask-later manner. She did not see the surgeon right away. She began her argumentative drill immediately, demanding to know why she was paged STAT, at this early hour in the night, when she was in the cafeteria eating. Couldn't they handle things themselves? Just what exactly was the nature of the emergency that made her come up here STAT? That did it!

Dr. Singh stood up from behind the nurses' counter and shouted, "I am the reason for your being paged STAT! My patients are not going to be treated like this." This was unacceptable, intolerable, he was going to administration tomorrow, and if there was not a radical change in capable patient care in this institution, he would call the ambulance service and personally supervise transporting HIS patients to another hospital. This was not the only hospital in town.

As for right now, he demanded a CCRN nurse for HIS patient, one on one care, for she was a prominent lady, extremely ill, and needed attentive, skilled care, and nothing less, PERIOD!

"Is that clear?" he demanded in his uncompromising tone.

"Yes sir, Doctor," Mrs. Roth complied. She did not know how it would be accomplished, but, somehow, it would be done.

"One day they are going to start running this like a real hospital," the doctor stated, his final *coup de grace*.

Ezra had heard the doctor's tirade. That just further motivated him to get out of here. For the other poor patients who even happened to be semi-conscious in CCU, this diatribe certainly would not have made them feel better. And for any who might have been on the mend, a dark cloud of doubt now lingered over their heads.

Roth picked up the phone, instructed someone to start calling to get two more RNs, minimum, three preferably, STAT. If she could get a CCRN, she'd authorize an on-call bonus. Don't stop until she had rounded up two! Understand?

She at last got to sit down.

Roth then instructed the one and only CCRN in CCU to take over Dr. Singh's patient, but first to bring her all the patients' charts. They were going to have to make room to accommodate this lady, at least get her a cubicle. Were there any patients that could be transferred to the surgical floor? Kathy could foresee what was coming.

"What about this patient? He's the most stable one in here. He belonged in ICU, anyway. That's where critical orthopaedic patients were supposed to go, especially those in traction. They weren't prepared to handle traction in CCU," Mrs. Roth quickly asserted.

"But, Mrs. Roth, this patient coded in OR this morning during surgery. He had an MI while undergoing a total hip revision," the CCRN replied.

"Who's his surgeon? Dr. Weller. Good, he's not one of the," she glanced up to make sure the surgeon was gone, "assholes. Can you believe that son-of-a-bitch? Screaming at me? Yelling where all these patients could hear?" Mrs. Roth was still reacting angrily.

"But, Mrs. Roth, Mr. Jenkins hasn't been in CCU twelve hours yet. He has only been stable for the last five hours," the conscientious CCRN protested.

"We will transfer him to the room closest to the Nurses' station on the surgical floor and give them the head's up. We've got to do something now, do you hear? Until I can get some help. I don't know what they expect me to do. All these damn layoffs and cutbacks. And those jerks in administration get their bonuses. Bull shit!" Mrs. Roth was ranting to herself as she flipped through the patients' charts.

The only capable CCRN on duty just sat there shaking her head. Mrs. Roth's decision to transfer Ezra Jenkins prematurely from CCU to the surgical floor had been governed by expedient reaction to surgeons' temperaments, not patient need.

The only two orderlies available came and moved Mr. Jenkins to room 346 on 3 east, the surgical floor. 346 was eight rooms down from the nurses' station, contrary to Mrs. Roth's expressed compromise. On duty tonight on 3 east were one RN, one LPN, and one ward clerk. Currently, there were thirty-two, now thirty-three patients, with two more in recovery, soon to come. To say that this surgical floor, 3 east, was understaffed like CCU would be stating it mildly. There was only one qualified nurse capable of responding to any patient emergency. And Ezra Jenkins was in the next to last room at the end of the hall.

At least #346 was a private room. Maybe he could get some rest now. He felt really sorry for all those poor sick people back there where he'd been. It'd be a miracle if all of them got well, with all those beeping noises and everything going on— the doctor raising all that hell. It didn't bother him that much, because he was feeling better, but to those sick people, waking 'em all up. Maybe the doctor was justified in running the hospital down, yelling at the nurses like that, but not in front of all those others! As if they weren't sick enough, then to have the hell scared out of 'em. He sure was thankful that Dr. Weller 'wadn't like that, a real gentleman he was. Yes, and they'd have a serious talk in the morning. There was definitely something wrong with this place. Bad wrong! It was more different than a chicken and a hog since his last hip operation. Over six years ago, and this joint had gone steady to hell. People weren't near as nice either, 'cept for that one nurse. All of 'em stressed out 'n mean as hell. If they could come out and work a day or two with him on his farm, he'd straighten 'em out. Show 'em what good there was in life. Why they had even changed the name, Health USA, or something like that. They oughta' be shot for using the name of our country like this. Yep, naming this shitty hospital after our great United States of America, why that's worse than treason! Bad as this place is.

And with that warm, patriotic metaphor, he decided he would get some rest, thought of his wonderful wife, Naomi, his family, his farm, thanked the Good Lord for them and all his blessings, and dozed off.

Suddenly, Ezra waked up and could not breathe. He grabbed his throat, gasping for air. He tried to open his eyes, but they felt like they were rolling back in his head. He tried to call for help. He could not. He tried to yell. He could not. He gasped desperately. Where's that damn button? She said just punch the call button if he needed anything. Where in the hell was it? It was supposed to be here in his bed somewhere. Oh... hell. He could hear himself gasping. He grabbed at his throat. He grew weaker by the second...where was that damn thing?...there on his pillow! He grasped it with his once mighty hand, hit the button, kept punching the button down. He wanted to crush the damn thing. Where in the hell were they anyway? His mouth was dry, his lips parched. Why couldn't he see? He couldn't see a damn thing. He was still gasping, gasping, groping at his throat. He could not breathe. He could not see. He could only hear his own moans — gasps, sick gasps, the gasps of a desperate, dying man. *Oh, no...oh, God...I...pray...oh, Jesus...please...no...*

Finally, the nurse came in. It was the LPN. She immediately saw— his face blue, cyanotic, unquestionably in respiratory arrest. She hit the intercom and yelled **CODE! CODE! ROOM 346! CODE!**

The LPN started CPR. The patient was unresponsive to her frantic efforts. When the crash cart finally arrived, they got out the paddles and shocked the patient, but it was all in vain.

It was too late. The patient in room #346 was staring in icy silence at the ceiling, eyes frozen open by the cold finality of death.

Something had caused Mr. Jenkins' heart to stop, a critical medical emergency which required immediate response. It could have been, should have been responded to sooner. His death might possibly have been prevented, if not postponed. Had he been hit with all the modern medicines and electric defibrillation from the crash cart sooner, his heart may have stood a remote third chance.

But the tragic sequence of events in the operating room— the fractured femur, necessitating extended time under anesthesia, prolonged surgery, the subsequent use of bone cement, which caused his blood pressure to drop, possibly led to a fat embolus, precipitating the massive MI, leaving him with cardiomyopathy, permanent damage to the heart muscle, all the morbid after-effects of multiple trauma, and more — had extracted their toll. One unfortunate event lead to another; episode after deadl1y episode cascaded precariously down the patient's life-support system, the death threat increasing at each juncture, finally sending him into cardiogenic shock, resulting in renal shut down, and major organ failure. Ezra Jenkins' pre-op ECG was normal and his general health was rated excellent. But the synergistic effect of the surgical events, each progressively more serious, presented a lethal barrier from which his heart could not recover.

Had the patient remained in CCU, as post-MI treatment protocol prescribes, his emergency would have had immediate response, maybe not preventing his death, but, at least giving him a fighting chance.

This patient had died needlessly.

For one Ezra Nehemiah Jenkins, there was no tomorrow. He was admitted to this HealthCare USA hospital as a healthy, hard-working, sixty-three-year-old man who loved his family deeply, served his church faithfully, and lived according to his rigid moral principles. He contributed to his country and society, cared for the land that he tilled, and worked tirelessly on his farm, the farm that he loved as much as life itself, the farm that he would never work again, the farm he would never ever see again.

For Ezra Nehemiah Jenkins had just expired.

Something went wrong on this day, something fatally wrong. That gut feeling that Ezra Nehemiah Jenkins had that never failed him did not fail him on this, his last day on earth. For it told him that something was wrong, even when he was unconscious from anesthesia, things had gone wrong. A questionable hip implant, a questionable batch of bone cement, some questionable chemical, possible contaminant in the cement, the cascading culmination of which had impaired Ezra Nehemiah Jenkin's body precipitating cardiogenic shock, causing his untimely, unnecessary, premature death

In this jungle camp in the central mountains of Puerto Rico, Margarita brought James a cup of coffee in a pewter tin cup and said she would change the poultice dressing on his leg after she had fixed breakfast for the others.

James was amazed at his total recall of the events surrounding that farmer's untimely death. What was it that caused his cardiogenic shock? Why were the electro-etched size number and lot numbers changed and smeared on that implant that day? That femoral component had to be mis-sized— defective. It caused the femur to split. How did it make it through QC? Could that out-of-spec, "gooey" bone cement have magnified his drop in blood pressure, causing a fat embolus that precipitated his massive heart attack? Could the mismatched packs of bone cement have contained contaminants? *Damn.* The fall-out from defective bone cement could be greater than defective femoral components, since it is used on total knees also. With well over one million total joint replacements done each year, and bone cement used on approximately sixty-five percent of them, the consequences could be huge. No wonder these questions were never answered by Legal or Regulatory Affairs. A recall, that dreaded "R word," would have ravaged Werner's profitability, not to even mention its reputation and industry standing. *Oh, shit.* This was probably the very reason that they, whoever they were, had to get James Cantrill out of the country. And contain that evidence.

He had a lot of things to do— questions to answer, criminal activities to investigate, he needed to find out more about Werner's plant down here in Caguas, Puerto Rico. Yes, some total hips were manufactured there now! *Damn.*

But, first, he had to heal so that he could walk again, and the pain was now growing by the minute.

His mother and daddy used to say: you've got to crawl before you can walk. James had done enough crawling to last him the rest of his life. But, it was crawling that saved his life. His saviors in this camp had found him bleeding, clawing, and crawling through the jungle.

CHAPTER 28

...there is something about him,
which even treachery cannot trust.
Junius, 1771

"So, what are you telling us, Brice?" Walter Kagan, the President/Chief Operating Office at Brecken-Mersack Strauss, Inc., asked. He and his Chief Counsel, Arlen Loeb, had been summoned to this clandestine meeting in Newark, New Jersey, by the impertinent corporate counsel from their orthopaedic subsidiary, Werner, Inc. The pretense for this secret rendezvous was *his* alleged, sudden discovery of incriminating inside information regarding the unannounced visits from the Inspector General from the FDA. Official visits from the FDA to inspect for GMP, Good Manufacturing Practices, were a dreaded but expected routine; but unannounced, impromptu visits, especially from the IG's office, were absolutely the last thing that a medical manufacturer ever wants to incur. It would send shock waves throughout the bowels of any corporation. The FDA could initiate a regulatory inspection, force a product recall, publish it on the "Gray Sheet," and actually shut down a product line or a complete manufacturing facility.

"I'm telling you that the RMSs, the WESs and the OCPs on that batch, that huge shipment of material alloy, were altered. Furthermore, two of the QA inspection and QC rejection reports on femorals from Caguas, the femoral stems manufactured at our plant in Puerto Rico, were falsified."

"Hold it right there, Billups! Neither Arlen nor I speak in your Warsaw acronyms. Please use plain, simple English, so that we may fully understand," the President/COO interrupted.

"The RMSs, the Raw Material Analysis Specifications, WESs, the Werner Engineering Specifications, and the OCPs, the Operational Control Procedures, were all altered due to variances which were unacceptable. Had that huge raw materials shipment been rejected, as it should have been, it would have thrown production scheduling months behind and caused insufferable backorders on the entire total hip product line. It was just called 'a vendor problem,' records were altered, then swept under the carpet. Due to the material being out of spec, the WESs and OCPs *had* to be modified to accommodate the compromised RMSs. Then, out of this bad batch of raw, a major bulk gets sent to Puerto Rico, where QC is not the greatest to begin with. The production order was marked *Expedite,* further exacerbating a situation with already compromised tolerances, and the finished femorals come back way the hell below any acceptable parameters. I mean these damn prostheses..."

"Damnit, Billups! Slow down! Let's take this one step at a time. These are severe charges with grave consequences," Kagan stated, waving his right hand. "Arlen and I need to grasp each specific detail. First, Werner receives from their supplier a large shipment of raw material from which total hip femoral stems are to be manufactured. Correct? After random testing, normal routine, they find that this shipment does not meet their minimum specifications for this particular alloy of raw materials, their RMSs, as you called them. Okay, Arlen and I understand that much."

Arlen was nodding his head in agreement.

"Now, start from that point. And speak slowly and succinctly, Billups, like they taught you in law school," Kagan said.

Both Kagan and Arlen knew how sharp Billups was in court. They had debated about thanking him for his handling of two liability cases, getting favorable decisions for Werner and Brecken, which saved millions in litigation expense and punitive damages. But, they decided against it because of Brice's penchant for arrogance.

However, Walter Kagan felt that lawyers were the bane of his existence. His job of running this multibillion-dollar, international pharmaceutical corporation was far too often complicated by self-serving, unethical attorneys. Litigation expense had expanded beyond logical reason, especially with what were called "nuisance suits," those that were unwinnable in court by plaintiffs, but which were much too expensive for the corporation to pursue. It was more prudent to settle with the plaintiffs out of court for $5,000 to $10,000 or less, rather than try the case; hence, the term "nuisance suits." The tremendous growth in the number of attorneys per capita promulgated the increase of unethical lawyers, commonly called "shysters" or "ambulance chasers." While he held his old friend, Arlen Loeb, in highest regard, he had little patience with most of the legal profession, especially Brice Billups. Kagan's academic credentials were impressive with a science/engineering background.

"All right. A large lot of this bad raw material gets shipped to our plant in Puerto Rico, to Caguas, with an *Expedite* on the production order," Billups was pointing with both hands, like Puerto Rico was right outside the hangar. He had psyched himself up for his best judiciary power stance, to abstain from his habit of fingering his moustache. But he had gotten excited. "Now, as you well know, the Quality Control down there is suspect at best. The rejection rates of their finished product are always excessive. According to my contact in operations, they throw our Best Practices numbers all to hell, and jeopardize our ISO 9000 standards. Why it's common knowledge, that if it were not for Code 936 and all those tax incentives, that whole damn operation would be shut down. So, to send out-of-spec raw down there with an expedite is just asking for trouble. To add to it, as I found out, the WESs... the Werner Engineering Specifications and the Operational Control Procedures had to be deviated, modified to accommodate the substandard material. The alloy, CobaltChromeMolybenum, you know, for cementable femorals, had an above max .03% Carbon and a below min 9.7% Chromium. Now, I am not a metallurgist or a biomedical engineer, but, these two critical variances change the properties — ductility, flexibility, and fatigue strength. Also, that variance from specs, beyond tolerances, complicated the surface integrity badly for polishing, passivation, and corrosion resistance. This radical change in composition not only compromises the manufacturing process but the total QA, uh, Quality Assurance, of finished product."

"I did not realize that you had experience in operations, Brice," Kagan interjected. Billup's insolent presumptiveness irritated the President.

The fact was he really *did* know what the hell he was talking about regarding metallurgical properties and casting— ductility and flexibility, i.e. modulus of elasticity applied to 316 LCVM stainless steel; rigidity and yield strength/ultimate strength were the critical properties of Co-Cr-Mo.

"Well, I had to. I had to study, become an expert for that knee liability case, you remember?" Brice wanted to grandstand his greatest legal victory. "Since Regulatory reports to *me*, you know I was promoted and placed over Regulatory...last year?" Brice was so inflated with his own hubris that he failed to notice their disdain. "Well, I had to study the technology further to get up to speed with my promotion," trying again to emphasize the word, "which helped me to judiciously investigate this grave matter," Brice stated, smiling, consciously refraining from his moustache and thinking that he had been complimented.

"It replicates a Markov chain," Brice continued, more smug than ever, "I mean, with the WESs and the OCPs having to be altered due to bad RMAs on bulk raw, it's like a chain reaction, a snowball rolling downhill. Uh, it's really like a classic Markov chain. Do you know...?"

"I'm quite familiar with the Markov analysis process of sequential probability, Billups, and it is irrelevant to what *you* have surreptitiously alleged. It is totally irrelevant to those charges which we are here to discuss. I shall tell you once again, stick to the subject at hand and state your allegations in plain, simple language," Kagan admonished.

Brice Billups was momentarily taken aback by the scientific knowledge, powerful voice, intellect, and authoritative aura of the company president. But his malevolent impudence quickly returned.

"Well, to make a long story short, there was all this out-of-spec CobaltChrome Molybdenum, on which the RMAs were altered, then filed away. *Not* rejected, as it should have been, because some of the more common femoral sizes were already backordered, and further backorders, which this rejection would have caused, would have been 'catastrophic,' according to Shortt and Nodycki in Sales. They said they were already under tremendous pressure with declining sales and eroding market share, especially on Hips, and this would have been the 'the final kiss of death,' they called it. So, when this out-of-spec raw hits the shop floor to be manufactured into total hip femoral prostheses, the Quality Control reports had to be changed just so this substandard product could pass inspection." Brice stood up, straightening his best Bullock & Jones power tie and proceeded to preach to the jury, forgetting that his jury here was shrewder by far than any he had ever faced. "Now, the worst part..."

"Sit down, Billups! We're not in a courtroom, yet. This is a discussion," Kagan commanded.

"Well, the worst part was that the bulk of it was shipped to Puerto Rico, where Quality Control is strained at best," Brice continued, trying to tone it down. "From there, we get back a whole production run, this large lot of finished product that should have been rejected and scrapped. My contact said it was even *beyond* rework. But instead, all of it hit the shelf, was sent to the shelves for stock. All of those QC documents had to be creatively manipulated. Major, major changes had to be made. Top-secret cover-ups had to be enacted. Now, here comes the tragic part— that death, the patient who died at that HealthCareUSA Hospital in Kentucky had one of the questionable prostheses implanted in him. When the distributor called after the surgery, then sent in all of his *very* comprehensive reports, Regulatory stonewalled him— unbeknown to me at the time. The lot number on that prosthesis was definitely one of the batch manufactured at our plant in Caguas, Puerto Rico, the product run that should have been rejected. They had been living in fear that this was going to happen. So, they just stonewalled, hoping that nothing would come from it. Unfortunately, that raised the suspicions of this distributor, who first, protested, then pursued and documented it further. When he called Legal, I was out of town, on that Sarasota case, you know the one, Arlen," Brice again vainly sought praise for his greatest legal victory, but to no avail. "When I got back, they would not discuss it — not the death, not the MDR, not the distributor's calls. I mean nothing! No one would discuss it. They were under edict, passed down in my absence, even though they're my damn department, this 'Presidential order,' they called it — not to, under any circumstances, discuss it with anyone, including *me*. Can you imagine? Obviously, Salter issued the edict, the 'black-out,' it was called. Not cover-up. 'Black-out!' And they would always whisper, 'black-out.'"

An austere silence befell the room.

They were meeting in a small office in the Avitat Aviation Hangar at the Newark Airport. It smelled of oil, diesel, and rubber. Only the roar of jets taking off outside could be heard.

Kagan and Loeb avoided eye contact. The question raged in their minds, "And how many more of these are walking around in patients?"

Billups gloated as he rustled the stack of papers sitting on the brown, formica table in front of him. All the papers were stamped *"CONFIDENTIAL."* He *knew* he had just dropped a bomb. Ahh... mission accomplished, thought he.

"Ron Salter ordered this?" Kagan finally asked.

"Yep," Billups quipped.

"Did any of our people know?"

"Yep."

"How far up?"

"All the way," Billups boasted. He smiled, so cocksure of himself and his treacherous plot.

"Rob Hempstead knew. Here are the overheads he just used in the Warsaw quarterly review... " Brice actually puffed himself up, trying to swell his small, concave chest, and pointing his chin upward.

"And you have all of this well documented?" Walt Kagan was now cold, calculating, his brows furled, lips stretched.

"Yep. Right here. It's marked *'CONFIDENTIAL,'* right here," Brice bragged, moving the overheads aside and tapping the thick *'CONFIDENTIAL'* file with his left index finger.

"Was this not the distributor who was suddenly terminated?" Kagan asked sharply.

"Well...he was. That was George Driscoll's doing. That sudden termination, I mean," Billups answered.

"His name?"

"... James Cantrill. George did it."

"Why?"

"George said it was because of some sales associates' complaining. Uh, some problems with younger salesmen calling in, called him to complain, said he was too old-fashioned, called him uh, an 'ol' Grandad,' uh... " Billups' narrow, fish-blue eyes began to twitch.

"How long had Cantrill been with Werner?"

"Uh, twenty-nine years I believe. Yeah, uh, that's what Lenny told me."

"Shortt was in on this?"

"Yes. He tried to deny it, like he always does, but Rob nailed him on it, uh called him...uh," Brice was beginning to stutter, "uh...uh...*crawfish, yeah*...uh... crawfish, that was *it!* You know how, uh, Lenny is?"

Brice Billups' suffused demeanor of self-importance and cockiness was deflating. He could feel his power base slipping.

"And how old is he? Cantrill?" the reproachful President questioned.

"... fifty-five... uh, fifty something. I believe that's what Lenny told me." Brice squirmed, not liking the sudden reversal of favor with his power play. He squinted trying to stop his eyes from twitching.

"And you were present with George when Cantrill was terminated?"

"Well, uh, yes. George wanted somebody from Legal there, you know?" Billups nodded to Arlen Loeb, seeking some type of affirmation.

Arlen ignored him. He was just thinking— whoever it was, whether Judas, Brutus, Machiavelli, or Satan, the devil himself— whoever the demon was who had sewed the seed of deceit, duplicity, and incivility, the seed of treachery in Brice Billup's heart could be proud, because it had grown dimensionally. Arlen was dishonored to be in the same room with this despicable little man, whom he also considered to be an embarrassment to the legal profession, in spite of Brice's legal triumphs for Werner.

"So, *you* are telling me that *you* were there when all of this went down?"

"Uh, yeah. Yes sir. Uh, yes sir," Billups stammered.

"And I understand that Cantrill mentioned that fatality as he left George's office. True?" Kagan's affixed stare pierced Brice's vainglorious facade, his flaming brown eyes drilling holes through his small body.

"Yeah, but he was bluffing. It was a comeback. He, uh Cantrill had to... to say something. It was just a bluff."

Billups did not dare say anything more about James Cantrill. He would not look Walter Kagan in the eye; he could not look either one of them in the eye for fear they would notice his eyes twitching, perceive his sudden loss of resolve, the sudden explosion of his nerve endings.

Kagan said nothing. His abject disdain was overpowering.

Billups' eyeballs were now twitching like a fluorescent bulb flickering before it burned out.

Arlen Loeb sat motionless.

The solemn President looked down at the stack of papers marked "*CONFIDENTIAL.*" He very deliberately pushed the whole stack across the table to Arlen Loeb for him to take. Without a word said, the message was both obvious and ominous. The severe storm cloud which these tempestuous circumstances presented, the impending threat to the entire corporation, was first the paramount responsibility of the Chief Counsel of the corporation.

Walter Kagan stood up. He walked over to the door and opened it. He did not, *would* not shake Billup's hand. He despised him. For one dismal moment standing there, Walt rued the day he had ever heard the name Brice Billups, much less had the displeasure of meeting him in person.

He shook his head, turned without looking at him and said disparagingly, "We will be in touch, Billups."

Walter Kagan, President and Chief Operating Officer of Brecken-Mersack Strauss, Inc., the third largest pharmaceutical company in the world, walked out on the tarmac toward his Gulfstream-V corporate jet.

Arlen Loeb, Chief Counsel of the third largest pharmaceutical company in the world, followed his boss' example. He walked out onto the tarmac toward the Bell jet helicopter, waiting to take him back across the river to corporate headquarters in New York City.

Billups was left sitting alone, dejectedly staring down at the cheap, brown formica table. This was not the outcome he had planned. He expected to be thanked profusely— for his huge wins in the past as well as today's revelations. Praised for his due diligence, for his thorough investigation, his exposition of this evidence...for his bravery to come forward. He had envisioned himself as a hero.

Brice looked around the grubby room. Why did they have to meet in this dump anyway? Why not the Harvard Club? Where they meet with all their high-brow poohbahs? It had private rooms. *I deserve better than this. After all the money I've saved their ass? Fuck Walter. I'll teach him to disrespect me, by God!*

He glanced out. Through the fogged-up pane in the office window, he noticed a skinny, shaggy rat creeping into the corner of the hangar. He shuddered.

Nobody, but nobody, likes a rat.

CHAPTER 29

...was wont to say of perfidious friends, that
"We read that we ought to forgive our enemies;
but we do not read that we ought to forgive our friends."
Apothegms, 1624
Francis Bacon

Nightmares. Over and over and over. Again and again. Horrendous nightmares. The same recurring nightmares. James swore that he would try to stay awake, if the damn mosquitoes would let him alone. If these dreadful nightmares kept on, he made an oath to himself that he would fight the restful sleep he so desperately needed.

He was afflicted by pain of a different origin. This pain was internal. Deeply rooted within. Deep within his heart. And even deeper within his soul. And it was more acute than all the external pain. He had heard the mantra," *we're rescinding the offer. We're rescinding the offer.*" over and over and over again. Reverberating in a sound chamber, *"rescinding the offer. Rescinding the offer."* It had to resemble the DTs— the delirium tremens. It was so real. He was back there again in George Driscoll's office, with his trusted friend, confidant, and corporate protégé, Lenny Shortt. Then, the mantra starts over again, this time with that lifelong friend now turned traitor, Lenny. Oh, God, not him again. The *Phantom of Perfidy*. The perfidious one, who after betraying friends and fellow associates always craftily managed to insulate himself from any responsibility for his dirty deeds with a surrogate or a superior. Always shifting the blame, lying to make himself look good, turning himself into a *phantom*, perfectly—

perfection in perfidy. Yes, the hurt was still there. The heartbreak of betrayal— the betrayal of a lifetime by a close friend— would always be there. But, that's enough of Lenny and his sickening perfidy. Lenny no more. Could not his cursed existence be exorcized from James' mind and soul? His betrayal, his perfidy blocked out of total memory? That bastard! In this graphic nightmare it *was* a horror show. It was the *DTs*, without the booze, but with all the psychogenic horror.

James cried out in his dream. Like a broken record— George's guttural, monotone voice continually repeating, *"We're rescinding the offer,"* again and again, like a motor in his brain running down. James screamed. But no one heard him. The record would not stop. George's damn voice droning, *"We're rescinding the offer."* George and his lies, his patently false ethics, his flawed business "model," his monotonous bass voice, his repetitive, nauseous mantra. The mantra continued on and on in an echo chamber. Then, enter that little prick from Legal, Brice Billups, with a smirk on that smart-ass countenance of his. It all came back so vividly— Brice's treachery, his arrogance, his slimy, light blue, fish-eyes twitching, that sneer, his cockiness, his high-pitched voice— it was worse than snakes and monsters in the worst delirium tremens.

When James awakened with a jerk, it was the jolt of sharp pain that jarred him back to reality. It was still dark; he was on the cot in the bivouac infirmary; the *coquis* were still chanting their nocturnal melodies— *co-kee, co-kee*. Yet, it took him a while to convince himself that he was there in the Puerto Rican rainforest, not back in that damn office in Warsaw, Indiana.

But, the little *coquis* worked their magic lullaby again and he drifted back off to sleep, only to dream again. This time it was even worse— he dreamed about his first phone call to his wife, Trish, telling her the horrible news— that they had just *rescinded their offer*, that he had just lost his job, that he had lost his distributorship, that *they* had lost their business, been dispossessed of their very own business, after 29 years. No more business. No job. No nothing, her shock, her anger, at first. But then, the tears, her crying, her uncontrollable sobbing. James was helpless. He could do nothing, could not say anything to console his wife, his love, his partner in business, his partner in life. Her sobs, and James was powerless to help, rendered impotent. Psychologically, spiritually impotent. The dream, his nightmare brought it all back, reenacted the whole tragic happenstance. It was awful, just awful— her sobbing in the background. He would never forget *her* hurt, *her* pain. For that he would never forgive them, the no-good *bastards.* The low-life traitors! And this nightmare seemed longer than the previous one. Oh, poor Trish, his poor dear, sobbing so hopelessly. And he kept reaching out to her, reaching out helplessly. No matter how far he stretched, no matter what he said, he could not reach her, was unable to touch her in his dream. She could not hear him. He was totally helpless, powerless to comfort her. Why? *Why? Why* had they done this to her?

And, then the tears shifted to the waiting room back in the hospital—Ezra Jenkins' family, crying over his death. That poor farmer, who should not have died. Mrs. Jenkins crying fitfully, being comforted by her daughter, who was sobbing almost as loudly.

Margarita awakened him gently. She had brought him coffee. She said in better English that he had been thrashing, moaning, yelling, *"No! No!"* He was wringing wet, his shirt stuck to his chest with sweat.

"Pobrecito, pobrecito," she repeated softly, wiping the perspiration from his forehead.

The ubiquitous *coquis* were ending their evening songs as daylight was slowly peering through the canopy of the rainforest. It was like the *coquis* were on a time-clock, punching in at darkness, and punching out at first daylight. They represented the only constant in James' life, from day to night, night to day. With the blessed exception now of Margarita, his nurse, his comforter, healer, his earth angel. He discovered that he was actually looking forward to night, because with darkness came the music from these harmonic little green tree frogs called *coquis;* then he looked forward to day to see, hear, and feel the tender touch of his new friend and Florence Nightingale, the doe-eyed Margarita. How wonderful.

As he sipped the strong, hot coffee, he reflected on the nightmares. Was it not ironic? James had himself just endured the most gruesome of all tortures, his body mutilated, his flesh cut and burned. In the hands of the demonic, maniacal Dr. Horst Frommacht, James' flesh had been simultaneously incised, bled, and coagulated with an electrocautery Bovie blade powered by an electrosurgical generator. Carved, burned and charred extensively, his skin was grotesquely scarred for life. These hideous injuries were not only repulsive, but also debilitating— he would be deformed for life, as well. In addition, he had been in that terrible wreck in the van, which had fractured his left leg.

He looked over his arms and hands— the gory, bloody, black gashes. Deep, gaping wounds exposing his bones. James still could not bear to look at them for very long, so ghastly and nauseating. Yet, the most excruciating pain was elicited by those tormenting nightmares—nightmares of betrayal, by a lifelong friend, by his company. The betrayal of trust, of loyalty, of devotion, a lifetime of devotion to a cause, a way of life, a beautiful career that helped benefit his fellow man, a wonderful business that he had built through the years. His job loss, the loss of his *life-force,* his Distributorship, his business of twenty-nine years; then, Trish, his dear wife, the trauma to her, her devastation, her hurt, her pain, her sobbing. That whole scenario, its abhorrence, its revulsion, that entire horror show was far worse than the worst of his torture. Hard to believe? That the excruciating emotional pain in his heart, his mind and his soul far surpassed the intense physical pain from the torture and its resulting wounds. But, it was true, so true. Now a revolting fact of life.

As he was finishing his coffee, James could hear rapid bursts of gunfire in the distance. Moises and Major Henry were obviously conducting maneuvers again. Margarita, oblivious to the sounds of war, was going about her routine. She was preparing another of her special herbal poultices that she used for dressings on James' wounds. He did not know what kind of concoctions she used as ingredients, nor did he wish to question her about it. Because they were working.

As she redressed the cavernous I-wound on his right hand, James reached over with his left hand, which he could still move with some duress, took her left hand in his, held it gently, and said, "Oh, *gracias, Margarita. Muchas, muchas gracias.*" simply not knowing what more to say.

Their eyes met, frozen for what seemed like an hour, those big, soft doe-eyes of hers that made you want to melt. "*De nada. De nada, Senor James.*" And, she went back to the dressings.

He was so grateful for her attention, her diligence, her expertise in natural remedies, and her tender nursing care. Without any doubt, she was the best thing that had happened to him all week. She, the major, her brother, Moises, and his troops had saved James' life. Wounded, broken, bleeding, his immune system shot, his stamina gone, he would have died within hours stranded in the rainforest. How on earth could he ever thank them?

Moises came into the infirmary tent with black paint under his eyes, which flattered his thick, black mustache. Sweat permeated his fatigues. Though early morning, the heat of the day was already oppressive.

"So, how are you today, Mr. Cantrill?" he asked in perfect English.

"Much better, thanks to Margarita. She's amazing."

"I agree. She is a vital part of our effort, here. My compatriot, Frank, told me about your career and its heartless termination. It is very upsetting to observe how ruthless some corporations can be today. They don't seem to care about layoffs disrupting families, dislocating society, and ultimately destroying human lives. My older brother was an executive, a Senior Vice-President for a big, multinational bank in Europe. He lived in Spain and traveled all over the world in his business. He had been with them for seventeen years, joined them right after getting his MBA from the London School of Economics. The bank missed their quarterly earnings targets for two consecutive quarters, causing their stock to come under pressure. It took a big hit on the FTSE-100, the CAC-40 and the DAK stock exchanges. Juan Carlos came back to Madrid from a business trip to Buenos Aires, walked into his office, and was fired! He was in shock...still is. He and his wife have five kids— two in college in the states, one in boarding school in London, the other two in private schools in Europe," he lowered his head, shaking it back and forth, and exhaled slowly. "So, I can sympathize with you," he sighed sorrowfully, pulling a wooden, fruit crate over to sit on.

"With our situation up here, we have to limit communications, or I'd call him every day. We were close growing up together. I used to look up to him. The reason I share that family experience with you is, as I said, I empathize with you. What happened to you is not right. You were treated more abysmally and more egregiously than my brother. The aftermath, the brutal torture to which you have been subjected, was inhuman and barbaric. Of little recompense to you now, Mr. Cantrill, is the fact that your entire circumstance serves to reinforce our cause. We shall fight passionately for those principles we hold sacred. Our primary goal here is independence for Puerto Rico— independence for our people. Independence for the individual."

Moises paused, took a deep breath. Leaning closer to James, he lowered his voice, "with all the earnestness at our command, what we are really fighting for here is...independence. Independence for our island.

The independence of the *human spirit*. Yes, *James*, freedom for the human spirit."

His final statement lingered momentarily, then ended with a coda composed by a raucous, distant band of Puerto Rican parrots high in the trees.

"Thank you for sharing," James had to clear his throat. "My condolences to your brother and his family. I do know how he feels." James was moved by how articulate, how compassionate, how prescient this Puerto Rican man named Moises truly was. Major Frank Henry had not exaggerated about his friend. Moises *was* emulating his biblical namesake, Moses, by leading his people.

"And, speaking of families, James, I am certain that you would like to get word to your wife that you are alive. We have an extensive network in the states, actually, all over Latin America, a grapevine that works quickly. Would you like to explore that possibility?"

"*Yes!*" James exclaimed, rising up from his cot, yanking his IVs and tilting both make-shift IV poles. "There's nothing on earth I'd like better. Yes, thank you! Oh, thank you, Mr. Moses," a little embarrassed that he had called him mister.

Moises smiled, his white teeth gleaming under his large black mustache.

"But I'm sure they've got my home bugged and my wife under surveillance by now," he relented.

"Not a problem. We're accustomed to working under those conditions. Your surmise is probably correct, judging from your circumstance and condition," he said, gesturing toward the gashes on James' right arm. "Of course, I can't make any promises, but we'll try to get through. The old cliché goes, 'Where there's a will, there's a way.' What other family do you have, or very close, trusted friends?" he asked, completely unperturbed by James' suspicion about surveillance.

"I have a daughter in Texas, Austin, Texas. She's a paralegal in a large legal firm dealing mainly in real estate, commercial property. My son-in-law is a landscape architect there. He works in..."

"Perfect! Absolutely perfect," Moises interrupted. "We have an underground in Mexico with a pipeline all over the Southwest and West. Real estate law is an ideal, low-profile contact point. That's excellent,

James. You must be living right. We'll get to work on it right away. Anything else?"

"Well..." James hesitated.

"Oh, go ahead. Don't be bashful," *Moises* reassured.

"Well, my ex-manufacturer is supposed to have a plant in Caguas, Puerto Rico. Werner. I believe there might be a connection— with the compromised product I saw in surgery and with what happened to me afterwards. If it's not asking too much, I mean, you've already done so much for me, offering to get word to my family, my gosh..."

"Not to worry. We've got a lot friends and associates in Caguas."

"Muchas gracias, Moises."

"De nada, amigo. You just keep on the mend."

As he left, he gave his little sister a loving pat on the shoulder.

James thought that Moises' eyes did not just twinkle. They projected a virtual light beam that almost illuminated those to whom he was speaking. In this simple one-on-one conversation, Moises was articulate, yet compassionate, intelligent, yet humble. He *was* dynamic. His speech projected leadership. James could envision him on a stage, standing in front of a crowd of thousands, cheering, mesmerized, bordering on mass hysteria. No wonder his people, the Puerto Ricans, followed him so religiously.

"My man James, how much better you look!" Major Henry called out as he entered the tent. He walked with a pronounced limp, apparently from his land-mine injury in Viet Nam. It did not, however, impede his mobility or his energetic swagger.

"Thank you, Major. Margarita has worked wonders."

"She *is* amazing. Call me Frank. After sharing our lives the other day, after your career tragedy. Hell, after sharing our death-threatening experiences together, our near-death encounters, we are friends, pilgrims from the fiery coals of Hades. Survivors, man. We *are* long, lost friends, don't you think? Brought together by adversity. Funny, id'n it? How paths cross? Hell, yes. We're soul-brothers in adversity and faith, man. Yes siree! You and me, my man, James, ain't supposed to be alive. Man... oh, man," he whispered, "every single day is a gift. A precious gift..." His deep-set, dark green, emerald green eyes glistened under his Green Beret.

"Frank, I'm thankful to *all* of you," James reached over to shake Frank's hand. He winced, stopping short. "Moises was just here. He said that he might be able to get word to my wife. That he could possibly get in contact with my family." James smiled.

"And he'll do it, too. I told you that he was awesome, didn't I? Moises has built up a network, an underground that spans the globe. His followers are not just confined to Puerto Rico," he reassured.

"And, in addition, he's going to look into that Werner plant here in Caguas, where I suspect there's a connection to what's been happening." James smiled again. "Now, Margarita. She's one of the best nurses I've ever seen. Where did she go to school?"

"She *is* great. She trained at LSU School of Nursing and Charity Hospital in New Orleans. Had all kinds of commendations and job offers, but she wanted to come back home. Had a no-count boyfriend, who dumped her. Moises was glad to be rid of him. She went to work at the U.S. Naval Hospital over on Vieques Island. That's where she was before coming here. She approached Moises to come here, believes in the cause, and wanted to help. He discouraged her, said she had too good a job with a future where she was. But, she kept insisting. And, man, am I tickled she did! She has been a huge help and has actually lifted morale of the troops."

Margarita reentered the tent. She began changing his dressings, applying her special formulas, and checking his IVs. She and Frank started talking to each other in Spanish, much too fast for him to understand.

The good-natured paramilitary trainer limped out of the tent.

When Margarita had finished her nursing care, she asked if he was hungry, to which he immediately said yes. She was wearing a light orange T-shirt today. James felt guilty, like a dirty old man, for thinking what he was thinking.

She brought him a big, brown bowl of rice and beans. After the one which Ramon had given him for breakfast that morning back in the torture shack, James was excited. His salivary glands told him what he already knew— Puerto Rican rice and beans were delicious.

He thought to himself, " It's a great day to be alive, like my ol' buddy, Fitch, used to always say: it's a great day to be alive— in the sweltering rainforest of Puerto Rico. Thank you, Lord."

CHAPTER 30

...in the opening of the jaws of her Grief and avenging Cares have placed their beds...

Aeneid
Virgil, 40 B.C.

Trish answered the phone after the third ring.

"Oh, Chuck. I'm so glad it's you. Where are you?"

"I'm on I-65 heading towards Indianapolis and home," Chuck replied.

"Oh, I was hoping you were closer. I've really got some stuff for you. Let me go first, okay?" Trish was actually smiling, waving her hands. "... tell you what I found out going through all of James' files last night. I read his notes on that tragic surgery. I can't believe it! James suspected that the size on that PDL Hip had been smudged, altered to read 14mm. That hip component was actually larger than 14mm. And that's what caused that poor farmer's femur to fracture, 'to split.' Meaning, Chuck, that hip *was* defective."

"Oh, my God," he said.

"It gets worse. The bone cement was 'gooey.' 'Out of spec,' James said. He said the lot numbers did not match up. I don't completely understand about the cement— each box has two packs, a liquid and a powder that are supposed to match up. But these didn't. So, that could have caused the patient's heart attack. Can you believe this?"

"This is incredible, Trish. Good work," Chuck replied.

"There's more. Then I started listening to the tapes, the phone calls James made to Werner. There's no doubt he was getting the run-around—from Regulatory to Legal and back. Back and forth. No straight answers. But, the name that kept coming up..."

"Hold it, Trish. I've gotta bad tail-gater. Hey, watch it, you...Hey, *damnit!* He's trying to run me off the road..."

Bang! Bang!

Two shots rang out. Two ear-shattering blasts pierced through the phone.

"Chuck! Chuck!"

Bang! A third shot—

"Chuck! Are you okay? Chuck!"

Then all she could hear were crashing sounds, glass breaking, motors revving, metal crunching. Then, nothing. Just static. Only static.

"Chuck! Are you there?"

More static. Then a whirring noise.

"Oh, my God..."

Trish ran out of her bedroom. One of the FBI agents met her on the stairs.

"Oh, my God...did you...oh..." she stammered.

"We heard," the FBI man said. "My associate is calling the Indiana State Police right now."

"Oh, no. No. Tell me...please tell me...that wasn't..." Trish shook.

She collapsed on the bed, staring at the phone laying mute on the bed. She sat there, aghast, her mouth open, her breath, short, dry.

The FBI man gently picked up the receiver and hung it up.

"Oh dear God...no..."

The FBI man patted her shoulder, trying to comfort her.

But, it was useless.

Several hours later, Agent Misler with the FBI contacted Lt. Shapley with the Indiana state Police, who was at the scene of the murder on I-65 just north of Lafayette, Indiana. After identifying himself, he explained why the FBI was monitoring the phone line at the time of the fatal incident. He identified Chuck Thursgoode as a PI and a friend of the Cantrills, whom Trish had hired.

Once Lt. Shapley understood the FBI's involvement, he went ahead and gave Agent Misler further details about Chuck Thursgoode's murder. The body had been found in a field off I-65 sixteen miles north of Lafayette. He had been shot three times. The first had been a distant shot with a high velocity weapon, probably a Mini-14 .223, while he was still in his van. The bullet hit his left shoulder from behind and left a large exit wound with fragmented bone just below the collarbone on his chest. The second shot entered through the driver's window, missed Thursgoode, then burst through the windshield. The third shot hit the passenger's door. He managed to get out of the van through the passenger's door, and, leaving a trail of blood, made it some twenty-five yards into the field before the assassin caught up with him. He took two shots to the head. Judging by the extensive exit wounds, the back of his head was blown off, with 9mm hollow-points or dum-dums. It was definitely a professional hit and may have involved two shooters, who chose an isolated stretch of the interstate just south of the Iroquois River. No towns; only forests and farmland. The trooper said it was not a "clean" hit because Thursgoode, as an experienced ex-cop and PI, probably had seen it coming. The van's tire tracks, the skid marks, indicated that he had braked suddenly to pull off the highway: "We believe that he raised his left shoulder for protection while he drew his weapon from his shoulder holster under his left arm. That would explain the bullet's rear entry. We have not found his weapon yet." Their crime unit was currently on the scene.

Agent Misler asked in which direction the van was traveling. I-65 south towards Indianapolis; away from Chicago made sense from Chuck's last phone call to Trish, when he said he was headed to O'Hare Airport. The FBI agent asked a follow-up question, qualifying it as probably premature: "Were they able to pick anything up yet at the crime scene, such as footprints in the field or tire imprints from the assassin's vehicle?"

Lt. Shapley replied that they had not gotten that far, but asked if they knew whether Thursgoode used a laptop computer?

The answer was a firm yes, that he was quite skilled, quite sophisticated with computers, especially the use of technology in industrial espionage. That was his specialty, having handled many large international cases due to his expertise. Why?

There was an adapter still plugged into the cigarette lighter, but it was not connected to any device. Assuming that it was his laptop, it was now missing from the van.

Lt. Shapely then said they had found something unusual, uncharacteristic at the scene of a homicide. They were not sure whether or not it could even be regarded as a clue. They would have to await lab analysis.

Intrigued, Agent Misler asked what it was.

The Lieutenant apologized, said that he was on his two-way, and did not want to describe it until he was on a secure line.

Misler complimented the trooper on his awareness, and privately, to himself, could not believe that he was paying homage to an Indiana State Policeman. Was the trooper pulling his leg? Practicing brinkmanship? David Misler, career FBI agent, was accustomed to jealousy, resentment, and conflicts of jurisdiction on the part of other law enforcement officials. The whole gamut of turf battles and vast range of human emotion had occurred during his lengthy career. An unusual clue? Why bring it up? Why mention it? But, yet, his curiosity had been peaked. What could it be?

After hanging up, he went upstairs to check on Mrs. Cantrill.

Trish was once again crying inconsolably. She had assumed the responsibility for Chuck Thursgoode's death. That undeserved guilt was killing her. When she thought of Mona, Chuck's wife, and their children, she sobbed miserably, holding her wet cheeks with both shaking hands. She had pulled her hair back that morning, fixing it nicely. The gray-streaked auburn sheen looked beautiful. It was now falling down, disheveled on her face and neck.

Agent Misler tried in vain to console her. He attempted repeatedly to assure her that the murder was in no way her fault. That is a fact of life. It is what happens in the investigation business, and that Chuck Thursgoode, as a professional, accepted that risk. As harsh as that seemed, so did his family, as well.

The more he spoke, the more Trish cried. This anguish simply compounded the tragic shooting of Sheryl Lukens, the ransacking of Lynnwood's office, and the whole aura of uncertainty, the threat of harm to her dear, dear James. Had he been killed now? With the reality of murder fresh in her home, the reality of James' death menaced her heart and mind. Surrounded by assassinations, she knew the odds of her true love still being alive were bleak. Probably nil. *Oh, James...Honey...*

As Trish sat on the edge of her bed, her head bowed with hands on her temples, her jaw bursting with pain, she vacillated between perdition and petition— *oh damn. Damn... Please God...oh, please....*

CHAPTER 31

We have before us the fiendishness of business competition...
passion and wrongdoing, antagonism between classes
and moral depravity within them,
economic tyranny above and the slave spirit below.
The Word of God and The Word of Man
Karl Barth, 1957

Rob Hempstead caught the 5:44 AM commuter train from Greenwich into Manhattan. He needed to get to corporate headquarters early, because he was calling an emergency meeting of his executive committee with his legal counsel to resolve the horrendous problems at Werner, Inc. Before he left his office later today, no matter how late, he planned to have the strategic plan for Werner in place, with ongoing contingencies and a transition team to go forward. Tomorrow morning early, he planned to fly back to Werner, once again unannounced, and literally clean house, terminate all of the deadwood. Already having terminated Salter, he would begin with the Vice-President of Sales, Leonard Shortt, the crawfish himself. Rob found himself actually looking forward to firing Shortt, because he was such a detriment to sales, to sales management, to management, period, and should have been dismissed years ago. He shook his head, reminding himself that most major corporations have at least one — a middle manager or high-level officer who is the epitome of the Peter Principle, meaning that their position greatly exceeds their capability. In Shortt's case, however, it was even more invidious, since he enforced his own agenda through the betrayal of his peers. What the Group President had witnessed in the quarterly review meeting in Warsaw just a couple of days ago was the antithesis of Judson Werner's founding principles. And Lenny Shortt was high on the antithetical blame list.

Next, he shamefully thought how he would delight in personally firing that little pompous bastard in their Legal Department, Brice Billups. He found himself hoping that Brice would ring true to his petty, antagonistic character and protest, making hostile threats. Rob would have his legal counsel at his side, totally prepared. After all, it was Brice who was at the core of the questionable termination of the distributor in Kentucky, James Cantrill. All the circumstances regarding that inflammatory situation were still unknown and needed to be further investigated.

He had in the past regarded firing someone as an unpleasant and difficult part of the job, but these two pieces of work would definitely be an exception to the rule.

As he reflected back on his last few years overseeing Werner, he wondered how on God's green earth a billion-dollar corporation could self-destruct so quickly? How could such a great, well founded tradition corrupt itself and go down so fast? In place of Mr. Werner's principle-centered leadership, there were now self-centered agendas. Instead of *his* strong ethical values, there were now *their* self-serving dogmas. Instead of the founder's creative centripetal forces, pulling all distributors and employees together for the mutual good, there were now hundreds of centrifugal forces, pulling everybody apart in separate, selfish directions. Just, how in hell could such an innovative, wonderful business so beneficial to humanity turn so absolutely rotten? Thank God, he thought, that it had not all occurred on his watch or his butt might be in a sling.

As the train stopped at the Port Chester station, Rob began to reminisce again about Werner's rich history. What a visionary, what an entrepreneur Mr. Werner had been! And how ingenious the concept of his distribution network had been, getting product to market through commissioned, independent distributors. When young Judson Werner began his career as a splint salesman for the DuLuth Splint Co., he had to purchase the splint kits himself in advance for $12.50 each and sell them for $25, while paying all of his own travel expenses. He traveled on the railroad, and would be gone for three months at a time. A railroad porter once laughed at the frayed, green telescope case that Mr. DuLuth had furnished to carry his splints. That insulted Werner's sense of pride and professionalism. He was so humiliated that he came home from that road trip determined to quit as a "peddler." He firmly announced his decision to Mr. DuLuth and said there were only two things which might cause him to reconsider— first, to sell splints from samples provided to him at no charge with commissions paid to him on all his sales; and, secondly, to carry the samples in a handsome, leather display case. Old man DuLuth would hear nothing of it. So Werner quit the DuLuth Splint Company and went home. After two weeks, Mr. DuLuth stubbornly relented and called his star salesman to come back to work for him. Hence, it was Judson Werner's superb salesmanship, ingenuity, and hard fought negotiating skills that invented an industry. An industry was thus born in 1908 and it was young Werner's distributor/compensation model that greatly contributed to its tremendous growth for the rest of the century, as well as the stellar success Werner's own company was to achieve. That tradition grew and was passed down from distributor to successive distributor, employee to employee. Those commissioned distributors and their incentive-based sales associates rendered customer service second to none. Rob had really enjoyed the times he had interfaced with the current Werner distributors. Of course, there were a couple of bad eggs, but, overall, they were a shrewd bunch of businessmen and a dynamic, fun group to be around.

He started chuckling to himself remembering some of their stories. The one about that infamous crawfish, Leonard R. Shortt, was priceless. The story went that a particularly popular distributor out west happened to be on the Vice-President's "shit list" and was about to be terminated. In his usual form, Shortt had discharged the Regional Manager to do his dirty work. The Regional Manager, lacking balls just like his boss, quoted Leonard R. Shortt, repeatedly to justify the termination of this distributor. "Leonard R. Shortt said that you had not made quota in the last two years. And Leonard R. Shortt said that you had not met your growth targets for the past nine quarters. And Leonard R. Shortt said that you had not made inventory turns for the last ten quarters. And Leonard R. Shortt said that you had not sent the assigned number of surgeons to weekend workshops. And Leonard R. Shortt said that you had not met your receivables, your DSO, days sales outstanding goal for the last seven quarters. And Leonard R. Shortt said that you had not hit the balanced selling goals in *over* two years. And Leonard R. Shortt said..."

"Wait! Wait just a *damn* minute!" the frazzled distributor protested, having heard more than enough. "*Leonard ARE NOT short!*" he shouted. "*Leonard ARE LONG!!*" Which was entirely true, since Leonard R. Shortt was 6 feet 2 inches tall— or long, were he lying down.

Rob Hempstead laughed out loud recalling the story. That was just one of classic stories that typified the Werner distributors' collective sense of humor, their camaraderie and resilience.

As the train stopped at the 56th Street station, more and more commuters were piling in the silver and blue train. There had been fewer people boarding at previous stops due to the early hour. The chill in the thick morning air, heavy with rank, city odors, rifted into the coach as the doors shut.

Sitting directly in front of Rob was a smartly dressed female whose excessive perfume preceded her. It was competing effectively with her shabbily dressed counterpart's aftershave. The contest of allure presented by the incompatible blend of the two scents was pungent beyond olfactory tolerances. The man sitting in front of them had begun sneezing fitfully.

Rob tilted his head back on the seat, shut his eyes, and tried to stop up his nose, breathing slowly through his mouth to escape the piquant colognes. But, he could taste it— like cherry vodka. Yuk! If he could just relax, rest, maybe even dose off for the next few stops, it would be the solace before the storm of disruption on his immediate horizon.

When he arrived in his corner office suite, it was still dark outside. He ignored the messages placed on top of his desk. He picked up his phone and left urgent phone mail messages with each member of his executive committee, as well as his legal counsel, to meet in his private conference room adjacent to his office at 8:00 A.M. sharp. He then pulled a yellow legal pad out of the desk drawer and began writing up the agenda for his emergency meeting. He did not want to bother with his computer. He usually regarded e-mail as a distraction, one that he certainly did not need this morning. He had left a note for Iva, his secretary, even though she would routinely check in with him first, never failing to offer to bring his coffee. She was a jewel, so efficient, always in a good mood, and focused on the work at hand. Why couldn't Werner hire more employees like her?

Rob began writing out the immediate action plan with his terminations of Salter, Shortt, and Billups. That would follow with a short list of others to be terminated with recommendations from his committee officers. He then tried to focus his thoughts on the intermediate and long-term strategic plan for Werner. After the changes in management, they would have to reorient the new team to Mr. Werner's customer-centered philosophy. His "Distributors-make-the-sale, grow-the-business" dictum had been long lost in the current negative, backstabbing atmosphere. "Our sales people butter our daily bread," had been the bedrock of Mr. Werner's founding philosophy. There would need to be new sales increase incentives put into place for the sales force, to try to restore their morale, and get the business back on track.

He looked out the window, forcing himself to ignore the messages on his desk. The first light of day was peering through the thick fog hovering over the New York City skyline. The teeming mist had begun to descend far below on the millions of commuters hitting the streets. From his 47th story window they all looked like ants busily crawling about on their concrete slab ant mound. He mused to himself that is probably what all of them here in this city were— workers, secretaries, publishers, investment advisers, models, fashion designers, bankers, executives, all of them together— just a bunch of damn ants laboring frenetically each day for the metaphorical queen. And who was Rob's queen? Certainly, his wife, Fran, with whom he had not spent any time, not quality time for sure, in what seemed like months. No wonder she complained constantly. He was definitely going to have to do something about that. But, right now, he had to...

The knock at his door jarred him from his reverie. It was now 7:35 AM.

It was David Zuckerman, his Executive Vice-President.

"What's up, boss?"

"We've got to resolve the situation at Werner. Before this day ends."

"I am with you on that one, boss. It's hard to believe that things deteriorated so quickly."

"Round up the rest of our executive committee, and we'll meet in my conference room. I'll have Iva bring us some coffee and Danish."

His committee was assembled around the deep mahogany conference table. The smog was just beginning to lift to the east, barely making the torch of the Statue of Liberty visible. But, liberty and freedom, individual endeavor and free enterprise, were not on Rob Hempstead's mind this morning. The hallmarks, the veritable symbols of America were but distant figments in the mist, because he had an albatross hanging around his corporate neck.

"Gentlemen, I believe you know why I have called this emergency meeting of the executive committee. I do not need to waste our valuable time, nor insult your intelligence by giving you a long historic background. No, the reason we are here is simple. *It is* the deplorable performance and decadent state of affairs at our orthopaedic subsidiary, Werner, Inc. Werner is in an irreversible downward spiral, bordering on free fall. Before we leave this room today, we *shall* have the action plan for resolution of the problems at Werner in place, as well as the short-term strategic plan to go forward. I do not know how long this may take, but, we are committed to stay the course until we have a plan. If any of you had previous appointments, I apologize in advance. The gravity of this situation takes precedence. I have already called the hangar, told them to have my Falcon ready to depart at 0700 in the morning for Warsaw, where we shall institute the corrective actions and immediately begin the restructuring. Before we start, do any of you have any comments which you would like to make?" Rob's voice was low, self-assured.

"Yes, I would like to say something," David, his Executive Vice-President spoke up. "Your presentation at Werner's quarterly meeting was fantastic. Your speech, your oratory was absolutely spectacular, Boss. I have never seen you so eloquent. I have put that into my trip report, as has Terry. And, let me just say how proud I am to be on your team."

"Here! Here!" were the affirmations of all other executive committee members present, as they all raised their Haviland china coffee cups to toast their leader.

"Thank you, gentlemen. But, that pales beside our problem at hand. Let us start *right* at the top. My favorite expression, *"A fish always stinks from the head down,"* once again rings true. Ron Salter was my hire for President of Werner, Inc. For almost a year, I thought he was on track and performing well. But, I must say now, he has been a disappointment. It defies my logical explanation where he went wrong, where he lost it. Moreover, where did *we* lose our focus? Make no mistake about it, gentlemen, *we* took our eye off the ball. *We* dropped the ball." Their superior was also losing some of his objectivity. He used to be his own biggest self-critic. His previous assumption of the responsibility for Werner's woes had been a stretch. Realistically, the problems there, the dishonesty, the hidden agendas, the direct diversions of accountability, the poor performance, and the manipulated numbers, the false reports had preceded Rob Hempstead's promotion to Group President. Werner, Inc. had been "stuffing the sales channel," that is counting sales to the Distributors as revenue and miscounting Distributor inventory in the "sold goods" column for a long, long time.

"Russ, I expect you to take care of Salter's severance agreement, which should include minimal, the *absolute* minimal outplacement package—with *zero* stock options. When we take our first break at 10:00, you can get your staff started on the paperwork, for Salter, and others." Rob shook his head and took a deep breath.

"Next, and I shall also handle this termination personally. And take some justifiable satisfaction in so doing The person to whom I refer is Leonard R. Shortt, the Vice-President of Sales, who has never sold anything in his entire life. Regretfully Russ, with his tenure, Shortt, will have earned, uh, correction, gained full retirement benefits, but, his outplacement package, within ethical parameters, is also to be minimized, severely minimized."

"The final termination on my contiguous list is in the Legal Department at Werner. I refer to Brice T. Billups. And, this one, gentlemen, I'm sorry to admit, will bring me visceral pleasure. Billups' two legal judgments did save the company considerable litigation expense, but that's his job and those are past events, though not in his Napoleonic mind. The recent damage he has done to Werner is significant. For him to fire that distributor in the heat of a Regulatory investigation, which invites reprisal against us with culpable information, was imprudent and intolerable. The fact that he, along with Shortt, has been able to obfuscate his agenda, to actually get away with these unethical acts is indicative of the pernicious organism which infects our once proud subsidiary. The disease of rationalization, the cancer of corruption, the poison of betrayal, the mortality of mendacity, *each* and every *one* of the aforementioned *is* systemic throughout Werner. Brice and Lenny Shortt are both malignancies which must be excised. Russ. And I am ashamed to admit this— I hope that all of you here know me better than what I am about to say— Russ, I find *any* type of parachute, *any* severance package whatsoever for *this little asshole* reprehensible. I also plan to interrogate him thoroughly regarding the questionable termination of the distributor in Kentucky, James Cantrill, and, the aftermath, as well."

Lamentably shaking his head, *"and that's yet* another problem..." he let out a deep sigh, that emanated from the tips of his Allen Edmonds shoes far under the table.

"Russ, get with our HR Department, and select the toughest barracuda they've got to go with us tomorrow. I mean the meanest, most experienced layoff officer in the entire department. I expect the exit interviews with Shortt and Billups to be the most rigid that we've ever conducted. We *must* construct tight, litigious parameters for each, is that understood?"

The corporate counsel knew how serious Hempstead was and readily agreed.

"Now, I know that each one of you have your own judicious recommendations. I have only just begun with the three most obtrusive, most flagrant changes needed. Several of you have voiced your reservations about Werner's incompetent middle management to me in several of our discussions. Yes, David? Go ahead."

"My first proposed termination is that of the Director, or assistant Vice-President, or Sr. Marketing Manager, whatever in the hell his title is, the Director of Marketing, Nicholas Knodycki. He is, without a doubt, the most incompetent, unqualified marketing manager I have ever encountered in any corporation. The only thing that he has ever marketed effectively is polemics— his own unadulterated, undiluted polemics. His constant habit of interrupting, his vacuous argumentative interjections, his art of disputation, are absolutely *the* most disruptive, counterproductive forces to product introduction and a positive marketing effort at Werner. No wonder Werner was, *is always* playing catch-up in the major product launches. They were *always* behind initially, almost having to play a loss leader approach, due to his negative polemics. I mean, this guy is a world-class polemicist and belongs in St. Elsewhere, and I'm forcing myself to be polite. Rob, you questioned how Shortt has been able to feather his nest at the expense of others for so, so long and get away with it. And I heartily agree, as we've discussed many times– promoting his own agenda while sacrificing the good of others, especially the distributors, of whom he is envious. *Damn...*" twisting his face, "...as well as the whole corporation. Well, Knodycki, comes in a close second. The damage that he has caused —morale, lost business, and even worse, *lost* opportunity— is incalculable. His tenure also defies logic, integrity, and even mediocre management principle. He is the biggest, most worthless *sack of shit* I 've ever seen." The others, including the boss, laughed in complete accord.

"I agree, David. Next?" Rob asked.

There were sudden, staccato knocks at the conference room door.

An exasperated Iva rushed in, almost breathless, and blurted, "Pardon me, Mr. Hempstead. But, Mr. Kagan is waiting for you up in the Board of Directors' room. He *has* been waiting. Didn't you see my message on your desk? Nola, his assistant, left you phone mail, e-mail messages," she gasped for air, " in addition to the one I left on your desk." She was panting like a cocker spaniel.

"No, Iva, I did not check any messages this morning..."

"Mr. Kagan shouted at me, telling me to get you up there at once! Oh, Mr. Hempstead..." Iva was just about in tears.

"Don't worry, Ivie, I'll go right up. I wonder what's so damn important. You'll have to excuse me, gentlemen. I'm sure this won't take long. Please continue while I'm gone. We're off to a good start. Remember, we're flying to Warsaw at 7 o'clock A.M. sharp in the morning.

He patted Iva on the shoulder, trying to comfort her, as he walked out of his executive conference room to take the private, polished brass elevator up to the top floor.

CHAPTER 32

He shall come down like rain upon mown grass:
as showers that water the earth.

Psalm 72:6

It had rained continuously for the past four nights and five days. There was mud and muck all over the place. It had done more than just muddy their outdoor abode, it had also dampened the spirits in the guerrilla training camp. James had to remind himself that he was in a rainforest; daily rain was a natural occurrence. But a week of heavy downpours was too much. And the mosquitoes were horrendous.

They had to move James and the infirmary from the tent into one of the caves in the mountain. It was nice to be dry, but shelter came with a price. There was an overpowering stench that would not go away. It was the foul odor of bat urine. Of all the things James could *ever* think of— *bat piss!* At times it had the same pungent, penetrating effect on the nostrils as ammonia. He could see the bat droppings on the cave floor. Bat shit. How ironic! Trish used to pay a fortune for bat *guano* to use as fertilizer.

Relief from the tropical heat was also nice, but that, too, came with an unwanted side-effect— the cooler damp humidity had increased his pain. And he had a fever; with chills. Margarita still had his IV's going. She had injected something into the IV stopcock for his pain, which had helped a little. In addition to the hassle of having to move, she now had two more patients in the infirmary, both soldiers. One had slipped over a crevice in the mud and broken his ankle and leg; the other had malaria. So, Margarita had her hands full, but she remained in a cheerful mood, always humming this hymn that was familiar to James. But, he could not come up with its name. The melody played over and over in his mind; it was driving him crazy. Margarita's attitude, her tender care, her expertise...she *was* amazing, almost imperturbable.

Now James had company, his first in days, but there was a language barrier. They seemed friendly though, exchanging smiles, giving each other silent gestures of encouragement. Margarita had whispered to him that, while they hated being laid up, they were honored to be with the "*macho Americano con,*" she caught herself just in time before saying, "*con cojones grande.*" She snickered, her soft brown eyes twinkling like stars.

She tried to explain away her pause, "*nuestros nuevo amigo, la independista!*"

James noticed the two soldiers staring at the grotesque wounds on his arms and hands. Their training in guerrilla warfare had not been exposed them to sadistic mutilation, to this kind of exquisite torture. He could hardly blame them. They especially zoomed in on the gaping "I" crater wound on his right hand and wrist. It never failed— with each new encounter, their eyes always scoped out the "I" wound, the symbol of his rescue, his quasi-membership in the *Independistos,* and his bonding with the group. James later learned that many of the soldiers had "I's" tattooed on their chests.

Thanks to Margarita's miraculous pressure dressings and herbal poultices, the big "I" was beginning to heal. But, the healing process made it look even more gory than before— it had big brown scabs around the top, along the edges of the black, charred tissue, the brownish crust of dried blood, as well as red blood, yellow adipose tissue, and, last, but not least, the exposed bones in his hand— a rainbow of raw flesh, a cornucopia of colors, all representing different stages of brutal torture, gross injury, unconventional medical treatment *au naturale,* tender nursing care, the different stages of the healing process, and the pride of survival. Hence, James could hardly blame his fellow patients for gawking and staring. It was just now that he was able to allow himself to look directly at his mutilated limbs, to inspect his injuries. The scabs, a favorable sign of the healing process, however brought a new pain— a scraping, stretching type. In spite of their hurt, they looked good compared to the gory, bloody, ghastly wounds that had preceded them.

Due to the weather, things had been much more reserved in the camp. James had not seen the Major in several days and really missed him. Major Henry was always so upbeat with some kind of positive news that really lifted his spirits. Plus, he spoke English. There had been an immediate commonality with him, which gave James the first sense of continuity, of belonging, of belonging to something somewhere, anywhere. Anywhere other than that torture chamber. Other than that bottomless pit from Hell. Margarita, the Major, with his good friend, Moises, the leader, had given him his first shred of encouragement. And, the most important thing— hope.

Nor had he seen Moises in the last few rainy days. Though hesitant, he had asked Margarita about her brother and was informed that he had left the island on business. James later learned that was not at all unusual for Moises to do. He was seeking strategic alliances, procuring supplies, always negotiating for the future, for supplies, for personnel, for economic incentives. At other times he was leading rallies in churches, slums, and rural communities, bringing words of hope to the masses, to the underprivileged, to *his* people. According to Major Frank, they always had an ongoing want/need/must-have list that was added to and deleted from nightly. Margarita also had her own continual list of needed medical supplies and replacements. To be a rough-shod band of guerrillas in the jungle, they seemed to James to be extremely well organized. Their unity of purpose and *esprit de corps* were extraordinary. If only Werner could reverse its course, take note and emulate them. But, he stopped himself in that thought process. It was still too painful to him mentally, emotionally, and spiritually. He was *not* going back there. He had made progress. And, speaking of progress, look at what a motley group he had somehow fallen into! *They had* saved his life. What a radical change of events, scenery, and *persona non grata*. And what a blessing— the blessing of salvation, the sweet blessing of life.

It had started raining again. Already dampened spirits got wetter. And here came the pain again. Only Margarita humming her hymn softly seemed unperturbed. She just went about her business like a songbird going from flower to flower.

With a huge ka-slosh, the Major came dripping into the cave, wearing a hooded camouflage slicker. He threw back the hood and shouted, "*And the rain descended. And the floods came. And the wind blew...*" he smiled, "*...and beat upon that house. And it fell not, for it was founded upon a rock,*" and he framed the word, *rock,* with his outstretched arms and his eyes looking skyward, descriptive of their new stone home. But his smile did not in the least deter the solemnity of the moment. The Major's scriptural recitation was humorous, yet deeply serious; theatrical, yet liturgical; staged, but sincere. It was moving. And all of them within the rock-bound infirmary were moved by it.

And, at that very second, as if directed by an ominous cue, in a deafening burst of thunder, lightning struck dangerously close by. It shook the ground; dirt fell from the roof of the cave. One of James' IV bottles, suspended from a rocky overhang, fell and burst on the rock floor. Giant trees cracked, splitting, their leaves rustling as they fell to the ground in the rainforest. All of them shuddered, including Major Henry. It accentuated the profound clairvoyance of his biblical quotation and reminded them of the utter fragility of their humble human condition and its earthly abode.

With a change in voice and expression, the Major responded, "Whoa! Do ya think it's gonna rain?"

Everybody roared aloud in badly needed laughter; except for Margarita, who only smiled briefly, interrupting her incessant humming—was that hymn provident, also? It was almost as if she were saying, "see there, I told you God was here with us— *vaya con Dios.*" Then, with the Major's help, she began cleaning up the broken glass.

It took almost an hour for the infirm to resettle themselves in their shaken but safe infirmary. The Major had left to conduct night maneuvers.

As dusk came, the fever had hit James again. He was experiencing intermittent febrile attacks, shivering one minute, freezing to death, then burning up the next. They did not have the luxury of ice, nor air conditioning, nor, for that matter, any method cooling off, save a manual fan. In James' debilitated state, with his arms, he did not have the strength to fan himself. Multiple blankets were used for his chills.

In the night, the rigors became worse. The chills were severe. He was shaking so forcefully that his cot was shifting, making noise on the rock surface. Margarita had piled blankets on top of him, only to remove them shortly thereafter, when he was burning up with fever. James was moaning, shouting out, bordering on delirium. She was worried that he had come down with malaria. But, she was even more concerned that his rigors, his shuddering and shaking, his physical gyrations, would damage his fractured leg, as well as exacerbate his wounds, which had begun to heal. She had to constantly attend to his IVs, so that they flowed intact, as the tubing shook and quivered, too. She was bathing him off with a wet washcloth; he was wringing wet with sweat during the fever attacks.

"Oh, *pobrecito. Pobrecito,*" she said softly, crossing herself.

Moises came in just past daylight, very excited. He was bringing James a gift— two rolled-up newspapers written in English, *The San Juan Star.*

But, James was delirious, thrashing about, murmuring, calling out unintelligibly.

Margarita had spent the night in her sleeping bag beside his cot. Looking up at her brother, her forlorn expression said everything.

Moises needed no explanation of James' sudden turn for the worse. He knew malaria first hand, had seen its deadly force many times. It had killed some of his family members and deprived him of the abilities of some of his best recruits.

As Moises left the cave, he shook his head and made the sign of the cross on his large chest.

CHAPTER 33

Grief fills the room...

King John
Shakespeare, 1591

Trish was inconsolable, crying uncontrollably. Against of her friends' and family's advice, she insisted upon attending Chuck Thursgoode's funeral. She felt compelled to extend her personal condolences to Mona, Chuck's wife, and their children. It was certainly a noble effort, but in the process she had unconsciously assumed more self-imposed responsibility for his murder, adding to her own guilt.

Compounding it further, she imagined herself as the widow sitting at the grave-side service instead of Mona. She saw herself at James' funeral, not Chuck's. Once the vision fixed itself in her mind, she could not dispel it. It was so real. She was wearing the black hat that had belonged to her mother; her pleated black dress was similar to the one Mona wore. As the minister read the 23rd Psalm, she even envisioned their senior minister standing there. *Oh God, could it be true? Is this really happening? Is this an omen?*

Superimposed upon Trish's grief and guilt was her foreseen attendance at her own husband's funeral. It was too much for her—the emotional breaking point, the heartbreaking straw that broke her previously strong resolve. No matter how hard they tried, she was beyond help.

She tried to compose herself. She remembered reading somewhere: just as death demands a reason and murder demands a motive, disappearance demands an explanation. Was James' disappearance an act of God? An act of nature? An act of mere coincidence? Or was it an act of evil? Was it an orchestrated plan to get rid of him because of what he knew? Because of what he stood for? Was he still alive? Could he be? Or was she just grasping at straws? The *NOT knowing*, the torture of *not knowing* was excruciating. The mental torture of physical separation, of psychological deprivation, of cognitive disorientation was too much for her, too much for anyone.

Time, itself, was torture. Seconds were minutes, minutes were hours, hours were days, and days seemed endless. Every time the phone rang her heart stopped. Could it be James? News of his whereabouts? It was always false hope— her constant expectation quelled again and again, only to cause more disappointment and give way to darker depression. And now, all she could do was cry.

Even when Kathleen and Christine, came over to hug, love, comfort, and console her, it was to no avail. At first, she had tried to be strong. She *had* been unbelievably strong, too strong, but no longer. Ann, their daughter in Texas, had wanted to leave her job without pay, pay she badly needed to make ends meet, to come be with her mother. But, Trish insisted that she not. So, she called her mother at least twice a day to comfort her. Their children were great. No, they had been magnificent. They had responded to this crisis like champions, like the spiritually beautiful women they had each grown up to be. She knew how proud James would be...if only he were here. But, now she could not get a handle on her shattered emotions that were flowing like a river out of control, like the mega-flood of the Mississippi in 1927.

Would her life ever be the same? Would her life ever come back to her? Why had this happened? To her husband? He was honest. He was a hard worker. He cared about people. He took care of his people. She had been his partner, doing the books, paying all the bills, the taxes, filling in during vacations, sick days, helping out responding to emergencies, making emergency deliveries. *Hell,* she even took her babies to the bus station in a cab at night back when they only had one car, always going above and beyond. By *damn,* they had always worked hard. And they *had* succeeded! They had built the business, were tremendously successful; had *doubled* the business time and again— how many times did James say? *Damn, damn!* Why? Why had they done this? What had they done to her husband? Take me. Take me, but bring my husband back. Please God, bring him back. Without him, life would be unbearable. It would not be worth living. Oh, please...and she began sobbing again, her chest heaving, almost hyperventilating. The tears had dried up; her lacrimal glands were dysfunctional, had swollen shut. Her eyes burned from sobbing.

And here she was confined to her bedroom, constricted to her home. Once a partner in a flourishing business, a competent, independent person, a loving wife, mother, and grandmother, an active leader in their church, she was now a prisoner in her own home. She felt imprisoned in a suspended sense of worthlessness. She was powerless. Like never in her life.

Trish tried to go back to James' 'safe file,' to go back through the documents, to listen to the tapes, but she could not. She could not concentrate. Her mind was shot. And her emotions unanchored.

She had to get a grip. Presently, she knew she was no good to herself. To her family. To anyone. Even if James were to miraculously be returned to her, she could not let him see her like this. Yes, she had to get a grip.

Smoking. Why had she quit smoking? She hated herself now for quitting. And she hated the anti-smoking movement. She hated that whole *damn* crowd! At least she had quit before they had gotten started. But, that's of little consolation now. What she needed was a cigarette. A good, hot smoke would help. A cigarette would definitely help her get a hold of herself. That's it! She would inhale it way down deep, clear down to her toes. And blow it out *real* slow. Yep, she needed a cigarette. That was her answer. A cigarette! Did any of the FBI men smoke? No. *Damnit!* She would just have to go across to the shopping center to Kroger and buy a pack of cigarettes. Why hadn't she thought of this last night? Instead of resorting to her usual escape— a huge bowl of vanilla ice cream dripping with chocolate syrup, topped off with Cool Whip. It had made her sick. She almost threw up. She was always sorry afterward.

As she took off her old velour, maroon mourning robe to get dressed, she could not even remember what brand of cigarettes she used to smoke. It had been years. How many? Ten? Fifteen? It was a menthol. Not Salem. No, she had switched to another brand. What was it? Two names— no, finally, it came back to her— Doral Yes, Doral. She had switched to Doral from Benson & Hedges menthol, because they were so much cheaper. Generic brands. Ha! Lower tar and cheaper; better for you. The hell with it. She would splurge, buy herself a pack of Benson & Hedges menthol. She pulled on a pair of jeans and one of James' old Polo sweatshirts and headed out the door to her car in the garage.

The phone rang.

It was Ann calling from Texas. She tried to sound like her jovial self. But there was a serious tone in her voice, an air of urgency, extreme urgency.

"Mom, this is important. Don't ask questions. Go to a pay phone and call me at the office. Right now! Do it. Call me now from a pay phone... at my office."

As she hurried out of the house, Trish wondered what was going on. Why a pay phone? Because of bugs? Call her at her office? Electronic surveillance? Why? She could not believe that she was thinking like this. Her mind was confused, twisted...shot...just about gone.

As she drove down the street, she still wanted a cigarette.. That used to be the first thing she did after cranking her car— light up a cigarette. *Damn!* She missed it. Should she buy a pack before calling Ann? It would settle her nerves and help her to think; really think more clearly.

Why not?

CHAPTER 34

Pride goeth before destruction,
and an haughty spirit before a fall.
Proverbs 16:18 (KJV)

As Rob Hempstead rode the brass elevator up to the Board of Directors' room on the top floor, he found himself in a quandary. *What has Walter got up his ass this time?* His boss was usually calm and assured, but when he did fly off the handle, he would often call Rob. Rob respected Walter, admired him more than any superior he had ever had.

As the doors opened, he faced Rembrandt's *The Prodigal Son,* beautifully mounted on the wall. *The place smells like money,* he thought. *I belong here.*

When he walked into the plush suite, his quandary was subtly replaced with apprehension. There were no smiles, only stern expressions around the fifty-foot mahogany table. This was certainly not his usual greeting in the board room. Sitting there impatiently were Walter Kagan, CEO/President of Brecken-Mersack Strauss, Inc., Arthur Loeb, Chief counsel, Logan Glauber, Chairman of the Board, Louis Rabbini, CEO of Global Express, LLC, a long-term board member, and Frank Sweeney, the Sr. Vice-President of Human Resources. The attendance of Frank, the head of HR, foreshadowed the portent atmosphere hanging from the three Waterford crystal chandeliers suspended from the coffered mahogany ceiling.

Denied his usual seat at the table, Rob's apprehension quickly changed to fear. His eyes widened, his face froze.

"Sit over there." Walt gestured for him to be seated across the table, on the opposite side from all the others. The seating arrangement at these power meetings often conveyed the message— me against them. The handshakes were also conspicuously absent.

"Do you make a habit of ignoring your messages, Hempstead?" Kagan asked coarsely.

"No. It was because of the urgency of my Executive Committee meeting...that I just left..." Rob nervously straightened his Ermenegildo tie.

"*I personally* left two messages for you. We have been kept waiting now for almost thirty-five minutes."

"I am sorry, Walter. As I said, this was a critical meeting ..."

"So is this one!" Kagan strained to keep his voice low.

"I did not say that, Walter," Rob replied, trying with great effort to remain cool and reserved. He looked down at his Hermes pocket handkerchief.

"The reason you were called here should come as no shock to you, Robert. Turn it on," Walt stated, pointing to a chart just illuminated on the screen in the front of the room.

When Rob saw the very Market Share chart he had produced, showing Werner's wretched performance numbers depicted by the analysis which he had personally commissioned, his eyes bulged. His face flushed and a colossal lump hit his throat. It was one in the same that he had used in his presentation, his "dress-down" at Werner just a few days ago. *How had Walt gotten that chart? I thought I ...*

"I'm sure that this Market Share chart is quite familiar to you. The story that it tells should also be familiar to you, as well," Kagan grimaced at Rob, who had momentarily lost his focus.

"The root causes of the volcanic erosion of Werner's Market Share should not only have been known by you, the Group President, but the problems should have been corrected... diagnosed and corrected long before the precipitous decline..." he spoke slowly, concisely, repeating key words for emphasis. "...the decline to this level... this level of unacceptable performance. I don't need to remind you that Werner was once the unchallenged leader in the orthopaedic industry in the entire world.

They were also an important year-on-year contributor to our consistent earnings growth. I, *also*, do not need to remind you that when you were promoted to Group President over six years ago, your primary goal was to turn things around at Werner..."

"Why in the *hell* do you think I called the emergency meeting of my Executive Committee early this morning, Walter?" Rob interjected.

"Quite frankly, Rob, it is *too* little. And way *too* late. This decline has increased on your watch. There has been no visible improvement. None at all. Look at your chart, Hempstead. It has been reported to me— that they have been guilty of 'earnings management.' Guilty of 'revenue recognition.' Continually 'stuffing the channel." In other words, they have been 'cooking the books' for some time now. I don't need to inform you that this is against the law, a violation of SEC statutes, and a felony. We're in deep shit because of this— something *you* should have discovered, exposed, been on top of. And immediately reported to me and the board. It was part of your fiduciary and corporate responsibility. It's your *damn* job to..."

"That's exactly why..." Rob pointed to the chart. He started to defend himself, but choked. It was just as well, because the CEO had not finished.

"And, furthermore," Kagan continued, "speaking of Werner's distributors. A tragic circumstance has been reported to me regarding the wrongful termination of a long-term distributor in Kentucky, a Mr. James Cantrill. In addition to that, as I understand it, there have been mitigating circumstances since his dismissal that could even further complicate the situation."

"I *had absolutely* nothing..." Rob retorted.

"I am not accusing you of complicity. I am simply stating that Werner's performance is unacceptable, their conduct is intolerable, with some elements there totally out of control. And, as Group President in charge of The Medical Division, your performance, it saddens me to say, is disappointing. It is, Rob, simply unacceptable..." he lowered his voice, tightened his lips. "You have failed to turn this company around. You have *failed* to achieve the pre-set goal, and, I must add, the agreed-upon goal, which you signed off on with your promotion to Group President."

Rob looked away from Kagan's icy countenance to all of the other stern faces around the table. All were friends of his, so he thought.

He had thought that they individually and collectively respected him, appreciated the difficult job that he was doing.

"Therefore, Rob, you are, as of 8:00 A.M. this morning, terminated."

"I do not *believe* this! I have not been given the opportunity to defend myself," Rob angrily argued. "Even a common criminal is guaranteed that right by the U. S. Constitution..."

"Do you dare to deny the fact that their, that Werner's performance has been abysmal? And their conduct reprehensible?"

Rob sat silent. He shook his head, submissive to the undeniable truth. In his heart, he knew that they were right. But, they had given him no warning, none whatsoever. Why? Multiple performance reviews citing poor performance or unsatisfactory results usually precluded termination. It was standard management procedure. This was the first time it had been brought up to him. Previously, he had always taken the lead, gone on the offensives for corrective measures. Then, why this abrupt, mercurial firing? By his friend, Walter? By the *damn* Board of Directors? Was he the fall guy? The scapegoat for all this *shit?* He then started shaking his head, back and forth, slowly at first, in utter disbelief.

"I have given my whole *damn* life to this company. I have devoted, I have sacrificed...my family..." his voice trailed off.

"I regret this. But, I must repeat, as of 8:00 A.M. this morning, you have been terminated from Brecken-Mersack Strauss. Inc. In view of your twenty-six years of good service to the company, we have endeavored to enhance your severance allowances. Frank will conduct your exit interview forthwith, in the presence of Arthur. You will qualify for your current annual salary, uh," he glanced down at the folder to his right, "$435,775 per year for the next two years, and two additional months thereafter, since you have been employed at Brecken for twenty-six years. In addition, we are providing you with a much more extravagant severance package: your stock options will remain intact over the two years, totaling $1,333,967.95; your benefits coverage will also continue, with major medical for your family, and the disability/accident /life insurance on you, personally."

Rob Hempstead did not hear a word that was being said. He was in total shock. He was horrified. His brain was numb, his heart in his throat. They could have said $10,000,000, *ten* million dollars, or a *hundred* million. It did *not* matter. It did not phase him. He did not care. Because his life was over.

"You are completely vested in full in all the retirement plans— your 401(k), pension, profit-sharing, the Brecken Executive Plan, the 1983 incentive bonus plan, all of them," Kagan continued. "Of course, Frank will go into these in more detail in your exit interview. We will continue to pay for the lease on your BMW for the next two years, until it expires. We have also made special arrangements for your outplacement service with the best firm in the country, Bright Associates, for six months, versus the regular three months. Frank can itemize all these details further if you wish. I'm sure that you will look back on this one day and agree that we have really sweetened your package, that we have been more than generous with you, really stretched the envelope for you."

The word "generous" struck a nerve and momentarily jarred Rob out of his apocalyptic state; the auditory black-out had been selective.

He was in a daze, stupefied by the untoward turn-of-events. He did not hear, nor see; he could not react. Much of it passed right by him.

When Frank went through the formal exit interview, he hardly heard a word, only nodding when he had to.

Two security officers presented themselves at the boardroom door and escorted him out of the building. He was not even allowed to bring his briefcase. He was impersonally informed that all of his personal effects would be delivered to his home tomorrow by registered courier.

As Rob Hempstead, *ex*-Group President of Brecken-Mersack Strauss, Inc., left his corporate headquarters for the last time. He stepped out on the sidewalk of Park Avenue. There was no limo waiting for him at the curb.

He did not know which way to turn. He began walking along in a fog. He was intellectually paralyzed by disbelief. A disquieting sense of desperation saturated his being.

How could they do this to me? I devoted my life to this company. How could Walter? He was my friend, my colleague...my...that bastard! By God, they were going to pay for this!

The teeming crowds of people pushing and shoving on the sidewalk passed him by. The blaring horns of the bumper-to-bumper traffic, the jack-hammers of construction all fell upon deaf ears. A giant crane was hoisting a huge, steel I-beam up to the top of the skyscraper across the street.

Rob felt like he had just been hit between the eyes with that I-beam. It was like a head-on collision with raw steel and getting diagnosed with cancer simultaneously. He was blinded by the intense pain.

He passed a homeless person begging on the street with an outstretched hand. Rob didn't even see him as his hand brushed his leg. He was completely unaware of the madness of his surroundings.

Standing on the corner of Park Avenue and 57th in his $2,000 Armani suit, he was no better attired than the street person. Clothes were meaningless. Life was meaningless.

Rob Hempstead's sense of identity, sense of purpose, sense of meaning— all were lost. His life had become worthless. *Who? Who am I?*

Standing there smothered by the masses, he was a human void, suspended flesh in designer clothes— only displacing the hot urban air. The master of quota, the revered master of "the dress-down" had been just been dressed down.

Dressed down, out of his designer clothes.

Dressed down, all the way down—

CHAPTER 35

...oh, por favor, Dios...

Margarita, 1997

He had become much worse. Within the last few hours, the rigors wracking James' body had become more violent. Margarita was genuinely worried about him. Fierce contortions were now threatening all of his other injuries. The sequential attacks of chills, fever, and the sweats had also gotten longer. She thought that he had falciparum malaria, the most severe type that can be fatal. Delirious, his screams reverberated around the cave, which amplified them many times over.

His fever had climbed to 104.8, dangerously high, especially for someone in his debilitated state. The double dose of aspirin she had given him to check his rising fever had not yet done its job. She had asked the soldiers to keep two buckets filled with the cool rainwater from the runoffs, actual waterfalls in some places, caused by the nonstop rain. Using the cool water to bathe him was a weak attempt to lower his body temperature. What she would give for a block of ice. Packing him with it would cool him down, and maybe save his life.

She had given him chloroquine for the treatment of his malaria, but it would take at least twenty-four hours before it began to take effect. She hoped that it was not too late and prayed that he did not have the newer drug-resistant strain of malaria. If so, her treatment options were nil. She did *not* want to lose him.

During the night, in the midst of one particularly vicious shaking attack, he had dislodged the splint on his broken leg. This allowed the fractured tibia to move, impinging on the surrounding nerves. His resulting screams shook the cave, echoing and blasting out into the jungle canopy like an explosion. It awakened the entire camp, which turned out to be fortunate, because Margarita needed help restraining him. They had to hold him still while she repositioned and stabilized the leg splint. Aided by the physical strength of three men, she had been able to tend to his leg.

His IVs were another matter. She had to monitor them constantly. His jerks and gyrations wreaked havoc with the needles in his veins, as well as with the IV tubing. The constant flow of saline was even more critical now, because fluid imbalance and dehydration were an early cause of death with falciparum malaria. The other malaria patient had a milder case, probably because he was native to the tropics and had built up resistance. Thank God for that, or her time would not stretch.

The febrile paroxysms were getting worse. James' fits of delirium were compounded by convulsions. Margarita, usually the cool methodical nurse, humming her hymn, was different now- — troubled, intense, almost frantic at times. She was perspiring more, her hair matted to the back of her neck. Her soft brown eyes were blinking and squinting from stinging sweat, her gentle touch now rushed and firm. She was being challenged to the limit of her nursing capabilities. It reminded her of a Saturday night working in the ER at Charity Hospital in New Orleans during her nurses' training— gunshots, straight razor gashes, knifings, wrecks, "the Gladiator Trauma Express," they called it. But, there she was part of an expert team of doctors, nurses, technicians, all professionals; here she was all alone, strictly on her own. She wanted to take time out to kneel down and pray, but there was not a second to waste. She had to somehow abort the spread of the parasites in his blood stream. Otherwise, it would progress to the cerebral malaria stage, which would mean, with her limited supplies in this crude setting, certain death. *Oh, por favor, dear God,* don't let him die. She crossed herself again. She had given him the last dose of chloroquine.

James was shaking. His cot vibrated against the rock floor, making automatic, fluttering sounds. He was hallucinating, groaning, shouting. His disturbance of the other patients would have been a worry to

Margarita, but their sympathy for James prevailed. The two soldiers who had come to her aid with the splint had stayed to help, but they too were helpless in curtailing his rapidly deteriorating condition.

A rally of sympathy and concern had infiltrated the entire camp. They had rescued this *Americano con cajones grande* and their nurse, Margarita, had brought him back to life. In so doing, he had become the hallmark of their courage and bravery. This strange *Americano* with the "Big I" gouged into the flesh on his right hand, who lay wounded, tortured, and dying in the jungle, had been saved for a reason. They thought his gaping "I" wound was an omen from the saints boding good for their cause. The "I," in their minds stood for *"Independistos."* They had been told about his life crisis, his kidnapping, his inhuman torture, the sadistic mutilation he had suffered. Inspired by his fortitude, courage, and escape, they regarded James as a mythical hero. The men would sneak in to see the grotesque wound; invent excuses to see Margarita just to glance at it. Once seen, the sadistic mutilation could not be forgotten They talked about him, his wounds, and especially the proverbial "I" around camp.

Somehow, James T. Cantrill, the involuntary refugee from the corporate ranks of America, had unknowingly and involuntarily become the unqualified recruit of the guerrilla ranks in the remote mountains of Puerto Rico. He had passively become one of them— an unofficial *Indenpendista.* After all, it was their very own, their special nurse, who was so zealously trying to keep him alive. No, they did not want him to die. He was a fighter, just like they were. Were it not so, he would have died days ago in the jungle.

But, his prognosis was bleak. With all the earnestness at her command, Margarita was battling against the most severe type of malaria, which now posed an additional threat to James. He had not responded to the last dose of anti-malaria medicine, nor the aspirin for his raging fever, now 105.1. He was burning hot, hot even to the touch. At this rate, he could not survive. Could there be an additional cause? An infection from his wounds? That would make the fever worse. She had injected more antibiotic, but she was out of those drugs, too. Were there other morbid complications? She had no way of finding out. With no lab, no X-ray, no way to make *any* diagnostic tests, no nothing, her skilled, merciful hands were literally tied behind her back. Her hands were moving now at a breakneck pace, from the IVs to the wet wash cloths on his forehead, the sweat dripping from hers, to his leg splint, to his wound dressings, to the blankets, doing the very best that she could. She was anxiously, feverishly trying to practice medicine...but, without any medicine.

Where was Fernando? Fernando, an old hill peasant, along with his faithful donkey, was their official courier for replacement medical supplies. A devout believer in *Moises,* in the cause and the *Independistos,* he was their virtual supply chain. He was slow but always dependable. He was supposed to have returned yesterday. Even if they were only able to get partial refills, the usual shipment, it would be an improvement. Beggars could not be choosy. She was completely out of chloroquine, with two malaria patients in house, out of gauze for dressings, out of Mycitracin, out of NeoSporin, no antibacterial salve, out of antibiotics, low on aspirin, and down to her last bottle of lactate Ringers and saline. She could *not* function like this. She was frantic.

If James went into a coma, she knew— it would all be over. He would die after she had worked so hard to bring him back to life; die of complications that could have been prevented or, at least, treated. He would die needlessly. All she could do now was pray.

CHAPTER 36

A snake lurks in the grass.

Eclogues
Virgil, 40 B.C.

There were three of them, dressed in army fatigues, black paint under their eyes, armed with automatic rifles, an M-16, an AK-47, and an M-14 for distance. They moved single file through the jungle thicket with calculated precision, even muffling the sounds of their machetes. The steady rain of the last several days had accelerated the lush growth in the rainforest. The bamboo, kapok, calabash, and wild vines were doubly thick, as were the mosquitoes and cucubanos, the local fireflies. These mosquitoes loved rain, human flesh and blood. But, the three men were not phased by the hostile elements. Their hard, muscular bodies were coated with insect repellent, among other things, to ward off small attackers. They were totally prepared for their mission, which involved larger prey. Experienced in guerrilla warfare, skilled in jungle maneuvers, they *lived* by the law of the jungle. Their full combat gear did not weigh them down; their eyes were focused like a hawk's, surveying the entire landscape, yet able to detect the slightest unfriendly movement. Hired to do a job, they were assassins, men who killed for money. Their current mission— kill one American, a James T. Cantrill, and dispose of the body. The orders came from the top as a "DP," a "demand-performance" contract— to execute clean with no trace. In other words, it meant that failure was *not* acceptable. No excuses. If there was any screw-up, any degree of failure, contracts would immediately be let on the three of them, individually, as well as collectively. They understood that. That was their business; they were the ace assassins-for-hire in the world. And the higher the "DP," the higher the pay, just the way they liked it.

As they ascended through the undergrowth, a snake, the very poisonous fer-de-lance, dropped from a Sierra palm. Before it hit the ground to coil and strike, the lead man had drawn his Bowie knife, and in a single stroke, severed its head with fangs bared. The rest of its five foot body flailed and twisted away, trying to fight off the pangs of death. The entire action had taken place in less than thirty seconds. The snake killer was nicknamed "Scap," short for scalpel, due to his skill with a knife. Scap could throw a knife and hit his mark with bull's-eye precision from over fifty feet.

Further up the overgrown trail, at the mountain, they intercepted Fernando and his packed burro. Fernando was knocked to the ground, then interrogated by the snake killer, who also spoke Spanish. He would not reply. His loyalty to *Moises* and the *Independistos* was supreme. But, that loyalty and devotion had never been challenged in this manner.

"Donde esta el Americano?" he was asked.

And, again, Fernando would not answer, staring back at him defiantly.

The snake killer took his the long knife and savagely amputated Fernando's right thumb. His shrieks pierced the dense jungle canopy.

"Donde esta?" he was again asked, this time louder.

Fernando was still uncooperative and did not answer, hollering as he squeezed his right wrist with his other hand.

In a split second, Fernando's left hand was grabbed by the snake killer while the other two henchmen restrained him. Next, his left thumb was sawed off with the long, serrated knife. Fernando's screams rang out through the rainforest. He collapsed with two streams of blood gushing out from each hand. The mountain ferns and all of the rich surrounding flora were quickly changed from a verdant green to a crimson red.

The two *compadres* of the snake killer were unmoved.

"Donde esta!"

When Fernando did not answer, the snake killer very calmly and deliberately sliced off Fernando's left ear. Fernando immediately lunged. He reached for the left side of his head with his hands, splattering his face and body with the blood surging from his wounds. His diminutive, once strong body had become a mass of blood and gore.

With his courage depleted, shock rapidly approaching, Fernando finally gave in. Weak from the loss of blood, he reluctantly told them about the *Americano* in the cave, and its general location, pointing towards it with his right hand as it shot off a gush of blood in that direction.

The interrogator rewarded his subject. He slit his throat.

Fernando's trusted donkey, its throat slit, was pushed off a cliff, braying and bleating as it fell careening down into the valley below. The IV solutions in its backpack burst and splashed on the jagged rocks.

Fernando's bloody body was then tossed over the cliff. When it bounced off the ledge, the precious vials of chloroquine in his pocket broke, diluting the red-stained rock

Without a saying a word, the assassins proceeded up the path.

As night fell, they continued moving forward quietly. Not at all impeded by the cover of darkness, they instead used it to facilitate their approach. They came upon the proximity of the cave with confidence, as if guided by a map. With their night-vision goggles, they scoped out the perimeter. The *Independistos'* camp was about a hundred meters to the north. They estimated that there were about 250 guerrillas there with three sentries posted for look-out. The cave had no guard posted. Ideally, they thought that they would enter the cave, kill the *Americano* without a sound, along with the other occupants. They thought that they would accomplish their objective successfully without engaging any of the soldiers and be gone well before daylight.

With cold precision and rehearsed hand signals, they mapped out their strategy. As in effective tactical planning, the professionals also made contingency plans— Plan B and Plan C, should Plan A fail, including alternative escape routes.

The cave had three possible approaches— one from above, but the top would require rope and rappelling gear, one to the north, and one south. The entrance from the north led directly to the path to the guerrillas' camp. The three assassins chose to enter from the south.

They rechecked their automatic rifles but hoped they would not have to fire a shot. One would stand guard at the north entrance, the other two would enter the cave. According to the plan, Scap would go first and would do the dirty work with his knives, if at all possible, capitalizing on three of the assassins' favorite allies: surprise, silence, and darkness. All of their signals, both manual and auditory, were well known and rehearsed.

As the two entered the cave, the rancid odor of bat urine penetrated their nostrils. Creeping in the pitch black dark, with their goggles in place, they could see an unlit lantern on a banana crate. They could make out two cots with forms sleeping on them, their snoring amplified by the roof of the cave. They waited.

With stealth perfection, Scap and his associate advanced to the cots. They quickly slit each person's throat without a sound, muffling the gasps from their mouths.

Scap's partner tripped on a loose rock, which crashed against the wall, echoing loudly in the cave. The third assassin on look-out heard the sound and rushed in.

Margarita, sleeping back in one of the tunnels, was awakened by the noise. She drowsily rose to see what was the going on.

Her entrance from the back of the cave startled the assassins. The assassin at the entrance turned his rifle in her direction and fired in the semi-darkness. The rounds ricocheted off the rock walls. The sounds from the gunshots exploded from the mouth of the cave

One round hit Margarita. She screamed and fell.

Her scream reverberated from the cave, catapulting outward, penetrating the darkness.

Those who heard it in the camp recognized the unmistakable female cry from one of their own, the sister of their leader. The others were roused and rushed to get ready for attack.

The Major, always at the ready, was already awake, up and about, preparing for maneuvers before daylight. In a blink he was down the path, his night-vision goggles on, running as fast as he could, his limp hardly slowing him down. He held his M-16 in the firing position, the mode selector switch on the three-round-burst mode. When he saw the look-out standing outside the north entrance to the cave, he slowed, aimed, and fired, killing him instantly.

Arriving at the north entrance, he pulled up, stopped to catch his breath a minute, and stood with his back flat against the mossy rock wall. He rechecked the selector on his rifle leaving it in the three-burst mode and reset the clip. It was still pitch-black dark, the coquis going into their final chants before dawn. Knowing that it would be even darker inside, he checked the laser on his rifle, readjusted his goggles, squatted, and dropped to his knees, expecting the unfriendlies within to aim high. He threw a branch toward the south entrance to draw their attention, and hopefully their gunfire. Their response was immediate, the volley zinging sparks off the craggy rocks. He surmised that there must be two, maybe three, armed assailants. Waiting on his troops might further endanger Margarita, James, and the other two soldiers in the infirmary...if they were still alive.

He dropped down to his elbows and quickly belly-crawled into the cave. The first assailant was on the left. The Major took him out with one three-round-burst. The echo from the blast was deafening. The flash from his muzzle gave away his location on the rock floor.

Scap saw the Major, but his aim was deflected by the movement of his accomplice who rolled over from the impact. Scap's gunfire went off target, ricocheted, but one round hit the Major in the right shoulder. The snake killer was much more proficient with a knife than a rifle. Major Henry spontaneously returned the fire, getting off two bursts, hitting the snake killer squarely in his chest with both.

Scap half shouted, half gasped as he went down, dying as he had lived, in devout disbelief. Reinforcements from the camp had arrived, flanking the entrance to the cave in twos. Suddenly troops spilled over the proximity.

The Major had raised himself to a sitting position, but was bleeding profusely from his wound.

"We're clear here! Check the tunnels and the perimeter!" he commanded with some duress.

"Find Margarita and James," he shouted in Spanish. As he turned to brace himself he saw Margarita, prostrate, leaning against the far wall in a pool of blood.

"Margarita! Margarita," he called.

"*Si*. Okay. . ." she meekly answered, in her broken English.

Major Henry started to crawl over to where Margarita lay.

"Major, you should not move. You are losing a lot of blood. Here, let me see. Where is the wound?" asked Margarita, despite the pool of her own blood.

The Major saw the pool of blood around Margarita and immediately called for help. As daylight shone through the cave entrance, the cave was illuminated in shadow-framing light. For the first time, he noticed the vast bloody mural painted on the grayish-white rock floor and walls—blood in separate pools moving and weaving on the irregular, undulating surface like eddies swirling at high tide, each a different hue, the burnt umber, brownish drying blood underneath his two soldiers on the cots, the caking vermillion expanding around the three dead assassins, the gentle pool under Margarita, and the crimson red pouring out of his upper torso, saturating his fatigue shirt and vest red— the red blood of a genuine red-blooded American. It was a shocking site, distinctly different from those to which he had grown so accustomed— in Korea, in the killing fields of Viet Nam, red-stained rivers and rice patties, gore in villages, carnage in the jungles, massacre at every level of human wreckage. But, this blood was different, not that he was that appalled at the sight of his own blood which he had seen spilled on more than one occasion; no, this blood on a flat, rocky white surface seemed so much more profuse.

His adrenaline rush was fading, his hemoglobin diluted, his energy weakened, the bleeding taking its toll. He became dizzy, his vision blurred. The pools of blood began to run together, forming a rock-bottom red sea.

"Oh, God. . .where are You?" he asked, growing weaker by the second.

His head fell on his left arm. Blood from the bullet wound drenched his fatigues.

He passed out.

Margarita grew fainter by the moment.

CHAPTER 37

The telephone rang with a muted, low-pitched ring.

"Yeah," the gravelly voice answered.

"Line clear?" the raspy voice asked.

"Affirmative."

"Code 103. Stop. Code 103. Stop. G-5, YankeeAlphaNavaho739TangoCharlie," the raspy voice commanded.

There was a pause.

"Code 103? A G-5?"

"Affirmative."

"Check. Reason?" the gravelly voice asked.

"InterPol. InterPol now involved. InterPol inquiry," another pause, "Interpol inquiry triggered internal investigation. Must neutralize immediately. Cancel. Neutralize now. Period. Understood?"

"Check. Understood."

"Subject?"

"No report, yet."

"When?"

"By 17 hundred, tomorrow."

"Check."

"Code 103. Urgent."

"Check."

"Ditto?"

"Ditto." Click.

Click.

CHAPTER 38

Nothing so needs reforming as other people's habits.
Pudd'nhead Wilson, 1894
Mark Twain

When Trish dialed her daughter's office in Austin from the pay phone, she was still coughing violently. She had gone into Kroger's and bought herself a pack of menthol Doral cigarettes. Having asked for matches, she was given a book advertising Winston. Her father smoked that brand. He died of cancer. Was that ominous or what? Or just to serve up more guilt? But, she thought, *the hell with it. I need a cigarette.*

She had not waited to get back to her car to light up... in spite of her mother. She knew that it was considered improper for a lady to smoke while walking in public. Her mother would have killed her.

She stopped in the parking lot, pulled a filtered cigarette out of the pack, stuck it in her mouth, struck a match, and put the flame to it. The carbon from the match burned her nostrils. Then, taking a huge drag, she inhaled, sucking it clear down to her toes. Her reaction was unexpected. She coughed so hard that her eyeballs felt like they were blown out of their sockets. The force of the heave bent her almost double from the waste down, causing her to drop the cigarettes and matches. She was retching so hard that it took her four tries to get the key in the car door to unlock it. Awful, just awful. Was this what she had been craving so voraciously the last few days? Craving off and on for years? She was coughing so fitfully that she could not take another drag. She flicked the cigarette out on the parking lot; then, as an anti-litterbug, felt another pang of guilt. At least she still remembered how to flick it, before the era of political correctness and social hypochondria.

Her curiosity peaked between coughing spasms. Not actually the right word, it was more concern than curiosity. What else could go wrong? Why this sudden need for secrecy? From Ann? From Ann way the hell out in Texas?

She was still coughing when Anne answered the phone.

"Are you sick, Mom?"

"I just strangled on my iced tea. Why did you want me to call you from a pay phone?"

"Wait, Mom, before I explain, I want you to hang up. I'm going to call you right back. Give me the number on the pay phone."

What on earth is going on? Trish thought.

Trish just stood there in the heat, shaking her head. The maturing spring sun beamed down on the hot asphalt parking lot in the Lansdowne Shopping Center. Birds sang from the tree line behind the shopping center.

She picked up the phone on the first ring.

"Anne, just what in the hell is going on?" Trish questioned the daughter who had always been possessed with a blithe spirit and a penchant for improvisation.

"Okay, Mom, now I can explain it to you. We had to use a pay phone for complete privacy. I had you hang up so I could call you back after activating the scrambler here in our office. We have a digital encryption system we have to use sometimes on confidential legal matters," she talked faster than usual, "some of the megadeals that we represent. I can't emphasize the privacy aspect of this conversation too much, Mom."

"Okay, Ann. Okay. I get it!" her mother interrupted, losing patience, burning up standing there. "What is it!"

"All right, Mom. But, understand, what I'm going to tell you, you cannot tell anyone. And, you have to act like you never heard it. Okay?

"Okay, okay, Ann. I'm your mother! If you can't trust me, we are both in *big* trouble. Now, for crying out loud, tell me. I can't stand it!"

"All right. It's about Dad. He's alive."

"Wha. . ." Before she could utter the word, Trish's heart stopped. Her tobacco breath was sucked out of her, her throat constricted, her mouth parched. She was not expecting this. It was like she had been hit by a boulder and flattened on the hot asphalt. She was so dumbfounded that she could not express herself, her feelings suspended in the hot air of the phone booth.

"Mom, are you still there? Mom?"

Trish still could not speak. She was so overwhelmed with shock and disbelief— a part of her had reluctantly accepted the reality that James was dead, but another part held on to hope, refusing to believe that he had been killed. Conflicting emotions streamed through her like a swollen river— awe, denial, surprise, excitement, doubt, jubilation, love, thankfulness, gratitude— a profusion of passions hitting her all at once. Dumbstruck, she braced herself against the booth's clear plastic wall.

"Mom? Mom? I know this comes as a shock. Just like it was to me. . .Mom?"

"Oh, Ann. . ." and she began to cry again.

"I know, Mom. He's alive. Dad *is* really alive. Dad is still alive," Ann assured, joining her mother in tears.

"How do you know?" she muttered, wiping away the tears of joy.

"It's the strangest thing, Mom. I got this call from our office in El Paso, from a person I didn't know, a Mr. Gutierrez. I only know two people that work in our El Paso office, and this was not one of them. He first identified himself, and, said for the sake of protection, the conversation had to be private, and remain confidential. I answered that I was a professional associated with the same firm, thinking that it involved one of the big NAFTA deals or developments that we handle. Then, he asked me a question that blew me away: did I know someone named *Padre?* Well, my heart stopped, too, Mom. I swallowed so hard, I almost swallowed the telephone receiver and peed in my pants at the same time," said she, the daughter who was always given to graphic descriptions.

"After I finally said 'yes,' he told me that he had some information for me regarding *Padre,* emphasizing the secrecy again. And, moreover, that I could only share the conversation with one person, my mother. Then, he repeated that you were to be the only other contact, that to violate that strict privacy would jeopardize not only the life of the man called *Padre,* but also those protecting him. Of course, I agreed. He said the information had come from one of their trusted sources in Mexico; that he, as a native Mexican, current Texas resident, U.S. citizen, and attorney licensed by the Texas Bar, was to treat the information as client privilege, assuring them of that fact, and act as a proprietary conduit, with only one exclusive contact, in the Austin office, namely me." Ann, who was also very loquacious, was on a roll. "Are you with me so far, Mom?"

"Yes, yes, go on. Is Dad in Mexico?"

"No. He's in Puerto Rico. According to Mr. Gutierrez, he was kidnapped, then flown to Puerto Rico. And, Mom, brace yourself. . . Mom, they say he was tortured. . ."

"Oh, my God! No! Tortured?" Trish slammed the booth with her right hand.

"Mom, I am just relating what I was told. Let me finish. Yes, he was brutally tortured. He's not in good shape now, but, he is alive. And he is safe. And, *that, his* safety, as well as the safety of his rescuers, who are protecting and caring for him right now, those are the ones *whom we must* protect, *his* safety, and theirs. Let me go on with the story. After being tortured. . ."

"Oh, my God! Tortured? I bet I know who did it!" She held the phone away from her ear, yelling into it.

"Wait, Mom. Just a minute. Let me tell you the whole story. After being tortured, Dad escaped. He was rescued up in the mountains, in the rain forest, in this jungle high in Puerto Rico, by a band of guerrillas, this army of insurgents called the *Independistos.* Listen to this, I was sworn to say that word only once, and make you swear that you would never repeat it, okay? They are a growing movement, a strong force in Puerto Rico leading the movement to secede from the United States and proclaim Puerto Rico's independence. Hence, their demand, their absolute demand for our sworn oath of privacy."

"Oh, my. I don't believe it! Tortured? How bad off is he?"

"Mom, I don't know. Mr. Gutierrez did not give details, just that he was in, quote 'bad shape, meaning there were life threatening injuries.' Let me finish, Mom. He said that he was being taken care of, that they had, quote, 'some medical care,' and that, it was going to take time for him to recover, *but* that he would recover." A car horn blared from the street.

"You cannot tell *anyone! Not* even Kathleen or Christy. . ."

"But, I *must* tell your sisters, Trish. . ."

"No, Mom! You can't. Neither you or I can breathe a *word . . . not* to anyone. If the FBI finds out, they will automatically send investigators, and, you see, that is the last thing *we* want. Whether these guerrillas are illegal, rebels, insurgents, or whatever, makes no difference to us. Because, they are the ones who rescued Dad. And are caring for Dad, protecting him from those torturers. And we *must protect* them. Understand, Mom?"

"Yes, yes, I think so. God bless them for saving him. Who kidnapped him? Like I said, I bet I know. Did they say who it was? Who it was that tortured him? Oh, how horrible!"

Ann repeated the need to never say the "I-word," with phone taps, satellites, Big Brother listening, etc. She briefly described the Puerto Rican leader, the risk taken in rescuing and caring for her father and the bigger risk in letting us know that Dad's alive and safe.

"Well, thank God for him. He saved our. . .What's his name?"

"I asked the same question. He would not say. Said it better for us not to know at this time."

"Why can't I tell your sisters? They wouldn't say anything," Trish asked.

"I asked that question, too, Mom. The FBI is living in your home, twenty-four hours a day. They hear everything in your house. The phone calls are monitored. Everything. They would detect a difference in how you are behaving, particularly around your children. The FBI agents could and would perceive a difference in you. In your attitude. Okay?"

". . . okay. I understand," wondering how she would do it.

"Mr. Gutierrez said he would elaborate further on the next advisement."

"When will that be?" Trish asked.

"He said to not ask any more questions, not get antsy. That secrecy, the utmost in secrecy, and being cool were absolutely critical. That he would make contact when it was time. Understand, Mom?"

"I guess. It's so much. To be thankful for. . .to uh. . ..think about. I'm just overwhelmed," she replied.

"I know that it comes as quite a jolt to you, Mom. It hit me, too. But, I've had a little more time than you to digest and adjust. I'm so happy. I am just so glad, about Dad. . ." her voice broke.

"Oh, me too, Hon. Thank God. Just thank God he's alive. . ."

"Remember, Mom, I will be calling you at home tonight just like always, like we have not talked since last night. Okay? Not a word, not a hint about this. If you need to talk, you must call me from a different pay phone each time here at my office. Then, I'll call you back. Remember, we are dealing with professional assassins— *assassins! That* was the word that Mr. Gutierrez used."

The term "assassins" started Trish's mind racing with thoughts of vengeance. How dare they! These damn kidnappers, damn torturers, damned assassins, how dare they do that to her husband!

"Well, I love ya, Mom."

"I love you, too, Angel. And thanks. Thanks so much. . ."

They both hung up.

As Trish stepped out of the phone booth and looked around the parking lot of the shopping center, her mind was darting in all directions. She was surrounded by activity. People were parking, going in and out of the stores, busily moving about with their daily routines. She got in her car, the pack of cigarettes on the car seat. Her craving for them had departed, but her cough had not. She coughed, took a deep breath, putting both hands on the steering wheel. And, right then and there, Trish said a fervent prayer, thanking God that her husband was still alive. And that she was alive. She made a solemn vow to herself to live— to live one day at a time to see this through. To live one day at a time until she was reunited with her husband, until they could be together again. . .

But, how was she going to pull this off? How was she going to act out the part in her home? In front of Kathleen and Christy? She had never been much of an actress. Never liked it. And the FBI? She could barely go to the bathroom in privacy. Would they detect a change in her? This was not going to be easy.

Normal. Act normal? What *was* normal? With the enormity of the good news, how on earth could she ever act like things were normal? When she couldn't remember what a normal life was like?

She started her car, coughed again, and turned on the radio to her favorite oldies station.

It began playing "*Til.*" She could not believe it. It had been one of their songs. . .she and James had danced to it many times—

"Til the moon deserts the sky
til all the seas run dry,
til you're back in my arms again. . .

The memories inundated her.

And, she began to weep again.

PART IV

RENAISSANCE

"We are often troubled, but not crushed;
sometimes in doubt, but never in despair;
there are many enemies, but we are never without a friend;
and though badly hurt at times, we are not destroyed.
2 Corinthians 4:8-9 (*TEV*)

CHAPTER 39

For when I am weak,
then I am strong.
2 Corinthians 12:10 (NIV)

James awoke suddenly, in a state of anxiety, not knowing exactly where he was. The fact that this had become a habit did not make it any less disconcerting. He was no longer in the cave. It was daylight and hot. The camouflage netting was again suspended overhead, but lower than in the original infirmary. He felt different, weak, giddy. He noticed that Margarita was thankfully close by, asleep on the cot adjacent to his. He looked around and was shocked by what he saw. His eyes locked with those of his friend, the Major, who was lying on another cot in the infirmary.

"Well, looka here, *amigo!* And how *are* ya?" the Major asked.

"Fine," James answered. "What are you doing here? And where are we?"

The Major went on to vaguely explain what had happened— that they had had an attack; they had to move the camp and the infirmary along with it; that he, himself, had been wounded, "just a flesh wound in the shoulder, nothing to it;" that the only reason he was here was because of Margarita and "these damn IVs;" that Margarita had a minor wound from a round that ricocheted, but it was superficial, too, it had grazed her "left bun, uh, her left buttock," which only caused her a slight problem walking, a real problem sitting; that *Moises* had *made* her lie down and take it easy; that, all total, the casualties were minor, that they had handled the attack well, which complimented the Major, meaning his training with the troops was working; that they had just needed to relocate the camp to be on the safe side. No big deal. Not a problem. The main problem — " was *you*."

"What do you mean?" James asked.

"Damn, man. Keeping you alive! You had malaria, the worst kind, Margarita said. You were sick, bad sick— rigors, delirious...shouting, screaming. You scared the hell outta all of us. We were really worried about ya. Margarita was worried sick. We thought we'd lost ya. And might have if *Moises* hadn't miraculously come through with medical supplies. Margarita was out of stuff, including malaria medicine. Once she got it, she hit you with everything she had. . . and, last night your fever broke. I mean, the camp was praying for ya. They didn't want to lose their *Americano con cojones grande!*" he let go with another bolt of his obstreperous laughter. "You've come to be mean a lot to the troops— with your sudden arrival on the scene, scars, survival and all. . . you're kinda a mythical hero. Though most of these guys were brought up Catholic, they still hold on to some ol' island voodoo. That 'I's' an omen," he laughed, pointing to James' gaping wound.

Margarita was up now tending to James, adjusting his splints, his IVs, his dressings. He tried to ask her about her wound, to tell her how sorry he was, to sympathize with her, but she would not hear of it. She brought him some fresh-squeezed orange juice. It was the most delicious thing he had ever tasted— full of pulp, a bracing, pungent scent, like an orange fresh plucked from the tree. He drank three big mugs of it.

James felt a sudden surge of energy, like a slug of Old Forester in his youth, a rush of invigoration, something totally foreign to his body lately. It was like a youthful, spring day, like every breath was fresh and crisp, like being born again. He felt life flowing through his veins, thoughts flowing through his brain, positive thoughts, intuitive thoughts for a change. Still weak, the pain still there, but feeling great— buoyantly charmed with being alive. Alive!

Was this wave of rejuvenation due to orange juice? Vitamin C? No wonder Sam, his son-in-law, loved OJ, drank it all the time; never drank coffee, or soda, just orange juice.

Futhermore, adding to his rising nature, he noticed that Margarita had just washed her hair, which shone like wet onyx flowing over her shoulders. When she leaned over him, it grazed his flesh, tickling, feeling good. Captivated by a sophomoric enthusiasm, he was invigorated by other sensations previously dormant. Here she was administering to his infirmities, literally saving his life, and he was having lewd, lascivious thoughts all the while. It was similar to a fax— once it started, it couldn't be stopped. Once the visual and tactile image had stimulated his thought, there was no way he could stop it. He could disapprove of his thoughts, he tried to disavow them, but he could not prevent himself from having them. Did this mean he was human? With raw animal instincts? That he was returning to the human race with male libido intact? His thoughts were zooming. . .

"Well, I gotta go, good Buddy," the Major chanted, interrupting James' libidinous reverie, thank God, because it was proliferating. And he was feeling guilty.

Margarita tried to stop the wounded drill instructor from going anywhere. The Major resisted, assuring her that he was only going to supervise maneuvers, not physically participate. He promised her that he would take it easy. She then admonished him sternly in Spanish, adjusting his arm sling, tightening the strap.

James just could not believe how good he was feeling. Margarita cautioned him, repeating over and over in her broken English, to take it easy, "take it easy," that he had been very sick, and should rest. Then, she resumed humming her hymn.

What on earth is the name of that hymn? James asked himself again. Nonetheless, his brain, his gray matter, all of his thought processes were getting untracked, flourishing, he deemed, with furtive, poignant perspicacity.

Margarita offered the newspapers that *Moises* had brought to him. James was thrilled and relished the fact that he could actually read a real newspaper again.

As he read *The San Juan Star,* there were headlines everywhere in the newspaper announcing layoffs. It immediately brought back the pain of his own job loss, like it had happened just seconds ago— he looked up at the date— it had been over three months since that fateful Friday. *Damn.* It provoked him to reflect inwardly on his experience, as well as that of all his peers who were involuntarily retired. He felt for all those people. *All those layoffs— human lives reduced to numbers on newsprint.*

And every single, solitary one of the layoffs was a human life, an individual, just like me, men and women with families, experiencing all that pain, that despair, that immeasurable violation of self and self-worth, that state of feeling listless and worthless, that deep-down, excruciating pain that will probably not ever go away.

Moises came in and seemed genuinely elated that James was better. "You gave us a scare, my friend. You look like a different man, now. How do you like the *San Juan Star?*" he asked.

"It's great, thanks. Nice being able to read again. But, I can't believe all these layoffs," James replied.

"Terrible. And they're getting worse. Hard for corporations to resist when their stock price rises after the announcement."

"I know. And nobody cares— 'you lost your job. Too bad. So what?' Most people just don't care. Death and taxes, quota and job loss. . . in that order," James laughed, though he didn't think it funny.

"Yes, it's tragic. I told you about my brother in Spain. His situation, and these headlines bring back memories of case studies during my MBA. The objective of corporate downsizing is cost reduction; the unit of currency in corporate downsizing, the 'bought-and-paid-for-with,' is the employee— the individual, a human being, one human life. A life filling the space called 'job.' Simply put, it's eliminating jobs to save money, cutting payroll by eliminating employees, individuals, real live human beings, just to save money, " *Moises* sat down on his sister's cot. "Am I boring you? Is this too much?" he asked.

"Oh, no. I agree. This is great, keep on," James reassured.

"The company downsizes, announces the layoffs with sterile language, in their contrived corporate jargon— downsizing, rightsizing, restructuring, cutting. . .you've heard them all. . . reducing, slashing, dejobbing, delayering, each word so sterile, so impersonal, so specious— the headlines hit the newspaper, and, their stock goes up," *Moises* continued, his enthusiasm framed by his white teeth. "The company wins, the stockholders win, and the workers lose. But, no one cares about the poor worker whose life has been destroyed. Why? Because everyone else is happy. The stock has gone up, the stockholders are wealthier."

He *is* articulate, brilliant, James thought.

"The economists say that productivity has been increased, efficiency enhanced. And, the miserable workers are but a statistic, a statistic left in the wake of strategic process. . ."

"Yeah, they're just a number," James injected. "Nothing but a number, drowning in their own sorrow."

"Downsizing impacts so many lives, not only affecting those who are the casualties, but also the survivors, those who had survived the cut. Though they are still employed, they felt their trust, their loyalty, and commitment had been violated, and especially their sense of security. They feared for their own jobs, just waiting for the next shoe to drop. I can't think of the company in the case study," *Moises* paused. "The after-effect was far worse than they had estimated. The laid-off worker was decimated in the workplace, the corporation is praised in the marketplace, the stock market applauds the strategy, and the stockholder grows richer, some major stockholders, much, much richer. Meanwhile the worker and his/her family languish. The worker, the employee who used to be regarded by his company as an asset, finds himself now regarded as a cost, an inhuman entry on the spreadsheet, a cost to be eliminated. The *ex*-employee and his entire family are left to suffer interminably. My brother was just devastated. . .as you can understand. . ."

"Exactly," James said, wondering out loud, "Is there something wrong here? Is there something missing in the workplace? Is something missing in a society that not only condones downsizing, but promotes it often heartlessly? You betcha'! Something's missing. Like my ol' history prof, Dr. Clark, used to say, 'it's the *sense of community!* The sense of community. The major thing that society lacks today, that most people lack today is the deep-seated sense of community. Community means belonging, caring, compassion, continuity; community carries with it an unwritten, unspoken sense of security; community necessitates and nurtures sharing. Community combines the past, the present, and the future. It congeals the past with the future via the present; it welds the present to the existence of the soul. Community is the melting pot of people and principles, family and family values, church and spirituality, life and legacy,' I can still hear him." James considered himself so fortunate to have benefitted from such a wise statesman.

What would Dr. Clark, age 98, say today about corporate downsizing and the waves of workers with disrupted lives?

"Reminds me of a special prof I had at Harvard. Funny how some teachers influenced our lives permanently."

Bursts of gunfire sounded. *Moises* didn't even flinch. One volley answered by another, then another. Silence. Then, the rounds started again. The Major was back on the job, back in the trenches with his troops.

"Well, I've got to go. . ." *Moises* stood up.

"Wait," James said, "I want to thank you. Thank you again. . . for everything. Including the medicine."

"You're very welcome, my friend. Enjoyed talking to you. Just keep getting better." And, after paying his respects to the others in the infirmary, *Moises* left, giving his sister a pat on the way out.

Then, James thoughts continued. He couldn't help it. Loyal workers are shipwrecked on the island of disrupted dreams and desperation, the island of despair. Human beings are shipwrecked on this island. And the island is built of human wreckage— just like an island in the South Pacific after an attack, or an air raid during World War II, strewn and littered with human wreckage— except this island of human wreckage is constructed by the modern-day war of corporate attrition. But, he, thank God had his own human wreckage gratuitously rescued on this tropical island.

Then, James thought about the poor farmer who died— Ezra Jenkins, that wonderful old man, Ezra Nehemiah Jenkins, the hard-working farmer, the literal salt of the earth, who died before his time, died needlessly, mostly because of *his* company. *Damnit!* Because of Werner's defective hip component. And that bad bone cement. Both precipitated an avalanche of lethal side-effects from which Ezra could not recover. Was there a remote possibility that he could have been saved? If circumstances had been better within the hospital? Minus all the managed care crap?—Cost containment, staff cutbacks, economizing on vital patient needs and services, a nurse anesthetist with no anesthesiologist back-up, buying the cheapest medical supplies, sub-par quality control in manufacturing surgical products, out-of-spec products sold, medical/ hospital/ healthcare cost containment— all in the name of managed care.

And, speaking of sub-par quality control with implants, and poor Ezra Jenkins, he could not help going back again to that PDL hip component, it was never far from his mind — and Werner's plant here in Caguas. Could it have been manufactured in Puerto Rico? He knew some Total Hips were. Was there a connection? He *had* to find out. He really hoped that *Moises* had contacts there.

Total Hips, profit margins, cutbacks, managed care...another definition hit him. Another objective defined itself in a salient thought— "likewise, the objective of managed care is also cost reduction; the unit of currency, the 'bought-and-paid-for-with' is the patient, the individual, a human being, another human life.

With both corporate downsizing and managed care, the bottom line is cash and on the opposite side of the ledger, the bottom line is a life. Instead of the old double-entry accounting ledger where

Credit = Debit

the newly 'downsized' accounting ledger, the newly 'restructured' formula for profit was:

Cash Flow = Workers' Woe

Whether employee or patient, the unit of currency, the means of exchange, the 'bought-and-paid-for-with,' the counterbalancing factor, the debit on the ledger is an individual, a human being— one human life that can be negatively, irreversibly impacted forever.

Hence, we have two heartless institutions. Whether corporate or healthcare, both are institutions with no heart and with no soul. They have taken the employee and the patient and dehumanized them as cost, as monetary units—units of currency that they can easily eliminate. With a simple keystroke to the spreadsheet—hitting the delete button—they, these human units of currency, are totally eliminated. These heartless, soul-less institutions could care less that they are human beings...with real lives...with real families.

How tragic— lives in the balance. The corporate ledger of downsized lives.

A brown lizard running on the netting distracted James, but his mind was on a roll.

Globalization *is* now a reality— the technology revolution, creating new jobs, and eliminating others, all the great advancements of the 21st century— a monumental sea change in the marketplace. But, at what price? Without a doubt, the progress has been phenomenal; and he realized that progress usually carried a price. He remembered Joseph Schumpeter's economic theory of "creative destruction." He wished he had brought it up talking to *Moises*. Examples abound— the horse buggy replaced by the automobile, the candle by the light bulb, the #9 washtub by the washing machine, the mule and plow by the tractor, the typewriter by the word processor, etc., etc.

A little brown-spotted lizard darted across James' cot.

Granted, each object that was creatively destroyed was replaced by something better. But, what price did the wave of corporate downsizing and managed care exact? Or, rather, extract? What were they creatively destroying for the sake of progress? Were corporate downsizing and managed care really progress? Or were they simply a process? A process of cost reduction? Corporate restructuring, corporate downsizing, healthcare cutbacks, managed care— for the purpose of cost reduction, cost containment. But, at what cost? *The cost, the* unit of currency was easy to explain— it was, it is in the body of workers, employees, patients, individuals, human capital, expressly, human beings, human lives! Were they the sacrificial lambs? Are they the sacrificial lambs? Margarita was taking his pulse.

But, James' mind rolled on. The sacrificial lambs creatively destroyed in the temples of cost reduction? Are lives being sacrificed at the altar of corporate downsizing and managed care? The altar of profit enhancement and competitiveness? At the altar of corporate survival? What *is* the cost of one human life? What *is* the value of one human life? How productive, how competitive is a society when its constituents are being dispossessed of their very own sense of self worth? What are the cultural values of a society when compassion is being compromised by cost and competition? What *is* the cost of wrecking one human life? What *is* the total cost *of human wreckage?"*

In profound amazement, his thought repeated itself, *Just what is the gross cost of human wreckage?*

Speaking of human wreckage, he looked down and surveyed his own body, the gory gashes. He had lost his business and his job, he had been kidnapped, tortured, his flesh mutilated, his immune system threatened by malicious injury and most recently, the malaria, his bones broken. He was a mess, a maimed, mangled mess. But, by the grace of God, his spirit was *not* broken. Nor his faith. Nor his hope.

And Margarita just brought him another mug of fresh squeezed orange juice which reminded him of Trish.

Aw, Trish…Trish…how I miss you. Oh, Trish…honey…
…from Puerto Rico with love…

CHAPTER 40

To rest upon a formula is a slumber,
that prolonged, means death.
Oliver Wendell Holmes

Interpol! For Christ's sake. . .

Walter Kagan had taken off in his new Gulfstream V jet at 6:25 P.M., which was 12:25A.M. at his destination, Brussels, Belgium. His ETA was 8:45 A.M. tomorrow morning and flying at over six hundred mph would put him there in record time. Good. Expedition was the order of the day, the urgent order of the moment. He loved his new corporate jet. It was the only uplifting, positive environment he had entered in two days.

His sudden departure was indeed an emergency. The disaster at Werner, Inc., had grown worse, if that could be possible. Adding inflammable insult to injury just today, Interpol had entered the scene. Interpol. *Interpol,* for *God's sake!* Interpol, the international police force, had called on him at headquarters! Had made an official call on him, Walter Kagan, CEO of one the world's largest pharmaceutical companies, asking him questions that he could not answer, questions implying criminal wanton endangerment, extortion, money wire transfers, kidnapping. *Jesus Christ!*

That on top of the Inspector General from the FDA, making unannounced, official calls on Werner in Warsaw, then on Rob Hempstead in their headquarters in New York City. The absolute kiss of death. How had Rob been so blind? How in hell could he have allowed this intolerable situation to occur, much less worsen during his supervision?

Furthermore, there was the issue of possible product liability at Werner— the incident in surgery with the total hip, after which the patient died. *Oh, Christ!* And, as if all of that were not enough, there was the matter of the wrongfully terminated Werner distributor, who had intimate knowledge of the quality rejections on the total hip prosthesis associated with that patient's death. This was a grave threat. *How insane.* To terminate a distributor, a proven long-term distributor, who possessed culpable information? Information that demanded further investigation. And containment. *Idiotic.* If one tidbit, just one tiny tidbit of any of this was made public, it would cause Brecken-Mersack Strauss formidable problems.

Hell, the fallout from this could be so severe— he didn't want to think about it. He would *not* allow it. He *must* prevent it. At all costs. He had to get to the bottom of whatever in the *hell* was going on. He couldn't get to Brussels fast enough.

Leaning his head back against the soft black, Argentinean calf's leather seat, he closed his eyes, took a big sip of his Bombay gin martini, and began to reflect. And commiserate. Things had been going so well, extremely well with their core pharmaceutical businesses. And, then this shit with Werner has to happen. There was a total confusion of constituency within Werner. The key intimate distributor/customer, long-term relationships, which had grown and nurtured good will, those dynamic, established franchises were being undermined by self-appointed despots. Some of this info he had gleaned from Rob Hempstead's reports, but most of it he had gained himself from his inside sources. How could Rob, his friend, whom he had respected, have allowed these selfish egos, these self-defeating agendas, all these deprecating conditions to develop, much less worsen? Rob had been such a capable executive. How had he let this go on for so long? Had he been seduced by their endemic, pernicious denial? It had happened before— executives losing their focus, losing their balance, their objectivity. Had he rationalized the extent of the damage? Had he been seduced by his own false hopes? The false hopes that preceded each president he had hired? The false confidence in each one's set of restructuring plans, which never went far enough? He regretted having to fire Rob, but something *had* to be done.

And, speaking of something *having* to *be* done— something *had* to be done with Werner.

He would expedite the divestiture. He had made the decision to divest, to sell Werner over four months ago, but not aggressively. He had instructed his investment bankers, Goldstein & Gimbel, to discreetly study the market and to entertain any offers. He pulled his Airphone out of its console in the jet's panel, punched the direct number to Saul Benjamin at Goldstein and left a message on his confidential voicemail:

"Saul, Walter here. Expedite divestiture. Repeat. Expedite Werner divestiture. Pursue buyers aggressively. We've already discussed the parameters. I am en route to Europe. Will call you upon return, Thursday. If immediate prospect, you can reach me through Doris. She will get word to me. Thanks, Saul. This *is* an expedite. An urgent expedite."

Somewhat relieved and remotely comforted by his judicious call, he reflected once again on the inopportune timing of these horrible events at his subsidiary. *Jesus.* Just when his core business, his cherished pharmaceutical empire, was about to take a quantum leap. He was about to launch a tidal wave, a tsunami of dynamic growth never before seen in the pharmaceutical industry. He had worked all of his life toward this goal. This would soon be his finest hour. He was literally on the threshold of the realization of his lifetime ambition. And, now, suddenly all this with Werner threatened to destroy it all.

Walter took a sip of his martini, opened his Gucci briefcase, took out his Leonardo da Vinci, leather-bound journal, gold-embossed *WGK Confidential,* which he had removed from his wall safe before leaving his office. He began to read over his journal, his own personal memoirs. He *had* to get his mind off this Werner shit; he'd deal with it soon enough in Brussels.

He had built and dedicated a $500-million-dollar R & D plant in New Jersey that was the showplace of the global research science community. There, his exceptional staff of PhDs and MDs had formulated a drug pipeline that would become the pinnacle of the entire healthcare industry. He had no less than three blockbuster drugs, each of which could develop into multibillion-dollar producers, and one super blockbuster cancer breakthrough that could be THE drug of the next century.

The first, about to be released next month, would be the new Cox-2 inhibitor that was the first drug to attack rheumatoid arthritis on its own turf, in the synovium. There were already two successful Cox-2 -type drugs on the market, but each had side effects, fewer side effects though than the previous nsaid-type arthritis drugs. But, their new drug, *Arthrid*, not only had a great name, but was effective— very effective. The early results were better than expected.

Walter was listening to Puccini's opera, *Turandot*, coming through the exquisite sound system in the cabin— Bose speakers in the front, ceiling, side panels, and rear; surround sound enveloped him. Beautiful.

The second potential blockbuster was the result of his having recruited and hired the top research scientist from Britain in SNP gene-mapping— genomics. His team had succeeded in discovering the APO-E gene, thought to be a major player in Alzheimer's disease, and they would market that new drug as *Cogniflex*. This dynamic drug would not only delay the onset of Alzheimer's, but also retard its progress when administered in the early stages. *Cogniflex* represented a benchmark, not just for its effectiveness against Alzheimer's, but as an approach, a virtual pathway to many other neurologic diseases, as well.

The striking reality of the discovery of this miracle drug, the clinical trials, the marketing of *Cogniflex* was Walter! This miracle drug *was* Walter Kagan. All Walter. It showcased Walter Kagan, period, demonstrating *his* genius as a researcher, a visionary, a recruiter of exceptional talent, a shrewd strategic manager, and a worldwide corporate leader.

Walter shifted in his seat, looking around the plush cabin, burying his neck in the soft leather. He took a big swallow of his martini. The inner glow was reigniting his spirits, refiring his self-concept as a world leader, his self-image as a benefactor of mankind. Why hell, *Cogniflex* could lead to a cure for Alzheimer's, a cure for Parkinson's disease, a cure for schizophrenia, for manic depression. My *God!* A cure for muscular dystrophy. For all neurologic diseases. And all this crap with Werner could blow the whole damn thing. *Shit!*

The third blockbuster addressed a broader area in the number one killer, heart disease. Brecken already had two highly successful drugs on the market: one which lowered cholesterol was a proven blockbuster with annual sales of over a billion dollars; their other drug with sales of almost a billion helped to control high blood pressure. They were currently engaged in multi-center Phase IV clinical trials with their new drug, which seemed truly miraculous. They had lassoed a receptor gene, called FJH-receptor III, thought to predispose the formation of plaque in arteries. The controversial aspect, but paradoxical action of this process that the FJH-receptor III precipitated was— their discovery that the reaction was reversible. They had invented and patented a recombinant technique which enabled them to experiment with and harness this process, combining it with their proven cholesterol-lowering drug.

He stopped to make a note in the margin: FJH-receptor III = Buster Blaster

The serendipitous result blew the laboratory's entire research staff away— the result was a compound which lowered the LDL, the bad cholesterol, which raised the HDL slightly, the good cholesterol. And, furthermore, it attacked the plaque already laid down on arterial walls, breaking it up, and, at the same time, delaying the process of future plaque formation. So, what they had serendipitously, unexpectedly discovered was a multi-disciplinary, multi-functional drug that simultaneously attacked two of the major causes of heart disease, while augmenting the body's defense mechanism against it. This could be the most phenomenal drug discovery of the twentieth century. And in a $20-billion dollar market, too. The labs called it "the Buster-Blaster." Unbelievably, he had word from two of their secret sources that the FDA was anxious, eager to broaden this drug's labeling. Absolutely incredible! For the FDA to really want to expand the indications for which a drug could be prescribed. Unheard of! Increasing instead of limiting an efficacious drug's labeling. This would represent a historic first and an ethical feather in their rich R & D nest.

His G-5 hit a burst of turbulence, jarring him in his seat and shaking his empty martini glass. He had just eaten the olive, and replaced the sterling silver toothpick in the glass, which tinkled as the glass shook. His captain came over the intercom, apologizing for the rough air, saying that he would change altitudes from 39,000 feet to 33,000, which should provide a smoother ride. His steward served him another extra dry Bombay martini straight up in one of his special Waterford crystal martini glasses.

He returned to his memoirs. *CardiStat*— this miracle drug alone would save untold lives, enhance the quality of life of thousands, hundreds of thousands, millions, increase longevity, and, as he took a big sip of his fresh martini, last, but however immodestly, not least, this miracle drug would stand as a testimonial to one Walter G. Kagan. To Walter Gatton Kagan, Chief Executive Officer, Chairman-to-be, of Brecken-Mersack Strauss, Inc., the world's largest pharmaceutical company. Yes, by God, he'd drink to that! And he did. Another quaff of his delectable martini. Damn, that was smooth! Yes, by God, Brecken *would* be the largest pharmaceutical company in the world, hands down, with these new blockbuster drugs unleashed on mankind. Another lifetime goal achieved!

The speakers vibrated with Luciano Pavarotti singing the classic aria, "Nessum dorma" from Puccini's *Turandot*. It filled the cabin, reverberating the entire craft, seeming to uplift the jet, while inflating Walter's chest, not to mention his ego...

Then, the aria ended. Quiet ensued. The mood, the opulent ambience abruptly changed...

Harsh reality — with its ugly green head, just like the fat shiny green olive on the sheen silver toothpick glistening up at him through the 90-proof Bombay gin— popped his pompous reverie. The FDA, no matter how interested, how intrigued, how attracted to his new life-boosting drug pipeline, was at his door like a hungry wolf a couple of days ago. The Inspector General, no less! And the day before that, the IG threatened to shut down *his* subsidiary company, Werner, due to non-compliance, irregularities, arrogance, and God knows what else. *Shit!*

And, then today *Interpol!* At corporate headquarters. Aw, *Jesus!* Wanton endangerment? Kidnapping? Money transfers through the Caymans? Hell, everybody knows how high profile the Caymans are. They smell. Puerto Rico? Why Puerto Rico? He knew that he should have closed the Werner plant down there. Rob and Salter talked him into letting them have one more year to straighten it out. *Damn!* He *had* to get to the bottom of all this crap, definitely conduct his own investigation.

Upon arrival in Brussels, he was supposed to meet with Thierry Marchand, his Executive VP/COO of Europe/Africa. He knew he could trust Thierry because he had personally promoted him to his new position. He had known him and followed his career for years. He had also called Nigel Watkins, the Division Chief of Security, to the meeting. The two of them should be capable of penetrating any barriers to evidence. He was determined not to leave Belgium without a logical explanation for these bizarre allegations, and, more urgently, a reasonable resolution to them.

The steward freshened his martini, placed a linen table cloth on his table, and prepared to serve his first course for dinner, the appetizer, Beluga caviar.

His reading returned to his passion— his company's pharmaceutical research. Their primary core competency was, had been, and continued to be cancer research, and efficacious drugs for cancer. They were the world leader in the fight against cancer with drugs for chemotherapy, and targeted drugs for specific cancers, i.e. ovarian cancer, breast cancer, esophageal/ gastric cancer, lymphoma, and melanoma. Their newest discovery, top secret at first, but also serendipitous, came from a rare tree in the Amazon rainforest, a wild palm called the babassu. The babassu palm had been useful previously because of its oil-bearing kernels, which were used for industrial purposes. Brecken's office in Sao Paulo had funded a missionary clinic deep in the Amazon/Rio Negro valley, where the natives used the bark and leaves from the babassu on poisonous bites. Hearing about this and intrigued by the unknown medicinal properties, one of their scientists from Sao Paulo investigated this remote resource. It was discovered that the extract from the babassu bark was an astringent, an anti-carcinogenic with other healing properties, as well. They began harvesting the extract and testing it...

More turbulence. He almost spilled his martini.

...testing it in their labs. The initial results on bladder cancer, liver cancer, and pancreatic cancer in rats was extraordinary. By varying the concentration of the compound, according to the targeted cancer site, the effectiveness was increased. They called the new miracle compound baba-35, for 35 percent concentration, used on bladder cancers; baba-55, for 55 percent concentration on the liver; and baba-75 percent used on pancreatic cancers. They were already experimenting with other cancers— lung, prostate, colon, brain, and two types of leukemia. The early Phase I and Phase II results were astonishing, indicating that it might prove to have the broadest spectrum of any efficacious disease drug— truly a miracle drug. The uncanny success seemed to correlate to the presence of certain genes they knew caused certain cancers. For example, the Ras gene, known to be involved in lung, colon, and pancreatic cancer, was inhibited by baba-50 percent plus concentrations. They were coordinating their genomics research with Dr. Smythe with the clinical actions of the babassu extract. This entire new field of pharmacogenomics portended great advances, and they were on the cutting edge of this new technology.

To facilitate this extraordinary research opportunity, Brecken had formed several strategic, long-term partnerships — with a leading genetic engineering firm in Palo Alto, California, with a Massachusetts laboratory to test specific compounds known to actively inhibit cancer-causing genes, and with key oncologists at medical centers prominent in cancer research, such as M. D. Anderson in Houston, Sloan-Kettering in New York City, Brigham Women's and Children's in Boston, Lucille Markey Cancer Institute in Lexington, Kentucky, Mayo Clinic in Rochester, Minnesota, and UCLA Medical Center in Los Angeles. The consortium was impressive, if Walter did say so himself. And while he was in Brussels, he planned to finalize plans with The Louis Pasteur Institute in Paris and the Sodertalje Institute in Stockholm with the same objective.

They were proceeding with Phase IV trials with bladder cancer, Phase II with both liver and pancreatic cancers, and Phase III with the largest population of sufferers, lung cancer. If the results continued to be as positive as before, this could launch the greatest weapon ever in the battle against cancer. This drug could really be the mother of all blockbusters.

The culmination of these four breakthrough drugs was so awe inspiring that it was almost incomprehensible to Walter. The synergistic overall results would represent the zenith of pharmaceutical efficacy—they would prolong longevity and enhance life. Phenomenal! These first two innovative breakthroughs would attack the number one and number two killer diseases, heart disease and cancer; the third would attack and possibly cure the most prominent neurologic diseases; the fourth would attack the most debilitating disease of the elderly, Alzheimer's. No doubt about it, these life-saving drugs would certainly increase life expectancy. And, moreover, *his* extremely efficacious drugs would greatly enhance the quality of human life.

What had Neil Armstrong said when he stepped onto the moon? "One small step for man, one giant step for mankind." Well, Walter Kagan, CEO of Brecken-Mersack Strauss had just launched a moonshot for man. Walter G. Kagan had taken "one giant step for mankind." Yes! Walter Gatton Kagan, with these miracle drugs, had definitely taken "one great, giant step...one gargantuan step for mankind." When he got back home from this emergency salvage trip, he would contact their best public relations firm to coin *THE* phrase for the next century showcasing *his* miracle, life-saving drugs— to coin *THE phrase* for the next millennium.

As his steward served his main course, beef Wellington, and waited for him to taste and approve his dinner wine, De la Chaize Brouilly Beaujolais,1996, Walter sipped it and mused to himself, "a full bouquet, a great year for Beaujolais. Yes, it *would* be a great year, after he had taken care of all this crap with Werner, after he had divested it, gotten rid of Werner for good. Yes, a great year, indeed.

Then, the pathway would be clear, clear for Walter G. Kagan, the greatest pharmaceutical baron of all time, clear for him to launch the greatest life-saving, miracle drugs of the next century, of the nest millennium. And take 'one giant step for mankind.'"

As he swirled the luscious wine around in his mouth, the inner glow was broader than a moonbeam. He loved his accomplishment, his monumental accomplishment. He loved it, just the thought of it, the magnanimity of it, a masterful, quantum leap for mankind. Hell, it would not only establish Walter Kagan's genius and cement his legacy for eternity, it would transform the entire research process, transform disease research forever— truly a quantum advance for mankind.

And, then came his greatest thought of the day...

Why he could win the Nobel Prize. Yes! Walter G.. Kagan— win the Nobel Prize for Science. Why not? After all, he *was* the greatest drug researcher in the world, expanding the human life span, enhancing the quality of untold, of innumerable human lives. Hell, yes! Walter G. Kagan, winner of the Nobel Prize for Science.

What an honor. What a thought!

Walter G. Kagan...

The explosion hit with a velocity that was earth-shattering. The cabin disintegrated into thousands of pieces amidst the deafening eruption. The fuselage was immediately dissolved into red-hot color with no discernible shape. The once-sleek corporate jet projected a huge bright orange fireball in the black night over the North Atlantic. The giant orange sphere inflamed the darkness like a monstrous flare, and began to slowly descend towards the ocean leaving a burning, luminous yellow-orange wake.

Like a dazzling, shooting comet, resplendent in intense radiance, illuminating the heavenly universe...

But only the stars could see.

CHAPTER 41

True to the kindred points
of heaven and home.

To A Skylark
William Wordsworth, 1827

It was hard, really hard, another one of the most difficult things Trish had ever had to do— to conceal her excitement after learning from Ann that James was still alive. She had to act like nothing had changed. Like she was still totally miserable, distraught, despondent over his disappearance. Like she was still on the emotional rollercoaster. Well, she had never been an actress. She was a no-nonsense, down-to-earth kind of person. So, putting up this front was hard.

And, then, not to tell, not to be *able* to tell the kids, Kathleen and Christine. It was almost as excruciating suppressing the good news as it was dealing with the bad news. That was really tough, because her daughters knew their mother. Maybe they would think that her emotions, her grief had hit the limit, that it could go no further, and that now she had become withdrawn. Kathleen could hopefully perceive, diagnose, and grasp her mother's emotional transformation after all of her graduate work in psychology. My god, she had worked on the psych ward at Walter Reed Hospital as part of her internship. She would surely pick it up.

Yes, that is how she would play it. It was simply too much— like "I just don't know what else to do. I've done everything I can. I got an old friend, Chuck Thursgoode, killed by hiring him as a private investigator. I got our attorney's secretary, Sheryl, shot and almost killed, and Lynwood's office ransacked and practically destroyed. I have prayed until I have run out breath. I have cleaned, and straightened, and cooked for the FBI men. The best thing I've done is to begin my own investigation— getting James' "safe files" and those tapes. Well, I can't tell them that. Yet. I don't know what else I can do. I'm just beside myself, so distraught I'm inert." Maybe, just maybe, her daughters would buy that. She would try it. She *had* to try something.

But, she had so many questions now that she knew that he was alive. Where was James? How was he doing? Would he ever be able to return to her? If he did, she would take care of him like never before. Never let him out of her sight. She loved him so. How much she had taken her husband for granted, everyday, leaving home so early every morning, coming home from work so tired every night, so set in his ways, having to lay out his clothes every night, bringing her coffee up every single morning. Oh, how she missed that, missed him, the wonderful living he had made for her and the children through the years, what a good father he was, what a fun grandfather he was. Oh, so many things. How she missed him.

It *was* tough. But, oh, damn, was she ever grateful, so thankful for the news, so thankful that he was still alive. Oh, thank you, God. Thank you. But, handling this news, repressing her excitement, not telling her daughters, not being able to tell anybody, having all these questions, nagging questions about his whereabouts. James tortured? Tortured! How? By whom? She thought she knew. Little doubt about it after all of her research into James' files and tapes. Those tapes. James was ingenious to have done that. Slowly but surely she was connecting the dots. Especially, after listening to that last tape, twice. Bam! The name at Legal that just kept coming up— Brice Billups. But, he was just one. Lenny, the betrayer, had a hand in it, too. And others. Yes, they were at the bottom of this. Had to be. The kidnapping. Then the torture? How dare they, those asses! She could not let herself start that again, would *not* allow herself to go through that mental torture again. *Torture,* how inhuman! How monstrous! They *were* monsters. Doing all those abominable things to *her* husband. And, if it was the last thing she did on earth, it would be to make them pay. By God, they would pay for what they did to *her* husband! She would see that they got theirs. Those bastards!

She forced her thoughts to return to her husband. What was he thinking right now? Hidden away somewhere, probably not knowing where he was, physically hurting, emotionally drained. She knew that he had exceptional stamina, that he was tough, tough as a horse. But, this was more than any individual could endure. After losing his business, being fired, for God's sake, being dispossessed of what he had worked all of his life to build, how devastated he must have been. Then, to be subjected to God knows what else? Kidnapped, absconded, tortured, away from his family, not able to communicate, to express his feelings, not knowing what was going to happen to him, to his family? To his world? To his life? My love, if I could only hold you...see you, tell you how much I love you, and miss you.

As she settled down in her bed that night, it was with a warmth and tenderness, and her prayer reflected it— wherever you are, my Love, please know in your heart how much I love you. Please come home to me. Oh, please Lord, bring him home to me.

Their clandestine meeting took place at the Arby's on Harrodsburg road.

Dana had called Trish with an urgent need to meet in total privacy. She wanted Trish to hear the rumor that had just surfaced first hand from her. It was about James. The rumor was that James had taken the buy-out and skipped. That he had taken Werner's check and disappeared.

"*What!* That's *insane!*" Trish responded.

"I know it is... I can't believe it either! It's not like him...no way," Dana was panting like she had been running. "Now, here comes the worse part. You know who's spreading this crap— the ball-less wonder himself, Tom. The little shit has..."

"Why that little asshole!" Trish couldn't believe she said it. But that's what she liked about Dana, who was a year older than James, also from the school of ol' timey values. Even though Trish was the boss's wife, she and Dana had a lot in common and were friends.

"After all James has done for him," Trish continued. "Constantly bailing him out of situations..."

"You know how I feel about *him*, anyway. After hearing this damn thing, I confronted him, asked him where he had heard this," Dana paused to get her breath. "You know who's at the bottom... who started it?"

"No. Who?"

"I really had to threaten Tom, to get it out of him. Told him I wouldn't type anymore of his quotes. Or anything else. You know how he is..."

"I know. Who is it, Dana?" Trish asked, now as mad about this revolting news as Dana.

"It's J. M. You know..."

"Why, that bitch!" Trish's exclamation raised the eyebrows of the other patrons, who looked up in shock. It did not phase her. "That bitch. She never liked James. Was jealous of him, really. Couldn't stand it, that he was so well liked, had won those awards...why that..."

"She *is* a bitch. And we're not the only ones who think so. Nobody likes her, she's so...anyway, she's the one who told Tom..."

"There's no way it could be, Dana. James called me from the Cincinnati airport, you remember? He was headed to his plane. They were boarding the flight, I heard it..." an incensed Trish tried to explain.

"No. I mean, yes. I remember," Dana had been sucking on her straw and spilled iced tea on her chin. She was still out of breath. "There's no way he'd do that. It's just *not* James. You see, that's how stupid Tom is... she's using him...she's..."

"She's spreading a vicious rumor. And she's playing Tom, the little pissant, to do it..."

"Yeah, that's the truth. But, here's the good news. I made a couple of calls before calling you. To Warsaw. Hardly anybody's heard it. And those that have...well nobody believes it. You know how they feel about James up there," Dana said still dabbing her chin. "And how they feel about her...they don't like her worth a damn."

J. M. Corzone, the new token Vice-President, was more well known for her inexperience, incompetence, and petty personal agendas than anything else. The glaring exceptions were her less than covert attempts to discredit James.

"Well, I won't lower myself to call her, but Tom...you know, if it weren't for that one account, James would have had to let him go ages ago. I told James he ought to fire him, but..."

"You don't have to worry about him. I threatened him with his life," Dana looked around and leaned in closer, "I couldn't threaten to castrate him," she tried to inject a little levity into the discourse.

"That's the truth, Dana." They both laughed, in spite of their anger.

The air conditioning made it chilly inside Arby's on this warm spring day, but these two women were generating waves of heat.

"Well, I wanted you to hear it from me first, before it got out of hand. It's not even gossip, it's so ridiculous. Nothing'll come of it, but I wanted to call..."

"Thanks, Dana. I would have died if I had heard it elsewhere. Thanks for everything— your support, loyalty, for all you've meant to me and James."

"No, I should be thanking you all. James took the chance hiring me, after I'd been out of the workplace for over fifteen years."

They hugged and walked out to the parking lot, carrying their cups of iced tea. They continued talking standing there, actually laughing a few more times.

But, as Trish started her car, she was reeling mad. The very idea of that damn bitch starting something so malicious. And Tom, after all James had done for him, to be that disloyal. That back-stabbing ingrate!

She reached down for a cigarette.

CHAPTER 42

Now faith is the substance of things hoped for,
the evidence of things not seen.
Hebrews 11:1

The night was clear, calm, and cooler than usual. James could see the stars through the netting. Never in his life had he seen so many stars, all twinkling and blinking, as if they were winking down at him. It *was* a star-spangled night. There was a half moon, its light radiating down, filtering through the camouflage canopy. One of the moon rays shone down directly upon Margarita's face, reflecting off of her long black hair falling off the cot, on which she lay sleeping. A host of moonbeams illuminated the far corner, like non-pulsating strobe lights in a discotheque. It was like a miniature musical production with the *coquis* as the orchestra. He was nurtured, uplifted by the splendid sight.

The *coquis* were making such beautiful music. Their chant seemed to be more melodic than ever. These little green frogs with their symphonic sonatas had helped him through the insufferable nights and the many agonizing days when the pain was so intense, that all he could do was pray, count the hours, the minutes down to dusk. He dwelled upon the anticipation of darkness, which would bring their sweet lyric songs— the *coquis'* lullaby— and, maybe then, he could finally sleep. James' existence was filled with four constants: pain, his continuous, miserable companion; Margarita's tender nursing care, thank God for her; the nocturnal *coquis*, thank God for them; and prayer, simply— thank you, Lord. He knew if he could withstand another day of unbearable pain, he would surely hear the celestial music from his unseen friends upon nightfall. Never heard of before, the *coquis* had become a symbol of James' faith, his fortuitous, formidable faith. These magical little frogs became a basis for, a spiritual icon to his daily survival. Never seen, only heard, they had come to represent the evidence of his abiding faith. Verily, they were *"the evidence of things not seen...and the substance of things hoped for."* As long as he could make it through another woeful day, and make it to nightfall and their song, the perseverance gave him hope; hope, that essential, yet elusive desire filled with promise for the future; hope, so vital to his survival, that he *would* soon return to his family, live to embrace Trish, his daughters, his granddaughters, all his loved ones once again, embrace them like never before, and, finally, live to pursue his new purpose— to make the *truth* known. And get the son-offa-bitches that did this to him.

James could not believe how much better he was feeling. They had actually gotten him to walk yesterday. With the assistance of two soldiers and two homemade crutches, roughhewn from tree limbs, and Margarita's encouragement and supervision, he had walked. The dizziness and pain were staggering, relentless. But he had accomplished it. The throbbing from his fractured leg was overpowering, causing him to see stars during daylight. But, he was able to bear weight on his good leg, protecting the broken leg while taking several aching steps. His cot was a welcome relief after the great effort it required. Afterwards, he was totally exhausted.

But, what a boost it gave to his self-confidence, a self-confidence once strong, once so stalwart that it was able to withstand repeated rejection and slammed doors. His self-confidence had suddenly been attacked from all quarters. But, reflecting back on it all now, hell, it was a wonder that he was still alive, much less on the mend. But, his paramount pain, ever present down deep in his gut, his soul, his heart, and his mind, was psychological. The psychological torture of deprivation of his *life-force*— his job, his business, his means of making a living, of providing for his family, of providing jobs for others, of serving others. His *life-force* was his means of self-expression; even more so, it was the means of redemption of his self-worth every single day. Losing *it* was psychological torture that rivaled the physical torture. The pain from his life-threatening injuries and malaria was transient; the pain from his business loss was permanent. The physical pain would subside, waning from time to time.

But, the burn in his gut, the wretch in his soul, the torment within his heart, the anguish in his mind never diminished. Even when he slept, nightmares replayed the scenario verbatim, over and over, exacerbating his waking reality. That unremitting presence sharpened the clarity of the whole horror show. Would it ever go away?

But, now, to be able to get up and walk again, to be able to partially take care of himself, to shave, all the little things that he'd taken for granted. What an improvement. Ambulation fostered a new determined direction— to get better and make it home! And to avenge this myriad of injustices to so many, including himself.

As dawn was approaching, the *coquis* began to abate. Their chants became muted, fewer, and fewer, and further between. It was a phenomenal, momentous process from Mother Nature.

Margarita was up and starting her daily routine, which meant her strong coffee would soon be coming. He could smell it. Great Puerto Rican coffee beans— the best coffee he had ever had.

As daylight was breaking, a chorus of monkeys shrieked from the treetops. And an angel on earth served him his hot, steaming mug of that robust coffee.

With a swagger and that flashing, infectious smile, *Moises* came in carrying a mug of coffee, also.

"Well, James... you *look* so much better. Doesn't he, Margarita? Hey! You're a different man."

"Thanks to Margarita and her helpers, I walked yesterday," he replied smiling, his pride evident.

"Well, that's good news, indeed! And timely. There are some things I need to talk to you about. First— we were successful in getting word to your wife."

"Super! That's great! Oh, thank you." James exhaled. What a great relief. He knew how worried Trish would be. The last she had heard from him, the phone call from the Cincinnati airport, was weeks ago. Seemed like years. What must have been going on in her mind— not knowing, thinking the worst. *Oh, Trish, Honey...* "Thank you so much, *Moises.*"

"You're very welcome. Now, before your excitement overcomes you, I must explain to you what tremendous pressure this wonderful news places on them... and on you. And on us. Think about it. Your wife can tell *no* one. If the FBI finds out, it's trouble for the *Independistos* and for you. For your safety." *Moises'* electric smile was gone. "I must now tell you the truth about the attack on our camp. The three men were coming for you. They came to kill you. The three assassins were professional, real pros, with top-of-the-line weaponry."

"Oh, my God! *Damn!* Poor Margarita, limping around here. And the Major!" he interrupted, upset, feeling terrible guilt. *My god. I've endangered these people, my new friends. They saved my life, nursed me, brought me back from the brink, fed me, took care of me. And they befriended me. I owe my life to them...and then I get them attacked, shot at, wounded, almost killed? Oh my God...*

"*Damn.* I'm sorry. Sorry I got y'all involved in this."

"No, James," *Moises* interrupted, "you did *not* get us involved. We got ourselves involved. And are glad of it. You've come to mean a lot to us, here. Your courage and sheer toughness were— are— an inspiration, an example to my men. I would have paid good money for a real life drill like we had. We *are* professionals, and regard this as part of our job. We are *all* much the better for it, again including you. So, that issue is settled." He leaned forward and squeezed James' good leg, his dark eyes passionate and powerful.

"Listen, *Moises.* There's an Army...or a Navy base here somewhere, in Puerto Rico. Y'all can move me there. That'll help secure your camp. And the *Independistos,*" James offered.

"Wait, we'll discuss that in a minute. But, first, the second piece of good news regards your Werner plant in Caguas. We've been able to establish one contact there, a machinist. But, we are working discretely on another who might be in management. You were right— they *are* making total hips there."

James raised up from his cot. This confirmed what he already suspected. He wanted, needed to know more.

"But we don't know what type. Or brand. The specifics you'll have to write that down for me." He handed James a piece of paper and a ball-point pen.

"Now, for the bad news. Unfortunately, I have had two of my new, young recruits break our rules. They sneaked out of camp, went into San Juan to the Ricky Martin concert, had too much to drink, and said too much. They have jeopardized our location and our cause. We must move our camp again, logistics and operations. And, even though this is certainly not your fault, it renders us the opportunity to address your future. Your secure future is not here in the wilderness with us. It resides in your getting good medical care, better than we can provide, regaining your health, returning home to your family, and reconciling your inhuman treatment. As you told Frank, 'to make the truth known.' I wish you Godspeed in your endeavor. And achievement of that goal. Now, let me discuss our plan, and the arrangements I have made."

James eyes widened, as he sighed, still feeling badly about the attack.

"I realize that this is a great deal to hit you with at once, but we are going to have to move quickly. We have to break camp by 0900. I have made arrangements to carefully move you to the U.S. Naval Hospital—you were right— on their base on Isla de la Vieques, just off the west coast. There, you will get state of the art medical care, and, you will be safe. As a U. S. citizen, you will be under the full protection of the United States Navy. They know that you are coming. They do not know the exact details of your rescue. They think that, after your escape, you were found by a peasant family, which is partially true. We are nothing but ordinary people with an *extra-ord*-inary cause.

James handed the paper back to *Moises* with "PDL Femoral Components? Other Total Hip components? Compliance issues? Quality Control? Rejection rates? Thank you."

"Well, *Moises,* I still can't thank you enough. You, and Margarita, and the..."

Moises held up his hand. "I will be back to say good-bye before you go. And to further encourage you on your pilgrimage home. *Vaya con Dios, amigo." Moises,* the leader of his Puerto Rican people, departed with the same swagger with which he had entered.

And James was saddened, he'd really miss his new friends, but confronted by yet one more unknown.

CHAPTER 43

The telephone rang with a muffled, low-pitched ring.

"Yeah," the gravelly voice answered.

"Line clean?" the raspy voice asked.

"Affirmative," was the answer.

"Code 103? Status?" the voice asked.

"Code 103, check." the gravelly voice replied.

"Code 103 check?"

"Positive. That's a positive," the gravelly voice stated emphatically.

"*Grazie,*" the raspy voice replied. "Subject?"

"Unknown," was the answer.

Silence.

"Locate subject. Period. Eliminate subject. Period. Dispose of subject! *Clean. Period!*" the raspy voice shouted.

"Must appropriate additional assets," the gravelly answered.

"*Do it!*" the raspy voice screamed. "*Capiche?*"

"Affirmative."

"Or else..."

"Ditto."

"Ditto?"

"Ditto." Click.

Click.

CHAPTER 44

Your tongue is like a sharp razor.
Psalm 52:2 (NRSV)

The numbness continued. Rob was lost. He did not even know the way to the train station to catch a train home. His limo driver had always driven him everywhere. When he finally became aware, he was just standing on the street, not even knowing where he was. It was late afternoon. Still in shock, he had reached for his cellular phone to call his wife. He no longer had it. They had taken away his phone, too! The reality of his unemployment only came in increments. It was the worst thing that had ever happened in his life.

He was dying in stages, slowly, one sensory system at a time. His stomach was alive, because it was wrenched into knots. His hearing was nonspecific, tuned out. The blaring horns and screeching traffic were inaudible. He could see, but it was a blur. He looked up at the street sign on the corner, 57th and 5th. How had he gotten here? His conscious memory had been deadened by the shock trauma of his sudden termination. His only recall was, "I am sorry, Rob, but, as of 8:00 A.M. this morning, you are officially terminated." It repeatedly sliced through his brain like a meat cleaver.

He had to call his wife. *Oh, God!* What was Fran going to say? How was he going to tell her? He was crushed— weakened beneath his manliness, stripped of his self-respect and personal dignity. What was he going to say to her? Would she...? He wanted to cry but could not.

He found a pay phone to call her. He picked up the receiver and could not remember his own number. He did not *know* his own phone number. Iva had programmed it into his cellular phone. He *had* to call information to get his own damn phone number. How much lower could he go? He looked down at his gold Rolex watch; it was 4:35 in the afternoon. Where had the time gone? Where had he been these last few hours?

"Hello."

"Fran? It's..."

"Where the hell are you? We're due at the club at 6. And you have to get on your tux. Remember we've got the Charity Auction, and then the symphony. Don't tell me you've..." she snapped, very perturbed.

"Fran...Fran?" Rob was so demoralized he could barely speak.

"What is it this time? Don't tell me..."

"Fran. I've been fired," he almost broke. The harshness of the word parting his lips for the first time left a bitter taste in his dry mouth.

"What?" she retorted.

"I've been fired. I've lost my job." It got harder as he went along.

There was silence. A long silence.

"Why?" she asked.

"... because of Werner, all that crap at Werner," he said.

"You remember, I told you not to take that damn job," Fran replied.

There was another prolonged silence. All Rob could hear was his own labored breathing.

"Fran, what we are going to do..." he finally muttered.

Another deathly period of quiet ensued.

"Well, I know what *I am* going to do. I am going to finally do what I should have done a long time ago— divorce you!" she stated, adamantly.

It was like a hand grenade had just blasted the phone booth. Rob choked, losing his balance. He thumped the glass of the booth with his elbow. It was all he could do to hold on to the receiver.

"You know, this is ironic," her voice was light, skippy. "I was just at my lawyer's office yesterday. I simply did not expect to file this soon. I have asked you, I have begged you, I have pleaded with you for years, for years for your attention, for you to spend time with me...time with our family. *Hell,* your two kids hardly know their father. We've been married twenty-eight years, and for twenty-six of 'em, you have been married to your *goddamn job,*" raising her voice. "You have not given a *shit* about me, much less your own children. All you have ever cared about was that *goddamn company*— next quarter's earnings, the next board meeting, year-end results, annual reviews, all that *bull shit.* I've heard it all. You cared more about your *damn* jet than me. When you just got your new plane, it was like having the grandchild that I yearn for. That *goddamn* plane was your baby. And, look at what it got you."

Her reaction sucked the breath right out of his lungs.

"I told you that promotion was a dead-end, a devious prescription for disaster. I *told* you that you ought to stay in pharmaceuticals, where you were really good. But, oh no, you wouldn't listen to your wife. No, who in the *hell* am I? You did not give a good *dog shit* for me. Nor your kids. Hell, Robbie tried to tell you, tried to talk to you about that new position when he was at Wharton, when they were studying case histories of the big global conglomerates. Even your son, your *own son* smelled a rat. But, not you. Oh, no. *THE* Robert Hempstead knew everything. No, you never listened to anybody."

Her tongue-lashing was loaded with double-barreled animosity. It knocked him on his ass, hitting him where it hurt. He was expecting her sympathy, hoping that she would reach out to console him in his time of need, but, instead, she launched into a tirade against him, assaulting him with the grounds for divorce! His brain was exploding within his skull, and his heart was being ripped out of his chest.

He was incapable of saying anything. He wanted to say, "You damn ungrateful bitch!" But, he could not, because he knew way down deep in his wrenching gut, that what she was saying was true.

"Well, I *am* sorry, Rob. After all these years of being married to a workaholic, I will be *damned* if I am going to be married to a loser. You may call Clarence, my attorney, and tell him where you want your clothes sent." And she hung up.

Loser. That word struck every nerve root in his body, reviving every single sensory ganglion with inflammatory response. It was like a seizure. He shuddered from head to toe, vibrating all over. Then, just as suddenly as it started, it stopped. He went numb. He had never been called a loser in his life. Stripped of his authority, his dignity, his prestige, his family. Now, a loser. It had penetrated the very last armor of his self-defense.

Look what they've done to me. The sons-a-bitches. That severance is nothing. It's irrelevant. Who am I now? A loser...

Rob could not move. He just stood there holding the phone to his ear, like a plastic figurine in a dark suit.

He stood there for what seemed an eternity.

A drunk banging on the clear panel of the phone booth jarred him back to reality.

And, he had thought back on the street before his call, that nothing worse could happen to him. For the first time in his life, he was out of a job. Rob Hempstead, king of "the dress-down." "Dressed-down" without an address. Out of work. Out on the street. And alone. All alone.

So terribly alone.

Alone with his own exclusive misery

— alone with his own elite, self-wrought despondency

— beside himself, beyond tears, beyond shock, beyond recovery, beyond salvation.

If he had a gun, he would shoot himself.

CHAPTER 45

When you pass through deep waters, I will be with you;
your troubles will not overwhelm you.
Isaiah 43:2(TEV)

The waves were splashing into the boat. A cold wind was blowing. Coupled with the spray from the sea, it was chilling to the bone. A full moon was shining down, its rays shimmering across the swells. But, inside the boat, it was dark. James could just barely see the Major with his night scope up in the bow. The sound of the outboard motor was rhythmically interrupted by the waves.

There were five of them in the skiff — the Major in the bow, two armed men on either side, another in aft running the outboard, and James lying down in the center. They had wrapped him in rain gear and covered him with a tarpaulin to shield him from the wash of the sea.

The plan was to deliver him safely to the beach on Vieques Island and leave him there to be picked up by the Navy SEALs. Some kind of covert arrangements had been made by *Moises* through his vast underground. Margarita had actually cried when James hugged her good-bye and kissed her cheek. He cried, too. My God, she had saved his life.

Looking back on it now, it all overwhelmed him — the whole circumstance of his rescue, rehabilitation, and salvation— found by a group of guerrillas, lead by a man named after Moses, a band of insurgent rebels whose trainer was an ex-Green Beret Major, who had treated him like a long-lost brother. *Moises'* sister, Margarita, his Florence Nightingale, his earth angel, without whom James would *not* have made it. He would have died from any of many causes, blood loss, shock, infection, malnutrition, dehydration, and, lastly, that pernicious malaria. How would he ever be able to repay her? *Moises?* His friend, Major Frank Henry? All of the troops, who rescued him, defended him, helped him as physical therapists, pulled for him when he was down, even prayed for him. It was simply unbelievable— the entire, life-saving ordeal.

As they chopped through the waves with the drone of the outboard, it hit him! Finally... the name of the hymn that Margarita was constantly humming. It was *"Love Lifted Me!"* Why hadn't he been able to think of it before? He knew that hymn, used to sing it in Sunday School as a boy, used to sing it in church with his parents and grandparents. His grandmother used to play it on the piano. Its melody had nearly driven him crazy. Why on earth had he not been able to think of it? He could remember it now:

"I was sinking deep in sin
Far from the peaceful shore
Very deeply stained within
Sinking to rise no more
But, the Master of the Sea
Heard my despairing cry
From the waters lifted me
Now safe am I.
Love lifted me, Love lifted me
When nothing else could help ,
Love lifted me..."

Now, somewhere off the coast of Puerto Rico, in the Caribbean Sea, under a starlit sky, the words of the hymn came to him like a message from above. Incredible.

And suddenly, a great calm came over James. It was as if an almighty hand had reached out and touched him. In the coldness of the wind and ocean spray, a deep warmth immersed his entire body, enwrapped him in a effusive state of calm confidence.

The Major gave a hand signal. The outboard motor was immediately cut off. The silence was punctuated only by the waves hitting the inflated raft.

And, there in a rubber raft off the shore of Isla de La Vieques, under the light of a full moon, in the quiet, with the waves gently lapping, he knew. For the first time he knew that he was going to somehow make it; knew beyond any doubt that he had been gratuitously saved from a bitter death, from an acrimonious end. And, he knew, somehow "*now safe am I.*"

The men quietly rowed the raft up to the shore. With some duress, they lifted James out, carried him across the sandy beach, and carefully laid him on the grass against a tree.

The Major knelt down beside him, grasped him firmly, but gently with a big bear hug, and whispered in his ear, "Play safe or don't play, good buddy."

Just as deftly as they had brought him here, they departed. He could see their silhouettes in the moonlight and hear the surf against the large raft as they launched it back out to sea.

And they were gone.

James was once again alone in the darkness with his friends, the *coquis.* They were in their full melodic chorus, chirping before the dawn, now with the background accompaniment of the surf hitting the shore.

The Navy personnel had been very orderly and considerate in transporting him to the base hospital. He looked around the room. Coming from where he had been, he could not believe his new surroundings. The modern Hill-Rom hospital beds had standard Werner traction frames with trapezes on them. His bed was all electric with automatic high/low/gatch positions achieved by the punch of a button. The overhead horizontal bar had IV side bars from which his IV solutions were hung. Compared to his cot in the jungle infirmary, this was quite a change. He had a lightweight fiberglass cast on his broken left leg instead of the homemade wooden splints wrapped with stockinette and a used Ace bandage. Bathed, shaven, lying on clean sheets— it felt so good.

The obtrusive negative with his new domicile was his night nurse, a young male who was a little too nosy for James' comfort level. He had rehearsed his story with the Major before they parted. Everything that had happened to him up until being found by the *Independistos* remained the same. His story was that he had been discovered and cared for by a peasant family in the mountains whose daughter had been a nurse. It was not an outright lie. He *had* been among peasants, peasants with a cause. This male nurse, short on duty and attentiveness, was long on abrasiveness and inquisitiveness, and was asking too many questions.

However, his day nurse was as nice as she could be— very capable, very compassionate, and outwardly reassuring about his recovery. A First Lieutenant, Maureen was a career Navy nursing officer who was originally from Minnesota. She had been brought up on a farm milking cows and caring for the animals, which inspired her to go into nursing.

Maureen, too, went above and beyond the call of duty, assisting him with his rounds of Physical Therapy. The PT staff were patient, encouraging, and understanding about the rigorous pain he was experiencing.

"No pain, no gain," James chanted over and over, gritting his teeth. The pain was severe, but his gain was well worth the pain. He was now able to walk the full length of the long hall, with the aid of his new crutches. They said, with his continued conscientious effort, that he would be able to walk on a weight-bearing cast with only a cane next week. His previous excellent nursing care, now reinforced by the modern facilities were helping him to progress dimensionally.

The food was a little different than Margarita's delicious rice and beans. Their hospital coffee was not nearly as strong as hers, but it was good. Maureen went out of her way to see to James' care and assure his comfort. They were taking super care of him. And he had improved a lot.

James reflected back to the devoted personal attention, the tender bedside manner he had received from Margarita, and now Maureen here. Once again, it was safe to say that *managed care* had not yet hit the medical unit at the U. S. Naval Hospital on the island of Vieques off the coast of Puerto Rico.

CHAPTER 46

Oft expectation fails, and most oft there
Where most it promises.
All's Well That Ends Well
Shakespeare

Why had she done that? Trish thought she had messed up? Kathleen had to know. Kathleen had to know something, that there had been some kind of change. She knew her own mother too well. What else would explain her bizarre behavior?

Trish knew that she should not have bolted when the phone rang. She had even practiced with the FBI to wait until after the third ring before answering. And, while sitting there talking to her daughter, she had almost blown it. The phone rang. She bolted, grabbed it on the first ring, much to the chagrin of the FBI. Thankfully, it was a wrong number. She had been thinking about Ann, thinking that Ann was calling with a signal for news about James, and she momentarily lost it.

After she realized her mistake, she attempted to explain it away. And that only made it worse, really made her look worse— not exactly the bereaved wife, distraught about her husband's welfare— but more like a flake on amphetamines. It looked as though she had grabbed up the phone with a premeditated purpose.

Kathleen was taken aback by her mother's reaction. It was also apparent how preoccupied her mother was the whole time they were talking prior to the call.

Trish apologized to the FBI agents. They were extremely perceptive, trained in all aspects of human behavior. Had they noticed, as well? Or, was she just paranoid? Well, hell, she *was* already paranoid, but was she getting to be an obsessive-compulsive paranoid?

It was just that she could not stand it. Knowing that her husband was still alive meant everything to her. But, having to pretend that she did not know, that she was totally depressed like before, just didn't cut it. She just hated acting. Even as a child, she was not good at playing pretend. Then, having to put up a front with her own daughters was compromising, and uncompromisingly tough.

When Ann had called last night, it was a routine call to check on her mother. She had tried to carry on a normal conversation, as if nothing had happened. It was awkward, extremely awkward. Talking about her granddaughters' activities helped, but with every call being constantly monitored, it was eerie. Could the FBI detect a difference from their usual dialogue?

Ann had been on her mind every waking minute. Previous to learning the news, naturally it had been James constantly on her mind. Now, Ann was simply a substitute, an envoy for information about her husband. Now she was totally dependent on Ann for information. It is just that she thought Ann would have heard something else by now. It *had* become an obsession. And that obsession had become a compulsion, a compulsion for accessing any shred of future news.

Hence, her fanatic behavior. Darting for and seizing that ringing telephone was not like her.

She was going to have to get a grip on herself. Calm down. Step back. Count her blessings that her husband was still alive. No matter where on earth he might be, oh thank God, he was still alive. He would be back with her one day. No matter what shape he was in, they would be back together. She would nurse him, take care of him, fix him the "power breakfasts" he used to love. Oh, how she missed him! How she had taken him for granted for so many years. He had been such a wonderful provider, a wonderful partner, just a wonderful man and a loving mate.

She wanted a cigarette. But decided to go get a cup of hot coffee. Walking into the kitchen, she saw the FBI agent whom she did not like sitting in *her* chair at the kitchen table. Approaching the coffee pot, she noticed once again that her kitchen counter was a mess— coffee stains, mounds of creamer and sugar caked up on top, Sweet'n Low wrappers strewn about, in between dirty spoons.

"Damnit, I'm sick and *tired* of this— *this damn mess* in *my* kitchen every *single* day!" As she slammed a cabinet open getting out a sponge and the spray Lysol, she shouted, "for months now, I've had to clean up after you, every *damn* day!"

She was wiping down the counter, still cursing to herself when Agent Misler came running into the kitchen. The other agent was just standing there, his eyes wide.

"Mrs. Cantrill. I'm sorry. We should be more considerate...I'm very sorry. Here, let me help," he offered.

"No. I'll do it," she replied, gritting her teeth, her TMJ mesmerizing her jaws. Her internal pressure cooker was boiling over— the pressure of not knowing, now knowing, of trying to act normal, of losing it, of being upset with herself, of simply having to carry on day after day, trying to be upbeat for her children, of having her whole life ripped apart. The weight of this entire excruciating saga was too much.

Misler signaled with a shake of his eyes and head for the other agent to leave the kitchen. He opened the compacter and tossed in Sweet 'n Low wrappers and dirty napkins.

As Trish continued rubbing down the counter furiously, she slowly began to regain her composure.

"I'm sorry. We'll be neater...as we should've been," he said, softening his voice, "all along."

Trish took a deep breath. "I'm sorry...for losing my temper. It's just b-... I'm just..."

"Listen, this is an intolerable ordeal for you. You've held up beautifully. I think you're amazing, Mrs. Cantrill," Misler reassured. "On top of being so hospitable to us, while we're living here in your lovely home, which I know is not easy. We've done this before. It's never easy. But, you've done well, amazingly well. You're a wonderful lady...and a strong person."

"Well, thank you. I'm...sorry..."

"Don't mention it. We're the ones who need to apologize. We'll not let this happen again."

Trish took her coffee and went back up to her bedroom, feeling guilty again.

She began working on James' files again, trying to concentrate.

How could she be so happy in one respect? So thrilled that he was alive? And, yet, so miserable? So strung out and disgruntled. Was it the knowing and having to act not knowing? Was it a collision of consciousness? Was she becoming a split personality? The swings of emotion were killing her. Was she the only woman on earth being forcefully pulled in opposite directions at the same time? She felt like it. Why did it have to be this way? After she had suffered so much, after crying her eyes out, day after day, night after night, sleepless night after sleepless night. Then, to get the greatest news of her life, and not be able to tell anybody, even her other two daughters. And to have to hide it, as if nothing at all had happened. *Damn.* It was almost as agonizing now as it had been before.

Think. Back to her investigation, where she was really making progress, especially with the tapes. The last two were very compelling, revealing James' reference to an additional tape of his most recent conversation, which seemed to penetrate Werner's cover-up. He had taken it downtown to Barry Milner's to have it copied. This had to be *the* tell-all piece of evidence. She would head down the first thing in the morning.

Trish was headed out when the phone rang.

"Mrs.Cantrill?"

"Yes?" she answered.

"This is J. M. Corzone. I just wanted to call ... to tell you how sorry I am about James. I would have called sooner, but..."

Trish, in total shock, said nothing.

"Mrs. Cantrill?"

Dumbfounded, Trish remained mute.

"Mrs. Cantrill? Trish?"

The receiver was shaking in Trish's left hand.

"Trish? ... Mrs. Cantrill? Are you there?"

"...I have nothing to say to you," Trish said.

"But...I don't understand. I'm just calling to say I'm sorry..."

"This conversation is *over.* Good day." Trish hung up the phone.

Her lips dry, drawn, her hands shaking, Trish was fuming mad. The idea of it! That bitch, having the audacity to call her. After all she had done. Against James. The lies...starting that rumor... that damn bitch! Unbelievable.

J. M.— what a name for a female— J. M. Corzone. Her actual name was Jenny Mae, but no one dared call her that, lest they incur her wrath, synonymous with the wrath of Jezebel. No, she was to be called only by her two initials. J. M. knew absolutely nothing about the orthopaedic business, probably knew very little about business, period; probably never had sold Girl Scout cookies, never had a lemonade stand as a kid, or a paper route, or any idea of running a business, much less a growing multi-million-dollar business. She was an example of yet another Werner incompetent in a management position, a position of unbefitting authority— assumed authority over James that backfired on her. So, she *had* to stab him in the back. That damn bitch.

The fact was that controversy was J. M.'s constant companion. It followed her wherever she went, from the workplace to the dry cleaners, the grocery store, everywhere. Controversy fit her personality like a glove. She was called Jezebel behind her back, by secretaries, as well as the distributors and sales associates. J. M. came to stand for "Jezebel May" — "Jezebel May" do this, "Jezebel May" say that. According to the majority of her peers, she *was* Jezebel reincarnate.

Now, Trish was mad at herself. She was so shocked by the call— at the improbability, the implausibility within a respectable person's conscious realm, that a bitch like that would actually stoop to pick up the phone and call. It was simply unthinkable that a person would have the sheer guts, the arrogance, the brass balls to call up the man's wife that she had just undeservedly, unethically sabotaged. It defied sober, civil explanation.

Yes, Trish had been a lady, much the opposite of the calling party. But was being a lady in a matter of false witness, in a matter of character assassination this flagrant admirable? Was being civil with an uncivil antagonist honorable? Was exercising restraint in a confrontation so treacherous something to be proud of? Or should she have vehemently told her to *go straight to hell!*

Had all this emotional trauma, this constant worry over her husband anesthetized her strong resolve? Had all she had been through softened her? Weakened her? Shrunk her self-knowledge? Diminished her defenses? Was she losing it?

It did remind Trish of what James used to always say about the number of incompetents at Werner. These "officer wonders," as he used to call them, had their own agendas which they were determined to enforce regardless of the negative effect on others or the overall good of Werner. They deemed themselves a special gift to the orthopaedic industry. James would rile at their egos, their unnecessary demands, and costly blunders. J. M. was a glaring example of that incompetence. And her call, her employment in a position of authority reinforced James' contention that they were the cause of the constant spasms of mismanagement. Oh, James...

Yes, Trish needed to focus, *had* to think about her husband— the wonderful news, he was alive! Get back on track with her investigation. Head on downtown and get those tapes. She was getting closer and closer to finding out the truth.

She couldn't get to Barry Milner's fast enough.

CHAPTER 47

...and the rocket's red glare, the bombs bursting in air,
Gave proof through the night that our flag was still there.
The Star Spangled Banner

The bombs had been exploding for the last three hours. The deafening blasts had made James flinch in his bed, riddling him with fresh jolts of pain. Slowly, he was beginning to adjust. The nurses and staff in the naval hospital were oblivious to the clamor. Maneuvers with live rounds by the U. S. Navy on Vieques Island were a daily routine.

While the noise was unsettling at first, it had become a source of pride and inspiration for James. It was very comforting to be back under the aegis and protection of the United States of America. It was difficult to describe the wellspring of security it enkindled. Coming from where he had been, going through the ordeal he had endured, it was more than comforting— it was heart-warming, awe inspiring.

Health-wise, he was making measurable progress— he now had a lightweight fiberglass cast on his fractured leg, padded aluminum crutches, clean pajamas, clean sheets, and a bed! With a Werner overhead traction frame. The horrendous gashes on his hands and arms still looked ghastly, but were healing nicely. He still tired quickly but his strength and stamina were improving. His day nurse, Maureen, had been fantastic. Much of his rapid improvement had been due to her kind, gentle, constant care and encouragement. She had personally coordinated his physical therapy sessions and worked subtly behind the scenes with his doctors, constantly going above and beyond with his care and recovery. Without any doubt, Margarita had saved his life, and now another fabulous nurse, Maureen, was helping him recuperate and put his life back together again.

The Navy doctors had been quite capable and professional, too. They had asked him with interest about his career as a distributor of orthopaedic and surgical equipment, particularly the orthopaedic surgeon, Dr. Charles VanderMeer. Dr. Van, as he was called, was from Michigan, went to medical school at the University of Michigan in Ann Arbor, and did his residency at St. Luke's Presbyterian in Chicago, where he had used more than a few Werner Total Hips and Total Knees. He seemed to be quite familiar with their product line, which he enjoyed discussing with James.

He was especially inquisitive about Werner's manufacturing operations in Puerto Rico due to Code 936. Dr. Van was as much intrigued by the tax incentives granted by the special U. S. Tax Code 936 as he was the quality of the actual hip implants made there. Though familiar with all of the pharmaceutical companies in Puerto Rico, he did not realize there were medical device companies, much less orthopaedic manufacturers, on the island.

Dr. Van had obviously been informed about the circumstances preceding James' fortuitous arrival in Puerto Rico. As for his long tenure with Werner and his sudden termination, the doctor was appalled. Back during his residency, he had been on a plant tour of Werner and remembered meeting Lenny Shortt, then a Sales Administrator. He was unimpressed by Shortt but very impressed with the manufacturing and quality control. However, his loyalty to Werner was founded in the excellent service and relationship he had with Sidney Lake, Werner's Chicago distributor. Hence, Dr. Van had a real history with Werner, which served to elevate his disbelief. He was genuinely dismayed, shaking his head, really shocked at Werner's treatment of a long-term distributor. He had deemed Werner an ethical company who valued their high caliber sales force. He could not imagine that Werner had any part with the kidnapping and torture, which horrified him. He had treated battle trauma routinely as part of his practice, but was overwhelmed by James' injuries and amazed that he was still alive. Even more so, he was proud of James' marked progress in a such a short time.

"Well, James, it *is* a small world. I am distressed to learn all of this about Werner, which I had regarded as an upstanding company, and, even more distressed to hear about your distributorship. Maureen told me. What they did to you after so many years. Unbelievable. . ." he continued shaking his head, stroking his chin. "But, the main thing is, you *are* on the mend, your fracture's healing nicely. There is slight possibility of malalignment which I'll show you on the X-rays tomorrow, but the main thing is it is laying down good callus and healing. If it continues, we'll be able to put you in an orthotic boot soon. I want you to begin toe-touch, partial weight-bearing, carefully with your crutches as the strength returns in your arms. The wounds on your arms and hands are better, too, with the infection under control. I wish I could call in our plastic surgeon to consult on those wounds, but we lost him due to cutbacks in the military budget. We were downsized, losing several of our specialists. Before, when I was in private practice, I was getting hammered by managed care, so I reenlisted in the Navy. Now, I'm getting squeezed by budgetary cutbacks. No matter where I go, I can't practice the quality medicine that I was trained for. Damn." Dr. Van stopped himself. "I'm sorry, James. I get upset easily by what is happening to health care. And I tend to protest. Anyway, your fluids are more in line, much better, and your blood work's stabilized. I want you to continue with PT. And just keep on moving in the upward direction. You are a very positive, spiritual guy, so just keep on making progress. And rest easy. Uh, I see on your chart you haven't taken any pain medication in a couple of nights. And Maureen tells me that you are not trying to be a hero. Well, don't. Rest easy, and I'll see you tomorrow."

"Doctor Van?" James asked. "I need to ask you. . . I want to call my wife. I really wanna call my wife. . ."

"Do you have a quarter?"

". . .you mean I can?"

"Yes, of course. She already knows you're here, and safe. Maureen's called her. She's been giving her your good progress reports. We wanted to wait, to make sure you were stable, both medically and psychologically. We've had cases of post-traumatic shock in patients much less impaired than you. If so, it might have been even more traumatic for your wife, which you wouldn't want to happen. And on you, as well. We just needed to make sure first. . .I hope you understand," Dr. Van explained.

"When can I?" James asked, nodding his head.

"Right away. Let me go arrange it."

And, the doctor left the room with a smile and a twinkle in his eye.

James' heart was pounding, his mind bouncing off the walls. What was he going to say? There was so much. It had been so long. I-love-yous seemed inadequate. He knew what he should *not* say— how he had craved the sound of her voice, the touch of her hand, the sight of her beautiful face, the smell of her hair, the kiss of her lips— and how many times he thought he would *never* hear, *ever* see her again.

Maureen took him down the hall into a small staff conference room, sat him down at a table against the wall, and handed him the phone, glowing as she left the room.

"Honey?" James said.

"Oh, Darling. . .it's you. . ."

Trish's sweet Southern voice sounded like seraphs singing in heaven.

"How are you?" James asked, fumbling for words.

"I'm fine. . . but, but how are you?"

"I'm better. . .lots better, but, I still don't look too hot," he tried to laugh.

"Oh, Darling. I can't believe it's you. I love you. . .so much. I've missed you. . .so. . .my. . ." she was crying softly.

"I've missed you, too. I can't tell you how much," James tried not to choke.

A brief, awkward silence followed. Then they both talked at once.

"It's just wonderful. . .hearing your voice," he said.

"Oh, Darling. . .my Darling. . ." Trish sobbed, "I'm sorry. . .I just—"

"Don't apologize, Honey. We've got so much to catch up. . .on" he wanted to say "thankful for," but it didn't come out. "I love you so. . ."

Another silence, punctuated by a few sniffs. The phone conversation resembled that of two smitten adolescents self-conscious of what to say next.

"How are you doing? Darling? What. . .did they do to you?" now sorry she'd asked.

"I'm okay, now. We'll talk about it. . . later. How are the girls doing? And my precious little ones?"

"Oh, they're doing fine. Our little granddaughters are sweeter than ever. . .all missing their 'Padre.' They're going to be so excited to see you. And I can't wait. . .either. I wanted to fly down there, soon as I heard, to be with you, but, they thought it was better to wait. . .I'm so glad you're better. . .I just love. . .I've missed you so much, Darling. . .that I. . ." Once Trish finally started talking, she couldn't stop. "I just want to see you . . .to hold you— "

"I can't wait to see you, Honey— "

"When do you think. . .?" she wished she had not asked, but she couldn't help herself.

"Soon. Soon as I'm able to travel, Honey, I'm outta here."

"Oh, good. It's just so wonderful. . .to know. . .to hear. . .oh, I. . ."

"I know—"

"I love you so much— "

"I love you, too. See you soon. . ."

When he hung up the phone, his cheeks were drenched with tears, his hands clammy.

When Maureen came back in to get him, James could not get up. He was drained. Totally drained— physically, emotionally, spiritually. This was the culmination of a longing so acute, a dream so vivid, of his love, his wife, his life.

Maureen had to wheel him back to his room in a wheelchair. She understood.

As night was falling, maneuvers were starting again. The explosions were formidable, causing the traction frame and bed to vibrate.

What a contrast in symbolism. Previously, back in the wilderness, the unimpeded nocturnal song of the magical little *coquis* came to be the symbol of James' undaunted faith. When he was as good as a dead man, tortured, maimed, bleeding, close to shock, it was the *coquis'* melodic chant that helped him maintain consciousness and persevere. When he was delirious from the falciform malaria, it was the symphonic chorus of the *coquis* that helped him pull through. Now, it was the detonation of awesome power that inspired his pride and faith. He felt safe under the protection of *his* country, the most powerful nation on earth, the United States of America. From chipper chirps to bomb blasts, these two meaningful symbols reinforcing one man's faith could not have been more dissimilar. The only similarity of the two was sensory. Though both were auditory, they each registered at opposite ends of the decibel scale.

From tree frogs to frogmen, from Margarita to Maureen, from dead man to convalescing patient, he was definitely a lucky guy. No, a blessed man. A truly blessed man.

With the discharges growing more distant, their blasts dissipating, James nodded off, very proud to be an American, thanking the God of his understanding for life, and praying to be home soon with his wife and loved ones.

James was gently awakened by Maureen.

"Yes? Oh, hi."

"Sorry to awaken you, dear. This envelope was anonymously delivered to the hospital with an 'URGENT' post-it stuck on it. I thought it might be important," she said. She handed him the envelope.

And, before James could say thank you, she was gone.

James flipped on the light, opened the envelope, and anxiously pulled out the folded paper.

He sat straight up in bed, trying to ignore the nails of pain. *Unbelievable.* This was *exactly* what he was hoping for. Marked *CONFIDENTIAL* at the top, it was a memorandum from the V.P. of Manufacturing at Werner, Warsaw to the Plant Manager in Caguas, the subject: "Compliance Issues/ PDL Femoral Prostheses." He read it:

CONFIDENTIAL *CONFIDENTIAL*

TO: Ruiz Castillo, Plant Manager
FROM: Tom Tomjonavich, V.P. Manufacturing
SUBJECT: Compliance Issues/PDL Femoral Prostheses
DATE: April 1, 1997

"As discussed previously, the QC rejection rate on PDL Femoral Prostheses is unacceptable. Mean rate of 43.6% far exceeds Warsaw norm and negates cost advantage afforded by Tax Code 936. Of particular alarm is last production run on 14mm PDLs where product fell outside the dimensional tolerance limits (+/- .0035"), which should have caused the

> entire batch to be scrapped. These specifications had already been deviated. Unfortunately, it has come to my attention that some of the components were mistakenly passed through QC to sterile packaging. I do not need to state the gravity of this. We do not want to be put in a position to have to use the "R" word. We do not want to see our name on the Gray Sheet. Ruiz, the cost prohibitive reality of Caguas productivity has now become secondary to medico-legal considerations. OCP initiatives and Operational imperatives which you were to immediately implement have been ineffective. After your current production run, I hereby order you to suspend production of PDL Femoral Prostheses, all sizes, immediately."

James was overwhelmed by this news. This explained everything—the smudged "14mm" on the stem of the PDL Femoral that fractured Ezra Jenkin's femur, the stonewalling, the cover-up by Werner, Brice Billups' errant, unethical behavior. This confidential memo, beyond any shadow of doubt, confirmed his worst suspicions. That Total Hip was defective. It, along with the questionable bone cement, was a contributing factor to that poor farmer's death. All of which were the underlying reasons for calling him to Warsaw, firing him, kidnapping him, torturing him, trying to get the tapes, which were now more important than ever. Those tapes were incriminating evidence. *Holy shit!* How many more of these defective PDL hips were there? How many were walking around in patients? They *were* walking time bombs!

James had to get this information to the right place to prevent further complications. To prevent further possible deaths.

As badly as he needed rest, as precious as sleep had become, he would not be going to sleep. Not tonight.

It was almost daylight. James had Dr. VanderMeer paged, urgent. He had been up thinking about the best action plan most of the night. When the good doctor came into his room, James swore him to secrecy. He explained the entire sordid saga of Ezra Jenkin's surgery and death. James related in detail the circumstances of the hip revision surgery, the mis-etched 14mm PDL, and the split femur, which Dr.Van fully understood. James conveyed his worst suspicions on the cause of death, then presented the doctor with the unequivocal confirmation of the incriminating evidence— the Confidential Werner memo.

After allowing Dr. Van to get over his initial shock, James explained what he thought to be the best course of action to prevent further surgical complications and fatalities.

Dr. Van agreed.

"You've made a humane, judicious decision, James."

Still shaking his head, Dr. VanderMeer left James' room. He was headed to the Administrative office to fax the memo into the Inspector General's office at the FDA.

CHAPTER 48

The telephone rang with a muffled, low-pitched ring.

"Yeah," the gravelly voice answered.

"Line clean?" the raspy voice asked.

"Affirmative," was the answer.

"Subject. Code 936. Status?"

Silence.

"Currently missing..."

"*What!*" the raspy voice shrieked.

"Missing. Additional assets conducting sweep; complete sweep. Location unknown. Subject could not have departed island," the gravelly voice tentatively stated.

"*Shit!* I thought I was dealing with professionals!"

Silence.

"Containment in force. Perimeters secure. Subject *must* be on island. Uh...just matter of time to locate..." the gravelly voice continued.

"Final. This is *fuckin' final! Locate.* Period. *Eliminate.* Period," the raspy voice shouted into the phone. "*Eliminate! Capiche?*"

"...ditto."

"Ditto." Click.

Click.

CHAPTER 49

Oft expectation fails, and most oft there
Where most it promises.
All's Well That Ends Well, 1603
Shakespeare

Trish called her daughters and told them about their dad's call. Spontaneous tears of joy and gratitude flowed through the telephones. After all the jubilation subsided, there were the daunting questions about his condition, particularly the torture he had endured. Trish told them that they had not discussed that subject; that, much to her chagrin, she had asked, he gracefully declined; then she felt ashamed.

They asked how he sounded.

"Yes, girls, he sounded different," Trish answered.

"What do you mean, Mom?" they each asked.

"Well, he was serious. . . more serious than usual. Unlike his old light-hearted self. And quieter. A lot quieter. Just think about it, girls. After all that he's been through— as if getting fired, losing his business was not enough. You know how he loved his business. Then getting kidnapped. Flown out of the country. Then tortured. My God! Lord, we're lucky he's alive! I mean blessed. We're so blessed that he's alive. Our prayers have been answered," she assured.

She explained to her daughters that he would be home as soon as they would let him travel. They already knew about his broken leg because the nice nurse had told Trish about it on one of her calls.

Trish stood at the front door as the FBI left, hauling out all their equipment. After having lived under her roof for months, she felt unexpectedly sad, especially with Agent Misler, who was very gentlemanly in departure as well as presence. As for the impertinent agent whom she did not like, he was even polite thanking her as he left. Her house was so quiet now that she hardly knew how to act. But, it was still not the home she loved, because her husband was absent.

So, when would he really be able to come home? How soon? Real soon, she hoped. When would he be well enough to travel? How bad off was he? What all had happened to him? Tortured? For God's sake, why had he been tortured? James never hurt anybody. Why had they done this to him? Who on earth had tortured him?

She thought she now knew. After picking up the tapes at Barry Milner's, she could not wait; she pulled into a UK parking lot to listen to them. James' last phone calls to Werner made it clear that Brice Billups in Legal had somehow taken over the case from Regulatory. It was also obvious that Billups was stonewalling, not returning James' calls, actually refusing to talk to him. James had left repeated phone mails for Brice, taping each one. He corroborated the fact that Brice had been put in charge of the Jenkins' surgical incident, from multiple people in Regulatory, as well as with the nice secretaries at Legal, and had recorded each conversation. James had meticulously constructed a paper trail— all the MDRs, Surgical Incident Reports, forms, etc. — along with the even more inculpatory audiotape evidence.

All the trails led to one person— Brice Billups in Legal. The buck stopped at Brice. No wonder the little son-of-a-bitch wanted James fired. But, he was not alone. Others, Lenny especially, had betrayed James. Those other asses at Werner had done it, too. No, they *had* it done. She knew that she had to be right. She hated 'em. Genuinely hated them. And then, J. M. having the guts…no, the balls to call her. After stabbing James in the back, repeatedly. That damn bitch. The entire pathways to and from Werner were strewn with mendacity and deceit. And now kidnapping and torture?

She tried to sleep, but couldn't. Her brain was screaming out— one burning thought after another, one nagging question after another.

She was still sitting straight up in her bed. She looked over at her clock. It was 11:43 P.M. She had to lie down and go back to sleep. Yes, she needed her sleep so she could clean her house tomorrow, get it ready for her love's blessed homecoming, and reorganize James' files. Thank God she had been able to sleep a little. What a welcome change. Sleep, something else we take for granted. That is up until that diabolic call from J. M., that two-faced back-stabber! What a, how damn. . .no. Stop it, Trish. Don't start on her again or you'll be up all night. Don't let her do that to you again. No, that hussy is not worth it.

She needed to get some rest. She had to settle down. Shut your eyes.

Midnight. She had to get back to sleep. Ann's contact, from Mexico. She'd have to write him a thank you note. After the FBI's. Why wouldn't they let me go down there to be with James? After all, I used to live in Mexico City. I speak Spanish, I could be a help, a help to him, a help with the people, an interpreter, with Spanish. Well, I guess they do speak English at the Navy hospital. Why did they take him to Puerto Rico? Why did they do that to him? James had just been fired. It was Werner; and she knew it had to be them, the asses. But what would they want from him? Want badly enough to kidnap him? That's a federal offense, serious. Big-time serious. Why would they take such a great risk? She now knew.

Midnight. She was having one hot flash after another. She got up, went to James' dresser, and got out one of his T-shirts and put it on. Sure, her old red flannel was her security nightgown, but she was burning up. His T-shirt felt good. It gave her a sense of his being close. Why hadn't she thought of this before?

And, then, in the darkness of her bedroom, the motive became clear— it had to be the death at the HealthCare USA hospital. James had worried himself to death over it, even though it had not been any fault of his or his staff. He had been overly conscientious with his compliance and follow-up in its aftermath. Then, faced with no cooperation and stonewalling, he painstakingly documented Werner's cover-up. Brice! That. . .

Get back to work. She needed to reorganize all James' files and tapes, now that she had been through most of them. She had conducted a good investigation on her own. She was proud of herself for that. She needed to put them in order, in a chronological order, for them to make sense.

Who was she going to present them to first? The FBI? With Lynnwood there?

Brice, Werner, all of them—she still had a hard time believing it. Trying to sweep all that crap under the rug, their typical reaction in the past. But, a patient dies for an unexplained reason with something definitely wrong, and they treat it like a non-event, just like nothing ever happened. James could not believe it. He was awake night after night. Thank God he had taped all those long-distance phone calls to Werner, saved all the documentation, and copied everything for Lynnwood, except for the last tapes at Barry Milner's. He had conferred at length with their attorney about the incident and all the events, and this damn cover-up that followed. He had gone to great lengths to make sure his file was current. Yes, James was very shrewd in that regard. He was always cautious, protective. . . downright savvy in those kind of matters. She was proud of him, his business acumen.

Yep, if they were the ones who had kidnapped him, and they probably were, that had to be the reason. If it was the last thing on earth, she would make them pay. But how. After torturing her husband. Brice. She remembered James talking about his fiendish behavior— screaming at two different distributors on the phone. They had reported it to James as Ethics Chairman. That little bastard.

And Lenny. Their friend? Betraying James like that. That low-life. If she could just get her hands on them herself. The law would be too kind to them. The courts usually were. Criminals got off too easy. She'd make them pay. She'd have Lenny, the snake, tied up, then make him explain his actions to her, face-to-face, eyeball-to-eyeball. Then she'd claw his eyes out with her own hands. Yes!

And Brice— after firing James, having him kidnapped. Then tortured. After everything he's done to me? The loss of income. The loss of my love. The not knowing. The mental anguish— mental and emotional torture. I've been literally living in hell these last months. What he's done to my entire family? To Sam, my son-in-law who worked for James? *Damn.* To Dana? To all our employees? Nothing could mete out the justice Brice deserves. She would. She'd hang him from his heels, have him castrated, then watch him bleed to death. . .yes! *Lord, forgive me. . .*

And, now for the supreme bitch, J. M.? Jezebel Mae? What had happened to Jezebel in the Bible? What was her punishment? She was put to death by Jehu. How? Was she beheaded? That's too kind. Maybe Trish'd just fight her one-on-one. Pull all her hair out by the roots. Then claw her eyes out. No. Physical pain was too kind. For her. J. M.'s only desire was power and dominance. Total dominance. And delighting in the subjugation, the misery she had caused. No, physical punishment was far too kind for her. She needed something deeper. More strategic. She'd have good ol' J. M. fired in disgrace. With no severance. With such a negative employment history that she would never be employable again. With charges of espionage or embezzling or something sinister leaked to the *Warsaw Times Union*. Then the *Wall Street Journal*. Yes. A paper trail that she could never escape. Leave her all alone, to sulk in her own misery. Yes! That's the only thing J. M., the miserable bitch, could understand.

Oh, God. Why am I thinking like this? Please forgive me. Here I've just learned that my true love' s alive. Safe after all this time. And I thank you, Lord. Oh, how I thank you! And then to think like this. To be so vengeful. No. Help me, god. . .

She had to think about her husband, her husband only, stay focused on him. Oh, how blessed she was to have him, to have fallen in love with and married him. How long had they been married? Thirty-five years now. What a life they had together, their three daughters, and five granddaughters. Oh, yes. And now, looking back— how often she had taken him for granted, taken this wonderful, loving hardworking man, her husband for granted. Damn! If she ever got him back, that would never happen again. Where, oh where could he be? If only she could, she would go to him, nurse him, take care of him like never before. She knew he needed her. Why couldn't she go to him? Nurse him? Fix him her 'power breakfasts,' that he loved so much. And bring him home when he was able to travel? Why all this super secrecy? Well, she knew there was a good reason. She had to be respectful of it. Yes. And be so very thankful that he was still alive. She needed to think about that.

Go over to the office and talk to Dana to see if they had any more of those hip components or that bone cement in stock. No, on second thought, she could not do that. That would raise all kinds of questions, and Dana was so conscientious, a real worrier. That would worry Dana to death. And raise more red flags. She could not do that. Should not do that. She would have to continue on the exciting positive course.

And continue to get all these tapes organized. She now understood James' intentions, but she had to arrange them so that they made logical sense in chronological order to law enforcement types.

It was 3:25A.M. and she could not stop her mind. It was running away with her. And running away from her. She couldn't help it. Her thoughts were rampant. Some of them were even good ones. Maybe she would turn on the light and work on those files. She had tried that many times before, and all it did was to make her wider awake. And make her mind go faster. And make her madder. She could not concentrate well right now. If she still smoked, she would be having a cigarette right now. Why had she quit? Hell, a cigarette would be great. Then, she could go right back to sleep. It used to be when she was worried about something— about money, being able to pay the bills for the office back when they were struggling, just trying to make ends meet, or worrying about one of the kids, and it would awaken her, she could smoke a cigarette and then go right back to sleep. Maybe she should have bought two packs when she called Ann that day. The desire was still there. She wished that she still smoked.

At 4:47 A.M. she made a decision. If she was still awake at 5:00 o'clock, she would just go down to the kitchen and turn on the coffee. It was preset to start at 5:45 AM anyway. She wouldn't wait. Good idea. Best idea of the night.

She punched the on button. She couldn't wait. She was standing in the kitchen in her old robe. In the darkness, she looked at the little red light on the coffee maker, waiting for it to quit perking. It seemed to take forever. What was it her grandmother used to always say, "a watched pot never boils."

She was too antsy, pacing like a caged tigress. She had to get out of the house. The garage door closed. It was 8:45 A.M.. Dressed, she had to go to the grocery. To get ready for when James comes home. Stock up with his favorites— meat loaf, macaroni and cheese, plenty of *insalata mistas,* pasta, all his favorite ice creams, make a big pot of spaghetti and meat balls.

Well, thank God James was okay. And getting better. Yes, and thank God for the good news.

Before she got out of her car to go in Kroger's, she looked around the parking lot again. The car with the two men looked suspicious. Or was it just her. Was she really getting too paranoid? It was a plain, dark blue car, a sedan, a non-descript, official-looking car. She hadn't been able to notice the tires, whether it had blackwalls or not. She had seen movies like this and knew about blackwalls and unmarked cars. She would and could outsmart them.

As she drove away, she was craning her neck, looking around the parking lot and the street, but she did not see them.

One thing is for sure, when she got home, she would call the FBI about the car. It might have been two of them. My God, who could she trust?

Pulling away from the light, she answered herself— she could trust no one. . .except her husband, and he was not here. *Please, oh please Lord, bring him home safely to me. . .and soon, before I lose my mind.*

CHAPTER 50

To no man will we sell, or deny,
or delay, right or justice.
Magna Carta, 1215

As James limped into the large conference room, he was somewhat apprehensive and did not know why.

He had just left his doctor and new friend, Dr. VanderMeer, who looked like pure hell, totally different from the surgeon who had enthusiastically faxed that memo to the FDA.

Dr. Van said he had been in surgery all night, that two of the Navy Seals had been wounded, one critically. As to the nature of their wounds, he said that he could not comment. Navy policy. That's what worried James. Hell, the Navy Seals could swim with sharks. They were the toughest of the tough, land, sea and air. Not to take away from his old buddy, the Major, a Green Beret in the Army Special Forces, all of whom were super skilled at land combat. But, the Seals were multi-geographical aquatic experts. What had really happened to them?

It looked like the Inquisition. As James was seated, he was first told that this was only a preliminary investigation. He was introduced to everyone in the room. He had never seen so much brass in his life. The U.S. Navy went first. There was the Lt. Commander of the Vieques Naval Base, the Chief of the Medical Staff of the Naval Hospital, and three officers from the Judge Advocate General's office. Next came the Deputy Attorney General of the Commonwealth of Puerto Rico, the Chief Detective and the assistant Deputy of Puerto Rican Bureau of

Investigation, and the Sheriff of Caguas County, Puerto Rico. Lastly, there were two men and one woman from the FBI. The latter were the only ones not in uniform, unless a dark suit, dark tie, and white shirt could be considered a uniform. They explained how disturbed they were over the illegal, forceful circumstance of James' arrival in Puerto Rico and their shock at the horrendous injuries that he had suffered and endured since being brought there. However, they were relieved that he was now getting good medical care and had been progressing so well. It was now their duty to coordinate the investigation to apprehend the perpetrators of these heinous crimes. There were multiple and conflicting jurisdictions involved; they hoped that he could understand the reason for the number of officials present.

Since they had politely asked for him to start at the very beginning, he did so.

James began with his being called to Werner headquarters in Warsaw, IN, on that fateful Friday and related all of the events chronologically thereafter. He described the torture house, the deranged Dr. Horst Frommacht, who tortured him on three different occasions with an Aspen electrosurgical Bovie machine, which was explained to the others by the Chief of the Medical Staff. Without saying anything, the Sheriff nudged his Puerto Rican counterparts at the mention of Dr. Frommacht's name, indicating a quasi-familiarity. James then described his two guards, Alfredo and Ramon, the trip in the van, the wreck with the peasant's cart and donkey, and his ensuing escape. He said that he did not remember too much from then on, due to his compromised, morbid condition. Obviously, he had been found somewhere in the wilderness by this wonderful peasant family, who literally saved his life. He stated that he would prefer not to reveal their identity, because they had made that simple request of him, and he was bound to honor it, because they *had saved* his life. They had made arrangements for him to be brought here to the Naval Base, which they said had a fine hospital where he could get excellent medical care.

James then passed out copies of the Confidential memo which he had Dr. VanderMeer fax to the FDA. In flashback, he described in detail all of the background leading up to the memo — the total hip revision surgery that he had stood in on, the patient's tragic death, his diligence with the post-op, post-mortem reports, Werner's stonewalling of the entire event, his suspicion that the femoral component was defective, his fervent concern complicated by his disbelief and anger over Werner's mishandling of the matter, and the fact that he had documented and tape-recorded their unethical response. He fast-forwarded through his firing , kidnapping, and torture to connect the sequence of events together— how that patient's death precipitated by that defective hip was undeniably confirmed by this confidential memo. And furthermore, how that substantiated the motive for his kidnapping and torture— to get the tapes, because they were the incriminating evidence.

He could not judge their reaction at first. But, then their line of questioning demonstrated that they understood the magnitude of that memo. They asked a lot of questions about the FDA, and manufacturing/ surgical protocol governed by the FDA. They quickly comprehended the correlation of events and evidence. That was their business, their profession— criminal investigation.

They asked a few questions encompassing the entire spectrum of the whole scenario. It surprised James that they focused so much on Werner's business, their global presence, particularly Europe. They inquired about their manufacturing operations, including Code 936, the Puerto Rican plant, the restructuring of their distributor network and sales force, their morale internally and externally, their products, i.e. Total Joints, and their market position in the managed care marketplace. He was amazed at their knowledge and understanding of business in general. They seemed to be interested in the big picture as well as motive and the minute details of each separate constructs.

Overall, it had been a good session. All present had been professional, considerate, and sympathetic. They said other questions would arise as the investigation proceeded and they would need to consult with him from time to time.

They wished James well and continued progress in his recovery.

James felt confident that he and they were all one step closer to making the truth known.

But, he left with some of the same apprehension with which he had entered. He could not explain the eerie feeling he had. Did it have something to do with Dr. Van and his all-night surgery on the Navy Seals? For some reason, he thought there was more to it. He had worked with surgeons for over thirty years, been with them in trauma surgery into the wee hours, seen and sympathized with them when they had been up all night, but Dr. Van was somehow different. Something else was bothering him. It was not just fatigue and lack of sleep.

What was it? Could there have been another attack? Like the one when the Major and Margarita were wounded? Could more assassins have been sent? Could the Navy Seals have been wounded by professional killers? Assassins hired to kill him?

How could he find out? He had to know.

He was exhausted. As he limped back down the hall, another thought from his last conversation with Dr. Van crept into his mind— death and quota. Sick. He needed the sanctuary of his hospital bed. But, then he heard something that stopped him cold. CNN was announcing Breaking News on a TV monitor in a sitting room:

> *"Walter Kagan, CEO of Brecken-Mersack Strauss, Inc., one of the world's largest pharmaceutical companies, has died. According to an unidentified source, he was en route to their corporate office in Brussels, Belgium when his private jet crashed in the Atlantic. This tragic accident, now under investigation, has shocked the entire global drug community. Kagan, a leader in pharmaceutical research, was alone on the plane with only his pilot, copilot, and an attendant, whose names have not yet been released. . ."*

Oh, my God! That was no accident, James' thoughts were racing. *Is there no limit to how far they will go? Kidnapping, torture, murder. They are worse than ruthless— they are evil. But, who could it be? Spearheading all this? Who's in charge? Who is this mean? This is all. . . just unbelievable! And very dangerous.*

He had to find out more about that plane crash.

When James got back to his room, his whole body ached. He clutched his crutches tightly, his arms throbbing. The pain pulsated from his leg, up his torso, through his shoulders and collided with the pain radiating up both arms. And his mind. It screamed from fatigue and overload.

He yearned for the comfort of the bed , but stood frozen, focused on the circle "W" — the "W" logo on the traction frame on his bed. Werner. Werner, his company. He looked down at his hands, the gashes.

His arms, scarred for life. Permanently disfigured. The pain pumping into his brain. His broken leg. He'd limp the rest of his life. Be a cripple. A horrendously scarred, crippled shell of a man.

Look at me. What did I do to deserve this? I had my wife, my family, my health, a thriving business. And look at me now! A maimed cripple. My life's been destroyed. And they did it to me. Werner. To me. Why?

With a sudden surge of anger James swung his crutch at the vertical bar clamped at the foot of the bed.

A huge crash brought the entire overhead traction frame down. James swung again making another flying hit. The vertical bars, upper and lower clamps hit the floor with a clatter. The long horizontal bar cracked the overhead light on the wall sending glass shattering. The long bar landed across the bed, the trapeze swinging just above the floor.

James fell, cursing, hitting the floor with a thud. The pain riveted his body.

A clamp lay beside him on the floor. The "W" on the clamp knob stared up at him like the evil eye. He picked it up and flung it against the wall.

When Maureen ran into the room, James was about to swing the other crutch.

She gently touched the back of his neck and shoulders, patting him.

"I know. . . it's just too much," she said quietly. "It'll be alright, dear. What they did was wrong . . . but, it'll be alright," she reassured in her soft voice.

As she helped get James up, helping him to the chair, she said it again, almost in a whisper, "It'll be alright."

James let out a deep breath, holding on to the arms of the chair, his arms and hands trembling.

"It felt good," he said.

CHAPTER 51

Big doors swing on small hinges.
Running Into a Dead End While Escaping
Reed Polk, 1990

As soon as "Breaking News" announced the violent death of Walter Kagan, the CEO of Brecken-Mersack Strauss, Inc., pandemonium broke on the floor of the New York Stock Exchange.

Arlen Loeb was standing in his 47th floor office gazing out the window at all the umbrellas on the street below when his assistant informed him of the news. He tuned in the CNBC Financial channel on his television recessed in the bookcase. *Oh God. Poor Walter. . .and he was on his way to resolve our woes— all those infernal Werner woes. I told him to sell that damn company over two years ago.* In his state of depression Arlen's first impulse was to jump out the window, impossible nowadays because the windows in skyscrapers don't open.

Brecken's stock plunged 15 percent within 20 minutes, going down from 87 ½ to 74 ½. The story on the wire services stated that the CEO was en route to Brecken-Mersack Strauss' European office in Brussels, Belgium, when, at 11:19 P.M. EST, his Gulfstream V corporate jet suddenly disappeared from radar. When search planes were sent out, they found the debris from his plane floating in the Atlantic. Two sections of the jet's fuselage were spotted. They later confirmed that there were no survivors. According to the FAA flight plan filed, the plane was occupied by three crew members in addition to Mr. Kagan. It also stated that the

NTSB, the National Transportation Safety Board, and the FBI had already left for the crash scene to begin the investigation.

Rumors were rampant that an explosion had caused the Gulfstream-V to disintegrate.

Their stock, symbol BMS, had hit a new high the day before with the news of the release of their new cholesterol drug, CardioStat. This miracle drug was supposed to lower the LDL, the bad cholesterol, while simultaneously elevating the HDL, the good cholesterol. Further, there was clinical evidence of its having a cleansing effect on plaque in the arteries. This boded well for the broad spectrum usage of CardioStat, making it the newest blockbuster drug with potential sales in excess of $1 billion. This would greatly enhance the pharmaceutical giant's already impressive drug portfolio and elevate their position of global leadership in their industry. The day before, BMS had hit its third consecutive intraday high and closed at 87 ½, which helped fuel the rise in the entire hot pharmaceutical sector. But, yesterday's news of the new miracle drug's release had little effect on stemming the huge downward spiral of BMS' stock. The 15 percent tumble with their stock had erased over $26 billion from Brecken's market value.

A company spokesperson stated that Brecken's Board of Directors had convened in an emergency meeting to begin seeking a replacement for Walter Kagan; that the Chairman and ex-CEO, Logan Glauber, would act as interim CEO and oversee operations. The company was greatly saddened by the tragic loss of its Chief Executive Officer, who had contributed so much to the dynamic growth of the company over the past two decades, as well as helping to transform the whole scientific process of pharmaceutical research and rational drug design. The spokesperson also reiterated the company was under sound management and there would be no operational interruptions; and said the outlook for the company going forward remained strongly positive.

However, in the wake of the statement by the company spokesperson and the Board of Directors, another "Breaking News/Developing Story" came across the wire:

> *"It was just learned from a source who wished to remain anonymous that there were internal problems with Brecken-Mersack Strauss' orthopedic subsidiary, Werner, Inc., in Warsaw,*

Indiana. The source stated there had been alleged irregularities in manufacturing triggering an inquiry by the Inspector General of the FDA. It was also alleged that there had been accounting irregularities which may be investigated by the SEC. The reports of these irregularities resulted in the firing of Werner's President Ronald Salter, and the next day the termination of the Medical Group President, Robert Hempstead, a long-term Brecken senior officer. Neither Salter nor Hempstead could be reached for comment."

As soon as this hit the NYSE floor, Brecken's stock tanked, plunging an additional 12 percent. The stock price went down further from 74 ½ to 64 1/8.

The floor manager for PaineWebber and the senior analyst at SalomonSmithBarney looked at each other in shock. It was one of the many transient seconds of extreme angst that occurred at the exchange each day. The distinguishing characteristic of this moment was the fact that their respective firms owned significant blocks of the drug blue chip. Shouting, with their hands and arms flailing in the air, they both frantically attempted to hedge their positions.

But, a half hour later, at 1:05 P.M. EST, trading in the stock of Brecken-Mersack Strauss, Inc., was halted. At that time, BMS had fallen precipitously, down 31 percent, from its 87 ½ open to a close at 60 3/8.

Traders on the New York Stock Exchange floor along with the electronic Financial Networks were thrown into a frenzy of wild speculation regarding the reason for the blue chip stock being halted. Rumors circulated that it was due to some dark conspiracy to manipulate and control human gene mapping. Some said a "Dr. Mengele-type" was at the root of the evil plot. This only exacerbated the pandemonium flying around he exchange.

The other large cap pharmaceuticals declined in tandem with the fall of BMS. The hit that BMS was taking was painting a black swathe across the entire pharmaceutical sector, taking it down also. The Pharmaceutical Manufacturers' Index, symbol PMA, which traded on the American Exchange, had reversed its daily rise to a record high 308 ½ and fallen 73 ½ to close at a yearly low, 235.

The rest of the blue chips were also dragged down by the unsettling news with Brecken-Mersack Strauss, Inc. The Dow Industrials had declined 163 points.

At 3:25 PM, 35 minutes before the closing bell, the undesirable explanation came across the wire in yet another "Breaking News." It stated:

> *"At 1:05 PM EST today, trading in the stock of Brecken-Mersack Strauss, Inc., symbol BMS, was halted by the NYSE. It had been discovered that questionable large-volume short positions in BMS stock had been transacted by Burinz AG, a global broker in Brussels, Belgium, and in its offices in Kuala Lumpur, Malaysia. Both of these short positions were sold on the day preceding Mr. Kagan's tragic accident. The sudden, steep decline in BMS stock resulted in this suspicious trade realizing hourly profits of 1.7 pound sterling, or $2.6 billion in U. S. dollars. An investigation of insider trading has been launched by the Securities and Exchange Commission and Interpol."*

At 4:00 P.M. EST, according to the usual daily routine, the closing bell on the NYSE floor sounded. However, on this day, the closing bell did not end the turmoil among the traders, the brokers, and the shakers and breakers on Wall Street. This series of alarming news releases on one single pharmaceutical manufacturer, the Brecken Mersack Strauss Company, had served to create chaos on the trading floor, resulting in the huge decline on the Dow Industrials of 355 points. Even the technology-rich Nasdaq Exchange declined concomitantly by a record 78 ½ points.

Hence, with the announcement of the untimely and tragic death of its CEO, Brecken-Mersack Strauss, Inc., the world's third largest pharmaceutical company, had lost over $54 billion of its market capitalization in a period of less than four hours. This multinational, multibillion-dollar conglomerate, one of the world's leading corporations, had unobtrusively lost over $54 billion, 250 million dollars in its overall value.

The ill-fated death of an executive precipitated the ill-fated death of a corporation. The death of a man begot the death of a company. Death begot death.

Arlen Loeb, Chief Counsel of what *was* the world's third largest pharmaceutical company, had progressed from depression to despair. *Oh Walter, why didn't you listen to me? I told you Werner was a can of worms. . .* He now wanted to slit his throat before jumping out the window...which would not open.

CHAPTER 52

I saw that there is nothing better than that all should enjoy their work, for that is their lot; who can bring them to see what will be after them?
Ecclesiastes 3:22 (NRSV)

Could the morale at Werner sink any lower? Most employees thought not. Freshly traumatized by the layoffs of their very own fellow workers, the survivors lived in fear. Their jobs, once a source of pride and security, were now a fountain of distrust, anxiety, and dread.

The first layoffs came unexpectedly, catching all employees off guard, literally shocking the hell out of them. After all, they were the first layoffs *ever* in the history of Werner. The official press release, prepared by the company and published in the *Warsaw Times Union,* said "only 169 employees." But the brutal fact was that many of those 169 dedicated, loyal employees were second and third generation workers at the plant. When Mr. Werner started his company and hired their grandmothers and grandfathers, aunts, and uncles, the hiring implied a lifetime contract. If the employee was honest, worked hard, and did their best everyday, they were not only hired for life, but they became a member of an extended, proud family.

Hence, the first layoffs violated what they felt was their lifetime agreement— a giant umbrella shielding their sense of security, their sense of community, of belonging, their pride, dignity— their veritable way of life. Morale suffered terribly. It left a pervasive core of denial, anger, anxiety, and fear with the rank and file, middle management, and upper management, though the latter would not admit it. However, there were three exceptions: two glowering exceptions, Brice Billups and Lenny Shortt, and one more constrained exception, that of George Driscoll.

The bars at Plato's and Stokey's were deserted. These were the watering holes for Werner employees after work, who came into unwind, drink beer, and shoot pool. It was tradition. But the sudden layoffs not only disrupted the lives of these fiercely loyal employees, but also disrupted their tradition. It had instilled fear in their hearts, driving them from socializing to seclusion. They now retreated to their homes where they wanted to shut out the harsh reality— attempting to quarantine themselves from the world that had betrayed them.

Orlee Scheaffer, the owner of Plato's, had had to layoff two waitresses and his night bartender, which saddened him greatly. He called Ron Johnson, the owner of Stokey's, to commiserate and learned that Ron had been forced to do the same thing. The fallout from the layoffs at Werner was mortifying throughout the entire community. A way of life had died. Instead of *the* historic sense of community, it was the death of community.

Brice Billups was totally preoccupied with his own delusions of power, consumed with plotting his next move and countermove. It was too bad about Walter Kagan, but, after all, Brice *had* given him a chance, had tried to help him, had gone out of his way to give him the benefit of the doubt. And Kagan had not only been ungrateful, but had treated him with disdain. Too bad, Walter. Wish you had recognized *my* talent. Hell, you caused me to bust my budget. A corporate jet's a "high-level hit!" Cost me $250,000, for Christ's sake. Knocked the hell out of my slush fund. Shit, Walter, if only you'd listened.

It was like when he was running track in college— just when they thought he was going to lose the race, when they had counted him out, that's when he'd gut it, suck cinders, turn on the after-burners, and win! He would win this one, too.

Regarding Rob Hempstead, he got what was coming to him. How dare he raise his voice to me. That will teach him to speak to *the* Brice Billups, the next President of Werner, the next President, hell, the next CEO of Breck-Mersack Strauss, Inc., with disrespect.

As for the perfidious Lenny Shortt, he was more intensely engrossed in self-preservation than ever. This time it was not simply a matter of betraying a fellow associate or another friend to make himself look good. Nor was it another one of his Machiavellian schemes to insulate himself from controversy, blame, and guilt. No, this time he had dual imperatives: first, to set himself up as the next President of Werner. After all, they had passed over him, not once, not twice, but three times! He was superior to any and all of the last three Presidents, all of whom had to be fired. Didn't they know a good thing when they had it? When he was right under their noses? Now, with Rob Hempstead, whom he never liked anyway, fired, and Walter Kagan gone, the opportunity for his promotion was ripe and of the moment. Second, in the event of a worse case scenario, he had to absolve himself of any involvement in this inundation of adverse circumstances — *damn Brice anyway! That little prick! Getting him involved in all this.* Yes, he *had* to distance himself from Brice. And maximize his retirement benefits and stock options next year. He had to make himself look good, no matter what the cost, at whomever's expense, so his retirement would not be jeopardized in any way.

The Senior vice-president of Sales, George Driscoll was totally obsessed with his new business model— it was *not* working. Sales were still declining, morale bad. He would not dare admit that his ideal model was failing. He was thoroughly engrossed in rationalizing the reality of eroding market share, declining sales, and deteriorating morale. His private excuses for failure were growing more vacuous with time. He just *knew* that his model would work, and that it would be his ticket to becoming the next president of Werner.

The remaining 1,335 Werner employees, were waiting for the next shoe to drop. The only question they had was when. And how deeply it would affect their personal lives.

The other shoe *did* drop at 4:15 P.M. Tuesday, May 8th, another Black Tuesday.

Werner announced an additional round of layoffs totaling 293 employees. The shock waves struck the entire plant like a flaming meteor and a tidal wave simultaneously. The news hit individually and collectively— all employees were devastated. The reaction of the employees who did not get pink slips, the survivors, was almost as agonizing as those who did, the casualties. The still employed, were hit all at once with a profusion of emotion— immediate, heartfelt sympathy for their coworkers who had just lost their jobs, further violation of their trust and security, and fear, a deep-seated fear for their own jobs, fear of the unknown, fear for their own sense of security, fear for their families— an ever-present, foreboding fear, an ominous fear that was paralyzing.

They stood in hallways whispering to each other, looking over their shoulders, their eyes darting about. They crouched in their offices, not wanting the phone to ring, wishing the world would go away. In the past, most of the people could not wait to get to work. The camaraderie was infectious, the card games at break, the bets on ball games, the scuttlebutt— now, they dreaded it. They were possessed by worry and fear, at work, at home, and in between. Many wished they had never heard of Werner, much less gone to work there. Their prideful pursuits each day had been infected by a plague— a plague of perfidy, of corrupted values, a plague of fear. Their daily lives, previously challenging and fulfilling, had been rendered barren, debilitating, and reproachful. Their sense of identity and personal dignity had been desecrated— their dignity was no longer rooted in who they were, but had become rooted in what they did. It had transcended through the generations of families being employed in the local orthopaedic industry, particularly with the leader, Werner, Inc.

Their cherished home-away-from-home had been converted into a betrayal chamber, a burial vault containing their pasts, the archives of their lives, their hopes and dreams, the chronicles of a strong Midwestern people who were proud of their history, work ethic, community, and their basketball. Their jobs were synonymous with their prestige and their involvement with their community. Jobs, identity, position, self-esteem, self-worth, and personal dignity— all were integrated and interdependent. All were one. It *was* their way of life. It *was* their life. But no longer.

Another source of community pride was grounded in the fact that last year, Werner, Inc. had finally achieved an unspoken goal— bumping L. M. Dunleavey & Company as the largest employer in Warsaw, Indiana.

As of the close of business yesterday afternoon, that certainly was no longer true.

After two rounds of layoffs totaling 492 employees, Werner, Inc. had dropped from being the leading, largest employer in Warsaw, Indiana to, not second, but third, all of which was of little consequence to 492 loyal workers who had just lost their jobs, whose lives had been disrupted, devalued, and, in their eyes, devastated.

In a small community the ripple effect from 492 dislocated lives was tidal. The multiplier from job loss swallowed up entire families. Friends of families. Whole congregations.

It was the death of a town.

CHAPTER 53

Today is not a rehearsal.

Anonymous

The armed guards were a little discomforting, but James did not care. He was being escorted by two Navy MP officers and two FBI agents. Five men, the two up front in uniform, commanded a lot of attention. People stopped to stare.

His armed escorts had been very explicit with their instructions. He was not to be alone or out of their sight at any time. He certainly couldn't run away from them, even if he wished. He was still wearing the ortho-boot and limping along with a cane. He still had flexion contractures in his right hand, was unable to straighten out his four fingers, which meant he could not shake hands. Dr. Van said that he might never recover full use of his right hand due to the damage to the ulnar nerve; but, the hideous wounds on both arms and hands were continuing to heal, and he was regaining his stamina. All in all, he was much better. By golly, he was alive. He had survived, and he was going home. He did not care if he had to crawl on his knees and swim across the Caribbean to get there, he would do it.

As they drove into San Juan, James' excitement grew. He had not seen cars, traffic, highways, buildings, skyscrapers, high-rises, people, or houses in months. Civilization still existed. It wasn't that he had thought the world and life in general had ceased to exist; it was that the life he had always known no longer existed. He had been so detached and secluded. Forced to focus on his own survival, to utilize his every cell and fiber to concentrate on just staying alive, he had become disconnected. Trying not to die had taken all of his mental, physical, and spiritual strength.

Had San Juan grown? It looked like a teeming metropolis to him.

After they had checked in for the flight at the San Juan Luis Munoz International Airport, James asked to stop off in a souvenir shop, a strange request his escorts thought. When he explained that when he traveled, he had always brought his daughters home a little trinket, a "happy," which had later grown to include his five little granddaughters. He *had* to get them something.

When he walked into the gift shop, he got an eerie feeling. Things looked different. The usual trinkets had changed. But, suddenly, there it was! *Coquis!* The little green, felt frogs were each in a small box with a picture of a real live *coqui* on the outside and an insert explaining their history in Puerto Rico, as well as their *co-kee, co-kee* melodic chant. Perfect. He bought five of them, one for each granddaughter. No, six. He should buy one for himself. The little green frog that became the symbol of his faith, his melodic token of hope, his literal bridge of faith and hope.

He also bought four T-shirts with giant Puerto Rican parrots in rich colors on them— one for Trish, and one for each daughter. They loved to wear them as night shirts or just to bum around. He paid with his American Express card, which he had hidden in his left shoe.

The excitement overwhelmed him— to be alive, to be going home, to Trish, his family, his loved ones— those three beautiful daughters, each one totally different, but so special, and those precious granddaughters, all five of them. He could not believe he was actually going to see his family again. As they boarded the Delta flight for Atlanta, James was grinning, glowing. The joy was simply too much for him to contain.

After being seated between the two FBI agents, James reached down into his pocket, felt the fuzzy little frog, smiled, and whispered under his breath, "*Co-kee, co-kee*...I made it."

As the stretch Boeing 767 took off, James tilted his head back on the seat and closed his eyes, like he had done so many times before, on so many business trips, for so many years. But this time, it was different. The release, the deep breath, exhaled, the ensuing relaxation were all the same. The sense of anticipation, whether going to a meeting or coming back home, was similar. The difference was an effusion of anticipation, excitement, and adrenalin, but all contained compactly within a crucible of continuity and fulfillment, rebirth and redemption. It was about perseverence and endurance. It was about so many things— about heart and soul and mind; about faith and hope; about spirituality and salvation; quite simply, about God's grace; about life and love and family; about essence and depth and meaning; about principles and values and integrity; about good and goodness; about caring and sharing; about roots and ancestry and legacy; about faces and places. It was about home. Home, where the heart is.

The stewardess' approach with the cart jarred James from his reverie.

"May I get you something to drink?" she asked.

"Yes, I'd like an exotic drink," he replied, catching her by surprise. "May I have a Diet Coke with a lime?"

"That *is* exotic," she said, laughing.

As a matter of fact, it *was* exotic. James had not had a soda in months. For that matter, previous to the Naval hospital on Vieques, he had not had ice cubes, either. It is amazing the things that we take for granted— ice, drinkable water, air-conditioning, showers, toilets that flush, clean sheets, safe, edible foods, and, the biggie— ice cream. Oh, yes, the best of all— ice cream!

Suddenly, there was commotion in the rear of the plane. Without a moment's hesitation, the two FBI men were in the aisle with weapons drawn. The two MPs stood up, posted themselves in front of and behind James, weapons drawn, at the ready too. As everyone craned their necks to look toward the rear of the plane, James was admonished to sit still and face forward.

The FBI guys catapulted over the drink cart as the airline attendants got out of the way. The aircraft alarm system illuminated and the announcement came over the intercom: "The captain has illuminated the Fasten Seat Belts sign; please return to your seats and remain seated with your seatbelts securely fastened."

All the passengers were in a frenzied state of anxiety. What was going on? Nobody told them anything. The entire cabin was borderline panic— nervous, apprehensive, and scared. No one knew what was happening and, the more they asked, the more confused and wary they became.

James thought he knew what was happening. This incident and their quick response explained why he was under such a beefed-up armed escort. There had been another assassin attack. This also helped to explain his doctor's anguish about the Navy Seals back at the U.S. Naval Hospital. Obviously, they had been wounded in some kind of unscheduled combat, some unexpected attack by hit men sent after him, just like the attack back at the *Independisto's* camp when his friends, the Major and Margarita, had been wounded. Now, they had come after him on the plane. These were, as he had been told, some highly professional, very dangerous adversaries. He felt guilty about these severe consequences, these awful things happening to people who were completely innocent—like all these passengers on this plane. While he knew it was not directly his fault, it was because *of* him that these unwarranted attacks were occurring. And innocent people had gotten hurt.

Then, almost as quickly as the disturbance had begun, it ended. The two FBI agents returned to their seats, as did the Navy MPs, sitting on either side of James. It was a false alarm. A passenger who had too much to drink got belligerent with a flight attendant. It snowballed to involve two more passengers sitting in an adjacent row. But, as soon as it became apparent that the FBI was there, the disturbance was resolved very quickly.

For the rest of the flight, the only excitement on board was contained within the breast of one passenger— a man who had endured inhuman travail, a miracle man undeniably endowed with faith, hope and love— a deep abiding love, that had sustained him through an abhorrent ordeal, the love of life, the Lord, and the undying love of his family, the warmth and abundance of which he anxiously yearned for on this his prodigal return home.

CHAPTER 54

Happiness is an activity of the soul,
based upon excellence, and guided by virtue.
Nichomachean Ethics
Aristotle, 346 B.C.

When James flew over the white barns of Calumet Farm on the final approach into Bluegrass Field, he was overcome with heartfelt gratitude. The sight of the familiar, the pristine beauty of the white fences and horse farms overwhelmed him. It was fall in Kentucky. The leaves on the trees were in full, blazing colors. "The sun shines bright on My Old Kentucky Home" played inside his head. He had been gone seven months. Seven long months. Countless times during those months he knew that he would never see his home or his family again. His death was assured. But, he had survived.

As he hobbled off the Delta jet into Gate B-2 in the Bluegrass Airport in Lexington, Kentucky, he was home. And, there they all were!

"Welcome home, Love," Trish murmured, tears on her cheeks. Her hug was so tight that it transcended words. It signified everything—a lifetime of love that had been tested to its depths, a relationship, a union that encompassed far more than emotion, sharing, distance, time, comfort.

"I love you, Honey. I'm so glad to be..." James choked. Very quickly, it became a group hug, a giant embrace from all his family smothering him at the center.

They were all there— with cheers and tears, hugs and kisses, and Welcome Home banners and balloons. And his love, his darling Trish, in his eyes, more beautiful than ever. Kathleen, Ann, and Christine. His sons-in-law, Sam and Tom. And all five precious granddaughters. Their friends. His pastor, all five ministers from his church. His employees, his salesmen, Dana, business associates— even his competitors. Unbelievable!

And a baby named James! An additional blessing, an unexpected blessing— one that he did not know about— a grandson! His first grandson. His namesake. Imagine that?

And...CNN. As he squinted in their bright lights, he thought, *I should have known.*

What a homecoming. What a joyous homecoming! And what a glorious miracle.

Shortly after they arrived home, James, the big James now, distributed the little "happys" to each one of his five granddaughters. Allie and Annie, the two youngest, hugged their little green *coquis* immediately, and with no rehearsal, all five launched into the *co-kee, co-kee, co-kee* melodious chants in unison. He leaned over, kissed his little grandson for the first time, reached down into his pocket for the other little green frog that he had bought for himself, and gave it to little James. Kathleen, Ann, and Christine, with tears glistening in their eyes, embraced their dad with their Puerto Rican parrot T-shirts in hand, as they were reminded of his "little- happys" tradition one more time. Life could not be better. Oh, how much he loved them.

Later, after the grand celebration, James excused himself, said that he had to check on something. He left and went to his office. The key on his wife's key ring still worked. First, he pulled three packs of bone cement off the shelf in the stock room. Opening the two separate sterile packages of monomer and polymer in each of the three packs, he had his worst suspicions confirmed— the lot numbers on the liquid and powder were all different, just like the "runny" ones used in Dr. Weller's surgery on Ezra Jenkins. All this bone cement was out of specification. In other words, it was defective.

Next, James pulled two 14 millimeter PCL Femoral Hip Prostheses off the shelf. In opening the double sterile pack and checking the size electro-etched on the stem, he once again confirmed his nightmares—

the "14 mm" had been smudged, indicating that it too had been altered. That was the reason Mr. Jenkins' femur split during his surgery when Dr. Weller was inserting the component. The diameter of the stem was actually larger than fourteen millimeters, the "14 mm" electro-etched on the stem, causing a spiral fracture of the patient's femur. It confirmed everything! They knew they had defective product. It was a giant cover-up. And he, James Cantrill, was the living threat to expose everything. *Damn.*

He put all of the defective products in a box. He was scheduled to testify before the Grand Jury at 9:00 A.M. tomorrow morning and he definitely planned to take these with him as evidence.

Returning home, he hugged Trish again, then limped up to his bedroom. He picked up the phone and dialed the number without having to think.

"Hello, you have reached the phone mail system at Werner. The party you have called, 'George Driskell,' is not available. 'Leave your message at the end of the tone'..." The sound of that monotone voice made James grimace.

"George, this is James Cantrill. I am back," James stated with deliberation, choosing his words carefully, "I made it...I am alive..."

He hung up and redialed.

"Hello, you have reached the phone mail system at Werner. The party you have called, 'Lenny Shortt,' is not available. 'Leave your message at the end of the tone, and I'll get back to you'..." The voice of perfidy, the voice of duplicity and betrayal made James grit his teeth and want to puke.

"Lenny, this is James. I am making this call to inform *you*, a person whom I once held in high regard... whom I once called friend..." he paused, enunciating each word for emphasis. "I am calling to inform you, '*the* 20th-Century Judas,' that I survived. I *am* alive. I *am* back. And I suggest that you get yourself an attorney."

James shook his head and redialed again. "Hello, you have reached the phone mail system at Werner. The party you have called, 'Brice Billups,' is not available. 'Leave a message at the end of the tone'..." The voice of impudence and arrogance had not changed.

"Brice, this is James Cantrill speaking," he paused. "The purpose of this call is to inform you that I *am* alive," he spoke with precision and force. "I made it...and I *am* back," he paused again. "I suggest that you do something that is completely foreign in your life...that is, get yourself a good attorney."

He hung up. But it felt inadequate, incomplete. He knew that Regulatory Affairs reported to Legal.

He picked up the phone again and dialed information, first in Warsaw, Indiana. No Brice Billups. Then Ft. Wayne. No listing. Then, South Bend. Bingo. The operator gave him the number. He dialed it.

"Yes," the raspy voice answered.

"Brice?" James asked.

"Yes," the raspy voice replied.

"This is James Cantrill speaking. I *am* alive. I am back. And I know," he said, lowering his voice, "about the Total Hips, the PDL Femorals. *I know.* About the whole cover-up. And the bone cement, too— "

"You can't prove a *fucking* thing, Cantrill!"

There was silence.

"How could you, Brice?" James implored. "Patients have died. People are dead, murdered."

Again, silence. Only the sound of raspy breathing could be heard.

"Patients... have died. People have been killed. Brice? How could you?"

Another brief silence ensued.

"A recall would have bankrupted Werner," Brice stated contemptuously. "After all, I will *not* be, would *not* allow myself to be*come* the president of a company with worthless stock options."

James shut his eyes, turned his face from the receiver, shook his head, and shuddered.

Then, Brice shouted, "You've got nothing, Cantrill! Nothing!" His raspy, high-pitched voice shot out of the earpiece. "You are nothing but a disgruntled employee! Remember *I was* there. *I* was the one who fired you! And it's all your *fucking* fault!" he screamed. "Your...threat... about the *truth? Shit,* I *had* to tap my slush fund! You...*you...*" he slammed down the receiver.

James hung up, removed the micro-cassette tape, carefully labeled it with the exact time, date, the name, "Brice Billups," and placed it in its plastic holder.

He walked out of the bedroom, stood at the top of the stairs, and smiled.

Lord, it was good to be home.

He could hear his granddaughters playing with their little green frogs downstairs—

"co-kee. . .co-kee. . .co-kee. . ."

THE END

EPILOGUE

And ye shall know the truth,
and the truth shall make you free.
John 8:32 (KJV)

James T. Cantrill's testimony before the Grand Jury lasted for two and a half days. His testimony corroborated that of previous witnesses, as well as the taped conversations, which his attorney, Lynnwood Ingle, had made available during his deposition. As a result, multiple indictments were issued.

James limped down the corridor of the Federal Courthouse using his walking cane. He was wearing a short-sleeve shirt per the instruction of his attorney, who was at his side. He rounded the corner to an unexpected event.

He found himself facing Brice Billups, who was being escorted to the courtroom by three U. S. Marshals.

Brice glanced down at the horrendous gashes on James' hands and arms. His eyes immediately began to twitch.

"At last," James said, glaring fiercely at Brice, whose hands were cuffed, his ankles shackled. It was a moment frozen in time. All of the humiliation, pain, torture, resentment, outrage, and hatred James had suffered over the last seven months welled up within his chest. A million thoughts raged through his mind. His first instinct was to kill the reprehensible little man, but he somehow restrained himself. He felt Lynnwood's hand on his shoulder.

Brice avoided direct eye-contact, instead looking down at the orthotic boot on James' broken leg, then back to his own chains and shackles. The marshals, one on each arm, forcefully prodded him toward the double doors of the courtroom.

As Brice shuffled on, the chains clanked loudly, echoing in the marble hallway.

James said nothing, took a deep breath, squared his shoulders, and stood erect. *I am who I am no matter what Werner has done to me,* he thought. He and Lynnwood walked slowly into the courtroom.

As they entered, James saw Lenny sitting slumped at the defendant's table, slack-jawed, looking like an old faded wooden sculpture. He too avoided eye contact.

James later learned the reason Brice was brought to court in shackles. He had stabbed a guard in the eye with a ball-point pen in an attempt to escape.

The trials proceeded without a hitch. The incriminating evidence presented by the prosecutor was irrefutable.

Brice Billups was found guilty of kidnapping, torture, conspiracy to commit murder, embezzlement, extortion, terroristic threatening, mail and wire fraud, securities fraud, and international terrorism. He was sentenced to three consecutive terms of life imprisonment without parole to be served consecutively. The only reason that he was not given the death penalty by lethal injection was that the jury felt that three terms of life imprisonment without parole was a more commensurate sentence. The presiding judge concurred with the jury— in lieu of the sequence of multiple guilty verdicts, that death by lethal injection would be the lesser punishment and sentenced Billups accordingly. In addition, the Inspector General's office of the Food and Drug Administration had just indicted him for six violations of FDA statutes. The penalties for these would be forthcoming. He is incarcerated at the maximum security federal prison at Marion, Illinois.

Leonard R. Shortt was found guilty of criminal conspiracy, criminal exploitation, accessory to kidnapping, accessory to attempted murder, and wanton endangerment. He was sentenced to three separate terms of five to twelve years to be served consecutively. He would not be eligible for parole until the third term of the sentence. He is currently incarcerated in Sing Sing Prison in Attica, New York.

Ronald L. Salter was convicted of violation of four FDA regulations by the Inspector General of the Food and Drug Administration. These resulted in a fine of $575,000 and two sentences of five to ten years. He is currently incarcerated at the federal prison in Atlanta, Georgia.

George Driskell was given the choice of signing his own resignation or transferring with the position of Product Manager to the Werner office in Seoul, South Korea. He chose the latter.

Robert Hempstead was last seen in a soup kitchen in the Bowery in New York City. All of his severance checks were returned "Addressee Unknown."

Werner, Inc. was ordered to pay an $87 million-dollar fine for non-compliance and violation of five regulations of the Food and Drug Administration. The company was finally sold by Brecken Mersack-Strauss, Inc. to an Indonesian tobacco conglomerate for less than one times sales, which continued to decline.

About the Author

Bill Kimbrell spent 31 years building his own surgical equipment business. Before that, he attended Millsaps College in Jackson, MS and graduated from SMU in Dallas.

Most recently, Mr. Kimbrell attended INSEAD University in Fontainebleau, France, where he became qualified and certified in Blue Ocean Strategy.

As the son of an English teacher and English major, both infatuated with the English language, Bill has long wanted to write "the Great American novel." *CODE 936* is his first novel. He is busy working on his second book, *10 CORE PRINCIPLES: from the Depression, through the Recession, throughout Life...*

He and his wife have three daughters, eight grandchildren, and live in Lexington, KY.

Visit his website at www.blueoceanglobalstrategy.com

Manufactured By: RR Donnelley
Breinigsville, PA USA
April 2010